THE HAILING SIGN

Steven Fink, President of Lexington Communications, is one of America's leading authorities on crisis management, and frequently appears on TV news shows and business programmes. He lives in Los Angeles. *The Hailing Sign* is his first novel.

The Hailing Sign

Steven Fink

HEADLINE

ISBN 0 7472 3175 3

Printed and bound in Great Britain by Collins, Glasgow

HEADLINE BOOK PUBLISHING PLC
Headline House
79 Great Titchfield Street
London W1P 7FN

**Dedicated to the memory of
Louis Davis
and
Gilbert MacKay**

**They were my friends,
They were my guides,
They were my Brothers. . . .**

*The beings who live below
say that God is on high;
while the angels in Heaven
say that God is on earth.*

—THE ZOHAR

The Hailing Sign

FOREWORD

O N November 4, 1979, the United States Embassy at Tehran, Iran, was seized by a band of militant Iranian students.

Much has been written already about the hostages' four hundred and forty-four days of captivity, and so this narrative will not dwell on the more well-known aspects of that ordeal.

But in the early days and weeks of the embassy's capture, there was a great deal of confusion and uncertainty as to exactly how many Americans were being held. That "confusion" was intentional on the part of two opposing governments: the United States and Iran.

Simply stated, there was a daring rescue of an American hostage by a private U.S. citizen.

The American government knew about it in advance, tried to stop it, but failed. The Iranian government knew about it in advance, tried to stop it, but failed.

And so, to avoid embarrassment for the Iranians, which might have led to threatened retaliation against the remaining hostages, and to avoid embarrassment for the United States, which would have found itself in the unenviable position of trying lamely to explain to its citizens how one man could accomplish what the powers of the nation could not, these two governments did the only thing they thought logical: They conspired to cover up the rescue.

This is the story.

PROLOGUE

On the beach at Netanya, Israel —October 1973

F ROM a distance it appeared to be a picture of harmonious, familial contentment.

A husband, a loving wife, and an adored five-year-old son stroll hand-in-hand near the calm surf along a deserted stretch of beach. The husband pauses momentarily, turns his back against an early evening breeze, and struggles to apply a lighted match to a cigarette before the flame is snuffed out. His brief moment of victory is quickly humbled by a disapproving glance from his wife. Chastised, he nevertheless manages to inhale deeply, twice in rapid succession, filling his lungs with the warm smoke, before flipping the cigarette into the sand. He watches sadly as the burning ember is quietly engulfed by a lazy, rolling wave.

The woman squeezes her husband's arm and reaches up to kiss his cheek, unobtrusively slipping a thin, glass tube into his shirt pocket. She steps out of her sandals and into the surf's edge, gritting her teeth against the sudden chill. The sea air approaches her trim figure and, for a moment, runs through her long black hair. Like her ancestors before her, she has the high cheekbones, aquiline nose, and full, sensual lips so common to Sabra women. As a young girl she played on this very beach under the hot Israeli sun. But now she wraps her arms in front of her and caresses her elbows as she wards off the cold and watches the setting sun fill the horizon. Her husband gently drapes his short military-style jacket across her shoulders and continues walking along the beach with his son.

And from a hilltop in the distance, through a pair of powerful army binoculars, they seemed impervious to the cares of the world.

"I still don't understand why we're chaperoning them," said the private.

"Shh! *Sheked!*" cautioned his sergeant. "Voices can carry on the wind."

The private lowered his voice. "Doesn't the Israeli Army have any better way to waste the time of two soldiers? Don't they know there's a war going on?"

"It's because of the war that we're here, chaperoning as you put it. The woman's brother is some big *mahoff* in the Mossad, I was told."

"He must be big," the private said. "This whole beach has been declared off limits to the public. What's the story?"

"All I know is that the family down there is leaving the country tonight. The husband used to be some hotshot in a branch of U.S. Intelligence, but that was before he got most of himself blown up in Vietnam. Now he's retired. For some reason—don't ask me why—he asked his brother-in-law in the Mossad for permission to bring his wife to the beach this afternoon. I think she used to live close by."

"That's it?" The private was incredulous. "We've been freezing our tails off just for that?"

"That, and because it's orders," replied the sergeant. "I wouldn't want to be us if, God forbid, anything should happen to them."

"What could happen?"

"Daddy, why is Mommy crying?"

It was an innocent question spoken by a confused, five-year-old boy. The father squeezed his son's hand a little tighter as they continued their walk along Netanya's chilled beach and farther away from the boy's mother, who freely let her tears mingle with the Mediterranean surf.

"Mommy's just a little sad because she's saying good-bye, Josh."

Joshua turned his head to see his mother looking out to sea and was even more confused than before.

"Why is Mommy saying good-bye to the water, Daddy? Won't there be any water where we're going? Will I be able to go swimming in 'Merica?"

"*A*-merica, Josh. Say *A*-merica," his father corrected him, artfully avoiding the latest barrage of the boy's questions.

"Ah-merica," the lad practiced. "Ah-merica."

"Your English is really getting good, Josh. In fact, I think you can speak English better than I can speak Hebrew," the father said with pride.

This last was more a statement of fact than the confidence-builder it was designed to be. Ever since they had decided to return to the United States—more precisely, *he*

5

had decided; his wife, Beth, had reluctantly acquiesced—they spoke only in English in order to help their son's command of his new language.

"Mommy's English is good, too, isn't it, Daddy?"

He tenderly released his son's hand while he fished in his shirt pocket for a cigarette. It was almost the end of his second pack of the day, and it was not quite six o'clock.

His wife had done everything she could think of to get him to stop smoking, at one point even going so far as to threaten that she wouldn't go with him to the States unless he stopped.

He tried—"God knows I've tried, Beth"—but his minor, half-day successes were eventually dashed each and every time. "If not for me, then stop for Josh," she had pleaded. "I don't want him to grow up as an orphan with his father dead of cancer. As it is, you're winded whenever you climb a flight of stairs."

He reached in his shirt pocket for a match and pulled out the glass tube his wife had placed there just moments ago. It contained a cigarette with the inscription: Break Glass in Case of Emergency.

Her sense of humor brought the day's first smile to his lips.

I love you, he thought to himself. I love you more than life itself.

"Huh, Daddy?"

"What was that, Josh?"

"I said that Mommy's English is good, too. Isn't it?"

"Yes, Josh." He picked his son up in his arms. "Mommy went to school in the States and she worked there. . . ."

"I know. I know," the boy said, anxious to recite. "Mommy worked as a nurse and you met Mommy when you were wounded and in the hospital. Right, Daddy?"

He had been in a coma for months after Vietnam and she had nursed him, changed his bandages, bathed him, and rolled him over to prevent bedsores. And hers was the first face he saw when he awoke, and the last face he wanted to see before he died.

When he finally was discharged from the hospital, her work visa was expiring. So he followed her to Israel, met her family, married her in Cyprus because he wasn't Jewish and couldn't find a rabbi in Israel to marry them, and settled down to recuperate.

But the Vietnam episode had left him with so many emotional scars and frightening nightmares that when the latest Israeli war broke out, he felt he had to escape the sights, sounds, and smells of a country at war. She understood. She wasn't happy, but she genuinely understood.

He kissed his son tenderly as the October air began to pick up slightly.

"Cold?" he asked the boy.

"A little."

They had almost reached the base of the hillside. The father turned toward his wife, who was now little more than a whisper in the distance. Still, he could tell that she stood motionless as he had left her, on the water's edge. He kissed his son again and lowered him gently.

"Let's head back," the father directed.

Anyone looking at them knew they were father and son. They had the same rich brown hair with a touch of waviness, and the same piercing blue eyes. The youngster had the same freckles his father had had at his age, and perhaps still had, although it was hard to tell through his bushy beard.

He had grown the beard in a pique of restlessness during his recuperative period, and swore to shave it off when his hospital stay ended. But Beth had grown fond of it. Now he took pleasure in stroking the growth when he was pensive.

He had covered half the distance back to his wife, mindlessly pulling down on both ends of his mustache, when, out of the corner of his eye, he saw the muzzle flash from the sea. An instant later he heard the shot shatter the air.

And then he saw Beth fall.

No one was ever able to explain how a black rubber raft with six terrorists managed to cross the sea undetected. No one ever discovered what their mission had been. No one ever tried. This was wartime in a small country and explanations were pointless.

"Oh, God! The woman's been hit!" the private yelled.

"Quick! Get the hell down there," the sergeant commanded. "I'll try to cover you from here and radio for help. *Move!*"

The private began to scramble down the hill.

"Beth! Oh, sweet Jesus, *Beth!*" He screamed at the top of his lungs.

"Daddy, what happened? Daddy, Daddy!"

"Josh, as fast as you can, run to Bubbah Goldie's over the hill. Hurry, Josh!"

He left the boy standing in terror and started to run as fast as he could toward his wife. But he turned his head and saw his son still standing as he had left him, crying and petrified.

"Daddy! Don't leave me!" He clenched his little fists together.

His father stopped only long enough to scold the boy.

"*Joshua!* Do as you're told, young man. *Now!*"

The boy knew his Daddy was angry because he had called him by his full name. But he was rooted in abject terror. His Mommy had fallen and his Daddy was angry with him. Why? He continued to cry, but did as he was told. He started running toward the hill. He was running to his Grandmom's house. Bubbah Goldie wouldn't scold him. He ran as fast as his little legs would carry him—away from his hurt Mommy, away from his mean Daddy. And then he heard a lot of gunshots. He screamed as his small hands flew to cover his ears.

He heard the bad, loud noise from behind him, toward the water. And he heard the bad, loud noise from on top of the hill where he was heading. But he froze in his tracks when he saw the man with the big rifle heading toward him, coming right down from the hill where his Daddy told him to go.

At that instant the boy's bladder burst out of fear, but he was oblivious to it.

His confused child's mind churned with doubt and panic. He didn't know what to do until the man with the rifle started to call him. The boy's tears obliterated the familiarity of the Israeli soldier's uniform. But he didn't know this man. This man was a stranger, and his Mommy and Daddy and Bubbah Goldie had always cautioned him about talking to strangers. Suddenly he knew what to do. He turned on his heels and started to run to his Daddy.

He knew his wife was dead.

He hadn't even reached her, but he knew in his heart that she was dead. He had known the instant he had heard the shot that a piece of him was gone from his life forever.

He ran so hard that the weight of his lungs began to crush

against his chest. Sweat formed of fear permeated his clothes and his heart beat out a sporadic rhythm in his arid throat.

The cigarettes—*the goddamn, fucking cigarettes*—sapped his strength and he could no longer feel his legs as they churned up the sand beneath him.

The raft paddled closer to shore, but he ignored it. More shots cracked from the vessel, but he couldn't think about it. Another gun, maybe two, sounded from behind him, but he was oblivious to it. His sole mission was to reach Beth and breathe life back into her.

"Daddy, don't leave me" echoed in his ear, but he knew his son was heading toward safety, so he blocked it out of his mind.

He was close enough to see the blood on Beth's forehead when he took a bullet in his right thigh. He willed the pain away. He had no wind left. He had no strength left. But he ran. Oh, how he ran. A bullet slammed into his right shoulder, but he told himself it hadn't happened.

"Beth, oh, Beth," he cried when he reached her. "Please don't take her, God," he sobbed.

He kissed her and wiped away the blood, but she would not respond. He dragged her from the water's edge, deluding himself into believing that that might do some good. He cradled her head in his lap and rocked her gently.

"Beth, my Beth," was all he could say.

His son's voice grew louder, but he told himself it was only his imagination. His son was heading toward safety. Josh was all right; it was Beth who needed him. Soon, God would see He had made a terrible mistake and He would correct it. God would make another miracle in the Holy Land. God would bring his Beth back to him. Oh, God, please hurry, he prayed.

But he didn't hear God's voice; he heard Josh's. And it was close. Too close.

"Daddy! Tell them to put me down! Let me go! I want my Daddy!"

The terrorists had grabbed his son and were dragging him into the raft.

"Noooooooooooo! LET HIM GO!" he commanded at the top of his aching lungs. "HE'S MY *SON*, YOU ANIMALS!" He felt his heart stop.

But the raft started out to sea. And a father went after his son.

"Come back!" he screamed. "Come back with my boy!"

He dove into the cold, dark water, ignoring the two bullets lodged in his body and unaware of the blood he was losing. His body felt nothing as he tried to swim, his right arm flailing about helplessly, his right leg a deadweight beneath him.

"DADDY! DADDY! WHERE ARE YOU, DADDY?"

"I'M COMING, JOSH," he managed to yell. "JUMP, JOSH! JUMP!"

"DADDY! DON'T LEAVE ME, DADDY!"

"I'm not leaving you, Josh. I'm coming, son."

He heard hideous laughter in front of him, and horrific gunshots behind him coming from the beach, from Israeli soldiers.

"Don't shoot," he tried to say. "They've got my boy!"

He heard the distant roar of planes overhead as he struggled to keep pace with the raft. He looked up for an instant and saw a terrorist holding the boy by his hair, swinging him from side to side, taunting him.

A large wave caught the raft for a brief moment and flung it backward into his face. The combined force of the wave and the raft pounded him under the water. He swallowed water but fought to reach the surface. Blinded by the saltwater and his tears, he lunged forward with one massive stroke of his left hand and caught the edge of the raft. He tried to entangle his hand in a rope dangling from the side. A knife sliced through the back of his hand, but still he held tight. The butt of a rifle cracked the bridge of his nose. But his left hand would not let go; for some reason he could not locate his right hand.

Then the business end of an oar smashed against his hand, once, twice. His broken hand, his broken fingers would no longer obey. He screamed, not out of pain but in temporary defeat.

"Don't! Don't hurt my Daddy!"

He could hear the hysteria in his son's voice as he slipped beneath the water again.

He rose to the surface and gasped air as bullets whizzed around him. He tried to tread water with one leg while attempting to get his bearings. He could no longer see the raft, but through his blurred vision he swam in the general direction of his son's pleading cries. His wrecked body tried to move on instinct alone, on sheer willpower. The sound of his son's voice gave him an added second of strength.

"Daddy!" The voice was growing fainter. "Daddy, don't let them take me away. Please, Daddy. I'll be good."

Oh, Josh, my son. You are good, Josh. Did he say that? He couldn't tell. He wanted to, but he started to go under again.

He fought to keep his dead legs kicking, his dead arms churning. He could no longer see, but he tried to will his body to move in the direction of a ringing bell. What is that bell, Beth? What, Beth? I can't hear you. Where's Josh, Beth? Tell him to come in now.

"Daaaaadddddy."

Yes, Josh. What is it, son? Tell Daddy.

The bell was getting louder, Josh's voice growing weaker. He thought he heard the boy hiccup.

Don't cry, Josh. You always get hiccups when you cry. Hold your breath, Josh.

His left arm reached out and struck something. It was a buoy with a ringing bell. He grabbed for it as he started inhaling water.

"Daaaaadddddy."

He struggled to bring his right hand up to help his slipping grasp on the buoy. How far had he come? He could no longer see the lights from shore. The bell pealed again and the thought that he was blind crossed his mind. He looked up. Was that another plane? A helicopter? Searchlights in the sky?

His lips were blue, but the icy water did not feel cold. He had no feeling left in any part of his body. His breathing was labored under a death-rattling wheeze. He knew he was delirious, but how can I be delirious if I know I'm delirious? He wanted to laugh at the absurdity of the question. He knew his body was no longer functioning. He wanted to just let go of the buoy and float along with the waves.

The bell rang out again and again and again.

Oh, God in heaven, he thought he said. Would You harm a poor shepherd's son?

Ein-Sof, he heard himself say. Ein-Sof, Ein-Sof. What was he saying?

The sun was down, the sky was black, the sea was ink. His head bobbed up and down with the buoy, over and under the water.

"Daaaaadddddy." Now barely more than a mournful wail on the wind.

"I'm coming for you, Josh," he vowed over the din of the bell.

Then he removed his hand from the buoy.

1

Philadelphia—May 2, 1979

THEY came in their tuxedos. They always did.

Alone, and in small groups, they silently entered the western portal of one of the oldest and most ornate buildings in the world. They passed between the Byzantine pillars, over the Seal of Solomon, and under the twelve signs of the zodiac. They always did; it was the only way to enter.

They climbed a small flight of stairs under the watchful gaze of the guards who nodded silent hellos to the familiar faces but stood ready to challenge any who did not belong.

The few who were armed surrendered their weapons unasked to the guards. They didn't have to, of course, since the guards never knew which of them carried weapons. But it was part of the code—part of the Obligation to which each of their lives was dedicated for all time—not to bring anything offensive or defensive into the Assembly. And the code—the Obligation—was never violated. In any way.

At the Tree of Life some of them parted company, the younger ones opting to scale the luxurious staircase while the older ones invariably trod the long, richly carpeted hallway to the elevators at the rear of the building.

They would meet again on the second floor outside of the Assembly Hall, where they would sign their names in an oversized ledger. Then they were permitted to enter the vast Hall in single file, leaving their footprints in the sand upon the floor so that other, less knowledgeable Brothers of the Craft could follow their trail in safety.

The Hall was triangular shaped, but the Brothers occupied benches on only two of the three sides, leaving, as always, one side in symbolic darkness. The throne at the triangle's apex was reserved for the Master of the Mystery, the *Ba'alei Ha-sod*.

It was almost seven o'clock, and a few latecomers scurried into the Hall before its huge oak-carved doors were shut and bolted for the duration of the Meeting. This being the annual night of initiation, they would not leave until the long ceremony concluded. They would not leave until midnight.

A golden altar in the center of the floor reflected the light cast upon it from three groupings of burning tapers, each placed in triangular form about the altar. *Emet*, or Truth, could be read through the fires of the first group of candles; *Emunah*, or Faith, appeared through the second; and *Hokhmah*, Wisdom, sparkled from the third.

Directly in the center of the ceiling was an opaquely clouded blue glass circle, representing the blue vault of

1 6

heaven, with the golden orb of the sun casting its illuminating rays out over the assemblage.

A huge pipe organ situated in a hidden loft played in the background over the hushed tones of the Members' voices. And as the ornate pendulum clock built into one of the walls slowly inched its way toward seven o'clock, the Master of the Mystery stepped out from his private chamber located behind his throne, walked solemnly to his podium, and surveyed the vastness of the room before him. He was pleased with what he saw.

The Hall was overflowing with Members tonight, out of respect for him, and out of respect due the Oriental Chair he occupied. He, John Sinclair, Master of the Mystery, Master of this Lodge of Brothers of the Craft, and a Master among Masters, had waited for this night for twenty-one years. Tonight was to be no ordinary initiation ceremony. Tonight the candidate was to be his son, Lee.

Tonight he would greet his son in a new way, not as a father but as a Brother. Tonight he would introduce his son to a new way of life, a way of life that would grant him everlasting protection throughout the world. Tonight he would initiate his son into the mysteries and rituals of the Brotherhood of the Craft.

Tonight he would introduce his son to God.

But for the son, the ritual in which he was about to partake had actually begun seven hours earlier.

Following the instructions given to him verbally by a messenger that morning, along with half of a torn dollar bill, he appeared at precisely noon at a designated street corner in downtown Philadelphia, just as the office buildings were emptying for lunchtime. He had been told to expect several people to approach him but to leave only with the person who presented the other half of the dollar bill.

A few minutes after the noon hour, an elderly man stepped up to him from behind and whispered into his ear, "The whole of the Torah is the Holy Name."

Lee Sinclair spun around quickly, but the man had meshed into the crowd and was gone from sight as mysteriously as he had appeared.

About ten minutes passed when another elderly man approached from across the street. Lee saw him coming but was still surprised when the old traveler walked up to him and placed his gnarled hands on Lee's head and said, "The Ineffable Name was written in black fire on white fire. But tonight it shall be yours." And then he, too, disappeared into the ever-growing throng.

Lee's eyes scanned the crowd for every elderly face he could spot. But he was not prepared when a large black sedan pulled up to the curb and a youthful-looking fellow, not much older than he was, stepped out from the backseat. He placed his left hand on Lee's shoulder and presented a torn dollar bill in his right hand. Lee fished his half of the bill out of his pocket and satisfied himself that they matched.

The stranger then said, "I am your friend. I am your guide. I am your Brother. I am a shepherd's son."

Before Lee had a chance to even think of a suitable reply, a black bag swooped down over his head from behind and he was thrust into the backseat of the car.

Where he was driven he could not say. How long he was driven would have been only a guess. But deprived of sight, he was chauffered throughout the city while passages of Scripture were recited to him by different voices. How many voices he could not determine, but as each voice began to speak, it started by introducing itself in the same cryptic manner as before: "I am your friend. I am your guide. I am your Brother. I am a shepherd's son."

Some hours later the car stopped and he was gently escorted out from the backseat. He was taken into a building and into an elevator. It troubled him that his senses were unable to tell him whether the elevator rose or descended. But the doors soon parted and he was guided through several passages and, finally, into a small, poorly lighted room. He was seated in a harsh chair while his ears picked up the sound of a match being struck.

"You are in the Meditation Chamber, Brother. All that you require is before you. Use the time remaining wisely. You may remove your hoodwink at any time." And then he heard the door close.

He waited for a moment, unsure of what to do. The only sound reaching his ears was that of his own labored breathing. He began to raise his hands to remove the hoodwink, but suddenly felt more secure lowering his head to his hands. When the cloth bag was removed he took a deep breath and looked around the small chamber. He was not prepared for the ghoulish sight that befell his eyes.

All four walls of the room were draped in heavy black cloth. Before him, on a small writing table, burned a lone candle that cast an eerie glow on a carafe of water, a long loaf of uncut bread, a pen, and some paper. The top sheet of paper read simply: Last Will and Testament. Clearly, he was to fill in the rest and sign it.

He stood stiffly and carried the candle to examine other areas of the darkened chamber, but bumped his shin against a long wooden box. He lowered the candle to it and realized with a gasp that it was a coffin. A small brass plate on the lid was inscribed *L. Sinclair*.

His hand shook as he debated whether or not to open it.

19

Finally, screwing up his courage, he lifted the lid with his foot, standing as far back from it as he could. The coffin was empty.

A small shelf above the coffin contained a human skull alongside a few books. He examined them and discovered a bible, a copy of the Koran, and a five-volume series of something called The Zohar.

He returned to the stiff-backed chair and contemplated the seemingly innocent series of events that had brought him to this point. All he had really known about the organization he was about to join was that his father belonged to some sort of fraternal organization, and had belonged for years. The name Brotherhood of the Craft meant nothing to Lee. He supposed it was similar to other fraternal organizations he had heard about, such as the Masons, the Knights of Columbus, or the Elks. Whatever he had expected—and he asked himself repeatedly what he had in fact expected—was nothing like this. Nowhere in his mind did he ever conjure up such things as being blindfolded and spirited away in broad daylight; or Meditation Chambers; or coffins; or wills.

The will. He picked it up and examined it, but it was virtually empty, awaiting only his bequests.

The thought of him having anything to leave anyone almost made him laugh aloud. He had shared his father's home until he dropped out of college in his freshman year and joined the marines. He was still a marine, about to be shipped overseas. And he was as penniless as he had been since he went through the rather meager inheritance he had received when his mother died.

His father, of course, had money, and Lee had never wanted for anything. But when it came right down to listing his assets in black and white on a will, he could think only of his four-year-old Corvette that burned oil badly, his high school graduation ring with a garnet stone, and a wristwatch that lost two minutes each day.

Nevertheless, he dutifully filled in the blanks on the document, leaving everything to his father, and signed his name.

He then removed the bible from the shelf and flipped through the pages searching for familiar passages. It had been so long since he had attended Sunday school that the words no longer had any meaning for him.

But he closed his eyes and the bible, leaned his head back, and prayed. He wasn't sure why he was praying; he just felt more comfortable doing it.

There was a current of electricity in the air as the clock struck seven. At that precise moment, the Master of the Mystery lifted the wooden gavel from its resting place on the ancient granite block and brought it down with tremendous force. The retort resounded through the Hall and all eyes immediately turned to the Master as he began the incantation of the ritual to open the Lodge—a ritual whose origins can be traced to the building of King Solomon's Temple in Jerusalem in the tenth century B.C.E.

In stony silence, the senior guardsman proceeded to seal the Lodge in carefully measured steps, ensuring that none but Members could gain admittance. Slowly, methodically, the Deacon—the Master's trusted messenger—passed among the members, exchanging grips and words with them all. Satisfied, he approached the altar and spoke: "My Lord, my Master. All present have earned the right to sit among us."

As the chaplain intoned a blessing, the Deacon slipped off to the dark side of the Hall and quietly entered Lee Sinclair's Meditation Chamber.

Lee stood when he heard the door opening, but the light just beyond the door was so poor and his lone candle so ineffective, that he could not see who had entered his small quarters. But he heard the door close and felt a comforting hand on his left shoulder.

"Do not be alarmed, Lee," said the Deacon. "I am your friend. I am your guide. I am your Brother. I am a shepherd's son. And I am here to prepare you for your initiation into the Brotherhood of the Craft."

"Uh, I've been thinking," said Lee, "and I'm not really sure if I'm ready for this. I mean, I didn't expect this sort of, well, this sort of thing."

"No one ever does, Lee," the Deacon said reassuringly. "But remember that what you are about to go through has happened to every other Brother of the Craft. And they all survived it."

Lee gave a nervous chuckle, thinking the Deacon was making a joke. But as he strained to make out the Deacon's face in the dim light, he could tell that he was not smiling.

"Lee, remove your shoes and socks and strip to the waist," the Deacon ordered, "and I will help guide you from your present darkness."

The candidate for initiation did as he was told and allowed himself to be gently guided through the door.

A voice he immediately recognized as his father's boomed out to him: "Behold a candidate in darkness! If he is worthy of our secrets, bring him forth to see the light."

The Deacon said to Lee: "You are in darkness and unsure of the way. But behold the ground before you and see that others have traveled this way before."

On those words the hidden organ began playing as the Members seated in the great Hall intoned in unison: "I am your friend. I am your guide. I am your Brother. I am a shepherd's son."

Lee looked down at his feet in the sand and saw footprints before him. Hesitatingly, he took a step forward.

As he did a voice cried out: "Blessed is the man that walketh not in the counsel of the ungodly, nor standeth in the way of sinners, nor sitteth in the seat of the scornful. But his delight is in the law of the Lord; and in his law doth he meditate day and night."

Feeling more sure of himself, Lee slowly continued to track the steps in the sand, each one bringing him closer and closer to the light of the great Hall.

And the voice cried out again: "And he shall be like a tree planted by the rivers of water, that bringeth forth his fruit in his season; his leaf also shall not wither; and whatsoever he doeth shall prosper."

And the Members in unison replied: "I am your friend."

Then the voice again: "The ungodly are not so: but are like the chaff which the wind driveth away."

The Members: "I am your guide."

The voice: "Therefore the ungodly shall not stand in judgment nor sinners in the congregation of the righteous."

"I am your Brother."

"For the Lord knoweth the way of the righteous: but the way of the ungodly shall perish."

"I AM A SHEPHERD'S SON."

The footsteps stopped and Lee looked up to see his father, who stood raised before him. And his father, the Master of the Mystery, asked, "Who shall ascend into the hill of the Lord? Who shall stand in His holy place?"

And the Deacon, replying on behalf of his charge, answered, "He that hath clean hands and a pure heart; who hath not lifted up his soul unto vanity, nor sworn deceitfully. He shall receive the blessings from the Lord, and righteousness from the God of his salvation."

And the Master asked of the Deacon: "Who are you to vouch for this novitiate?"

The Deacon replied, "I am his friend. I am his guide. I am his Brother."

"And who is he who stands before me?"

"He," said the Deacon, "is a poor son of a faithful shepherd who, rather than divulge the secrets of the Brotherhood entrusted to his safekeeping, suffered himself to be ignominiously slain."

And so began the ancient ceremony for which John Sinclair had waited. He was about to obligate his son to the Brotherhood of the Craft.

It was a long and beautiful ritual, mostly didactic in nature and form, but one that imparted wisdom and light and truth. Much of its beauty came from the mere fact that the spoken portion of the ritual, close to three hours in length, was completely memorized by the Master, as nothing in the Brotherhood of the Craft is ever written down. Ritual—all ritual—is esoterically handed down by word of mouth from generation to generation. Having the mental capacity to confer the degree of initiation is considered an achievement by all Brothers.

And tonight, John Sinclair's oratory had never been better. The few times he stumbled over a word he was able to recover quickly before any of the elders of the Brotherhood had a chance to correct him.

Lee, for his part, stood motionless and spellbound by his father. He had never in all his twenty-one years seen his father in such a commanding role.

His father began his lecture simply, tracing the history of the Brotherhood of the Craft to the remotest ages of the world. Back in time to Moses, to David, and to Solomon.

The Master explained how the earliest Members of the Brotherhood practiced the Solar Mysteries of the Egyptians, which eventually broke off into two separate groups, the Lesser Mysteries and the Greater Mysteries.

He touched on how the evolutionary process developed into such secret societies as the Pythagorean Mysteries of Greece, the Mithraic Mysteries of Persia, the Adoniac Mysteries of Syria, the Diocletian Mysteries of Rome, the Dionysian Artificers of Phoenicia, the Comacine Masters, the Cabbalah and, ultimately, into the Brotherhood of the Craft.

"And we," said his father, "are children of the King's palace. We are *Benei Heikhala De-Malka.*"

And with those words, the Master of the Mystery began to spin an incredible biblical tale of wonderment, devotion, idolatry, greed, envy, and murder. And as he did so, some of the older Members closed their eyes and relived the memory of the night they had received the Word for the first time.

As Lee listened to his father's words, he became aware of the existence of a pencil point of light just above his father's head. The light began to move and shift gradually and Lee was helpless to avoid staring into its relaxing shapes. As his father's biblical tale grew, so grew the light and its various forms and pleasant colors.

Lee's powers of concentration became so acute and he was listening so intently to his father that he was caught completely by surprise when he was suddenly and violently grabbed from behind.

He tried to struggle but was helpless against the huge bulk of whomever it was who had pinned his arms. He looked at his father for help and was about to call out. But before he had the chance, he was spun around where he was confronted by someone wearing a grotesque rubber mask of some kind.

As his head began to clear from the severe jostling he had just received, he realized that his father was still talking, as if nothing unusual had happened. He strained to hear what his father was saying.

He tried to turn his head to the side to see his father, but a pair of unseen hands behind him set his head firmly in place, facing this evil, menacing creature before him.

His father began talking about golden rings and then began describing an assault on an individual, some type of ancient shepherd in service to a biblical ruler. Lee quickly surmised that *he* must be portraying this shepherd, that he was the principal player in a fast-unfolding drama.

He was almost beginning to enjoy the tale when the pitch of his father's voice began to rise with alarm. His father was detailing how this "villain" attacked the shepherd, and with each detail of the assault, the personage before him simulated the attack on Lee.

He tried to raise his arms to defend himself, but to no avail. They were securely pinned to his sides. He tried to think of his military training, but the blows came too swiftly.

And the instant the attack ended, he was spun around again. Another grotesque mask confronted him. Another demand for golden rings. Another refusal. And another attack.

Again and again, he was confronted by men wearing tuxedos and horrible rubber masks. Again and again he was attacked. And still his father's voice droned on.

But suddenly his father's voice became muffled. He stole

a look at his father and saw that he, too, had donned a mask. The light above his father's head was brilliant now and spinning wildly.

He became aware of a strange, sweet odor in the room, like perfume but more intoxicating. He allowed his lungs and his head to fill with the dizzying aroma. It was becoming increasingly difficult to follow his father's words. His brain was becoming thick and fuzzy and he felt light on his feet. Once, when his knees buckled and he thought he was going to fall, he became painfully aware of the unseen hands holding him firmly in place, almost lifting him off the floor.

The odor, the dizziness. My God, they're gassing me, he thought. He tried to shout out but somehow couldn't find his voice.

Quickly, he managed to glance at the floor before his head was snapped back to attention. No, he wasn't floating; it just seemed that way.

Gas masks, he thought. That's why the facial features are so strange. They're all wearing some kind of gas mask under rubber masks. Oh, God, why is this happening to me? he inwardly screamed. How could it? How could my father allow me to be hurt?

His vision was starting to blur and now everything seemed to be happening in slow motion. His father was telling about the final and fatal blow to the shepherd who steadfastly refused to divulge the secrets entrusted to his safekeeping. But this time, as his father described the last assault, he was struck a final time, viciously, it seemed. And this time he was going to fall, and no one was there to catch him. Then everything went black for Lee.

When he came to, his first reaction was to try to get his bearings. As he slowly opened his eyes, he realized that he was flat on his back and he felt warm and cozy, the kind of warmth one feels on a cold winter morning under a pile of blankets, he thought.

After just a few moments, when he realized that he felt no pain on any parts of his body where he had been struck, he also noticed the pleasant sensation of feeling quite refreshed, as though he had just had a much-needed nap.

He became aware of a gentle weight pressing uniformly on all parts of his body below the neck, and soon adjusted to the unnerving realization that he was in a deep pit, almost completely covered over with dirt. He was, in fact, lying in a grave.

He then recalled the last words he heard before being knocked unconscious (did I faint?): ". . . and caused his immediate death!" Apparently, he was still playing the unwilling central part in this fascinating drama.

When he looked up and straight ahead, the first face he saw was his father's. But as he averted his eyes slowly to the sides, he also saw that he was surrounded completely by Members of the Brotherhood, all solemn-looking in their black tuxedos. (Mourning clothes? he wondered.) The masks were now gone from sight. And no telltale gaseous odor lingered.

As he squirmed slightly, he was aware that his clothes had been removed and the cool fabric completely encircling his body was silken. (A burial shroud?) On top of where his chest should be, a small spring of acacia or evergreen rested in the dirt.

He had not been aware of the organ playing in the background until it stopped suddenly and his father began his oratory once again.

The Master of the Mystery confirmed that Lee represented the son of the shepherd who, rather than divulge the secrets of the Craft entrusted to his safekeeping, suffered himself to be ignominiously slain. And it was made abundantly clear to Lee that he was under a similar obligation.

The biblical legend continued on, with the Master of the Mystery explaining how the assassins buried the body and how, eventually, they had been captured, tortured, and brutally executed.

As each piece of the story was revealed, a group of Members acted out each development—the capture, the execution, and the search and discovery of the shepherd's body. But it was during the "discovery of the body" that a most curious thing happened.

The Master of the Mystery explained that the body was nowhere to be found. The search party had traveled far and wide on its mission, but to no avail.

"Ein-Sof," said one of the tuxedoed mourners standing around Lee Sinclair's still-prostrate form. "Ein-Sof," a small chorus chimed in.

"They invoked the ineffable name of God," the Master explained. "They did not pray to God as perhaps they should have. Rather, by invoking His name in such a manner, they were *commanding* God to lead them to the body."

"Ein-Sof," the chorus began to grow and grow, more voices joining in the rhythmic chant. "Ein-Sof, Ein-Sof, Ein-Sof."

"And this angered the Lord," the Master said. "And He spake sharply: 'I will lead you to your shepherd, but I will speak to you no more.' And God kept His word. He led them to the body, but He spoke to them no more."

At this juncture, some of the Members, still acting out the drama, began to clear away the dirt and debris from Lee's body as the Master's lecture continued.

"And as they viewed the body in that unhallowed grave,

they were shocked to discover that the assassins had muti-lated part of the shepherd's body: The two middle fingers of both hands had been chopped off.''

Lee's shroud was being removed and he glanced at his own hands: The middle fingers of both of his hands were missing.

He gasped suddenly and was about to cry out when he realized that his eyes had to be deceiving him. In an instant he logically reasoned that his father was missing no fingers, nor was anyone else he had seen tonight. And he recalled the Deacon's words about every other Brother of the Craft going through what he was about to experience.

Slowly, he raised his hands and turned the palms inward, greatly relieved to see his two middle fingers securely taped down. He let out an audible sigh of thanks.

But as he was examining his own hands, he noticed that each and every Member surrounding his body had raised their hands far above their heads, and that they were drop-ping their two middle fingers.

''Behold the Hailing Sign!'' bellowed the Master of the Mystery. ''It is a signal of distress for your everlasting protec-tion. It is to be used only in life-threatening situations. But if your life is ever in danger, and if you have the ability to give tl . Hailing Sign, it will be answered by a Brother who is obligated to try to save your life at the very risk of his own.''

At the conclusion of these words, Lee's body was lifted from his grave and carried to the altar. He was stood upright while his shroud was tied at his waist, leaving his upper torso bare.

His father stood across the altar from him while the Mem-bers formed a circle around both of them, father and son, Brother and Brother. One of the Members unfastened the tape binding Lee's fingers while another Member appeared with a bleating lamb, which he placed upon the golden altar.

"My Brother," said the Master of the Mystery to his son, "much of our tradition comes from the bible. And the bible tells us over and over how sacrifices were made in the name of God and always on momentous occasions. Tonight is such an occasion, and this lamb will be offered up as a sacrifice. The honor belongs to you, if you so desire." And his father offered him a jewel-encrusted dagger.

Lee wasn't certain what to do and he opened his mouth to speak but found it difficult to discover his voice. He had not said a word for hours on end.

"Would you like a drink of water, Lee?" his father asked.

"Yes, sir. Please," Lee responded, suddenly realizing that his father was back to being his father again, or at least he appeared to be his father again. The formality of his father's performance tonight seemed to be gone.

A glass of water was handed to Lee by one of the Brothers. After he drank it down and passed the glass to an unseen hand, Lee's father asked him again, "Would you like the honor of sacrificing the lamb, Lee?"

"Dad, are you serious? Do you really want me to kill this animal?"

The poor lamb, as if sensing that his continued good health was being openly debated, began bleating even more loudly.

"No, Lee," his father said. "You don't have to do it if it will trouble you. I'll do the honor for you."

And before Lee had a chance to react, his father had taken the sacrificial lamb in his left hand and deftly slit the animal's throat with the dagger in his right hand. Immediately, blood covered the altar, pouring forth freely from the lamb's neck where the Master of the Mystery still held the dagger in place. He pulled the dagger free and the lamb was quickly removed from sight.

Lee was in shock at his father's behavior. He never would have believed that his father—a man who scorned hunting as cruel and vicious—would have the ability to cold-bloodedly kill that lamb.

Still holding onto the dagger, John Sinclair, resuming his demeanor as Master of the Mystery once more, intoned, "The Lord teaches us about sacrifices in the book of *Genesis,* chapter 22, when He commands Abraham to sacrifice his only son, Isaac, atop Mount Moriah."

Lee suddenly went white with fear.

"Dad," he began to say softly, but he was quieted by a Member nearby.

"Have no concern, my Brother, my son. It is not for me to sacrifice you. It is for you to demonstrate your faith in God. Take the knife, Lee."

His father placed the bloody instrument in his hand.

"My Brother, all that is required to complete the ceremony making you a Brother of the Craft is for you to take the knife I have just given you and plunge it into your belly."

Lee laughed aloud in spite of himself. "You want me to kill myself? Dad, this has gone far enough, hasn't it?" He was whispering so that the other Members would not hear.

"My Brother, there comes a time in every man's life when he must demonstrate his trust in his God and his faith in a friend. This is your time, my Brother."

Lee could barely believe what he was hearing. His own father was telling him to take his own life; he was trying to kill him. Earlier, he thought, his life had been in danger; but that was merely illusion. He could see no illusion now, nor the hope of one. He saw his father slaughter the lamb. The animal's blood was still on the altar, still on the blade he held firmly in both hands.

"Dad." He was trying to keep his voice low and calm but it cracked. "Dad, are you listening to me? I could get hurt. Christ, I can kill myself." But the Master of the Mystery would not respond.

Lee turned to look at the Members assembled about him. Maybe they weren't aware of what his father was asking him to do. He found the Deacon in the crowd—the only face he recognized—and tried to reason with him.

"Did you hear what my father asked me to do?"

But there was no response.

"Trust in God," said an anonymous voice.

"Trust in your Brother," said another.

Lee spun around and tried to confront the unseen speakers. "This is insane," he cried. He was drenched in sweat but he tried not to panic. There had to be a way out of this nightmare, somehow.

A voice from behind him said softly, "I am your friend."

Lee turned quickly. "Don't feed me that shit! This has gone far enough. Friends don't do what you guys are doing."

"I am your guide," said another voice.

"Oh, yeah? Well just guide me to my clothes and let me get the hell out of here," he shouted, his voice too shrill for his own liking.

"We cannot do that, son." It was his father talking, softly, comforting. "We've come too far, Lee, and we cannot turn back. We've imparted too many of our secrets to you."

"Dad," he whispered. "Dad, please. I'm—I'm scared."

"If you trust in God, you have no need for fear. The bible informs us that they who put their trust in God shall never be confounded."

"Dad, please stop talking like a preacher. I trust in God. Honestly, I do. But I also trust that this knife could kill me if I listen to you."

"Think, Lee. Think about what you've been taught tonight."

His mind raced through the myriad alien activities that had consumed almost the last twelve hours of his life, looking frantically for a clue. As possible instruments of salvation, he alternately considered, and discarded, torn dollar bills, passages from Scripture, wills and coffins, footsteps in the sand, biblical murders, missing fingers, and what is, or what used to be, the real name for God.

Missing fingers. The Hailing Sign when his life is in danger. Jesus, it was so simple he couldn't believe he hadn't thought of it before. These guys just gave me a lecture about what to do when my life is in danger, he reasoned to himself, and then they put my life in danger to see whether I was listening to what they said.

He tried to remember what he was supposed to do. Something about raising his hands over his head and dropping some fingers into his palms. But which two fingers? He looked at his hands—surprised at first that he was still holding onto the bloodied knife—and noticed the tape marks still on the middle fingers of both his hands. Quickly, he let the knife drop to the floor and he thrust his hands over his head. Then, carefully, he lowered the designated digits. But nothing happened.

Lee didn't really know what he was expecting to happen, but he certainly was anticipating *some* response. His action was met with silence.

"Isn't this right?" he questioned everyone and no one in particular. "Isn't this it? Huh? Aren't I supposed to do this?"

But they just stared at him.

"Dammit to hell! Won't anyone talk to me? What am I supposed to do?"

He was oblivious to the tears that began to well up in his eyes. "Please, I'm begging you. Tell me what to do."

"Trust in your Brother," said a soft voice.

"Ein-Sof," someone else whispered.

Lee began to repeat the foreign-sounding word, first to himself and then out loud. And to his surprise, each time he mouthed the word a sense of comfort he hadn't felt all night swept over him.

"Ein-Sof," he said, over and over, as if asking for guidance, divine intervention, a signal.

He dropped to his knees in front of the altar and picked up the knife, grasping it with both hands, blade pointed toward his stomach.

"Ein-Sof," he murmured, turning the blade around as the candlelight danced on the hilt and then returning the angle so that the knife pointed at his midsection once more.

He steadied his right hand in his left, looked his father in the eye, and took one last deep breath and thrust the knife into his belly with every ounce of strength he possessed.

The next few moments were confusing for him. He felt the blood gushing onto his hands before he had the courage to divert his eyes downward and see the wound. But he also saw his father break into a huge grin and clap his hands together. And he heard an uproarious cheer and much applause from the Members.

But what he noticed most was that there wasn't any pain.

It was when this fact sunk in that he had the courage to look. As he pulled the knife away from his body, he saw that the blood came not from his belly but from the knife—a trick knife with a collapsible blade that squirts blood. And a knife, he was sure, that couldn't even hurt a lamb.

"Order, Brethren, order!" It was the Master of the Mystery once more, and his voice was law. The Members quieted down immediately.

"Congratulations, my Brother. Your accomplishment here tonight is not to be taken lightly. Because we have all gone through it, too, we know full well how difficult it is to plunge a knife into yourself. But this action was done to teach you the one fraternal tenet that cannot be stated too often: A Brother will never harm another Brother for *any* reason. There are no exceptions to this Obligation.

"The Hailing Sign you threw was not answered because your life was never in danger. However, we were pleased that you had enough presence of mind to think of it."

The clock began to chime midnight and the Members dispersed from the circle they had formed, after stopping where Lee stood and patting him on the back or shaking his hand.

It was over at last.

He was a member of the Brotherhood of the Craft, the oldest and largest secret fraternal society in the world, whose membership extends even behind the iron curtain, and whose past and present rolls have included kings, presidents, prime ministers, and even popes—as well as less noble men—among its ranks.

It was over.

He was a Brother.

2

▼

—May 3, 1979

EARLY the next morning, Lee broke the news to his father that his orders had come through. He was being assigned to the marine detachment at the U.S. Embassy in Tehran, Iran, and would be leaving within forty-eight hours.

Later, after Lee had left the house, John climbed up into the attic and found an old shoe box of photographs. There were tears in his eyes when he came across the picture he had taken of Ruth and Lee the day he had brought them both home from the hospital.

"I'll be with you soon, honey," John thought. "Soon."

He wasn't aware of how long he had been in the attic,

looking through old memories, but when he came downstairs the early-afternoon mail had already been delivered.

He tore up the letter from the doctor without even opening it.

3

Washington, D.C.
—December 23, 1979

THE Palestinian diplomat who had been called away from the embassy party to take the phone call listened intently to the voice on the other end of the line. The caller was one of their moles inside the U.S. State Department, but the message was frustratingly brief.

"Again, if your please," ordered the member of the Palestine Liberation Organization's unofficial delegation, which operated out of cramped quarters in the damp basement of the Lebanese Embassy. "I am not sure I heard you correctly."

"You heard me all right," said the whispered voice. "I said that someone called for Alexander Mycroft's file today."

"But *who?*" the Arab demanded. "And *why?* Is he still alive?"

"The 'who' is someone in the Decoding and Cryptography section. I don't know why, but I do know that right after he signed out the file, he had his secretary book him a seat on tomorrow morning's nine o'clock Metroliner to Philadelphia."

"Yes, yes," muttered the diplomat. "Give me his name and anything else you know. And please be quick." The Arab wrote down the information.

He terminated the conversation and immediately placed a call to Beirut, surprised that he was able to get through in under fifteen minutes. The diplomat discussed the information he had just received with his superior, a bearded man who sat in robes on an oversized divan and drank hot tea from a cracked glass. He allowed his tongue to toy dangerously with the crack as he tried to process the incoming information.

"I agree," said the voice from Beirut at last. "The man must be followed. Perhaps he will lead us to Mycroft."

"If he is still alive," said the diplomat. "But we don't even know what he looks like today."

"How much could he have changed in—how long has it been?—five years, six? What is important is why the government of the United States would be interested in the services of Alexander Mycroft? What are they up to? What is *he* up to?"

"I don't know," the PLO diplomat responded. "I just know that we must act swiftly if we are to act at all."

"Who can we send?"

There was an awkward silence followed by a long sigh before the diplomat answered. "That is the problem. We have only the girl."

"But she is perfect! She has been in the United States for years. Ten years, twelve years. She speaks the English language with no accent. Her mother was French. She has no outward appearances of Middle Eastern or Asian traces. She is—How do they say that?—American as apple cakes? And she is ruthless. Send the girl."

"But she is unstable."

"She is perfect. Send the girl."

"But she knows Mycroft; she hates him."

"We don't know if he is alive. And besides, we are sending her only to see where this State Department person leads us. No more. At least for now. Send the girl. And keep me informed." And with that they were disconnected.

"Pie," said the diplomat to himself. "Apple pie, I think."

The Palestinian diplomat walked down the hall of the basement and entered a room at the far end without knocking. As always, he stared at her for a few moments when he first came into her presence. Her beauty made his heart race and he always needed just a moment to inwardly compose himself before speaking. He had this constant fear that his voice would crack like a schoolboy's whenever he spoke to her.

She possessed naturally luxuriant black hair, dark eyes, and full lips that never knew lipstick or needed to. With almost equal parts European, Asian, Middle Eastern, and Latin blood coursing through her veins, she had the sort of cheekbones and sensually flaring nostrils that high-fashion models would kill for.

He knew how perfectly formed her body was, too. When they first met several years earlier, she seduced him and granted him one opportunity to fulfill any fantasy he could conjure up. But he had been so overcome by her beauty and her offer that even in her naked presence he was unable to achieve an erection. She masturbated in front of him but

4 1

refused to use her legendary tongue to assist him. She climaxed, dressed, and departed, and never gave him a second chance nor a second look.

This evening she sat at a small table wearing headphones, eavesdropping on a conversation somewhere in the embassy and tape-recording it. He picked up a spare set of headphones and placed one side of it to his ear. All he could hear was breathing.

"Who is it?" he asked quietly, trying to keep his voice under control. "The congressman?"

She removed the headset and shook her head. "No. He could not make it tonight. It is one of his aides. But he is not a very good lover. Most American men aren't."

He switched off the tape recorder and sat across the table from her. He wanted to be close to judge her reactions. Beirut could be damned. If *he* thought she was unstable about this assignment, he wouldn't send her.

"We have a small task for you," he began.

She sat forward intently with her hands in her lap under the table. She was bored and craved diversion, excitement. "Yes?"

"There is a man in Washington who will be taking a train to Philadelphia in the morning. You will follow him and see where he goes, what he does, whom he talks to."

She sat back in her chair, dejected. "That is the assignment? Just something a kid could do? Why are you wasting my time?"

He mulled one of her phrases over in his mind: "Just something a kid could do." He was fluent in English but had never been able to really master idiomatic phrases with ease the way she had. It was impossible to tell she had not been born here.

"There may be more to the assignment. The man works

for the State Department and today he took out an old dossier from the file room. We are curious about the file.''

"Do you want to see the file?''

"Oh, no, no. We have seen it many times in the past. It is the subject of the file that we are curious about. We thought it was a 'dead' file''—he smiled at his small pun—''and we want to know why someone is interested in it.''

"What's the file?'' she asked. "Whose file is it?''

Now. The moment of truth. He sat forward. *Alexander Mycroft.''*

She blinked several times as if her brain's retrieval system was searching for the name, the memories. In truth, it was shock that caused her to blink. With her hands still in her lap, she began digging her nails into her palms to try to keep her composure. The diplomat was disappointed. "Are you telling me that he is alive? I will gladly correct that oversight.''

He slapped her without warning. "Pay attention! Your job will be to collect information. You will follow this man from the State Department and try to find out why he requested Mycroft's file. If Mycroft is alive, we want to know. We want to know why the U.S. government is interested in him after so many years. Are they sending him on an assignment? Where? Does it have something to do with the situation in Iran with the American hostages? You know how important it is for us to maintain good relations with Iran. Have you forgotten so quickly that Chairman Arafat was with Khomeini just last month? If Mycroft is being sent on a secret government mission to Iran, don't you think our new Iranian friends would be in our debt if we could stop Mycroft, or at least warn the Iranians in advance? And if this is so, then what is the mission? And why use Mycroft? Why would they use someone from the State Department to con-

4 3

tact him? Mycroft was never a diplomat. And why use some-one from"—the PLO representative consulted his note—"the Decoding and Cryptography section to contact him? Do they want him to send messages, receive messages? From where? From whom? We want information. Is this 'just something a kid could do,' or shall I continue?"

She rubbed her cheek but remained silent. He noticed a trace of blood on her face but didn't think he had hit her that hard. He grabbed her hands and held them toward himself, seeing where her sharp nails had broken the skin and drawn blood.

"As I thought so," he cursed. "You are wrong for this assignment. Your emotions are still too attached to what this man did years ago. I will find someone else." He started to get up to leave.

"NO!" She screeched and pushed the table aside, throw-ing herself into his lap, forcing him back into the chair. "It was just the shock of hearing his name. I am fine now. Really, I am fine." Almost without thinking, she began kiss-ing his crotch softly and caressing him through his trousers. "You know, we never did finish what we started a few years ago," she cooed, knowing he could be bribed. "I can help you." She started to undo his belt buckle and pull down his fly with excrutiating slowness, almost tooth-by-tooth. "I can help you achieve the largest erection of your life."

His heart raced so that he had trouble finding words through his parched lips. "You'll have to take Moussef with you," he said in a cracked voice.

She stopped. *"Moussef?* Never! He smells. He never bathes and he never shaves. He is dirty and too unpleasant to be around. I don't need him and I don't want him. I refuse!"

"Very well, I will find someone else to do this assignment.

You can continue listening to congressional aides making love badly." He started to throw her off his lap, but she placed her hand inside his pants and he sucked in his breath.

"Please." She was cooing again as if nothing had happened. "I will work with Moussef. I was hasty. I was rash. Please. Let us finish what we started." He relaxed and she freed his penis from his pants. It was limp.

This may take all night, she thought. But she would be successful. With her tongue and talents, she never failed. And for this assignment, it would be worth it even if it took a week.

She began her work.

—————

4

▼

—December 24, 1979

A S Alexander Mycroft walked briskly up Philadelphia's Chestnut Street Transitway, one arm laden down with an oversized shopping bag filled with Christmas presents and the other entwined by the gloved hand of a shapely blonde whom he had met just the night before, there were only three things on his alcohol-fuzzied mind: Would he get laid tonight? Did he get laid last night? And why the hell was he being followed?

As much as he despised parties—especially holiday-type parties that carry with them the forced air of joviality—he had surprised himself last night by accepting a last-minute invitation. He had attended primarily to drink himself out of his annual preholiday depression and had been well on his way to oblivion when the pretty blonde approached, took him gently by the hand, and led him out of the party and down the hall of the apartment building to her own place.

The next thing he remembered was awakening to the noontime serenade of the church bells of the Cathedral of Saints Peter and Paul, which aggravated his hangover, and to the smell of freshly brewed coffee. He was naked and alone in the queen-sized bed but found a one-size-fits-all terry-cloth robe at the foot of the bed and slipped it on. At first, he couldn't remember whose apartment he was in and he quickly checked to make certain his wallet was still in his pants. A moment later, after spying a framed photograph on the highboy, he recalled the attractive blonde but not her name.

His lungs ached for a cigarette and he had to remind himself—again—that he no longer smoked.

Mycroft parted the closed bedroom drapes and briefly peered outside. The sun was shining brightly, casting a near-blinding reflection on the light snow covering the ground three floors below. He padded out of the bedroom in the general direction of the coffee aroma, crossing over a plush beige carpet that felt warm between the toes of his bare feet. His bones creaked noisily.

The combination living room-dining area was well furnished and well appointed, and a single coffee mug awaited him in the kitchen alongside a not-quite-full automatic drip coffee maker. Evidence of someone—the blonde, he assumed—having already had the first cup of coffee was resting in a soiled mug in the sink. Other than that, the rest of the kitchen was spotless—even the ashtray. He had hoped that, perhaps, the blonde was a smoker. He could have used a whiff of even stale tobacco odors to calm his morning jitters.

He peeked into the yellow refrigerator only to discover that it was barer than his own.

Mycroft poured himself a mug of black coffee and downed it quickly—enjoying the pleasant surprise of a hint of cinnamon—while scanning the morning's paper that rested unopened on the small two-seater kitchenette table.

He was alone in the apartment—alone with the damned church bells. Their incessant ringing brought a slight nervous tic to his left eye.

After pouring a second cup, he retraced his steps in search of a much-needed bathroom, which he discovered adjoined the lone bedroom.

A note taped to the bathroom mirror read:

> Hi!
>   Make yourself at home. There's coffee in the kitchen and bathroom stuff on the vanity below.
> Towels are in the linen closet behind you.
>   Be back real soon. Please wait.

He wished she had signed her name.

Looking down, he found a still-packaged disposable razor and toothbrush, toothpaste, and shaving cream. He couldn't help wonder how large his hostess' razor and toothbrush supply was, and how frequently she had the opportunity to offer them to spontaneous overnight guests.

Mycroft was sipping his second cup of coffee more slowly than the first and thought that as much as his reflection in the mirror told him he needed a shave as soon as possible, the unsteadiness of the hand holding the coffee mug dictated that a shower first would be more sensible.

Having been married once, he was not surprised at the large variety of shampoos and other assorted hair conditioners and bath oils lining one corner of the shower ledge. Nor was he surprised that the vaguely familiar sweet aroma over-powered the small bathroom. It made him feel uncomfort-able and closed-in.

But he was taken aback when the sliding glass shower door parted and his hostess stood before him wearing a heavy woolen fisherman-knit sweater and carrying a small bag of groceries.

"Hi!" she said brightly. "How do scrambled eggs and bacon sound?"

"Love some," Mycroft responded, trying to act non-plussed while realizing how truly lovely she was.

"That's good, because it's about all I can do in a kitchen, and it's what I just bought at the store," she said. "Have everything you need?"

"I'm just fine," Mycroft said, wondering again about her name.

She let out a low throaty whistle while her gaze shifted downward. "I'll say," she replied, then winked at him. "Don't be too long." She closed the shower door and de-parted the bathroom.

After shaving, Mycroft donned the slacks, sport shirt, sweater, and Frye boots he had worn the night before. Out of habit, as he buttoned his shirt, he patted his pocket gently, assuring himself that the small glass tube he always carried close to his heart was still there. His mind tried to review the events of the past dozen or so hours, but it was no use. He couldn't clearly remember a thing after having left the party. Remember her name? He couldn't even recall whether he and the blonde had made love the night before. Jesus, he thought, I've got to cut down on the booze.

He examined himself in the full-length mirror before leav-ing the bedroom, displeased with his image. True, his stom-ach had only a slight paunch that he had been working on.

But his premature gray hair, which replaced the once brown, wavy hair, made him look older than the forty-five he was. From a distance, his blue eyes still looked clear; but when he moved his muscular six-foot frame closer to the mirror, he saw bloodshot eyes and crowsfeet at the corners. The last six years had really taken its toll on him.

Mycroft grabbed his camel-haired sport jacket from the hanger, but casually tossed it on a living room chair as he made his way toward the unpalatable smell of burnt toast.

"Need any help?" he inquired.

"Nope, it's all ready," she replied as she approached Mycroft and kissed him casually, but naturally, on the lips. We must have made love, Mycroft reasoned to himself. I wonder how I did?

"You can sit here," she said, pulling out a chair for him.

Mycroft passed on the offer of black toast, but he dug into the overcooked eggs. Accompanied with overcooked bacon, it was like eating rubber and cardboard, but he politely lied when she asked whether he was enjoying breakfast.

Cooking isn't everything, Mycroft daydreamed. We could have a great relationship, get married, have a kid or two, and hire a full-time cook. He took another bite of the questionable eggs. Cooking isn't everything, he argued to himself. It's the relationship that counts. You have to have someone you can trust, someone you can lean on, someone who gives you love and warmth and understanding in return. What the hell was her name? he wondered. He absentmindedly reached for the bread basket despite his earlier misgivings. His bite of the burned toast was noticeably crunchy and loud to his ears, but she didn't seem to notice. Besides, he reasoned, we could always order out. He liked the way this one looked and hoped it might last more than a few dates. At least, he hoped, it would last through the holidays.

Mycroft laughed with her and was pleased to find himself enjoying the small talk. She was easy to talk to, and he started wondering whether she liked him. And the longer they talked, the harder it was for Mycroft to even think of a way to ask her her name. Their conversation flowed on. But when she asked him a few obligatory, personal questions, Mycroft tensed and gave her the canned, greatly abbreviated version.

He told her that he had spent almost twenty years in the army but didn't tell her he had worked primarily in Military Intelligence; he told her he had been severely wounded by a rocket grenade in Vietnam and had spent nine months in three hospitals but omitted the fact that one of those hospitals was the psychiatric unit of Walter Reed where they tried to help him cope with the nightmares of his capture and torture by the Vietcong, nor did he mention that the last hospital was in the Middle East and that he was recovering from wounds that had nothing to do with his military service. He told her, for instance, that he retired from the army with the rank of Lt. Colonel (following several well-deserved battlefield commissions) on a full medical disability, but he lied when he said the only disabilities he had were some physical scars not mental ones; and, lastly, he turned his head slightly to avoid looking into her eyes when, in response to her question, he told her that his former wife and child had died in an accident in 1973 but didn't elaborate.

His right hand casually fondled the object in his shirt pocket, bringing a warm smile to his heart but not his lips.

By two o'clock they had finished the pot of coffee, and Mycroft was still amazed that anyone who could make such great coffee could be responsible for such disgusting bacon and eggs.

He was enjoying himself immensely and hated to leave,

but he did have to pick up several Christmas presents at a department store before closing time. Mycroft was wondering what the best way would be to say good-bye without making it sound so final, when suddenly the blonde said, "Well, where do we go from here?"

"I have to do some shopping—" he started to say.

"Great! How about if I tag along? I'm a great shopper and, if you're not doing anything tonight, we could pick up some food at the market and I could make us a quiet dinner here, right under the mistletoe or something like that. What do you say?"

Mycroft liked everything but the dinner suggestion. He didn't know whether his stomach would ever recover from breakfast, so he said, "I'd love to have the company and I'm not doing anything tonight. But I insist on taking *you* out to dinner."

"It's a deal," she said. "Just give me a couple of minutes to get ready."

That was almost three hours ago and ever since they left the small apartment building on the Parkway and walked the few blocks to the City Hall shopping area, Mycroft had the uneasy feeling that they were being followed.

It had been a couple of years since anyone had any reason to tail Mycroft, so at first he wasn't sure whether his imagination was playing tricks on him. He felt better than he had felt in a long while—owing mostly to the blonde's presence. He thought he still might be feeling some of the effects of last night's drinking.

However, he learned a long time ago not to ignore his hunches. And after a few well-designed twists and turns among the crowded aisles of John Wanamaker's Department Store, he was able to isolate the tail with certainty.

He was inwardly pleased that the old moves and instincts that had come with years and years of training and experience were coming back to him so easily. Once he and his date had entered the Market Street entrance of the department store, it had taken Mycroft exactly seven minutes and two escalators to positively identify the man on his trail.

Mycroft's ego felt certain that if his companion hadn't been with him, he could have done the task even sooner, but he didn't want to alarm her or give her any indication that anything was amiss. So his meanderings through Wanamaker's heavy shopping crowd had to have the appearance of purpose.

The man Mycroft eventually identified as the tail was of medium height and appeared to be in his late twenties. He had to be an amateur, thought Mycroft, if only for the conspicuous absence of even a shopping bag. The kid, as Mycroft now thought of him, didn't even give the appearance of shopping or of being in a hurry. This was, after all, Christmas eve.

Mycroft finally picked up the packages that he had ordered previously and he and the blonde found their way through the sea of bodies to the Chestnut Street exit. The tail was not far behind.

It did not escape the realm of Mycroft's possibilities that his date was being tailed and not him. But he decided that who was being followed was of considerably less importance than the act itself.

He knew he couldn't shake the kid without letting the girl know what was happening. He thought of trying to isolate the kid and take him out. But he wasn't "carrying" (always a slightly naked feeling to which he had long ago resigned himself) and didn't know whether the kid was armed either. He'd have to do it carefully and wondered whether he was too out of practice.

He quickened their pace up the Chestnut Street Transit-way and suggested to his companion that they stop for a drink before dinner.

"Are you sure your hangover can take it?" she asked.

"Positive," he replied. "I don't usually drink as much as last night," he lied slightly, "but I could go for some Christmas cheer right now. How about you?"

"I'm always good for an eggnog," she laughed, but Mycroft didn't. Just the mention of eggs made him momentarily ill.

They slipped into a little bar above Sixteenth Street that was quickly filling up with holiday revelers. Mycroft managed to find a small table near the rear and took the seat facing the door.

"What's your drink?" Mycroft asked.

"A glass of white wine, thanks," she replied.

Mycroft signaled the waiter and ordered. "A glass of chablis for the lady and I'll have a Stolichnaya on the rocks with an orange slice," he said.

Mycroft looked past her and spotted the kid coming in the door and taking a seat at the bar facing them across the crowded room. It was the first clear look Mycroft had at the tail, and he began to think he knew the person from somewhere in his past, but he wasn't sure.

"Listen," Mycroft began, unsure of exactly how to phrase his thought, or his fear, "you wouldn't by any chance have a jealous boyfriend, a young guy, say in his late twenties, medium-build, sandy-colored hair, would you?"

"No," she said. "Why on earth did you ask that?"

"Well, there's no reason to be alarmed, really, but ever

since earlier this afternoon, someone fitting that description has been following us. Now I don't know if he's tailing me, you, or both of us, but it's about time we found out."

"You're serious, aren't you?" she asked, and sounded genuinely concerned.

Jesus, he thought, how's she supposed to sound? Here she is with a guy she just met and he tells her they're being followed.

"I'm serious," Mycroft said, "but I'm going try to find out who he is and what he wants."

She grabbed his hand and pleaded, "Don't! Please, I don't want anything to happen"—after a beat she added—"to you."

Her skin was soft and her hand felt warm and comforting on his. He tried not to remember the last time someone held his hand that way, but it's hard to forget someone you loved. Especially, he told himself, when you begin to have feelings for someone else.

As much as he didn't want to pull his hand back, he did and quickly reached for the glass salt shaker on the table. He dropped the shaker into the handkerchief he had opened on his lap, folded it, and casually slipped them both into his pocket.

"Tell you what," Mycroft said, "it's too crowded in here for him to try anything if he means us any harm. So I'm just going to go into the men's room. If he's after me, he'll probably be stupid enough to follow. He hasn't been very smart so far."

She started to protest, but he cut her short. "Trust me," he said, and meant it. "I promise I won't let anything happen . . . to either of us. I've handled plenty of punks like this before. Be right back."

As he made his way to the men's room, he could feel his adrenaline starting to flow, and as much as he hated to admit it, he felt good—his senses were alive and he was feeling stirrings of things he hadn't felt in years. A lot of things.

There was only one person in the men's room as Mycroft entered, and he was on his way out. Mycroft took a fast survey: no windows, one urinal, one stall, one sink, and lots of graffiti. He checked to make sure the mirror above the sink wouldn't give the tail a view as he entered.

He quickly slipped off his boots and placed them inside the small stall in front of the toilet, facing out. Then he reclosed the stall door and loosely draped his jacket over the top of the door, after removing the salt shaker and handkerchief.

He next took off his belt and wrapped part of each end around both hands, then stood behind the bathroom door with the handkerchief clenched firmly between his teeth. He knew if someone other than the tail came in first, they'd think he was either crazy or a mugger, but he put that thought out of his mind and waited impatiently. He'd only give it a minute or two. If the tail was going to make a move—and Mycroft had a hunch he would—he'd move fast.

He could feel his pulse quicken as the door began to open slowly—too slowly, he thought, for someone coming in on ''legitimate'' business. The door opened slightly further, but no one entered at first.

Then Mycroft caught a glimpse of him through the crack of the door and tightened his grip on the belt. As the tail stepped into the bathroom, he stooped just low enough to see the bottoms of Mycroft's boots in the stall.

When he stood up and came further into the room, Mycroft demonstrated years of military training in a handful of seconds. He deftly slipped the belt around the kid's neck, jerked him upward and placed his right knee in his back to knock the wind out of him.

Grabbing both ends of the belt with his left hand, Mycroft quickly took the handkerchief out of his teeth with his right hand, feeling the weight of the salt shaker.

He pulled the kid backward toward him and placed the back of his own body firmly against the men's room door to prevent anyone else from entering.

The whole move took less than ten seconds, Mycroft estimated. Not bad, he thought, for being out of practice. He loosened the tension of the belt a little, just enough to keep his quarry from passing out from lack of oxygen.

"I'll only ask you once," Mycroft hissed in the kid's ear. "Why have you been following me?"

The young man took several deep breaths before answering hoarsely, "Would you harm a poor shepherd's son?"

A chill went through Mycroft's spine. It had been a very long time since he had heard those commanding words spoken.

Without thinking, Mycroft responded automatically. "Give me the Word!"

"How can I give what He has not imparted?" he answered correctly.

Mycroft removed the belt and turned him around. He was sure he knew him from somewhere.

"Who are you?" he demanded.

"I am your friend. I am your guide. I am—" he began, but Mycroft cut him short.

"Okay," Mycroft conceded, "we're Brothers. But why the hell have you been following me?"

"I'm sorry about that," the young man answered nervously. He wasn't used to being attacked, nor had he ever before been put in a situation that called for him to follow someone. "Really, I am sorry. But I had to see you alone and was just waiting for the right opportunity. You see, you've been with that girl all day and—"

Mycroft grabbed the kid by his lapels. "Brother or no Brother, I want to know right now: Why the tail?"

"You are summoned," the young man struggled to get the words out. "Tonight at seven."

Mycroft removed his hands from his Brother's lapels. "What's it all about?" he asked, knowing it was a foolish question. He had never before been summoned to an assembly of the Brotherhood of the Craft. No one is, unless it's very serious. And, more often than not, it's a life-or-death situation.

"Please, Brother Mycroft, you know I am only a messenger," he said, looking quizzically at the handkerchief in Mycroft's right hand. "I have to go now."

Mycroft splashed some cold water on his face and examined his hands. No shaking, he was glad to observe.

He slipped his boots and jacket back on, reflexively reaching into his inside left coat pocket for his cigarettes. He discovered the pocket was empty before remembering that he had smoked his last cigarette six years and two months ago on a deserted stretch of beach in Israel. It bothered him that after all this time he still reached for cigarettes out of habit.

He pulled the glass tube out of his shirt pocket for the umpteenth time. Break Glass in Case of Emergency, he read, although the writing was starting to wear thin. He stared at the cigarette, wondering for a moment whether a six-year-and-two-month-old cigarette would taste great or putrid. He slipped the tube back into his pocket and examined his reflection in the mirror. He thought his eyes were a little clearer, but his hair seemed grayer.

He wanted to think about why he had been summoned to the meeting, but someone entered the men's room and he realized he had left his date alone at the table. She undoubtedly had seen the messenger leave and was probably wondering what was taking him so long.

As he exited the men's room, he tried to think of what to tell her about having to cancel their plans for the evening.

But he needn't have bothered. She was gone.

5

▼

THEY came in their tuxedos. They always did.

Alone, and in small groups, they silently entered the western portal of one of the oldest and most ornate buildings in the world. They passed between the Byzantine pillars, over the Seal of Solomon, and under the twelve signs of the zodiac. They always did; it was the only way to enter.

For the first time in many years, Alexander Mycroft was among them.

He'd had barely enough time to rush back to his town house in Society Hill and change into his formal clothes after questioning the waiter about his date's disappearance. When Mycroft returned to the table from the men's room, both drinks were sitting untouched on the small table. After waiting a few minutes, he slipped a waitress a few bucks to check out the ladies' room. She wasn't there either.

But then a waiter came over and said, "Are you waiting for the blonde?"

"Yes," said Mycroft. "Where is she?"

"Can't say," he replied while cleaning off a table. "She started to ask me to give you a message and then she said to me, 'Oh, hell! Forget it. I don't even know his name!' And then she split."

"Nothing else?" Mycroft demanded.

"No, man; the lady just seemed pissed, you know? I mean, you gotta treat them with kid gloves today, you know what I mean? I mean, once you find a good woman, you gotta do all you can to keep her, you know?"

"Yeah," Mycroft sighed. "I know."

But he couldn't help wondering whether maybe there was some connection between his being followed and her leaving. Or maybe she thought I was just a kook playing cops and robbers and decided to leave before any trouble started, he considered.

He mulled these thoughts over and over in his mind while inhaling deeply of the driver's cigarette smoke as he rode silently down Market Street in a cab headed toward his home.

When the cab turned onto Pine Street from Fourth and pulled up to Mycroft's house, he promised the driver an extra ten dollars to wait for him.

Back in the cab headed up Market Street, he managed to put thoughts of the afternoon aside and focus on the reason he had been summoned to the Lodge. It had never happened to him before, and he was personally aware of only two other instances involving other Members, both serious transgressions that ultimately resulted in Lodge trials and eventual expulsion from the Craft. However, he believed they had been summoned by mail, and certainly not by dispatching a messenger to issue a summons in person. Although he could think of no logical reason to be summoned in such a manner, he was sure that it was a serious matter and that it was a summons he was obligated and duty bound to obey. No excuses were permitted.

When the cab pulled up in front of the seemingly nondescript building entrance, he alighted and fell into place with other similarly attired Brothers entering the gates. He recognized a few of them, but there was no conversation once they passed the Byzantine pillars located just inside the outer gates.

Mycroft decided the stairs would be faster and took them two at a time, grateful for the windpower to do so. However, when he went to sign his name in the ledger, he discovered the book was absent from its customary place on the marble writing table. In its place was a single evergreen sprig to inform those capable of interpreting such symbols that there would be no record made of tonight's Meeting, nor would there be a trial, since trial proceedings in the Craft were always recorded meticulously. In a word, the sprig meant trouble. But whether it meant trouble for him or for another, he would have to wait to find out, although he was silently betting on himself.

As he passed the upstairs guard's station, he was approached by the young Brother who had followed him earlier in the day. He didn't look any the worse for wear, Mycroft thought; in fact, dressed in formal wear and the particular regalia of his Craft office—a Deacon—he almost looked like one of those male models Mycroft would spot on occasion in the pages of the Sunday *New York Times Magazine*.

"Brother Mycroft," the Deacon said, "I am to escort you to your assigned seat for the evening. However, the Master of the Mystery asked that I first take you to him in his chambers. We haven't much time," he said glancing at his watch. "It's almost seven. Frankly, I would have thought you'd have been here earlier."

There was a touch of scorn in his voice, which Mycroft chose to ignore as he fell into step behind his escort. They proceeded across the sand-covered floor and down the dark side of the triangular room. Mycroft noted with curiosity that the dark side contained a large concave screen—the sort he had seen in many bars featuring seven-foot screens for watching sporting events. But the mere notion of watching a ball game amid the starched formality of a Craft Meeting was unthinkable.

When they reached the Apex, they climbed three steps and slipped through a door just to the side of the ornate throne.

"Brother Mycroft, Master," announced the escort, who then silently closed the door behind him as he left, leaving Alexander Mycroft facing a very pale and obviously distraught John Sinclair.

"Alex, thank God you're here," said Sinclair as he embraced Mycroft in a greeting of fellowship.

Mycroft was astonished. True, he hadn't seen his old friend in a number of years, but he wasn't prepared for a vision of a near-feeble old man sweating profusely. He decided to ignore it for the moment.

"Did I have a choice in coming, John?" Mycroft asked rhetorically.

Sinclair dropped his gaze to the floor, slightly embarrassed. "We both know the answer to that, Alex," he said. "But next time, try not to strangle my Deacon."

"If there ever is a next time, John, try not to have me followed. It makes a person edgy. By the way, I am curious to know why I've been summoned."

"Alex, there's so much I have to tell you. That's why I wanted to see you before the Meeting. But now, dammit, we don't have time. It's almost seven and the Meeting can't start late.

"Look," he said, struggling to properly knot a bow tie, "I can't even tie this fucking thing. Help me, will you?"

Mycroft's fingers deftly completed the bow as John said, "Almost everything will be explained to you in the Meeting. But you must meet me back here as soon as the Meeting's over. It's imperative, Alex!" He grasped Mycroft's hands as he said this, then released them. "I'll fill in the other details that I can't go into out there. Thanks," he said, admiring the finished bow in the mirror while slipping on his tailcoat. "Now hurry and take your seat. The Deacon is waiting for you outside the door."

As he turned to leave, Mycroft paused at the door. "John, you really look like shit. Will you be okay?"

"Alex, besides some irritating chest pains, I've never been more afraid in my entire life. Now get out of here. I'm late."

Mycroft really didn't need an escort to find his seat since all of the seats were scarlet except the empty white chair awaiting him—the guest of honor. But he dutifully followed the Deacon and sat down just as he heard the loud retort of the gavel hitting the granite block on the podium. It was exactly seven o'clock and the Master of the Mystery was opening a Lodge of the Brotherhood of the Craft in ancient ceremony.

Despite his years of absence from Craft Meetings, Mycroft found the words of the opening ritual coming back to him with ease. It was true what they said, he thought: Once learned, the rituals are never forgotten. But his mind quickly diverted from rituals as his eyes focused on one of the burning candles. It reminded him of the first Friday evening after his marriage to Beth. She had just lighted Friday night candles in preparation for the Sabbath and he, unaware of the significance of the candles, casually walked up to them and lighted his cigarette from one of the flames. She was furious at him for that, he recalled with a silent laugh. He caressed the glass tube in his pocket and thought how he would have loved to have had the chance to bring his son, Josh, into the Brotherhood of the Craft. His reverie ended when the opening concluded and the Master directed attention to the screen.

The images were immediately recognizable as television news footage of the recent takeover of the American embassy in Iran. Scenes of tens of thousands of screaming Iranians, blindfolded Americans, and rifle-toting militant students flickered to life on the screen. These scenes were all too familiar—the same foreign scenes that had repulsed all America each night on the news for the past two months.

"Brethren, I know we are all aware of the deplorable situation in Iran," the Master began as the TV announcer's voice started to fade. "The United States Embassy has been taken over by a bunch of Iranian hoodlums and they are holding American hostages. I don't have to tell you that, ordinarily, this would be of no concern to us as Brothers of the Craft, as much as we may feel revulsion as American citizens. But I want you to very carefully watch the scene coming up in a few moments; you'll see that the Craft is indeed involved.

"Most of these scenes were filmed by American news crews. However, some of them—like this one, now watch carefully!—were filmed by Iranians and were given to American news companies. This particular footage was just shown recently on American TV.

"The Iranians wanted to demonstrate to the world that stories of mistreatment of the hostages were not true. They wanted to show the world that the hostages were being well taken care of, so they released this footage of them inside and outside of the embassy building.

"See, here are some scenes of their living quarters and coming up is some of the first footage of some of the hostages. Then I guess they took some of the men outside of the building for exercise. Okay, here it comes. *Watch!*"

The screen was depicting the scenes John Sinclair had just described and the camera—apparently being held by someone who was not too familiar with a videotape camera's operations—was shakily panning the faces of the hostages, occasionally zooming in, then out.

Suddenly, the fuzzy, grainy picture of a young man in a military-green T-shirt and blond, military-style haircut came into view. The camera operator was trying to focus on him, and the picture would alternate between blurry and perfect.

"Keep your eyes on *this* one!" the Master commanded.

The young man at first appeared to be unsteady on his feet as he stood in place and appeared to survey his surroundings. He seemed to spot the camera and turned to face it, haltingly at first, as if he wasn't sure he was allowed to do so. He seemed to glance around to see if he was being observed by his captors, then turned to face the camera again.

Then, as if he was about to do some exercises, he put his hands on his waist and pivoted his upper torso a few times from side to side. Next, he raised his hands above his head, very slowly, very deliberately, as if he was doing some stretching exercises.

But when his arms were fully extended over his head, he slowly turned his hands to face the camera and carefully dropped the middle two fingers of both hands into his palms. He repeated the maneuver once more before the camera panned to face another captive.

The videotape stopped and the room was thrown into complete darkness for a moment until the lights came up slowly. There was an undercurrent of excited conversation among the Members. There was no doubt as to what they had just observed.

But the Master waited patiently for silence instead of gaveling the meeting back to order, and then said, "A Brother is in distress. A Brother's life is in danger. A Brother has thrown the Hailing Sign. And we are duty bound to obey!"

Again the murmur of voices, the hushed but frenetic tones of the assemblage. This time, John Sinclair did not wait for the conversation to ebb. He banged the gavel down upon the massive granite block with such force that a small chip of wood flew off.

"He who has been summoned will approach the altar!" commanded the Master, without using Mycroft's name, as was the custom in such circumstances.

Mycroft could feel all eyes on him as he slowly rose from the white chair, crossed to the altar, and stood directly below the golden inscription, *Fait Lux*.

"My Brother, we are not fools," said the Master, talking directly to Mycroft. "And we are not readily given to foolish talk of miracles. But two things are certain: First, a Brother has thrown the Hailing Sign and it is our sworn Obligation to hasten to his rescue if there is even the remotest chance of saving his life—even at the very risk of our own lives. This Obligation is sacrosanct.

"Secondly, my Brother, you possess certain, uh, skills and experience that are known to us. Your judgment in accurately assessing the situation and determining if there is a chance of rescuing our Brother is vital.

"But due to the unique circumstances of this particular situation, you may decide right here and now that the situation is beyond even *our* vast control. *And your decision will be final!*"

Alexander Mycroft began sweating under his arms and at the same time silently cursing John Sinclair to eternal damnation for having ever placed him in this predicament. What he was asking was unreasonable, to say the least. How the hell could Sinclair possibly expect one man to accomplish anything when the entire United States government had been able to do nothing except sit around looking helpless.

Sure, he had certain "skills and experience." Yes, he had been on dangerous missions in his life and had even managed to break a few people out of foreign jails and prison camps. But there were some important differences. In the past, he had trained army personnel on his team, accurate intelligence and counterintelligence reports, the backing of his government, and virtually unlimited resources.

What the fuck did he have now? he cursed to himself. True, he would have the support of the Craft's worldwide network of Brothers, but he had no grand illusions that that would amount to anything. He didn't have to look around the room to see that the overwhelming majority of the Members in this room alone were over sixty-five years old. What did that say about their counterparts in other countries?

But there was something else he had: a sworn Obligation to do what he could, even if that meant that nothing could be done. He was at least grateful that Sinclair had given him that out and a way to save face if he decided it was too risky.

He tried to study Sinclair's face, as he could sense everyone else in the room trying to read his. He wished he had gotten to the Meeting earlier. Maybe if Sinclair had told him then what he promised to impart to him later, it would have made the decision easier. One way or the other.

All he knew now was that Sinclair's eyes seemed to be imploring him. But imploring him to do *what?* Oh, well, he thought.

Mycroft took a deep breath, reached for the jewel-encrusted ceremonial sword on the altar, raised it high above his head with both hands, and spoke with conviction in a loud and clear voice the rallying cry of the First Crusades, signifying the mission was God's will: *"Deus vult!"*

Every member in the room clapped their hands together once, signifying thunder, and said in unison, "So mote it be."

Mycroft thought there were tears on Sinclair's cheeks, but the Master grasped his chest as he painfully uttered the words, "It is my will, it is my hope," then keeled over.

At first no one moved, partially due to shock and partially because their subconscious reminded the Members that no one could approach the Apex without the Master's express invitation or command. But Mycroft, seeing a friend lying on the floor, reacted instinctively and bounded toward Sinclair's prone form. The Deacon arrived almost as quickly, followed closely by a swarm of other Members.

The Secretary picked up the phone attached to the side of his desk, quickly called the guards downstairs and ordered them to bring in the emergency equipment and phone for an ambulance.

The Deacon was loosening Sinclair's tie and shirt collar

while Mycroft removed his own jacket and made a pillow for Sinclair's head. The Master's open eyes spotted Mycroft and he called to him in whispered but urgent tones.

"Alex, Alex."

Mycroft tried to cut him off. "Don't try to talk, John. Help is on the way. You'll be fine," he hoped aloud.

But Sinclair persisted and grabbed Mycroft by the shirt front and pulled his head down.

"Alex, it's Lee," he implored in a raspy whisper. "Please help, Alex, *it's Lee!* It's my boy! See Deacon. Be careful. Watch out for Christie, Alex; she'll stop you if she can. See Deacon." He stopped to catch his breath as he fished a small white box out of his jacket pocket and thrust it into Mycroft's hands.

Mycroft thought it might be a pillbox and started to open it. "What is it, John, medicine?"

"For later, Alex. Put it away."

He tried to say more but just then the emergency team arrived and immediately clamped an oxygen mask around John Sinclair's mouth while beginning the first vigorous thrusts of CPR. Within another couple of minutes the ambulance arrived and whisked Sinclair to Hahnemann Hospital just a few blocks away.

Mycroft was so troubled by the events of the past few hours that he absentmindedly left his coat on the steps at the Apex and blankly returned to his seat in just his shirtsleeves—an unthinkable act under normal Lodge circumstances. And he was beginning to question whether he'd ever see anything resembling "normal circumstances" again.

The Members filed out in silence, leaving Mycroft alone. His reverie, however, soon was broken by the Deacon, who approached him holding Mycroft's tuxedo jacket.

"Lee's his son, in case you didn't know."

"Thanks," said Mycroft as he laid the jacket across his lap without looking up. "How many others knew that John's son was a hostage in Iran?"

"Some of us knew," the Deacon replied, "but John was kind of under instructions from the State Department not to talk about it publicly. Our government doesn't want the Iranians to know exactly whom they're holding hostage. The Iranians think some of the hostages are spies, but they're not sure who. That's why the State Department has never released the names or the exact number of hostages."

"You're not trying to tell me that Lee Sinclair is a spy, are you?" asked Mycroft.

"No, of course not. He's in the marines and was stationed at the embassy when the takeover happened," the Deacon said. "He was just caught up in things. Christ, he didn't even have bullets in his gun. None of the marines did. It's policy."

"How do you know so much?" Mycroft inquired.

"I work in the Cryptography and Decoding Section of the State Department, presently assigned to the special Iranian task force. John ordered me to give you a briefing, or as much of a briefing as I can."

"What do you mean he 'ordered' you? Are you as opposed to this suicide rescue mission as I am?" Mycroft asked.

"More so," said the Deacon. "Look, let me be completely honest with you. I'm torn between my duty to my country and my Obligation to the Craft. I don't have to tell you that my Obligation to the Craft comes first. But until now, the Brotherhood was never in conflict with my patriotism."

"And it is now?" asked Mycroft.

"Only to the extent that your actions—if you decide to take any actions—may jeopardize what the country is trying to do behind the scenes. We've broken off diplomatic relations with Iran, naturally, and we're trying to negotiate the release of the hostages by using the Swiss as our intermediaries. The Iranians are very touchy and nervous and the slightest thing can blow the discussions. And a rescue attempt—even a suicide rescue attempt—is not exactly slight. Frankly, I was praying you'd take the out John gave you and just declare on the floor of the Lodge that any rescue attempt would be futile.''

"Well, we don't know that for sure, do we?'' said Mycroft, resenting anyone telling him what could and couldn't be done. "We don't know anything for sure until I do a little firsthand reconnaissance.''

"You mean you're actually going there? It's crazy!''

Mycroft stood up and put on his jacket. "Probably.''

"Okay, I know how you feel—''

"No, Deacon, you don't know how I feel,'' Mycroft said. "But I'm gonna tell you. I feel like I'm being manipulated—by you, by John Sinclair, and maybe even by our government. I feel like I'm being pulled in a half-dozen different directions. For me, that's par for the course. But when I came home after Vietnam and was down at Walter Reed, it was John Sinclair who came to see me three and four times a week for months on end. John helped me through a very rough time. He sat with me and at times he held me in his arms when all I wanted to do was scream and beat my head against a wall. I don't especially want to go out and get myself killed, but I owe John something, and I owe the Craft a lot. We *all* owe the Brotherhood, Deacon.''

The Deacon only nodded and then asked Mycroft to wait while he got his briefcase.

As the Deacon was on his way back across the Lodge room, the guard stuck his head in to report that he'd just heard from one of the Members at Hahnemann Hospital. Sinclair was in the cardiac-care unit. He was alive but he was unconscious.

When the guard left, the Deacon said, almost under his breath, "It'll almost be better if he goes this way."

"What're you talking about?" Mycroft demanded.

"Sinclair. He's terminally ill. Cancer," said the Deacon.

"Jesus," was all that Mycroft could manage.

"I think that's really why he asked you to help. Before this thing in Iran happened, he was planning to go over there and visit Lee. Kind of 'one more time' or so. Now I think he's under the delusion that you and the Craft can pull off some kind of miracle rescue and bring Lee to him before he dies."

"That's probably what he wanted to tell me after the meeting," said Mycroft.

"Huh? What do you mean?" asked the Deacon.

"When I was talking to him just before the Meeting began, he asked me to meet him back in his chambers after the Meeting. He said he had to talk to me about something that he couldn't talk about in the Meeting. Something that would explain things to me more. It was vital to him and I'm pretty sure it was scaring the hell out of him."

"I don't think his illness was it," said the Deacon. "John wouldn't tell anyone he was sick, especially you. He didn't want sympathy and he wouldn't ask you to risk your neck as a personal favor to him because he was dying. You know him better than that. When he was showing that news footage, he never once mentioned that it was his son in the pictures. This is either a fraternal Obligation or nothing."

"You may be right," answered Mycroft.

"Most likely he wanted to warn you about Christie."

"She's one of his daughters, isn't she?"

"Yeah, the older one."

"John's mentioned her to me," Mycroft said, "but why would he warn me about his daughter?"

"Christie and her brother, Lee, are very close," the Deacon explained, "and she was devastated when he became a hostage in Iran. Late last night, John telephoned her and confided in her. He told her what he planned to do—that he planned to ask you to try to rescue Lee. She didn't take the news very well, to hear John tell it."

"What do you mean?"

"She told her father that his actions—*your* actions, actually—could get Lee and other hostages killed. And she threatened to go to the authorities, to the State Department, even to the White House if necessary. The last thing she told John was that she'd stop you herself if she had to."

"Great. That's all I need. Where is she?"

"She had been working in Europe and was there last night when John spoke with her. Right now? Who knows where she is. She could be on her way over here even as we speak."

"All right," Mycroft conceded. "If she shows up I'll watch my ass. What other information do you have for me?"

"Plenty, and I hope you're a quick study. Because if all you know about the situation over there is what you've been reading in the papers or hearing on the news, you don't know half of what's really going on. And if you're serious about going there, you need a hell of a lot more information about the situation."

From his briefcase he removed a map of the embassy compound and a score of other papers marked *"TOP SECRET"* and began unfolding them on the floor of the Lodge.

"All right," said the Deacon, "let's try to do this fast. I've still got a Christmas tree at home to put up for my family."

They worked diligently for the next two hours. Mycroft memorized every detail about the several different buildings within the large compound where the hostages were being held. He scrutinized the original blueprints of the Chancery Building where the State Department's latest intelligence informants *thought* Lee Sinclair was being held. He familiarized himself completely with maps of Tehran and the country of Iran. And he most especially studied possible escape routes.

It was the subject of escape routes and the remembrance of a previous escape from a foreign country that jogged Mycroft's memory into recalling where he knew the Deacon from. But he waited until the Deacon had concluded his briefing before saying anything.

"You were in Vietnam, weren't you?" Mycroft asked him. But the Deacon merely gathered up his papers and stuffed them hurriedly into his briefcase. "We were in the same POW camp, right?"

"Yeah," answered the Deacon without turning around. "You could say that."

Mycroft heard the hostility in his voice. "Look, I'm sorry about this afternoon. Jumping you in the men's room, I mean."

"Forget it, okay?" He started to leave, but Mycroft caught up with him.

"Listen, I said I was sorry. You don't have to—"

The Deacon spun around fast. "Look, Mycroft, you don't get it. It's not the men's room, it's Vietnam. Yeah, we were in the same POW camp, only I was there for eighteen months. You were there about two weeks. I know you were sent in on a mission but you left us there when the bombing started."

"Wait a minute," Mycroft interrupted. "You don't know the whole story. You don't know—"

"But I do, Mycroft. I do know the whole story. I know the perverse tortures I was put through. I know that you ordered the bombing and you left Americans behind. And I was one of them. Most of my buddies died in that bombing. I guess I was lucky. *That's* the whole story, Mycroft. That's what I live with."

"But it wasn't like that."

The Deacon headed for the door again but stopped just before leaving. "You're my Brother and I'm obligated to help you. That doesn't mean I have to like you. I'm against your going to Iran. I think you'll wind up getting people killed and if you're one of them, I can't say I'll shed any tears. But I've given you the best information I have. I've honored my Obligation. And now I'm going home to my wife and son. You probably don't understand about families, Mycroft, but to me that's all that really matters." And then he was gone.

Mycroft sat for a while. His bones felt brittle, but he felt too drained to move at the moment. For the second time that day he thought of Beth.

He supposed that, in a way, he was always thinking about her and Josh. Everytime he craved a cigarette he thought of them. Somewhere in a dark recess of his mind—a deep niche where the light of logic never reaches—he once told himself that if only he had never smoked and hadn't gotten so winded that day on the beach, he would have been able to save his son.

His common sense, on the other hand, told him how illogical that was. His common sense reminded him that he had taken two bullets and lost more blood than he had a right to lose and still expect to live. And his common sense never let him forget that he did, in fact, reach the raft eventually, although it was overturned when he crawled on top of it and everyone aboard—"Fuck 'everyone aboard,'" he had screamed when he came to a week later in an Israeli hospital. "I only care about my son. What happened to Josh?"—was presumed dead.

Still, he hadn't had a cigarette since, and not a day passed when he didn't want one. When his hair started turning gray prematurely, he used to joke that he had a gray hair on his head for every urge he had for a smoke.

Without thinking, he started to stroke his upper lip—a habit he had developed when he still had the beard—and tried to put the disturbing conversation with the Deacon out of his mind. He had his own nightmares about Vietnam and didn't need to hear about anyone else's.

The Deacon's charges merely served to remind him that the quiet life he had sought for himself six years ago was a fantasy. He would never be able to escape the past completely. There would always be a Deacon somewhere. There would always be something to remind him of Beth, someone to remind him of Josh. There would always be a maddening urge for a cigarette. He caressed the glass tube in his shirt pocket.

Maybe the Deacon was right, that he shouldn't go to Iran. Now he stood a good chance of having the sister of the young man he was supposed to try to rescue all over him like eggwhite if he tried anything in Iran. She could turn into a distaff Deacon. What was her name? Christie. What was the blonde's name? That one he couldn't recall, if he ever knew it in the first place.

He stretched to work out a kink in his back, and felt the small box in his pants pocket. He had forgotten that John had given it to him and he now opened it.

Inside was a small golden ring, easily mistaken for a wedding band except for the engraved image. It was an equilateral triangle, minus one side, containing within it the Hebrew symbol for the mark of God.

He turned the ring around in his hand and found the inscriptions he knew would be engraved in triplicate on the inside of the ring. The inscriptions were written in three ancient languages: Syriac, Chaldaic, and Egyptian—the three known languages of the tenth century B.C.E.. And although he couldn't translate it, he knew from the ritual of initiation all too well what it said in each language:

> Blessed be he who shall welcome and assist this
> worthy ring bearer.

Mycroft suddenly felt the room get very warm and he noticed a slight tremble to his hands. Of course he knew the story and the meaning of the ring, as did all Brothers of the Craft. But he had always believed it to be mere legend, never supposing that such a ring ever existed.

Could it possibly be real? he wondered. And if it was genuine, how in the world did John Sinclair ever come by it?

But if it was fake—and he feared such was the case—he could easily get himself killed trying to pass it off as authentic. And Sinclair, of all people, would have to know that.

Slowly, as he was supposed to do, he slipped the ring onto the third finger of his left hand and gasped aloud as he felt a current—almost akin to a small electric charge—surge within him, traveling first up his left arm, across his chest, then down his right arm. When he grabbed hold of his left hand with his right, the sensation passed immediately.

It hadn't hurt him, just surprised him. And, he admitted to himself, in some inexplicable way it somehow felt comforting. Nevertheless, he wasn't about to allow himself to be lulled into a false sense of security just because of a piece of jewelry. He would not allow it, certainly, to be the deciding factor in whether or not he actually tried to rescue Lee Sinclair.

And almost convincing himself that he had in fact felt nothing more than his own imagination, Alexander Mycroft departed the Assembly Hall.

6

THE Deacon walked briskly and with a slowly sub-
siding anger as he crossed the street to enter City
Hall courtyard as a shortcut to get to Suburban
Station and the last Metroliner back to Washington. If he
hurried he could still make it; otherwise he'd have to ride
back in a regular train, which he did not enjoy doing. The
Metroliner afforded him more of a relaxing trip and one with
a much-needed bar car. Maybe a few drinks would help him
wash away the encounter with Mycroft.

He heard footsteps behind him but could tell from the
high-heeled gait that it was a woman. He turned briefly
without breaking stride and saw a woman's outline perhaps

ten yards back. If it had been a man he would have been nervous, he admitted to himself. The courtyard was dark and deserted and not the most secure place in the city after nightfall. Still, he switched his briefcase to his left hand in order to keep his right hand free, "just in case."

He was glad, too, that it wasn't a man behind him because he would immediately have thought it to be Mycroft. He was unhappy with the way the "briefing" had gone. He meant everything he had said to him but he just had never planned to say it. The conversation was replaying in his mind when he heard his name being called.

"Bill. Bill, please wait."

It was the woman. He was puzzled so he slowed his gait, looked over his shoulder, and tried to see who it was. But it was too dark. She called out to him again as she increased her speed.

"Bill. Please wait a minute. We need to talk, Bill."

Who the hell could it be, he wondered, as he slowed his pace to a virtual standstill. "Who is it? Who are you?" He was walking backward.

She was almost abreast of him now, but it was still too dark and his eyes had yet to fully adjust to the absence of light.

"Bill," she said softly, as if not wanting to disturb anyone, although there was certainly no one around. "Has it been so long that you don't remember me?"

The voice had a familiarness to it. "Christie? Christie, is that you?"

She had reached him now and they were almost face to face.

"Christie, it's too late. I've already given Alexander Mycroft the briefing. I happen to agree with you about his not going to Iran, but your father insisted—Oh, my God! Your father! Christie, your father had a heart attack and they rushed him to the hospital."

She was still obscured by darkness but she stared intensely into his eyes. "Hello, Bill. It's so good to see you again," she cooed. "It's been far too long, don't you think? We've got so much to talk about, to catch up on old times. We can start with Christie, for instance. She sounds like an interesting subject for the first part of our talk."

"Wh-what is this? Who the fuck are you?"

"Tsk, tsk. Such language, Bill. It's unbecoming. Look at me closely, Bill. I haven't changed so very much. You know me, if you try to remember. Think very hard, Bill. It will come to you." She moved a little closer so that he could see her.

"Look, lady. I don't know you. I don't know how you know my name. But I know that I don't want to have anything to do with you. I have a train to catch." He started to turn his back on her.

But from the shadows came the unseen hand of a man with a scraggly beard and strong body odor. He grabbed the Deacon from behind in a hammerlock. His briefcase fell to the ground.

"Moussef!" the woman scolded softly. "Don't be too rough on Bill. He was not really leaving, were you?"

"What do you want?" he demanded with such force that his own confidence surprised him.

"I admire that in you, Bill. You want to get right down to business. I thought we could renew old acquaintances for a while. But I must respect your wishes. To begin with, Bill, I want you to tell me everything you can about Alexander Mycroft. Why were you meeting him? What assignment has the government given him? Why is the government using

Mycroft after so many years? Does this assignment have something to do with the Iranian situation?"

The Deacon just stared at her incredulously. "Fuck you and the horse you and this smelly fleabag behind me rode in on."

"Moussef," she said softly, ignoring the Deacon for a moment, "Bill, here, is absolutely right. You must begin to improve your personal hygiene habits, and my nose and I would suggest you begin with daily baths. I do apologize, Bill. Please don't let Moussef's aroma affect our discussion."

He struggled against the hold, but the smelly Arab only increased the pressure of the grip, forcing the Deacon to involuntarily cry out for the briefest of moments.

"Careful, Moussef," she cautioned. "Don't harm Bill."

"Listen to me, lady. I don't know who the fuck you are and I don't care. If you want to kill me, fine; go ahead and kill me. You want this animal behind me to break my arms or my neck? Tell him to do it, all right? But whatever information you think I have is staying right with me. I don't give two fucks what you do, either."

"Well spoken, Bill. Truly it was very well spoken. I'll see that someone knows how brave you were."

She continued talking in the softest, most seductive voice as she removed her gloves.

"Bill, we are not stupid. We know that yesterday afternoon you called for Alexander Mycroft's dossier from the file clerk in the State Department. We know that you came to Philadelphia this morning to find Alexander Mycroft. We followed you as you followed him. We know that your earlier encounter in the bar was far too brief for you to have imparted any information to him."

She unbuckled his coat and his belt buckle and began to pull down his fly. His knees started to give way, but Moussef held him firmly in place, the Arab's beard alongside his own face. The Deacon's eyes opened wide in terror, in unbelieving recognition; his jaw hung slack.

"And we know that tonight you were with him for several hours. Tonight you gave him his assignment. We can kill him anytime if we want to. But first I want you to tell us exactly what you told him tonight, Bill. I want you to tell me everything."

She slid down his pants and began to fondle his penis. "Oh, Bill, it's so lovely but so soft. Watch me make it grow, Bill."

He was having trouble speaking. "I—I—I know who you are. It—It can't be possible. Oh, dear God, help me. It's *you!*" His eyes were at their widest opening; they could not blink.

"Yes, Bill," she cooed. "Of course you know who I am. That's what I've been trying to tell you. And because you know who I am, we both know that you are going to tell me everything I want to know. Isn't that right, Bill?" She smiled broadly, then slowly dropped to her knees.

She took his prick into her mouth and began to suck ever so gently, caressing it with her mouth, her tongue, her hands. He tried to kick her away.

"Moussef! Pin down his legs," she ordered.

The Arab wrapped one of his legs against the Deacon's.

"Please be careful, Bill. I really don't want to hurt you." She resumed her activities.

"Noooo!" He screamed at the top of his lungs. "Please stop it. Please stop it. Please, you must stop it. No, No, NO, NO!! Oh, please God, please make her stop, please. Please. Please, anything, but not that. Oh, please, dear God in heaven. Oh, please stop it. Please, I'll tell you anything you want to know. Anything. I swear. Only please stop it. Please." He started crying.

His tears brought her up.

"Oh, Bill. Poor Bill. I know I wasn't hurting you, was I? Don't cry, Bill." She began to kiss away his tears.

"Please have mercy on me," he begged. "Please just kill me. Please don't do what you were going to do."

"Now Bill, I know that most men enjoy that sort of thing. I know that I can please you if you let me, Bill."

His eyes filled with tears. "Please have pity on me. Haven't I been through enough? Tell me what you want to know. I'll tell you anything. You want to know about Christie Sinclair? I'll tell you everything I know. You want to know what Mycroft is going to do? I'll tell you. I'll tell you everything, but you've got to promise me that you won't get on your knees. Please, pull up my pants. Please. Please don't do that anymore. Please." He was crying again.

"All right, Bill. I only want to be your friend. I only wanted to please you. I wouldn't hurt you. I'll pull up your pants in a few minutes. I'll just keep your cock warm with my hands while you talk. Now let's dry your tears and have a real nice long talk. Tell me everything I want to know, Bill."

"Tell me *everything*."

7

▼

—December 25, 1979

MYCROFT didn't particularly want to stop off at the hospital on his way home but felt obligated to do so. And Obligations were an important part of any Brother's life. He was exhausted and almost feared that at the mere sight of a hospital bed, he would just collapse into it and sleep the night.

There was a Brother on night watch—and there would be a Brother with John Sinclair at least until the Master was moved out of the coronary-care unit—who told Mycroft that Sinclair's condition was stable and he was sleeping. Mycroft asked the Brother to call him if there was any change during the night.

As he walked out onto Broad Street, the City Hall clock

tower was just beginning to strike its midnight medley of chimes. It occurred to him that he had awakened exactly twelve hours earlier to another set of chimes. But when he began thinking of how his life had been turned upside down in only half a day, it made him feel all the more tired.

He searched in vain for a cab as he walked but knew it was hopeless. It's Christmas, he thought, and shook off a shiver of depression before it overcame him.

During the thirty-or-so-minute walk home, he had the streets and his mind to himself, but neither afforded him much comfort.

Mycroft reasoned that if he was crazy enough to travel to Iran, he would probably not succeed and would most likely wind up as another American hostage, or, more likely, dead. However, it did not escape his former spy-brain mentality that often one well-trained man *can* sometimes succeed in impossible missions where entire nations have failed. His past experiences, plus the fact that he was still alive, was itself living testimony to that point.

He rationalized that he owed it to John Sinclair—as a good friend and Brother—to at least supply him with as much reliable information as possible. Knowing firsthand how governments operate—especially the U.S. government—John was probably getting increasingly angry and frustrated by typical bureaucratic, Foggy Bottom runarounds. Perhaps if he could just manage to obtain reliable intelligence reports from some of his foreign counterparts—intelligence such as how the hostages were being treated, what the real chances of a negotiated settlement were, and how soon such a settlement might be reached—that in itself might be sufficient to fulfill his Obligation to John and to the Craft.

His mind began assimilating and systematically discarding lists of contacts throughout the world who might be in a position to help. But since he had been out of full-time service for a few years, even though Military Intelligence still called upon his talents periodically for light duty whenever he traveled abroad, he wasn't altogether sure which of his contacts was still operative. He knew, however, that he couldn't approach the United States.

He thought about the Deacon, too, who made it quite clear that he was taking a tremendous risk in supplying classified data to Mycroft. The Deacon's words and suggestion that any outside intrusion might screw up already-tenuous talks between the U.S. and Iran also weighed heavily on Mycroft's mind.

It began to snow again just as Mycroft turned down Pine Street. Shit, he thought, a white Christmas.

As he was about to place his key in the front door lock, Mycroft noticed that the door was slightly ajar. He coaxed the door open slightly with his left foot. Someone had done quite a vicious number on his home and he was sure—judging from the destruction—it had not been a routine breaking and entering. It, in fact, did not appear to be so much a burglary as a looting—furniture overturned and slashed, pictures ripped and torn from the walls, lamps shattered on the floor, drawers and papers strewn everywhere.

But Mycroft's shock soon gave way to horror and nausea as he noticed the message that had been left for him. What held his attention was the graffiti spray painted on the far wall. He didn't know what it meant or why it was there, but he knew that the one word had not been selected at random or by coincidence. He read it again and again, hoping the word would change or go away. But it leaped off the wall at him and buckled his knees:

"Joshua."

8

THE telephone immediately woke Mycroft from a fitful sleep. He was awash in his own perspiration, at sea in a recurring nightmare. His breathing was labored, as if he had just completed an exhausting run, which, in his dream, he in fact had. His lungs ached for a cigarette.

The phone rang a second time and he quickly sat up in bed, looked around the hotel suite's bedroom, and tried to get his bearings. He recalled checking into the Fairmont Hotel in the middle of the night. All they had available was a suite and Mycroft had taken it. The sun glared through the window; it had to be late morning or early afternoon, he deduced, but couldn't quickly fathom who would be calling him.

He grabbed the instrument on the third ring and instead of issuing a conventional greeting, cautiously asked the caller, "What number do you want?"

"Three-five-seven and nine," came the proper fraternal response from his friend and Brother, Police Captain Stanley Harris. Mycroft quickly remembered that he had called his friend about the break-in as soon as he had checked into the hotel. He wanted the police to know but wasn't yet prepared to make it official. He knew that "Cap" Harris would investigate and keep it under wraps for a while.

"Hiya, Cap," Mycroft responded groggily. "What do you have?"

Cap could hear the sleepiness in Mycroft's voice. "I hope I woke you, Alex. It'll make us square for you waking me at two in the morning."

"Sorry about that, Cap."

"Yeah, well you may be sorrier for a lot more than that if you don't get yourself some new playmates, Alex. I've never seen a place turned the way your place was. Anything missing?"

"Not that I know of."

"What do you make of the name on the wall? Mean anything to you?"

A small pause, and then: "I'm not sure, Cap. I'm really not sure. Joshua was my son's name, but he's dead. Has been for years."

"Alex, you and I have been friends for a long time. If you're in trouble, let me know, fella."

"You know me, Cap. I'm always in trouble," Mycroft answered, trying to lighten the conversation a little.

"Sure, sure. Make all the fuckin' jokes you want. Just tell

me what you want me to do. I can have the lab boys do a once-over, but I doubt they'll find anything of use. Or if you can give me some more info—something I can work on, like a possible suspect or motive—maybe we can make it safe and cozy for you to go home."

"That's just it, Cap," Mycroft replied. "I'm not going home. Not for a while, at least. I'm going to be out of town— out of the country—for a while. Keep an eye on the place for me, will you, Cap?"

"Anything for you, good buddy. Just tell me where to reach you if anything comes up."

"You can't, but I'll try to check in with you in a few days. And Cap, thanks. I owe you."

"What you owe me is a good night's sleep, which I intend to start catching up on right now." He hung up.

Later, after Mycroft showered, things were nagging at his mind as he finished dressing and started out of the room. He was pulling down on the outer corners of his upper lip, playing with a nonexistent mustache, and asking himself questions concerning possible connections between the Sinclair boy and his home getting the once-over. If there was a connection, it meant that his assignment was at risk. Someone already knew what he was planning and where he was heading.

The time had come to try to get his mind working the way it used to work when he actually earned a living risking his life on dangerous missions. The time had come to force his mind into being sharp. He could feel his senses had dulled in the past half-dozen years, his reflexes were no longer fast and his thinking had slowed, too. All from inactivity. Well, maybe there had been too much drinking, too, he conceded.

The Deacon and John Sinclair had rigged him up with a

British passport and had given him expense money in British pounds. Anyone else knowing that would know that Mycroft also had a plane ticket for London.

The first thing Mycroft resolved as he crossed the room was that he needed to go where he could conceivably lay his hands on some of the best intelligence data in the world. And London wasn't it.

The phone rang just as he began pulling the door closed behind him. Thinking it might be Cap again, he sprinted toward the phone and lifted it cautiously.

"What number do you want?" he asked cryptically.

But there was only a hollow silence and the echo of his own voice bouncing back at him.

"What number do you want?" he repeated.

First the silence, and then, softly a young voice said, "Daddy."

Mycroft's knees wobbled and he felt his bowels spasm.

"Who is this?" he demanded. "Goddammit, who the hell is this?" His voice was shrill and his heart pounded in his throat.

"Daddy. Don't leave me, Daddy."

"Oh, God in heaven," he pleaded, his voice—what he could muster of it—little more than a whisper under his struggling breath. "God, don't do this to me."

"Daddy. Don't leave me."

"Who is this?" he screamed, but he heard the click and the line went dead.

He sat down before he dropped and pushed his fingertips into his temples to massage the throbbing in his head. He clocked his pulse at 140 before heading for the liquor cart across the room. He took a hefty swig of vodka straight from the bottle and picked up a hotel-supplied cigarette and book of matches from a crystal box on the coffee table.

He propped the cigarette into his mouth (Oh, that feels so good, so natural, he thought) and even went so far as to strike the match. But he only stared into the flame as he waited for his pulse to lessen.

Then, wanting to kick himself for having been so slow-witted, he grabbed the phone and jiggled the receiver.

"Operator, operator," he yelled.

"Operator, may I help you?" was the nasal monotone reply.

"Operator, this is Mr. Mycroft in room"—he had to check the phone for his room number—"in room 773. I want to know if you can trace the call that just came in."

"One moment, please."

The wait, only a matter of seconds, was interminable nevertheless. And then, "I'm sorry, Mr. Mycroft. We have no record of a call coming in recently. We do have a record of a local outgoing call, though. Is that what you mean?"

"Of course that's not what I mean! I just got a call that sounded like long-distance, but I'm not positive about that. Please check again."

"I am sorry, Mr. Mycroft. We just have no record."

He hung up and tried to sort things out, pulling harder and harder on the corners of his hairless upper lip, allowing his thumb and forefinger to meet in the middle of his lower lip, pinching the flesh together.

He could fathom only two possibilities, neither of which afforded him any solace.

The first was that he imagined the entire incident. He didn't think it likely but entertained the notion only because of the nightmare he had just had about Beth and Josh, brought on, no doubt, because of the name "Joshua" scrawled on his wall.

The second was that it was a cruel practical joke played

by the child of a hotel guest—the operator would not have a record of room-to-room calls within the hotel. But that his room was selected at random was too bizarre to be a coincidence, and he long ago dismissed the thought that there were such things as coincidences.

A third possibility—that the call was legitimate—he would not, could not, allow himself to consider.

He poured himself a stiff drink and waited to regain his composure.

An hour or so later, still mulling over the call, Mycroft journeyed to the lower lobby level of the hotel in search of a sundries store for aspirins and toiletries. As his purchases were being rung up on the register, he picked up a copy of *The Philadelphia Inquirer* and scanned the stories with Iranian datelines.

Same old bullshit, he thought to himself. But suddenly a story and accompanying photographs just below the fold caught his attention:

GOV'T OFFICIAL FOUND SLAIN

Police this morning are investigating the murder of a man whose mutilated body was found late last night in City Hall courtyard. The victim, identified as William T. Gregory, a federal government official, was pronounced dead at the scene. Police have tentatively ruled out robbery as a possible motive for the slaying, saying that the victim's briefcase, wallet, and money were untouched.

Gregory, 34, a native of Philadelphia's Chestnut Hill area but who worked primarily in Washington, was apparently on his way to the Suburban Station train concourse when attacked, police officials theorized. The deceased leaves a wife, Rene, and infant son, Max.

Investigators say that Gregory's body was badly mutilated and that he most likely bled to death. Although police describe the mutilations as particularly vicious, they refused to elaborate.

Mycroft studied the accompanying picture of a younger Bill Gregory, obviously taken in happier days. Mycroft had never even known his name. The photograph was old and slightly blurred, but there was no doubt.

The Deacon was dead.

COLONEL Mycroft was unsure whether the airplane's turbulence was being caused by updrafts, downdrafts, or the enemy anti-aircraft shell fire that was exploding all around the fuselage. He had known the mission would be extremely hazardous (it had been stamped ''R.Q.'' for Return Questionable on the file jacket) but hadn't figured on the likelihood of getting killed before his mission actually began. He drew the parachute's cinch tighter across his chest and between his legs.

The intercom next to his head buzzed and he grabbed the receiver off the wall. He was, after all, alone in the vast cargo hold of the plane.

''Colonel Mycroft, we'll be over the designated jump site

in about sixty seconds," the pilot's squawky voice said. Mycroft couldn't help but be amazed at how calm the pilot sounded. "I'll give you the green light when we get there. Considering the fireworks, I'd suggest a long free fall before hitting the silk."

"My thoughts exactly. Thanks for the ride," Mycroft responded while reaching for his M-16.

"Good luck, sir."

Mycroft rose and stood by the open door, one eye on the red light. This was the part he dreaded most about jumping: waiting. Once he stepped out into the nothingness, he always enjoyed the feeling, the freedom, the flight, the sound and the feel of the wind rushing up to meet him. He was a fatalist and as such never once worried about his chute opening. Mycroft had made about three dozen jumps in his military career, almost half at night. But intentionally jumping behind enemy lines, five miles above the DMZ in North Vietnam, just to be captured, while the Vietcong used him for target practice, well, this would be a new one even for him.

His body clock was telling him that sixty seconds had almost elapsed and he fastened his helmet's chin strap and lowered the night-sight goggles over his eyes. He then placed both hands on the outside of the open door, ready to pull himself through and into the blackness of space the moment the green light switched on. Mycroft could feel rather than actually hear the pilot cut the right engines in order to avoid having a helpless parachutist sucked into the plane's tail wing.

The plane slowed, the green jump light came on, and U.S. Army Colonel Alexander Mycroft pulled for all he was worth.

The shell fire that immediately surrounded him was deafening and close enough that he received some minor burns on his hands and face from the explosions. But judging by the way the shells were trailing after the now rapidly disappearing plane, the Vietcong had not spotted his jump, and he was soon hurtling through the black night unobserved. He looked up in time to see black smoke pouring out of the plane right on schedule. From the plane's height, it would appear from ground level to have been hit. So far, Mycroft thought, so good. Now all he had to do was manage to get himself captured without being killed first. He would have only fourteen days in which to fashion his escape with or without his assignment in tow.

The shell fire stopped and Mycroft yanked the rip cord. The chute whooshed open with a rush and jerked him upward as the air caught and the silk billowed above. The night-sight goggles worked as they had been designed to do, and he spotted a small opening in the forest not far to his right. Mycroft pulled on the toggle and began drifting in that direction.

When he was about three hundred feet from ground level, rifle fire started whizzing by him, one or two shots hitting the open silk. Mycroft began swinging his body to and fro to provide as much of a moving target as he possibly could. He wasn't certain but thought the shots were coming from the left of him. He pulled hard again on the toggle and aimed more to the right.

At about one hundred-fifty feet, more sniper fire broke out and he began swinging his body frantically. More holes appeared in the chute and his descent began picking up speed. One bullet glanced off his helmet.

After dropping rapidly for about another one hundred feet, machine gun fire broke out. At this range, he thought they couldn't possibly miss but he soon discovered they weren't aiming at him. The spray of bullets were trained just above his head and began systematically slicing away his lifelines. At twenty-five feet, the bastards succeeded. The silk separated and Mycroft fell to the ground unfettered, miraculously suffering nothing more serious than two sprained ankles, but knocking himself out in the process.

He could not have been out for more than a minute or two, for when he came to, the Vietcong were still running up to him. Soon he was surrounded by rifles trained on him and a steady stream of high-pitched gibberish from the black pajama-clad enemy. Mycroft carefully pulled a white handkerchief from his pocket, waved it, and prayed for the best.

Although he couldn't make out any of what was being said, he soon got the drift that one contingent wanted to kill him on the spot. Another, however, apparently recognized his rank (which had been part of the mission's original strategic plan) and argued that he'd be more valuable alive than dead. Fortunately for Mycroft, that argument won out and he was jerked to his feet, stripped of his weapons, and forced to hobble along through the woods at gunpoint.

The arduous trek soon became unbearable for him. Walking on now balloon-sized ankles and with his hands tightly bound behind his back with chicken wire and a pungent-smelling sack over his head, he was alternately pulled and pushed through the thick foliage until, able to bear the pain no more, he collapsed along the trail.

He awoke some time the next day to find himself stripped naked and tied spread-eagle on the ground amid a small, hut-filled Vietcong village. His arms and legs were stretched to their fullest by leather straps securely tied to four stakes. Twice on the first day—at least twice that he could recall—a soldier approached and poured water from a wooden bucket onto the leather straps that the sweltering heat and sun combined to contract, stretching his limbs even further apart.

The inner part of his legs, from mid-thigh up to his groin, had been lightly cut by a sharp knife, just enough to draw a trickle of blood and thereby attract a ready host of ants, maggots, and other insects to feast on his blood and nibble at his testicles. At night the rats came out and replaced the insects at the banquet table.

The next day two fresh cuts were placed on either side of his neck, and the leather was soaked three times.

On the morning of the third day, Xian Ling, the notorious, sadistic, Chinese-born Vietcong interrogator, arrived at the village and immediately was taken to inspect Mycroft. Ling was furious that Mycroft was near dead and ordered him to be untied and his wounds tended to immediately. He let loose with a string of epithets and then departed.

During the ensuing week, Mycroft was nursed back to reasonably good health under constant armed guard. He was sponge-bathed twice a day, once in the morning and once in the evening, by two Vietcong women. His ankles were packed in clean rags, presoaked in cool water, and placed on cushions at the foot of his straw mat. His wounds were cleansed with an antiseptic that burned down to his inner soul and the dressings changed three times a day.

Water was almost literally spoon-fed down his throat, but initially he had no stomach for the rice they tried to feed him and vomited all over himself. The women would be summoned to clean him.

His delirium passed in two days but his fever raged on for three more. He had no control over his bowels or bladder and soiled himself regularly. Whenever this occurred, almost always in the middle of the night, the women were summoned immediately and wordlessly cleaned him off with soap and water. A fresh mat would be brought in and soldiers would lift Mycroft gently while the women replaced the mat.

In his ten days of captivity, no one spoke a word to him and he also remained mute. The only exterior sounds he heard from his thatched hut were the occasional screams of other prisoners.

He could see little through the doorway of his small prison but it didn't matter. He knew what was out there. Military Intelligence at HQ told him. Somewhere in that tiny village compound was Lt. j.g. Arthur vanSant, son of U.S. Senator William vanSant, ranking member of the Senate Foreign Relations Committee.

Mycroft's mission was (a) to locate vanSant; (b) get him out alive if possible; (c) kill him if rescue was impossible—"liquidate if RQ" the orders had actually read; (d) but under no circumstances leave him with the Vietcong. All in just fourteen days.

Mycroft surmised that Senator vanSant wanted his son to be a war hero, dead or alive. Having him captured and tortured by the Vietcong was not part of the senator's plans. Mycroft wondered whether the senator's wife knew of the plans and decided that she probably did not.

Mycroft was told there would be other U.S. prisoners but he was not to concern himself with their fate. Only vanSant. On that point, his orders were explicit.

Just before sunset on the tenth day, Mycroft heard a jeep pull up to his hut and a moment later Ling walked in.

"You are looking much better than the last time I saw you, Colonel Mycroft," said Ling. "Of course you are not surprised that I know who you are; your dog tags would tell me that much. But I also know that you are a very important officer in your government's Military Intelligence division.

Perhaps you have heard of me, too. I am Xian Ling," and he swelled his chest, arched his back, and brought himself up to his full five-foot-four-inch height as he said this.

"I have heard of you, yes," said Mycroft, his voice sounding raspy from ten days of nonuse.

"This is good that you know me. This will save us much time when we begin to talk. And talk we will, I promise you. We will get along well. My hospitality can be boundless, as you shall soon see. Tomorrow, however, will be soon enough to talk. Tonight you shall complete your convalescence with my blessings and my compliments, and tomorrow we shall talk again . . . seriously. Oh, yes, you are looking much better." Then he turned and left.

Later that night, when the two women came to give him his regular evening bath, Mycroft observed that they were not the same two who had visited his hut regularly during his captivity. These two were younger with exquisite doll-like faces, one of whom, Mycroft was surprised to note, was clearly occidental. Mycroft estimated they were no more than fifteen or sixteen years old, and later learned that they were Xian Ling's "daughters." Méi, the older of the two, had inherited Western European features, while Nguyen took after an oriental parent.

The stories about Xian Ling's "daughters" were legion in Vietnam and Mycroft's briefing papers had been filled with them. Some of the young women were Ling's actual offspring but others had been sold to him over the years and their origins were from a variety of countries. Some had come from China and Thailand and Cambodia; others had come from Egypt and Lebanon and Libya; still others had come from the backcountry areas of France and Spain and Portugal. The cultural mix produced children of breathtaking beauty. And these children ultimately grew into seductive temptresses with legendary sexual prowess.

They would be taught as children all the ways to please a man, and all the ways to torment him, too. They could be lovers of unequaled and unrivaled passion, or imaginative killers who derived as much pleasure from murder as from sex.

And they were slavishly and sexually devoted to their "father," who was their lover as well as their teacher. They traveled with him as a harem until a U.S. Air Force bombing mission wiped out all his wives and most of his daughters.

Now there were but two left, and they were in Mycroft's hut.

When the girls arrived, the guards drove four stakes into the ground at the four corners of his mat. The girls handed over some sort of furry strips of animal hide that the guards used to bind his hands and feet to the stakes. Once again he was spread-eagle, but for the first time since he had been brought into the hut, his limbs were not bound too tightly, just enough that he was securely pinned to the stakes and completely immobilized. The guards left.

The girls then undressed themselves completely and soon were as naked as Mycroft. Their black hair was thick and reached their waists. Undressed, standing in the soft glow of the hut's meager candlelight, they were voluptuous. They had nubile figures and each had a clean-shaven vagina.

They unrolled a mat—larger than Mycroft's—and laid it down beside his. The two girls proceeded to wash him in much the same manner as the other women had, except these two spent a considerably longer amount of time washing and rewashing his genitals, and the soap was sweetly perfumy and far less abrasive than what the other women had used previously.

When they had completed his bath, Méi, the occidental girl, laid down on her back on the mat alongside of Mycroft, facing the opposite direction, Nguyen, the oriental girl, then proceeded to wash her sister from head to toe, again spending a consciously extra amount of time on her pubic region and breasts. The occidental then rolled onto her stomach and her oriental sister completed washing her back. This being done, Méi rolled onto her back as before and spread her legs as wide as she could while her companion produced a small round brush that she lathered with the perfumed soap and water. Bending over her prostrate sister, Nguyen slowly inserted the brush far into her older sister and began to rotate and manipulate the brush so as to give Méi both pleasure and hygiene at the same time.

When the occidental girl was thoroughly cleansed and satisfied, the two reversed positions and repeated, step by step, the same ritual.

Reversing positions once again, Nguyen, on her knees, produced an array of perfumed oils and creams and began to apply them to her sister's prostrate body, beginning at her neck, working down toward her breasts, her smooth belly, between her legs, until her entire body glistened in the soft candlelight. And thus was the oriental girl similarly annointed.

They then carried the oil and lotion decanters to Mycroft and began to massage his naked body in a slow, circular manner, one girl beginning at his face while the other first kissed and then oiled each toe. As they began to slowly inch their way toward his center, each girl assumed a kneeling position on either side of his body and massaged his legs and chest with delicate hands, occasionaly raking their long fingernails along his inner thighs.

They reached his groin at the same time and that, too, they divided. One girl, the occidental, dispensing oil deep between his legs, inserted a finger far into his anus until, massaging his prostate gland, Mycroft unwillingly achieved the largest and most rock-hard erection of his life. The finger was withdrawn at the precise moment Mycroft felt his ejaculation building, and Nguyen, on cue, grabbed his shaft hard with both hands, applying tremendous pressure at its base, which halted his climax.

He was then covered, from neck to feet, with a white silk sheet that had a triangular patch cut out from its center. They put more cushions under his head to increase his field of vision. But being able to see nothing of his body except his penis standing rigid at attention only served to force every fiber of his body and mind to consciously and subconsciously concentrate on that one exposed area. The sides of the sheet were closely tucked around his body and small droplets of warm oil were slowly poured onto his erection.

While Nguyen massaged his temples with her fingers, Méi remained kneeling at his side and lowered her mouth to engulf him and massage the oil with her talented tongue. He could hold back no more and instantly came in waves.

A ring of some sort was placed just above his scrotum and tightened to prevent him from becoming flaccid.

The girl massaging his temples quickened her pace while her sister straddled her legs over Mycroft and positioned herself above his still-rigid penis. Inserting just the tip of his shaft into herself, she relied entirely on her internal muscles to rhythmically and methodically expand and contract until she had sucked him completely into her body.

She began to fondle the nipples of each of her own breasts as her lower body rose and fell and circled. The oriental girl stopped massaging his temples and crawled down and positioned herself behind her sister, also straddling Mycroft. She lowered her hands and massaged her sister's clitoris vigorously while the occidental closed her eyes and began to moan audibly. It was the first sound Mycroft had heard in the two hours the girls had been with him. Again Mycroft was powerless and he came in unison with the girl who had been riding him.

Even the coolness of the silk sheet could not prevent Mycroft from being bathed in a pool of perspiration that completely soaked the fabric covering the upper portion of his torso. The two girls dismounted, removed the sodden sheet, and commenced to provide him with the relief of a cool sponge bath and a much-needed rest. His body was then re-annointed with perfumed oils and recovered with a fresh silk, also missing a strategically located triangular patch.

While he rested and regained his strength, he watched in unbelievable awe as the two girls then proceeded to make love to one another with an energy and ferocity unlike any he had ever dreamed possible.

They fondled, caressed, nibbled, nuzzled, kissed, and suckled every conceivable mound and crevice on each other's bodies while emitting animal sounds of pleasure from deep within their throats. Their orgasms caused spasms and shudders, howls and tears, all designed to please and arouse Mycroft. And when they had released each other from their final embrace and Mycroft thought for sure they were spent, they oiled each other's bodies again and produced a large, human-organ-shaped dildo that they kissed and suckled in idol-worshiping fashion. This object of their devotion was at last strapped tightly around the hips of the oriental girl while the other assumed a position on all fours alongside of Mycroft to afford him the most unobstructed view possible of the savage fucking—for that was the only word to describe it—of his two concubines.

Their attentions were then shifted to Mycroft once again as he was systematically manipulated and brought to orgasm more times than he had ever believed himself capable. He had no recollection of the number of times he spent himself but he remembered being given fresh silks no less than three additional times. Just before he passed out from exhaustion at first light, each girl snuggled up to either side of him, resting their own weary heads on his chest while their hands lightly intertwined together at his groin.

When he awoke at midday, he was untied and, for the first time since he had been brought into the hut, completely alone. The girls had departed, leaving no evidence of their previous night's orgy. He was naked, as before, but discovered his uniform had been washed and left for him by the door. He rose slowly, testing his bones and muscles warily, and enjoyed a deep-felt yawn and stretch. He rubbed the sleep from his eyes, splashed some water on his face from the wooden bowl deposited alongside his uniform, and dressed.

Mycroft cautiously peered outside his small doorway, bending slightly to avoid hitting his head on the low frame. To his surprise and bewilderment, there were no guards posted. There was some light activity—soldiers milling around, some going out on patrol, some returning—but no one seemed to pay any particular attention to him. Not knowing when he might again enjoy such freedom, he decided to return the nonchalance being afforded him and engage in as much reconnaissance as possible.

His hut had been one in a small circle of six, none of which was guarded. Mycroft gave a cursory examination to his neighboring huts but uncovered no activity in or around any of them.

Circling the huts slowly from behind, he noticed two paths leading off into the forest at approximately opposite compass points from each other. The egress to one was blocked by a handful of armed soldiers, so he bypassed them unchecked and proceeded in silence down the other path.

After walking no more than fifty yards, the uneasy quiet of the noon was pierced by a scream of such terror that it raised the hairs on Mycroft's neck. He instinctively crouched low and listened but heard no more. However, from his reduced vantage point he could see, lying on the ground, the decapitated heads of what used to be two American soldiers, with their helmets loosely affixed atop the decaying, maggot-ridden flesh. He swallowed his bile and continued on.

Rounding a bend in the trail some few yards further along, he came to a clearing housing a number of long huts built upon stilts over a marshy swamp, accessible via a gangplank laid to reach the solid ground of a compound area. A few stockades—wooden cages, actually—each housed a small number of prisoners, and undoubtedly more were in the huts. There were Vietnamese soldiers freely entering the huts, from which an occasional scream was heard.

In the center of this activity stood Xian Ling, calmly directing and orchestrating the most hideous forms of torture to be carried out on his prisoners.

Mycroft stared in horror at the grisly scene before him. On one side of the opening, a handful of American POWs had been hung, like limp laundry out to dry on a line, by various limbs and digits of their hands and feet. The most wretched of these were still alive, but just barely. Once or twice he spotted bodies being flung through open floorboards of the huts into the swamp below. Whether these unfortunates were alive or dead, and what fate awaited them in the swamp if they were still breathing, he could not know. He stood frozen in revulsion until he felt the cold business-end of a rifle prod him in the nape of his neck. He gently was nudged forward and marched, hands raised, into the center of the clearing.

"Ah, welcome, Colonel," said Ling. "I was beginning to think you'd sleep the day away. Yes, you do look much better. I trust my daughters gave you the pleasure they have been trained to impart. What do you think of my little fun palace?"

"About what I'd expect from someone as sick as you are."

"Do not be too hasty to judge, Colonel. After all, you have not been treated too poorly, hmm? These men were all given the opportunity to receive similar treatment. These men, by refusing to cooperate, have sealed their own fate. You, too, will be presented similar options."

Mycroft was about to answer when he spotted a naked prisoner being led down the ramp from one of the huts. The soldier tried to break free but quickly had his hands tied and trussed up above him on a low-hanging branch. His feet were spread apart and tied to two stakes in the ground. His body was streaked with whip marks and scored with fresh burns, as though he had been used as a live ashtray. The face was much thinner than in the photograph Mycroft had engraved upon his mind, but he was sure it was vanSant.

Ling seemed mesmerized by the activity and never took his eyes from vanSant as he continued to speak to Mycroft. "Have you ever considered the wonders of the human body, Colonel? The penis, for example, is capable of providing so much pleasure, as well as so much pain."

As he droned on, Mycroft observed one of the girls who had entertained him the night before approaching vanSant. It was Nguyen, the oriental. She slipped out of her robe and knelt naked in front of vanSant's groin, taking him into her mouth as he bucked, trying to pull back. The girl threw both hands around his buttocks and drew him in even more.

Try as he might, vanSant was powerless to prevent the involuntary muscles from being aroused and soon had a very respectable erection. Mycroft knew just how persuasive this attractive young girl's lips could be.

Mycroft stole a glance at Ling, whose breathing had increased noticeably. Tiny beads of perspiration erupted on his forehead while his lips curled upward in a satanic grin.

Suddenly, the girl's tempo increased, and as vanSant's body shuddered with his ejaculation, Mycroft spotted the gleaming edge of a razor blade protruding from a corner of her salivating mouth. While swallowing his semen, in one swift movement of her head—a movement so sure and knowing that it could only have been perfected after years of practice—she lopped off his penis, retaining the severed member in her mouth. It had occurred so fast that vanSant could not have even been aware of it until she stood up and opened her grotesque mouth in a hideous smile, displaying the still erect penis and razor blade to his disbelieving face.

VanSant screamed when reality set in, then his head slumped forward on his chest as blood began to spurt forth from his loins. The girl began parading around the compound, displaying her trophy in cigar fashion, dangling from her lips. Mycroft threw up.

Mycroft didn't know whether vanSant had ever really passed out, but the instant he was freed, he immediately lunged forward and violently tackled the unsuspecting girl from behind. What he had hoped to accomplish wasn't clear, but as the girl fell forward, she began a yell that quickly was muffled and gurgled to silence. VanSant was shot almost instantly and died on top of the girl who remained motionless.

A puddle of blood began seeping out in all directions from under the girl's neck and when she was turned over, the razor blade was protruding from her throat, from the inside out.

*   *   *

For the next three days, Mycroft was subjected to an intense interrogation replete with physical and mental torture of such extremes that he began to doubt his own perception of reality and never managed to completely crumble the mental block he formed surrounding the full details of his ordeal.

Part of his mission had been accomplished for him and all that remained was to concentrate his every conscious moment on thoughts of his own survival and escape. This single-mindedness of purpose, coupled with his intense hatred for Xian Ling, gave him an inner strength that defied Ling's numerous interrogation techniques. How much longer Mycroft could have held out without revealing troop strengths, movements, positions, and supply information (or dying, whichever came first) he did not know.

He did know, however, that he had been given exactly two weeks to accomplish his mission. If he did not manage to return within that time, the American forces would begin shelling, bombing, and strafing the entire area, even if Mycroft and every other prisoner perished in the process. It would help his own chances immensely if he could somehow manage to signal his forces, to help pinpoint the exact location of the VC, and keep the fire diverted away from the internment center.

This he managed to accomplish several hours after nightfall on the fourteenth day of his captivity.

He had been fed and nourished then retied by the two armed guards who now stood watch over him. Xian Ling needed Mycroft alive, if he was to be of any benefit to the sadist, and took great care to keep him alive despite the torture. One of the guards, who had been in Mycroft's small hut many times previously, appeared nervous. Slowly, he positioned himself behind the other guard, then suddenly grabbed his fellow guard from behind and swiftly and expertly thrust a knife into his back, clamping the victim's mouth shut with his free hand.

Withdrawing the bloody blade, he threw the dead guard to the floor and quickly cut Mycroft free and tossed him the dead guard's automatic rifle and knife.

"Look not so surprised, my Brother," the guard said in English. "I would not harm a poor shepherd's son. I knew you were a Brother from some of the things you muttered while you were delirious and I have been looking after you as best I could since your arrival. Tomorrow, however, you are scheduled to be moved to the larger compound where I cannot help you. You may be killed escaping tonight but at least you'll have a chance."

"We can make it together," Mycroft said, trying to massage the circulation back into his wrists and ankles.

"You misunderstand, my Brother. I have no wish to leave. I truly believe in what we are fighting for. I will kill Americans without thinking twice, but my Obligation to the Craft will not permit me to knowingly allow any harm to befall my Brother. You understand this, of course."

Nodding in the direction of the slain guard, Mycroft asked, "How about your friend over there?"

The other guard merely shrugged. "He was one of Ling's men. I never cared for him anyway. I will say you managed to overpower us both and killed him."

"All right, then. I'll return the Obligation now. Before this night is through, this place will get the shit bombed out of it. Anyone here will go up with it. Now do you want to leave?"

His reply was instant. "I *cannot* go with you. My place is here with my people. I will lead you out, then we will part company."

"Wait!" Mycroft called out. "I want Xian Ling before I go. I want to kill that son of a bitch with my own hands."

The guard laughed quietly. "With that, I will gladly assist you. Ling is not one of us; he is Chinese. You must understand that. He and others like him are despised by us almost as much as we hate Americans. If you kill him, you will be doing us a great service. Come, I will lead you to him."

Silently, they made their way out of the hut and quickly skirted around it to the path running behind the huts. The guard stopped behind one and motioned to it.

"He is most likely with his daughter, Méi Ling," whispered Mycroft's guide.

Mycroft nodded and softly positioned himself against the rear of the hut, listening to the sound of passion coming from within. He moved around to the front and quietly entered Ling's hut. The occidental girl was on all fours and Ling was kneeling behind her with his back to the door. He never saw it coming.

Mycroft took a few fast steps into the room, grabbed Ling's head from behind, and quickly drew the guard's knife across his throat. A spark of recognition flashed in Ling's eyes as he tried to call out but could not. Ling was frozen. Mycroft then took a half step around him with the thought in mind of slaying the girl, too. But seeing that the girl's inner muscles had her father in a tight grip, Mycroft quickly drew his knife down between them, severing Xian Ling's penis.

"Poetic justice, you prick," Mycroft hissed. He spared the daughter's life and fled just as the girl turned and began to scream, as expected. He needed the diversion.

Mycroft rejoined his escort as the girl's screaming gained strength. As the other guards started shouting and running toward Ling's hut, Mycroft retraced his path and returned to his own hut. No one even looked at him as he stepped inside

113

and heaved one of the two oil lamps onto the floor alongside the back wall. The dry thatch caught instantly.

"What are you doing?" the guard asked frantically.

"Only what I have to," he replied as he grabbed the other lamp and set the adjoining hut ablaze.

The signal fires set, Mycroft turned to his savior and said, "Please believe me; nothing here will be standing in the morning. Come with me and I promise that if we make it back to my lines, I'll see that you're released unharmed."

"I believe you, my Brother. But here I must remain. Come. Let me lead you to the path."

In the commotion caused by the signal fires, Ling's death, and the screams of Ling's daughter, Mycroft and his guide calmly began walking toward the path that Mycroft had previously observed being guarded. En route, Mycroft saw scores of Vietcong soldiers running toward the huts from the direction of the internment center. There were no soldiers guarding the path, either.

Mycroft's guide stopped at the entrance to the path.

"Here we must part company, my Brother," the guide said.

"What is your name?" Mycroft asked.

"It does not matter. Go quickly."

"If you live through the night and are ever captured by the Americans, tell them you've been working for me. Mycroft. They'll find me and I'll help you."

"I'll remember. Now please go, Brother." He pushed Mycroft toward the path, then turned and ran in the other direction.

Mycroft crouched low and started running along the path as he heard the first of the planes overhead. But then he stopped in his tracks.

His orders had been clear. Get vanSant out or kill him.

There may be a few other Americans there, he was told; but he was not to concern himself with their fate under any circumstances.

How many times had it been drilled into his head that when you're on a mission, think only of the mission's objective. Missions fail when the operative allows himself to be diverted. But surely if they knew how many Americans were here and how they were being tortured and killed, they'd reconsider, he reasoned.

Never be diverted from your mission, men, a voice echoed in the recesses of his mind. Wear blinders if you have to, men. Get in, get out. One, two, quick, men. That's how you stay alive, men.

The sound of the planes was getting louder and he heard the first bomb drop before he saw the explosion.

Fuck orders, he said to himself and turned and headed back in the direction from which he had just come. He was still in a weakened condition and the going was difficult. At the head of the path he turned right and started toward the internment center. More bombs were falling and they were getting closer to their mark. He had to hurry but couldn't.

At the clearing, Mycroft saw only two guards standing together. He got into a prone position behind some brush and took careful aim with the rifle. It was the first time he examined it closely but was not surprised to note that it was Russian.

He dropped both guards with two short bursts but put two more shots into their heads at close range when he got up to where they had fallen. He picked up their weapons and tried to run toward the stockade area where the screams of the prisoners—fellow Americans—were intensifying in fear and panic.

Mycroft was near exhaustion. In his condition, it had

been doubtful that even he could have escaped alone; but now to have circled back to accomplish—what?

He stumbled and badly bruised his face in the fall. The bombing was getting closer, the prisoner's screams were getting louder. Not sure whether he could reach the stockade, he nevertheless forced himself up and began a halting run toward the prisoners. He saw a bomb obliterate one stockade before his eyes.

And then he began to hear rifle shots coming from behind him. A small party of Vietcong had heard Mycroft's shooting of the two guards and they had come to investigate. They were shooting in Mycroft's general direction, but he didn't think they were able to see him in the darkness sporadically illuminated by the bomb bursts. He continued on as best he could, crouched low.

Elsewhere, the Vietcong had begun to return air-fire power with anti-aircraft weapons. The village compound behind him was all ablaze.

Never be diverted, men, played a worn tape in his head. He mentally switched it off and stood up slightly to get his bearings.

And then the rocket grenade came out of nowhere and almost killed him. . . .

"Mr. Mycroft? Mr. Mycroft?"

He never knew that as he lay near death through most of the night, his earlier saviour—the Vietnamese guard, and Brother, who had freed him—came and searched for him, then managed to turn him over to American troops. . . .

"Mr. Mycroft? Please, Mr. Mycroft. Are you all right?"

. . . And he woke up in an army hospital a month later.

"Mr. Mycroft, please wake up. We'll be landing soon."

. . . And he knew he would open his eyes and see the hospital ward. But when he did manage to flutter his eyelids once or twice, he didn't see the nurse. He saw a Sabra woman, a native Israeli. Was that Beth, he asked himself? Beth, is that you? he thought to himself. Then he closed his eyes. No, that's not Beth. Beth is in the *other* dream. A silent tear rolled down his cheek.

"Mr. Mycroft, you're all perspired. I'm going to sponge off your face with this damp cloth. Please wake up, Mr. Mycroft."

. . . Oooohhhhh, those nurses really know how to make you feel good, he thought. He opened his eyes, but it wasn't a nurse sponging him off. And it wasn't Beth. But where was that Israeli music coming from?

"Oh, Mr. Mycroft. I'm so glad you're all right. You must have had the most dreadful dream," said the stewardess.

. . . I know that music, he recalled. It's *Alenu Shalom Alechem*, the song of welcome to the Jewish Holy Land the El Al planes always play when they cross into Israeli airspace.

The stewardess was sitting in the seat next to him, tenderly mopping his brow with a cool cloth. "Thank God you're all right," she said. "That must have been an awfully bad dream."

"Yes," Mycroft said, "just a bad dream. It hasn't happened in a long time," he lied in a murmured voice.

The plane's wheels touched down. He was in Israel.

The beginning of another suicide mission for Alexander Mycroft.

10

Philadelphia—December 26, 1979

"SURE, you can go in," said the doctor, "*if* you absolutely have to."

"We absolutely have to," said the shorter of the two men standing in the hospital corridor. He said it coldly, without a trace of emotion, as he slipped his identification back into his pocket. He only appeared emotionless; he was like a coiled spring ready to snap. The long hospital wait had been an effort.

The doctor curled up his stethoscope and placed it in one of the oversized pockets of his white coat. "Very well, but don't stay too long. And, for God's sake, try not to upset him."

He turned to leave to answer a page, and the two men entered the private room without knocking.

"Mr. Sinclair? May we talk to you for a few minutes?" The tall one, by mutual agreement, was doing all the talking.

John Sinclair raised his head slightly to study the two figures standing at the foot of his bed. He pushed the electric control button to raise the head of his bed to afford him a better view.

The tall one, he judged, was fiftyish with salt-and-pepper hair perfectly groomed in conservative fashion. He was meticulously dressed in a three-piece gray herringbone suit and carried his charcoal gray overcoat neatly folded over his left arm. He carried himself well, and Sinclair, although never having been in England, thought the man resembled his imagined version of a British gentleman on a country estate.

The other man, however, was more of an enigma to Sinclair. Although he, too, was tall, he had a way of standing— almost slouching—that belied his true height. He couldn't even venture a guess at his age. Depending how his face was turned, or how the light from the window fell upon his features, he could have been anywhere from early forties to mid-fifties. It was the same with his suit, which at times appeared to be varied shades of light blue to dark gray. His hair was usually sandy-colored, but it, too, was a study in browns, and his face was almost completely nondescript. Sinclair never did get a good look at his eyes. He was, Sinclair thought to himself, chameleonlike, and he thought the man would be able to blend into any crowd or any wall without attracting undue attention to himself.

"You're not doctors," Sinclair said. It wasn't a question.

"No, Mr. Sinclair, we're not," replied the tall one as he produced identification. "My name is Henry Peterson. I'm with the State Department. And this is Mr. Blake—"

Sinclair shot upright in bed. "State Department? Is it about Lee? Is he all right? Is he—are they . . . *out? Free?*"

"I'm sorry, Mr. Sinclair. No, I'm not here with any news of your son. I'm truly sorry."

Sinclair slumped back against the pillow. He looked at the man Peterson called Blake, who was doing his best to hold up the far wall of the small, antiseptically white room. "Are you with the State Department, too, Mr. Blake?"

Blake and Peterson exchanged a brief glance, and Blake walked a few steps to stand beside Sinclair's bed. He, too, produced identification but said, "No, Mr. Sinclair. My name is Otis Blake. I'm a special agent with the CIA."

Sinclair's eyes widened. "The CIA? What in the world does the CIA want with me?"

Blake ignored the question and turned to Peterson. "Get on with it, Peterson. We're wasting time."

He regretted saying it even as the words were rolling off his tongue. He regretted showing any emotion at all. He prided himself on his ability to withhold emotions of any kind, but he wanted to interrogate Sinclair fast and be on his way. The matter was still domestic and he had no real jurisdiction. But everything—including every fiber of his well-trained mind and body—pointed to it being international. He knew it in his gut, where it counted. And all he wanted was Sinclair's confirmation so he could take charge. He resumed his position against the wall.

Peterson, for his part, continued as though the brief interruption had never occurred. He searched for the right words. "Mr. Sinclair, do you—that is, *did* you—I mean, I—*we* understand that you knew William Gregory. How well do—*did* you know him?" Peterson muffed it badly.

"Sure I know Bill. But you make it sound like—" He never finished the sentence.

"I'm truly, truly sorry, Mr. Sinclair, but Bill Gregory is dead. He was killed on Christmas eve, two days ago. Well, murdered, actually." The words came out in a rush.

What little color was left in John Sinclair's face faded quickly. Peterson took a deep breath and began reading from his notes.

"We know that you and Bill Gregory were together early on the evening of December 24th. We also know that when Bill left his office that morning, he took some highly classified documents with him, as well as a classified file on an Alexander Mycroft. These papers were found on Bill's, uh, person; but we don't yet know if he took any other documents that were not found and we don't know if whoever killed him saw or photographed the documents." Peterson paused for a moment. It had been, for him, a lengthy speech.

"Now, Mr. Sinclair," he continued, "we do know certain things, but we require your immediate assistance in helping us make sense out of what information we do have. For instance, we know that you and Bill and Mr. Mycroft were together on the evening of December 24th—two days ago. We know that Bill was murdered. And we know that Mr. Mycroft has left the country. And, naturally, we know that you were hospitalized. But what we don't know, Mr. Sinclair, is how these events tie together."

Sinclair, although genuinely shocked at Bill Gregory's death, could focus only on what to him were the key words in Peterson's monologue. Without realizing it, he said in a whisper to himself, "Alex has left the country. It's started!"

CIA agent Otis Blake heard it, but Peterson, on a roll, continued. "Please understand, Mr. Sinclair, that Bill Gregory worked in the Cryptography and Decoding Section of the State Department. As such, he had access to extremely sensitive material and documents pertaining to the Iranian situation. Surely *you*, of all people, can appreciate that if certain documents or information fell into the wrong hands, it could jeopardize not only your son's life but the lives of the other hostages as well. It could also—I'm speaking very,

very candidly here—" he lowered his voice to a near whisper—"also jeopardize the lives of *other* Americans in Iran whom the Iranians don't yet know exist. You may think nothing is being done, but I assure you there is much work afoot. Much work."

He paused and, without asking, poured himself a tumbler of water from Sinclair's bedside table. Blake was growing impatient.

"Mr. Sinclair," Peterson continued in his normal speaking voice, "plans are being formulated that are, uh, tenuous at best. Now if Bill Gregory had merely *shared* certain pieces of information with you, well, naturally we'd be concerned, but not *overly* so. What I'm trying to say is we don't think *your* having bits of this knowledge would prove dangerous. But where we're really concerned—and this is the reason for Mr. Blake's presence—is because of the apparent involvement of Alexander Mycroft."

"I—I don't think I can help you. I think you should leave."

Blake took a step forward, his patience having worn out. "Look, Mr. Sinclair, Peterson here is trying to give you every possible chance to cooperate, but if my hunch is right, I don't have time to waste. *We* don't have time to waste. Now listen carefully because I don't want you to misunderstand what I'm about to say. I'm only going to give you one chance to tell me what I have to know or, so help me, I'm going to pick you up by your nightie and throw you the fuck out of this window!"

"Blake, *please*—"

"Shut up, Peterson! Sinclair, I don't give a shit about Bill Gregory. If he was screwing around with classified documents, he got what he deserved. And I care even less about Alexander Mycroft. What I *do* care about are the hostages and my operatives in Iran. If their covers are blown, I'm gonna hold you personally responsible. No matter what you may think, there are a helluva lot of people risking their asses to save your kid and the other hostages. They can do it, too—provided nobody screws it up. Comprende?"

"You have no right to talk to me like—"

"I have every fucking right in the world, Sinclair, especially where national security is at stake. Now you listen: Gregory lifts some papers and files from the State Department. Then you, Gregory, and Mycroft meet. Within hours afterward, Gregory is murdered, Mycroft hotfoots it to Israel, and you, you dumb shit, wind up in the hospital with a mild coronary, probably due to all the excitement you started in the first place."

Peterson intervened at this point to give Blake an opportunity to cool down.

"Mr. Sinclair, this is what we've been trying to tell you all along. The documents Bill took pertained mainly to the embassy compound and recent intelligence reports and the like. Bill had been decoding that material for a National Security Council review, in conjunction with the Iranian desk at State, of course. The file on Mr. Mycroft was extremely thorough and complete, I am told, and he had to requisition it from the file clerk. That's how we knew, of course. But you see—"

Sinclair finally managed to cut him off. "Are you sure that Alex went to Israel? Not England? Is that what you said? Why in the world would he do that?" He was looking at Blake when he said it.

The CIA operative looked at him suspiciously. The patient was genuinely confused and getting agitated. "Mr. Sinclair, we were hoping to get answers *from* you, not the other way around. A little while ago you seemed pleased that

Mycroft had left the country, but now you're upset because he went to Israel instead of England. What are you, his fucking travel agent?"

"Blake, please!" It was Peterson, trying to inject some order back into the questioning. But Blake ignored him.

"Listen, Sinclair, I personally don't care what's on Mycroft's travel itinerary as long as Tehran isn't one of the stops. And that's what you're going to tell me."

At that moment Sinclair's monitor went off, signaling a too-rapid increase in his heartbeat. A nurse came rushing into the room in response to the signal.

"I'm afraid you gentlemen are going to have to leave," she said.

"No," said Blake. "We're staying; you're leaving." And he forceably turned her around and shooed her out the door.

"Blake, you can't do that," protested Peterson.

But Blake again ignored him and approached Sinclair's bed. He knew he probably had gone too far and decided he'd better try another tack before the nurse returned with security guards.

He sat down softly on the edge of the bed and placed one hand on Sinclair's leg, in a gesture of comfort and support.

"Let me tell *you* what happened," Blake began in the voice of a confidant, "and you correct me where I'm wrong. Your frustrations over your son's captivity got the better of you. I don't blame you, Mr. Sinclair, really I don't. Frankly, I don't know what I would do if I were in your shoes. So you came up with some kind of scheme—I'm not sure what— that somehow entailed Bill Gregory supplying information to Alexander Mycroft. I honestly don't know how you got Bill Gregory to go along with you, but that's not my concern. But I know Alexander Mycroft. I know what he's capable of. I know all about his past military service and his Intelligence record. He can be ruthless, but he's not known to have a diminished mental capacity. I don't know what the three of you cooked up, but somehow it involves your son. A rescue mission? Maybe. Why Mycroft would attempt anything so stup—so, uh, foolhardy, I don't know. But somewhere things got out of hand. You wound up in the hospital. Someone killed Bill Gregory. And Mycroft takes off for Israel. *Something's* going to happen over there, Mr. Sinclair, and I *have* to know what it is before it's too late. Mycroft won't be able to do anything but muddy the waters for us . . . for you . . . for your son. I *have* to know what he's planning, where he's going. I have to *stop* him, Mr. Sinclair, and you have to help . . . help your son . . . help your country."

"Now, I want to show you a picture, Mr. Sinclair." Blake was smooth, now. Calm and smooth. He knew he didn't have too much longer before he and Peterson were evicted from Sinclair's room. "Your friend Bill Gregory died a pretty horrible death, but I just want to show you this picture of the upper part of his body and ask you whether the position of his hands and arms suggest anything to you."

Sinclair looked numbly at the picture but said nothing.

"Okay, Mr. Sinclair. It doesn't mean anything to us either," Blake said, misinterpreting Sinclair's silence for ignorance. "Not yet, anyway."

Peterson spoke up in a quiet voice. "Please, Mr. Sinclair. Please help us if you can. I can't stress how urgent it is."

Sinclair began to feel a sense of defeat and resignation.

Blake showed Sinclair one of the other pictures—one that showed part of the mutilation Gregory suffered. "This is how Bill Gregory died, Mr. Sinclair. He bled to death as a result of this hideous slashing."

Sinclair forced himself to look at the picture, then sucked his breath in with a loud gasp. "Who—who could have done such a thing?" He felt bile build up in his throat and turned the photo facedown with both hands.

"We don't know who and we don't know why," Blake responded. "What we *do* know is that it is somehow related to events that *you* put in motion. Whatever you thought you were doing by asking Mycroft to rescue your son—that is what you did, isn't it, Mr. Sinclair?"

Blake and Peterson held their breath while waiting for a response. Sinclair looked down at the sheets on his bed and nodded affirmatively.

Blake continued in a soft voice, gratified that his initial instincts that it was an international affair had just been validated and knowing that Sinclair was now pliable enough to give him any other information he might need. This justification would help quiet the inevitable protest from the hospital. "So, whatever you thought you were doing by asking Mycroft to rescue Lee, you actually set into motion a much larger chain of events. A chain of events over which you now have no control but which may prove detrimental or even disastrous to existing operations in Iran. You don't know what that chain of events is and neither do we. But with your help, it may not be too late to stop it and to at least make sure that no harm comes to your son."

Tears began to flow on Sinclair's face again as he asked in a soft voice, "What do you want to know?"

"First, why in the world would Mycroft agree to try to rescue your son, and why did Bill Gregory lift classified government documents from the State Department?"

Sinclair was silent for a few moments. "I'll tell you as much as I can, but don't ask me to explain 'why.' I won't tell you why. But I will tell you that neither Mycroft nor poor Bill wanted to help. They were both against it. I made them help; I forced them. Just say I blackmailed them, all right? If anything happens, I'm responsible. Just me. Just the way"—he started sobbing but continued talking through the tears—"just the way I'm responsible for Bill Gregory's death."

Blake sat closer to Sinclair. "If we knew who killed Gregory, we might get a better handle on things. Who else knew about the rescue plan?"

Sinclair's Obligation to the Brotherhood of the Craft permitted him only to say, "The only people who knew any of the details were me, Bill Gregory, and Alex Mycroft."

"How about any women? Did any females know about the rescue plan?"

"Women?" asked Sinclair, surprised, his tears momentarily abated. "Christie knew, but why do you ask? What does any of this have to do with her?"

"Who is Christie?" Blake asked.

Peterson answered: "His daughter."

Sinclair was getting agitated again and the monitor was beginning a warning beep. "Why are you asking about Christie, Mr. Blake?"

"Calm down, Sinclair," the CIA agent responded. "I'm not necessarily talking about your daughter. It's just that the police have good reason to believe that a woman was involved in Bill Gregory's death."

The cardiac-monitor beep started growing louder and faster. "Christie wouldn't do something like that. She was against the rescue attempt and told me she was going to try to stop it, but *murder?* No, no, no. It's just not possible."

"Where is your daughter now, Mr. Sinclair?"

"I—I don't know. Europe, the last time I spoke with her. But now, I don't know." He sank back against the pillows.

Blake was back in his role of confidant again. "Mr. Sinclair, for what it's worth, I don't think your daughter was

1 2 7

involved in Bill Gregory's murder either. But if she's trying to stop Mycroft, she could get in the way and get hurt. Badly hurt. You do see that, don't you?''

Sinclair nodded silently.

''So, what I'd like to do is have you tell me the story from the beginning, Mr. Sinclair. And please try not to leave anything out.''

Sinclair took a sip of water and cleared his throat. ''I'll tell you as much as I can.''

''Remarkable story,'' Peterson said as they were escorted out of the hospital together under the direction of the chief administrator and two burly orderlies. ''But why Israel instead of England, I wonder?''

''I know Mycroft,'' Blake said. ''It fits. And it's damned smart.''

''Blake, this is not really my line, you know. Tell me honestly, do you really think this Mycroft will try something crazy over there? In Iran, I mean.''

''No, Peterson. Like I said, I know Mycroft and one thing I don't think he'll do is anything crazy. But what scares the fucking shit out of me is that whatever he tries will *work*. And *then* what the hell do we do?''

11

Tel Aviv—December 27, 1979

THE walk through the barnlike openness of the building that served as Ben-Gurion Airport was uneventful, but Mycroft could feel eyes watching him. And just as he emerged at the curb, two men approached him, one from the front and one from behind.

"We have a car waiting for you, Mr. Mycroft."

"No thanks. I didn't order a car," Mycroft replied, knowing resistance would be useless.

The man from the rear took a step closer, one hand in his suit pocket. "But we insist."

Mycroft knew the drill, but it still played out in his mind like a scene from a old movie. "Oh, sure. My car. Right. Let's go."

"Sensible, Mycroft," said the man in back. "Very sensible."

Mycroft was piled into the back and the two men got in the front of the four-door sedan. There were no door handles on the inside of the rear doors. They took off and headed west toward Jaffa.

"I suppose it's pointless to ask who you guys are or where we're going," Mycroft finally said after ten minutes of silence, "to say nothing of why."

The man seated on the right in front turned his body to face the rear, with his back resting against the door. "That's right."

"Well, I know you're not Mossad. No, you're definitely American. From the cheap polyester of your suits and the typical aviator sunglasses, I'd say CIA."

"Shut up, Mycroft, and just enjoy the ride," said the driver, clearly annoyed.

"But if you're CIA you're pretty stupid to be operating alone. I know you guys have a little rocky relationship going with the Mossad, but you're sure as hell not going to be in their favor by pulling a stunt like this right under their noses."

"Look, Mycroft, I told you once—"

"After all, you don't really think they weren't watching, do you? And if this move had their sanction, they'd be the ones doing the driving, not you. No, the way I figure it, this is an independent operation, and in Israel, my friends, that can be very hairy."

"One more word out of you and—holy shit! *What's that!*"

The car had just completed a bend in the road and the driver jammed on the brakes, fishtailing the rear end of the sedan. Alex was thrown against the left door and the rider in front was similarly tossed into the driver's lap.

Just ahead on the road, a horse-drawn straw wagon had overturned, blocking the road and filling it with a thin covering of straw, causing the sedan's wheels to skid even more. A large pile of straw, however, was positioned just in front of the sedan.

As soon as the car had come to a stop, four men in complete Arab garb and brandishing Uzi submachine guns jumped from the straw pile and began firing into the car's grille and tires, totally decimating the vehicle while carefully avoiding shooting at any of its passengers. The two men in the front of the car instinctively reached for their guns.

"Don't be assholes," Alex said. "Your two peashooters against four trained submachine guns are gonna get someone killed—and I don't want it to be me."

One of the robed gunmen hollered to them in Arabic.

"What did he say? What do they want?" asked the driver.

"Your guns for starters," Mycroft answered. Another burst from one of the submachine guns amputated the side mirror and the two handguns quickly went flying out the two front side windows. Two of the Arabs approached the sedan from either side and opened the doors, front and rear, barking orders.

"They want us out," Mycroft said.

"Yeah, even I can understand that, wise guy."

When they were standing outside of the sedan, two of the Arabs pulled Alex away from the others and, with an Uzi in his back and hands raised, Mycroft was marched to the other side of the straw wagon and into the rear of a van. A short toot on the horn brought the other two Arabs, alone, and they drove off leaving a smoking sedan and two smoldering Americans behind.

Mycroft didn't know who his benefactors were or whether he had actually been rescued. He might have been plucked out of the frying pan and tossed into the fire, for all he knew. But he was still alive and the welcoming committee—for all their shooting—had been careful, Mycroft had observed, not to kill anyone. It was, at least, a hopeful sign.

He asked them whether they spoke English but got no reply. He tried a similar question in Arabic, what little of it he remembered, but was also met with silence. He didn't even bother to try Hebrew.

The van sped along the winding sea road toward the ancient town of Jaffa and somehow managed to navigate the incredibly narrow cobblestone alleys of the town. They pulled up in front of an innocuous stone building and Alex and two of his escorts alighted from the van while the two others drove off. They entered the dimly-lit building and were guided along a passageway that steadily declined. They approached a door that one of the guards opened and then stepped back from to allow Mycroft to enter alone. The door closed softly behind him and Alex listened for the sound of the door locking but was surprised when he did not hear it.

There was a man seated at a desk in front of him, but his back was toward Mycroft, who could see only a small round bald spot at the top of the back of the man's dark curly hair. Alex could barely contain himself, but then—

"Shalom, Alex, and welcome to the Holy Land!"

The chair spun around and Alex burst out laughing.

"Avi! Avi Blume! I'd recognize that bald spot anywhere."

The two old friends and former relatives met in the center of the room and embraced warmly.

You haven't changed a bit, they lied to each other, and it's so good to see you again, they said in truth.

"Tell me, Avi, how is the Mossad's answer to James Bond, huh?"

The Israeli agent's well-endowed ego took the comment

as a statement of fact rather than as a gentle ribbing. "How am I? I'm still saving your tuchus, that's how I am. It seems to be a habit hard to break."

"Well, don't feel obliged to break that kind of habit on my account. Do you know who they were?" Alex asked.

"But of course," Avi responded almost indignantly. "Do you think the Mossad are fools?"

"CIA?"

"Yes. The gall of them. The chutzpah! It is an insult to *me!*"

"Do you know why I was picked up?"

Avi turned back and sat down at the desk, indicating a chair for Alex. "That, I must confess, I do not know. Do you?"

"Yes . . . and no," Alex said. "If they knew why I was here, the answer is yes. But since they shouldn't know, I'd say no."

"Well, it's quite apparent their intelligence is not all bad. Obviously, they knew you'd be arriving and they know why. I, of course, knew you were arriving also. Simply checking El Al's daily manifest told me that. But as to why you are here, I must tell you that I do not like the CIA knowing something I don't."

"Avi, my dear, dear friend. Not only was I planning on contacting you the moment I arrived, but I plan to ask your assistance as well."

"So, tell me, Alex. What is the trouble?"

"Avi, a Brother has thrown the Hailing Sign."

Ten thoughts, perhaps a hundred, immediately jumped through Avi Blume's mind, but in his typical ability to cut through subterfuge and get directly to the essence of the matter, he asked only, "Why would this be of concern to the CIA?"

"The Brother is one of the American hostages in Iran."

"And you have been asked to respond to the sign? A wise choice on the part of the Brotherhood."

"Thanks for the compliment, but I haven't played this kind of major-league ball in a long time. I'm out of practice."

"Not so much so, I suspect. And you have me. How can I help, my friend?"

"Information, mostly. Intelligence reports, if you have them. A hot bath and a good meal."

"My manners! Forgive me for not thinking. You've had a long trip and a rude welcome. One of my men will take you to a guest house where you can freshen up and take a long nap. I'll pick you up for dinner later. Then we'll have a long talk. Come. We are going."

Alex awoke with a muffled start. Someone had a hand clamped over his mouth.

"*Sheked*, my friend, quiet," said Avi. "You were having a nightmare."

Alex nodded his acquiesence and Avi removed his hand from Alex's mouth. "Why the gag?" Alex asked.

"You were making noise and we have a visitor here."

"Who is it?"

Avi got up and started pacing the small confines of the bedroom. "That is what I want you to tell me. She has been asking for you, my friend."

"*She?* What is this, Avi? Who is she?"

"Come with me into the next room."

The two men entered a small, almost bare room with a two-way mirror on one wall. Beyond that wall, Alex stared at a woman of such exquisite beauty that she almost took his breath away. She had long flowing, rich black hair and piercing brown eyes. Despite the absence of makeup her lips appeared naturally full, red and sensual. Alex emitted a low whistle.

"She's gorgeous," Alex whispered. "Who is she, Avi?"

"You've never seen her before, Alex? From the way she was asking for you—actually demanding to see you—one would have thought you two were old lovers."

"I'm not that lucky. What's the story?"

Avi was watching Alex closely as he said, "She says her name is Christie Sinclair."

"Oh, sweet Jesus," said Mycroft, as he leaned back against a wall for support.

"Now, Alex, tell me: *Who is she?*"

"Her brother is *our* Brother Lee Sinclair—the Iranian hostage who threw the Hailing Sign. Her father, John, is the Master who asked me to respond."

"But what is she doing *here?* And why is she asking for *you?*"

"I think she's trying to stop me from rescuing her brother."

"Then I will send her home."

"No, wait. Let's not be too hasty, Avi."

"Alex, I can tell by that look in your eye, you're thinking with your fly open again. That's always been your biggest weakness: falling for women who were wrong for you."

"Does that include Beth?" Mycroft asked sharply.

"My sister was *right* for *you*, but you were *wrong* for *her*," Avi responded just as crisply. "Now, before this discussion goes where neither one of us want it to go, put your putz back in your pants and let's send this woman back home. You know who she is; you can look her up later when your mission is finished."

"Maybe she can help, who knows? Why are you so intent on dismissing her?"

"Your instincts are dulled, Alex. This woman shows up out of nowhere and claims to be the sister of the man whose life you are obligated to try to save, and you just accept that? She arrived at the airport this afternoon and stormed into the security office and demanded to see you. They never heard of you, she was told. But she insisted that you were here, that you were with the Mossad, and that she would create a big scene if they didn't take her to you. I was contacted and I told them to bring her here so we could both take a look at her. Now, we've both seen her, but you've never seen her before. And you just accept her as she is and with her story?"

"Why do you keep saying that, Avi? Who else could she be? And if you doubted her, why did you have her brought here?"

"Alex, my friend. Earlier today you tell me a Brother has thrown the Hailing Sign and you are obligated to respond. Later in the day, she shows up with your name on her lips. Why do I bring the two of you together? To see if there is a connection. All I see is a diversion from your mission, and my Jewish nose smells trouble."

"Maybe we will send her home, Avi. But first let's at least say hello before we say good-bye." He turned and left the room and entered the adjoining room where the woman sat alone. It happened so fast that Avi was still watching through the glass when Alex walked over to her and said, "Christie Sinclair? Hello. I understand you've been looking for me. I'm Alex Mycroft."

She stood and took a few steps in his direction until she was close enough for him to smell her perfume. He breathed in deeply and filled his senses with her loveliness. She stared at him hard and he could feel her piercing eyes penetrating deep into his soul. After an awkward silence, he put out his hand, but she ignored it and slapped him hard across the face.

"You son of a bitch! Because of you, my father is in the hospital and whatever crazy scheme he cooked up with you may wind up getting my brother killed."

He saw her lower lip begin to tremble as he began to raise his hand to his cheek. Thinking he was about to strike her, she flinched and recoiled slightly, then began to cry. Alex held out his arms and she came into them for comfort.

Avi had witnessed only the slapping episode and was rushing into the room when the tears began, so he was not prepared for the sight of Alex caressing Christie's hair as he held her tenderly in his arms.

"Oh, I'm sorry, so sorry," she sobbed on his shoulder. "I didn't mean to hit you, but I'm so scared. I never thought I'd find you, and when I did, I didn't know whether to be happy or angry. Oh, please forgive me."

Alex made appropriate comforting noises and allowed himself to feel intoxicated and somewhat aroused by the closeness of her body to his.

"Well, well," said Avi. "Now that we've broken the ice, let us go and break some bread and get to know each other. Although, by the look of appearances, it seems you two are getting a jump on things."

Somewhat embarrassed, Alex tried to pull back slightly from Christie, but she kept her arms around his neck just a seductive beat or two longer than necessary. He gazed into her moist eyes. I could *really* fall for *this* one, he thought to himself.

Dinner was at an outdoor Jaffa restaurant on a small cobblestoned patio surrounded by a low stone wall and overlooking the Mediterranean Sea. There they feasted on unkosher shrimp and squid delicacies. Avi poured freely from bottle after bottle of Carmel Mizrachi wine from the Rothschild vineyards of Zichron Yaccov, a small village on Mount Carmel near Haifa.

Not far from their table, in more conventional attire than they had worn earlier in the day, sat two of the Mossad agents who had snatched Alex from the CIA's clutches. They were keeping watch over them. When Alex had asked about this, Avi had merely shrugged his shoulders and said, "Always there is something. Some trouble. Some terrorist. Always there is something."

A calmer, more controlled Christie wasted little time in making her position and her feelings known. "This is madness. Absolute madness. Don't you see that, Alex? What on earth makes you and my father think you can rescue Lee? Why do you think you can succeed when the government is not able to do anything?"

Alex tried to reassure her. "Before you jump to any more conclusions, stop assuming that I'm going to be able to do *anything* in Iran. My, uh, Obligation to your father doesn't include getting myself killed."

"And how about Lee? What if *he* gets killed?"

"There's a very small chance of that," said Alex. "The last thing the Iranians want is American blood on their hands. So far, they've gotten as far as they have just by *threatening* to spill blood. If they seriously harm one of the hostages, the U.S. will retaliate."

"But I thought you were going to try to rescue Lee."

"Listen, the first thing I'm going to try to accomplish is to gather information. To see if he *can* be gotten out. But that does not necessarily mean getting him out by force. There may be other ways, peaceful ways."

"The government has tried negotiations," she protested, "and gotten nowhere."

"There are all different types of persuasion. But I promise you this. We have reason to believe—despite what our government says—that Lee's life is in danger. If that's true, anything I can do to alleviate that danger, I will do. I have to."

"Very well," she said through an unsuccessfully stifled yawn, "but if you're going to Iran, I'm going with you."

"Don't be absurd," Alex started to protest, but he was interrupted by Avi.

"Let us consider it," he said. It was one of the first things he had said all evening. "But let us not consider it tonight. Christie looks to be very tired."

The wine, the time change, and the earlier excitement were taking their toll on Christie, who began to yawn once again. This time she let the yawn run its full course.

"Oh, I am tired," she said. "It just came over me. I can't keep my eyes open. Will you both excuse me, please? I think I had better go back to the house."

Alex began to stand, too, but she stopped him.

"No. Alex," she said. "Please, you stay and continue talking with Avi."

"One of my men will take you back now," Avi said.

As she left, one of the Mossad agents fell into step behind her, just catching her arm as she proceeded unsteadily along the cobblestone path down to the house Avi had arranged for them to occupy.

"How much did you put into her wine?" Alex asked.

"Only enough to produce the desired result, I promise you. She will have the best night's sleep she's had in years and will awake tomorrow feeling like a new person. I'm glad to see your eyesight has not failed you, my friend."

"It wasn't hard to miss. But do you mind telling me why you drugged her?"

He shrugged his shoulders. "Call it instinct if you like."

"Come off it, Avi. You can't be serious. Stop looking for bogeymen everywhere. You saw her. What do you think she is?"

"I don't know what and I don't know who and I don't know why."

"Stop talking Yiddish gibberish."

"All right, I will. You say I saw her. Yes. I saw her. You saw her. But did we see the same thing? You saw a woman of exceptional beauty, but I saw a stranger. You saw her with your crotch and I saw her with my mind. But whoever is right, let's not discuss that now. The important question for now, my friend, is how may I be of service to you?"

Alex silently stirred his thick black Turkish coffee and reflected on the wisdom of bringing Avi into this matter. He was genuinely fond of his friend—his former brother-in-law—despite the six years since they'd seen each other last, although he was not altogether pleased that Avi had drugged Christie. But perhaps Avi was right to have done it, he thought. A good agent *does* suspect everyone. And as to the wisdom of getting Avi involved, Avi had already gotten himself involved when he rescued him earlier that day. And besides, he needed information—the kind of information he was certain Avi would have.

Mycroft resolved to tell Avi everything, save for the disturbing phone call from the little boy. It could not possibly have any bearing on the matter, he wanted to believe, and it would serve no purpose except to remind Avi that he had never forgiven Mycroft for the death of his sister, Beth, or his nephew, Josh.

"Where to begin." Alex sighed aloud while his right hand caressed the glass tube through his shirt pocket. "At the beginning, Avi. At the beginning."

*   *   *

"But this is incredible," Avi exclaimed an hour later when Alex had finished the story. "First, I can't recall a time when I ever actually heard of a Brother throwing the Hailing Sign."

"It's a rarity, all right. I've only heard of one other incident myself."

"And then the Master's heart attack and the Deacon's murder! There's much more here than we're able to see just now."

"I agree, Avi. And the only way I can see to flesh it out is for me to continue on with the rescue attempt. If I turn back now, we'll never find out what's really going on."

Avi thought for a moment. "Yes, that seems right. Now, let me see; I think I recall the name Sinclair from our intelligence reports."

Alex was inwardly pleased and gratified to hear Avi confirm what he had expected—the Mossad *were* monitoring Iranian activity. But whether they were doing so for themselves, for the security of their tiny country, or at the request of the United States, he didn't know.

"Ah, yes. One of the marines, I think," Avi concluded.

"Right. Look, Avi, I want to know honestly. Am I crazy for even thinking about a rescue? Is it possible?"

"Crazy? Alex, you will forgive me for saying this, I pray, but if anyone is crazy, it's your government, which is quickly becoming the laughingstock of the rest of the world. Listen closely, my friend. Do you think for one moment the Israeli government would allow madmen to hold even one of our citizens hostage? *Never!* Because if you permit it once—just once, mind you—others will try it, mark my words.

"Why do you think Israel always retaliates after a terrorist

141

raid or a bombing? Because we *have* to! We have not only to retaliate but we have to give them more than just measure for measure in return. Someday—please God, maybe even in my lifetime—we may live in peace with our Arab neighbors. But until then, we have to show the world we do not fuck around. We will no longer march quietly into the showers. You understand? You've heard the saying, 'Masada shall not fall again!' To us it's not just an empty phrase.

"Your country should have moved within *days* to rescue your citizens. What if they had failed, you ask; what if they failed? Then Americans would be dead. American hostages, American soldiers. Yes. But many more Iranians would be dead, too. You say to the world, 'All right, world, some of our citizens have died. But so have theirs. All right, world, you want this to happen to you? Just try screwing with Americans again. Anywhere in the world, we will fight for our people, protect them, defend them.' *That* is what you say. Everybody feels sad that Americans have died, but pfft,"—here he made a quick gesture with the back of his hand—"it is over. And at least the Iranians gained nothing. No advantage over you, no demands made.

"*Days?* My God, *months* have gone by already. And what does the once-mighty and once-feared United States of America do? Talk. Nothing but talk, talk, talk. Nothing but empty talk while a *meshugenuh* madman with a *shmatah*, a dish towel, around his head brings your country to its knees.

"Do you know what *could* have been done in two months? My God, Alex; in two months you could dig a tunnel into the embassy compound and no one would ever know. You could sneak in at night and gas the entire compound—I mean everyone, hostages and Iranians—never fire one shot. You could put everyone to sleep. And as they *shluff,* you one by one carry your people out of there and the next morning the lunatics wake up with their putzes in their hands.

"Crazy? No, my friend. You are not crazy. You've got chutzpah. And, more importantly,"—he swelled up his chest immodestly—"you've got *me!* Now, what assistance can I provide?"

Alex was about to ask Avi how well he knew the layout of the embassy compound when the sound of screeching tires demanded their instant attention. They turned in time to see a black Saab turning the corner near the restaurant, coming around on two wheels at breakneck speed, blinding them with the car's headlights.

"Get down!" Avi yelled and Alex reacted instantly. The Mossad agent at the table nearest the street crouched low and produced his Uzi submachine gun from under the table.

The car slowed only briefly, but as it passed by the patio, two machine guns protruding from the two right windows opened fire on them, sending broken plates, bottles, wooden table splinters, and a few lingering patrons flying in all directions. The Mossad agent began to return their fire, but his gun was silenced almost immediately. And as quickly as the car had appeared, that's how quickly it disappeared from view, down the cobblestone road and into the night.

When Alex picked himself up, he found Avi crouched down near the fallen Mossad agent, holding the young man's bloody head in his lap.

"Dead?" Alex asked.

"Yes. He was a good man. He was my wife's youngest brother, Yosef. Oy, God, how will I tell her?"

"Any idea who they were?"

"None. It was too fast. I couldn't see." He looked up at Alex and noticed the red on his shirt. "Alex, are you hurt?"

143

He looked down. "No, this is only spilled wine." He thought for a moment. "I feel responsible, Avi. What can I say?"

He stood up and covered the face of the fallen agent with his handkerchief and walked away with Alex. "We do not know for certain if they were after you, my friend. And I cannot believe the CIA would do this."

"Frankly, neither can I. But I'm still puzzled about the CIA's sudden involvement in this. I don't know for the life of me how they knew I'd be here or, if they did, *why* I'm here. There is something, somewhere, we're overlooking."

Avi absentmindedly turned his gaze down the cobblestone street and rubbed his chin reflectively. "Yes," he said mostly to himself. A siren in the distance heralded the arrival of the local police. "You, my friend, go to bed—and before the police arrive. There is no point in your getting involved with them. I can take care of things. We will talk in the morning."

12

Philadelphia

"**E**XCUSE me, John Sinclair?" Only the oversized head of the tall Police Captain Stanley Harris was visible as he sheepishly peered into the hospital room. "They said it would be okay if I came in. I'm Captain Harris, Homicide."

His six-foot-four-inch hulking frame dominated the room as he approached Sinclair's bed and fished around for his badge. He left his blue overcoat buttoned but courteously removed his porkpie hat and attempted without success to brush the few wisps of hair remaining on his head back into a semblance of order. There was too much area to cover and not enough material to do the job. As he moved between the bed and the window, his body seemed to grow larger as it absorbed almost all available natural light.

"You're also *Brother* Harris, if I'm not mistaken," Sinclair responded, "although I can't remember the last time I saw you at a Lodge Meeting, Cap."

The color rose in Cap Harris' cheeks as he took a chair. He was flattered that Sinclair remembered him and his nickname but embarrassed by his prolonged absence from the Brotherhood of the Craft meetings. It would have been inappropriate to make excuses, so he merely nodded and said he would try to attend more often. Then he quickly changed the subject.

"John, you probably know why I'm here. I'm investigating Bill Gregory's murder."

Sinclair stared at nothing in particular on the far wall and said, "I still can't believe Bill's dead. I hold myself responsible."

Cap took out a notebook and the stub of a pencil, which he briefly touched to his thick tongue. "Why do you think you're responsible?"

"Oh, that's right. You weren't at the meeting, so you wouldn't know." Sinclair paused to pour himself some water and then launched into his narrative. When he was finished, Cap let out a long low whistle but remained mute for a few minutes as he consulted his notebook.

"There are some pieces that are starting to come together," Cap said after a while, "but I'm still not quite there. There's got to be some connection between Bill Gregory's death and Alex Mycroft's phone call to me."

Now it was Sinclair's turn to be surprised. "Alex called you? Why?"

"Besides being a Brother, Mycroft is an old friend of mine. Damn good one, too. He called me the night Gregory got killed, but he obviously didn't know about it. Mycroft's town house had been ransacked and someone had scrawled

1 4 6

the name of his dead boy on one of the walls. He told me he'd be away for a while but didn't say why or where. But there's got to be some connection between the two events."

"Do you have any ideas?"

"Not yet, but I know I'll figure it out. There was a similarity in the savagery of the two incidents, too. You could tell by looking at Mycroft's place that whoever did it was *angry*. It wasn't just a burglary. In fact, Mycroft said he didn't even think anything was taken. No, this was vicious hatred.

"As for Bill Gregory," Cap continued, "well, it was really horrible. He was sexually molested, then castrated."

Sinclair sucked in his breath with a gasp.

"Sorry, but you've got to know, John. It was brutal, but he didn't die right away. Whoever it was left him to bleed to death. And it was what Gregory did during the time he had left that brings me here to see you."

Sinclair looked confused. "I don't understand."

"He crawled a short distance away from where the attack took place and died with his hands in the Hailing Sign."

"A cry for help?" Sinclair suggested.

"That's what I thought when I came in, but now I don't think so. I think it was a warning."

"Of what? To whom?"

"I think someone is out to kill Alex Mycroft."

13

▼

Tel Aviv—December 28, 1979

"YOU'RE a dumb shit, Johnson! The biggest, god-damned dumbest shit I've ever met, and boy, let me tell you someday about some of the dumb shits I've met in my time. But you take the cake!" Otis Blake was circling Agent Johnson, hurtling epithets at his subaltern who stood stoically in the center of the small room, suffering the verbal assault in silence.

"Well, aren't you going to give me some kind of dumb-shit excuse? How the fuck did it happen? How did he get snatched from you and that other dumb shit partner of yours?"

"Chief, it happened so fast. There were four of them. Arabs I think, but—"

"Arabs my ass! They weren't Arabs, you dumb shit. You think the Mossad are going to let fucking Arabs run around in this country? It was probably the Mossad who got Mycroft. They've got brass balls, let me tell you, and that snatch was just the sort of thing they'd do. They probably spotted you at the airport and set up the snatch on the spot. Shit, they probably used their greenest recruits just to practice on two dumb shits like you and Willoughby. Didn't you read Mycroft's file?"

"Yes, Chief. I read it. Willoughby, too. We both read it."

"Well, then you should have known that Mycroft's tight with the Mossad, especially with a guy named Avi Blume. I'm betting you find Blume and you'll trip over Mycroft."

Johnson knew that finding a Mossad agent in Israel was like looking for a drop of salt in the Dead Sea. "Sure, Chief. Got any ideas on where to start?"

"Don't get smart with me, Johnson. I'm not done with you yet; not by a long shot. How many men do we have in the general area? Or, how many men can we pull in, say, within twenty-four hours?"

"About a dozen, maybe more."

"Get on it. Immediately! I want Mycroft before he goes off half-cocked and gets about sixty or so Americans slaughtered."

"There's something else. Maybe it's related, maybe not. But last night there was a shooting at an outdoor café in Jaffa. The word is that a Mossad agent bought it. There was an American at the restaurant, too. It could have been Mycroft; the description fits."

"Was he hit?"

"No. He was with another man whom we think was Mossad, too."

"Blume. I'll bet anything it was Blume."

149

"Well, we're checking on that."

"Who was responsible?"

"We don't know, sir."

"Great. A dime'll get you a dollar the Mossad thinks the CIA did it to retaliate for the snatch. Way to go, Johnson, you dumb shit, you!"

14

Jaffa

"*BOKER TOV*," said Avi as he wished Alex and Christie a good morning in Hebrew when they joined him downstairs late in the morning.

"*Boker Or*," responded Alex, wishing his friend a traditional morning filled with light.

"I trust you two slept well while I was hard at work."

"I've never slept better," Christie said. "And the air. Take a deep breath, Alex. It's so clear, so clean."

"That's because we haven't yet managed to duplicate your country's well-developed pollution," Avi said with a smile. "But, we're ingenious. We're working on it."

"I heard you on the phone when we were upstairs," Alex said. "Were you able to find out anything about last night?"

Avi shot a quick glance at Christie, but Alex said, "It's okay; I told her."

"Well then, help yourself to some cheese and hard-boiled eggs and we'll talk over breakfast."

As they were putting food on their plates from the small sideboard, Christie asked Avi, "Is everything in Israel done while eating?"

"Only in the proper Jewish homes. Yes."

When they were seated at the table, Avi began talking rapidly while going through some notes.

"To begin with, an old friend of yours, Otis Blake, arrived in Tel Aviv earlier this morning. Does that tell you anything, Alex?"

"Only that the CIA is taking this seriously enough to put its best people on it. Whatever 'it' is."

"Ah, yes. 'It.' Well, naturally I can help you there, too. The CIA not only knows what your mission is, they know about me, also. Blake is heading up the operation personally—to find you as quickly as possible and to prevent you from getting into Iran."

Alex let out a mild curse. "They know about Iran?"

"Well, as far as we can tell, they know you are planning *something* in Iran. They do not yet know precisely what, or if they do, we don't know about that. But since they know *something*, one can assume they know *everything*. They are losing no time in bringing in more men, too. We will, naturally, keep them under close surveillance, but they may get lucky. One never knows about these things. Right now, their plan is simple: Find me, they find you.

"Something else, too. We know at least that the CIA was not responsible for last night's shooting. In fact, the CIA is as troubled by the incident as we are."

"But how can you possibly know all this?" Christie asked. "This information is fantastic."

"Well, it is really child's play for us. I would like to impress you and tell you what a wonderfully efficient intelligence group Israel has—which, of course, it has—but actually we have the CIA bugged. We have the whole conversation between Blake and his men from this morning on tape."

"Do you have any notion then who *was* responsible for last night?" Alex interjected.

"A few hours ago my men found the car and its former occupants. It was the PLO."

"If that's the case," Alex pondered aloud, "we can assume it was merely terrorism for terrorism's sake. In other words, it probably had nothing to do with me."

"Ordinarily I would agree with you, my friend. But I'm afraid such is not the case. When we searched their bodies, we found an old photograph of you on one of them, Alex. Last night was not terrorism. It appears that it was designed to be assassination: *yours.*"

Christie looked up. "Bodies? Does that mean they're dead?"

"Yes, I'm afraid they are. All three of them."

"Did they talk before your men killed them?" Christie quickly asked with a hint of animosity in her voice.

"Regrettably, they did not have the opportunity to talk. But why do you assume my men killed them? I assure you they did not. The three assassins actually took their own lives. My men discovered them in their room. Cyanide capsules, we believe. Archaic, but still quite effective."

Alex noticed that Christie's face was pale and the hand holding her coffee cup was shaking. "Are you all right, Christie?" he asked.

Avi couldn't help but notice the obvious caring sound in Alex's voice. He felt that his friend was starting to feel too much too soon for someone he didn't even know. It was not an uncommon pattern for Alex Mycroft, Avi knew, but it troubled him nonetheless. If Mycroft was going to be successful in Iran, he needed full concentration on his assignment. And Avi knew as well that the success of the mission might bring Alex back to life in other ways. The past six years of mourning and self-flagellation had taken their toll on Mycroft. But Avi's gut told him that casting the girl adrift would be a strategic error, too.

"Alex, I'm scared," Christie responded. "I told you yesterday that I was afraid people would die as a result of this rescue attempt of yours. Now look. Without even getting to Iran, four people are dead. And Lee could be next. Or you. Maybe we ought to turn back."

"I'm inclined to agree with Christie," Avi said softly. "Remember the Obligation: 'Only if there is a greater chance of saving a Brother's life than of losing your own.' You must weigh the consequences of your actions against the desired results of your mission."

"I'm not going back. But maybe you should, Christie."

"No!" It was Avi who answered just as Christie was about to object herself. "I apologize. I didn't mean to interfere with such an important and personal decision, but let me explain." He paused and when he continued, he did so haltingly.

"Christie is obviously determined to follow you if you go through with your plans to go to Iran," Avi said, "and it could be dangerous—to both of you—to split up. Alex, if Christie gets picked up by Iranian Revolutionary guards, who knows what they might force her to say? It could jeopardize your mission, your life. I don't think she ought to go, either, but better to go together and keep an eye on each other than to go separately."

"Good, that's settled," Christie said. "Now the question

is how do we get into Iran, and what do we do when we get there?''

"And what do we do about the CIA?" Alex threw in.

"To say nothing of the PLO." Avi offered.

15

Tel Aviv

"WE'VE located them. They're at a Mossad safe house in Jaffa." The sweat was coming through Johnson's shirt, partly from the heat of the early morning sun and partly from his own nervousness at having to deal face-to-face with Otis Blake again.

"Are you positive?"

"Yes, Chief. They're there all right. Three of them. Mycroft, Blume, and some girl."

"Who is she, do we know?"

"Not yet. But we'll make her soon."

"Any Mossad in the area?" Blake asked.

"We spotted two for sure, but there may be more."

"You can count on it. Okay; going in's too risky. How long will it take to set up a stakeout?"

"I've already got some men on the way. We can be fully operational inside of a half-hour."

"Good, good," Blake said. "Glad to see you using your head. Let's get going."

16

Jaffa

AVI Blume put down the telephone and said, "It's time to go. The maps I want to go over with you are in Jerusalem. And besides, I don't wish to be here when your friend Blake arrives."

"Does he know where we are?" Alex asked.

"Only for the moment," he said to Mycroft. Then turning to Christie he asked, "This is your first time in Israel? Oh, you will fall in love with Jerusalem. Everybody does, which is one reason why men have fought over it for three thousand years. Come, though. If we hurry, your first view of the holiest city in the world will be just as the noonday sun reflects off of the golden dome of the Mosque of Omar. It is breathtaking!"

The Israeli took Christie by the hand and started for the door, leaving Alex rooted to the center of the floor. Avi glanced over his shoulder. "Are you coming, Alex?"

He didn't answer at first, and then said, "Why don't you take Christie on ahead and I'll meet you inside the Jaffa Gate at noon. I—I have some personal business to attend to in Netanya."

Avi walked over and placed his hands on Mycroft's shoulders and smiled broadly. "I understand, and I am pleased. But let us agree to meet at three instead of noon. I do not wish you to feel rushed. One of my men will drive you." Then he quickly departed with Christie before she had the chance to ask any questions.

The old woman sat quietly on her porch watching Mycroft step out of the passenger side of the car. She lowered her embroidery work to her lap, covering a sealed envelope that rested there, the moment she heard the car pull up. Her white hair was pulled back well off her face, revealing the lines of age and worry that are so common to mothers, and grandmothers, who have known tragedy in their lifetimes.

Mycroft looked around as he got out of the car. It had been six years since he had been there last, but nothing appeared to be changed except the woman on the porch. She seemed so much older than the last time he had seen her. It had been at a solemn family dinner, a farewell dinner of sorts, with little conversation and lots of tears served up between liberal portions of chicken soup, chopped liver, roast beef, and kasha. After dinner, unable to stand the old woman's sobbings any longer, Alex had turned to his brother-in-law and asked him whether he could arrange it so that he could take his wife and son for a walk on the beach.

And after the dishes were washed and put away by the

women, and following a brief phone call by the reluctant Mossad agent to a command post somewhere, Alexander Mycroft took his wife and son—this old woman's only daughter and only grandson—for a last, leisurely stroll along a deserted stretch of Netanya's beach.

Six very long, very difficult, years ago.

"Alex, Alex, Alex," the old woman called out in a frail voice. "Come and give your Goldie a big hug and kiss."

Mycroft inwardly relaxed, relieved to hear that sort of warm greeting. He had neither seen nor spoken to Beth's mother since the tragedy, and he was unsure of the reception that he'd get. He completed the short walk to the house and took the two steps up to the porch in one jump.

"I've missed you, Goldie," he said sincerely as he bent over to kiss the woman's cheek. She flung her arms around his neck and kissed him repeatedly on both cheeks, tickling him with her whisker stubles.

"Come and sit down, Alex," she said. "I've made some iced tea for you and here's a little cake that I remembered you like. Oh, Alex, let me look at you. You're too thin, my Alex. Are you eating enough? Tell me the truth; you can't lie to your Goldie."

Mycroft laughed. "Still the same Goldie. I'm eating fine, but I still miss your cooking."

"Then you'll stay for supper. It's settled."

"I wish I could, Goldie. Honestly, I do. But I can stay only a little while this time. And—" he paused, unsure of how to phrase his next thought—"and I want to visit Beth's . . . I want to spend some time with Beth."

"Oh, my Alex, Alex. She'll be so pleased. Don't forget to take some stones with you."

"I'll remember, Goldie."

"Have you seen my Avi?"

"Yes, Goldie. I've seen Avi, and we'll be seeing each other later this afternoon. Otherwise, you know I'd stay for dinner."

"Well, when you see him, you tell him to call his mother once in a while," she said as she furrowed her brow in mock anger. "He thinks he's Mister Bigshot, but you tell him I'm still his mother. You tell him, Alex."

Mycroft burst out laughing. "I promise I'll tell him Goldie."

The old woman leaned across and took Mycroft's face in her gnarled hands and pinched his cheeks. "Alex, why haven't you been here before? Why haven't you written?"

He held the woman's hands against his cheeks and closed his eyes. "I've wanted to, Goldie. But I didn't know what to say."

They fell silent for a time, and then began to chat about life in the village of Netanya ("That butcher, that *goniff.*" she said. "His thumbs should fall off for what he charges for meat.") and her arthritis ("The doctor says I should move away from the sea, but what does he know?").

After a time, Alex rose to leave, kissed the woman several times on her cheeks, and started down the short path to the waiting car. And then something the old woman had said earlier sprang into his mind and he pulled up short.

Returning to the porch, he said, "Goldie, did you say you made that iced tea for me?"

"Yes, Alex. Did you like it?"

"Of course, Goldie. It was delicious."

"Let me put some in a jar for you."

But he ignored this and asked, "But you asked me if I had seen Avi. Didn't Avi call you and tell you I was coming by?"

"Oh, no, Alex. I forgot. It was the man who came by very early this morning. He woke me up."

Mycroft tried to keep the urgency out of his voice. "What man was that, Goldie?"

"He was a dirty little man with a scraggly beard. But he said he was a friend of yours and asked me to give you the letter when you arrived. Alex, just between us, you should get your friend to bathe more often."

Mycroft's nerves were quickly going on edge. "What letter was that, Goldie?"

"Oh, my, Alex. Did I forget to give it to you? What did I do with it?" She looked around the porch for a few minutes before remembering to lift her embroidery. There the envelope lay where she had put it, in her lap. "Here it is, Alex."

Mycroft turned the letter over carefully but could find no distinguishing marks of any kind on it, nor was there any name on it. He gingerly tore open the top flap and removed the paper inside and stared at the cryptic message:

"Alex, you don't look so wonderful," she said. "Are you all right?"

He folded the paper carefully and placed it back in the envelope. "A dirty little man with a scraggly beard, did you say? Yes, Goldie, I'm fine, but now I've really got to run." He kissed her again, this time on the forehead, and headed for the car once more.

She called after him, "Don't forget to have my Avi call me, Alex."

He smiled and waved good-bye as the car pulled away, but under his breath he said to the driver, "Give me a pencil and paper and *fast!*"

The drive toward Jerusalem was uneventful for Avi and Christie, except for their conversation.

Avi doggedly tried to get Christie to talk about herself, but she artfully sidestepped most of his questions. Instead, in the fashion of a woman infatuated with a man and eager for any morsel of information about him, she got Avi to reveal more about Alex than he would have ordinarily.

"Alex was married to my sister some years back."

"Are they divorced?" she asked.

"She's dead."

"Oh, Avi, I'm sorry. How did it happen?"

He looked over at her for a few moments before answering. "If I told you that Alex killed his wife and his son, you probably wouldn't believe me. But let me tell you the story. You have a right to know about the man you're getting involved with."

As they continued their drive, the Mossad agent narrated the story of the bloody deaths on the Netanya beach six years ago.

And when he concluded, Christie said, "But, Avi, that's tragic. How can you say he killed them?"

His Israeli temper started to flare and he raised his voice a bit. "Weren't you listening to me? I told him not to go. I warned him of the danger. And I told him I would hold him responsible if anything happened. And I do hold him responsible."

"It's cruel of you to say that, Avi. How do you know I won't tell Alex the minute I see him?"

" 'Tell him'?" Avi smiled. "Tell him what?"

"Why, tell him that he shouldn't trust you, that you think he murdered your sister."

The agent smiled. "I haven't told you anything that Alex doesn't already know. But we're also Brothers, in more ways than one. And I love him like a brother, too. God knows, I wouldn't be sticking my neck out for him if I *didn't* love him. He knows he can trust me. But that doesn't mean I don't blame him for what happened."

After driving a few more kilometers in stony silence, Christie asked Avi to finish his story.

"But I have finished."

"What happened to Alex? How did he survive? And how about his son?"

"Alex was found unconscious, clinging to the overturned raft. He had lost a large amount of blood and the only thing that kept him alive was that the cold waters had reduced his body temperature and, consequently, his blood circulation. Still, he remained close to death for a couple of weeks. As for Josh"—Avi halted his story for a moment while he dabbed at his nose and eyes with a tissue—"well, we don't know for sure. A storm came up suddenly and we assumed that the raft overturned and the boy and his captors drowned."

"But you're not sure?"

"When you don't find any bodies, it's hard to be sure of anything. There's a possibility that there was another raft and that they escaped in it. Or, maybe there was a mini-sub waiting for them so many kilometers offshore."

"You mean the boy may be alive?"

"I try not to think about it, Christie. It's easier for me to sleep at night believing that my sister's killers and my nephew and his kidnappers are dead and buried at sea. But, yes. The boy still may be alive somewhere."

"But that means—"

"That means *nothing*," he cut her off. "He was five when he was taken and that was six years ago. If—I say *if*—he is alive, he would have been with God-knows-what type of animals for more than half his life. I do not wish to think of what he'd be like today."

"What does Alex think?"

"Christie, I've known Alex Mycroft for more than fifteen years but I've never been sure exactly what he thinks."

It was a simple code and one that is widely known in intelligence circles. Still, Mycroft was disturbed that someone should be leaving cryptic messages for him . . . and at Goldie's! Who besides Avi knew he was going to be there?

He took the pencil and paper from the driver and began to jot down the deciphering key:

A	B·	C		J	K··	L		S	T···	U
D	E	F		M	N	O		V	W	X
G	H	I		P	Q	R		Y	Z	-

He remembered that each letter on the grid corresponded to a "letter" on the code, depending on how many dots were in each sector. Therefore, since each shape on the message had a corresponding shape on the deciphering grid, the number of dots in each cryptic mark dictated which of the three grids to search to find the right letter.

A perfect square shape containing one dot was an "E,"

two dots made it an "N," and three dots made it a "W." One dot in a "U"-shaped character stood for "B," two dots made it a "K," and three dots meant it was a "T." Mark by mark, he deciphered the message:

> YOUR SON ALIVE
> GO HOME HE LIVES
> CONTINUE ON HE DIES

Mycroft double-checked to make certain that he had translated each letter properly. When he was sure it was right, he told the driver to stop the car and let him out for a few minutes.

He stood near the tail of the car and supported himself against the trunk while he breathed in deeply. His face was bathed in perspiration and his hands shook almost uncontrollably. He continued deep breathing, waiting for the wave of nausea to pass, and looking around to see if he was being followed. There was no one else in sight.

The driver emerged to see if he was all right. "Just a little carsick," he lied. "Wait for me in the car. Please," he added.

He tried to make sense of it. Who besides Avi knew he was going to Netanya? And if Blume had arranged for the message, why?

If the Mossad had the CIA bugged, couldn't the CIA have the Mossad bugged, too? Otis Blake wanted to stop him from going to Iran, but why would Blake leave this kind of cruel message? More than stop him, they'd want to capture him. No, the CIA wouldn't leave a message; they'd leave a detail of agents to pick him up.

The PLO had been responsible for his wife's death and son's kidnapping and presumed death. But how in the world did the PLO figure into this? They couldn't possibly know about his actions or his plans, could they? And if they did—for whatever reason—why would *they* want him not to go to Iran? That made no sense.

A dirty little man with a scraggly beard? Who was he? *What* was he?

The Brotherhood? Ridiculous. It was because of the Brotherhood and his Obligation to the Craft that he was involved in the first place. If they wanted him home, all they had to do was say so.

Christie? He had been trying to figure out her motivations and match them against Avi's suspicions. She may have wanted to stop Mycroft, but how could she be responsible for the message? How could she know about Josh? She didn't seem to fit into the equation.

He began going over these thoughts again when a short toot on the car's horn interrupted him.

"Sir," the driver called. "We're going to be late if we don't get going soon."

Mycroft climbed back into the car. "To the cemetery," he said, and pensively pulled down on the corners of his lips as the car sped off.

Netanya's Jewish cemetery was small, but still he had to ask directions from the caretaker to find Beth's grave. It had not occurred to him until this moment that he had never been here before. He had still been in a hospital when Beth had been buried.

He stopped to scoop up five small pebbles and bought some flowers before heading toward the grave site.

Once there, he stood quietly for a few moments, not knowing what he should do, what he should say, what he should think.

He pulled the pebbles out of his pocket and, one by one, placed the five stones atop Beth's headstone in the old Jewish tradition.

Tears welled up slightly in his eyes as he recalled bits and pieces of their too-brief life together. He pulled the glass tube out of his pocket and rolled it gently between the palms of his hands as formerly shadowy portions of his memory gradually came into focus.

Then he knelt down and tapped on the headstone gently with the glass tube.

"Hello, Beth," he said aloud. "I wish you could tell me if Josh is with you. I wish—I wish—" and then he put his face in his hands and cried. "Oh, Beth. I miss you."

He allowed himself the luxury of a good long cry before regaining his composure.

"Beth, if you can hear me, please tell me what to do about Josh. Is he alive, Beth? What should I do? I have to go to Iran, but if there is even a chance in a million that Josh is alive, I swear I'll turn back. But what do I make of that note, Beth? Is it real? Is it fake? Who is it from? And if Josh is alive and I go home, will I ever see him again? Isn't there more of a chance that if he's alive and I go to Iran, whoever is responsible will show themselves? Please, God, Ein-Sof, let her answer me."

He remained kneeling for a little while longer, tormented by his uncertainty, as a voice from his past echoed through his mind: Never be diverted from your mission, men. Wear blinders if you have to, men. That's how you stay alive, men.

Fine, thought Mycroft to himself. That's how *I* stay alive. How does a five-year—he corrected himself—how does an eleven-year old boy stay alive . . . if he isn't already dead?

Mycroft had held himself responsible for Josh's fate six years ago, and perhaps he was still to be responsible for his fate once again. His decision could cost his son his life, if the boy is still alive. If. Sometimes the biggest word in all humanity, Mycroft thought, is If.

He began pulling up a few weeds in front of Beth's grave to make room for the flowers he had brought. And as he deposited the flowers, he saw the envelope. He hadn't seen it before.

He picked it up and examined it, although he already knew what it was. It was the same type of cheap quality as the one he had received only a short while before. Carefully opening the sealed flap, he pulled out an identical cryptic code to the one he had gotten from Goldie.

So whoever left it—this dirty little man with the scraggly beard?—*didn't* know he'd be at Goldie's for sure, or at Beth's grave. Whoever it was had played two hunches, both of which, it turned out, had been correct.

It neither increased nor decreased the possibilities. Someone still knew an awful lot about his past to be able to leave two messages—maybe more?—for him. It still could be almost anyone.

What was it he had said to the Deacon when the Deacon told him he'd read Mycroft's file? "Which one? There must be files on me in a dozen or more capitals around the world." Or something like that.

"I'm sorry, Beth. I'm sorry for so much, so much. But I promise you, if he's alive, I'll find him, Beth."

He blew her a kiss and then left to meet Avi and Christie in Jerusalem.

17

Philadelphia

"Y OU'RE crazy, Harris. Really certifiable. I don't
think you've got both oars in the water."

Cap Harris was having great difficulty control-
ling his temper and his huge shaking frame in the presence
of his superior officer. "Inspector, I know how it must
sound, but I'm *not* crazy. I knew there had to be some kind
of common denominator between Bill Gregory and Alexander Mycroft. I've checked these guys out from when they
were in their mothers' wombs until I found it."

"It's too far back to fit," Police Inspector Monroe countered.

"I'm telling you, Inspector," Cap pleaded, "I've been over

it a dozen times. It's all there in Mycroft's military and medical files.''

''Fine,'' said Monroe, ''but I ask you again: What was the motive?''

''I told you before,'' Harris replied sheepishly, ''I don't have it *all* figured out yet. I don't know what the motive was for icing Gregory. I just know *who* tortured him to death and how.''

''Okay, let's say you're right,'' the Inspector said, still not convinced. ''What the hell do you think *you* can do about it?''

''Well, for openers, I can try to prevent another death. I can try like hell to keep Alexander Mycroft alive.'' Cap took a deep breath, knowing the reaction Inspector Monroe would have to his next suggestion. ''I can go after him.''

''Go after him? Go *after* him? To *Israel?* To *Iran?* Oh, sure, Cap. Wait, let me get your plane fare out of petty cash for you! You know something, Cap: You've been working too hard; you've got toys in the attic, you know that? *Go after him?* Call him on the fucking telephone if you're so goddamned sure you've got it all figured out!''

''I tried but I can't reach him. I—I don't have any idea how to reach him, or where,'' Harris offered quietly with downcast eyes.

''Beautiful, Cap. Just fucking beautiful! You can't even reach him and you want me to let you go globetrotting after him. Whaddya expect him to do, meet you at the fuckin' airport or something?''

''Look, Inspector, I may not know where he is this instant but I do know one place he's *got* to show up *before* he can get into the embassy. I'd wait for him there.'' He knew it was hopeless.

"You really need an oil change, Cap. Your brain's rusted out. Now get the fuck outta here and take all these shit-ass medical and military papers with you. And don't come back 'til you start talking sense! You hear me, Cap?" The Inspector called after a slamming door.

Back at his desk, Harris picked up the phone and dialed a local four-digit extension in the Police Administration Building, commonly referred to as the Roundhouse due to its architectural design.

"Hullo, Personnel? This is Captain Stanley Harris. I want to know how much vacation and sick leave I've got coming to me. . . . Yeah, you heard me right: vacation *and* sick leave combined. And I want to know *now!*"

18

"JOHN, listen to me. I'm your doctor as well as your friend. You're going to recover from *this*, but you've got to start the chemotherapy for the cancer as soon as possible."

John Sinclair was staring out of the hospital window, gazing at the falling snow.

"John, are you listening to even one word of what I'm saying?" Dr. Paul Reid was growing annoyed and it showed. "I'm only trying to save your life, John. Won't you at least meet me halfway?"

Sinclair turned around.

"You're not trying to save my life; you're trying to give me a few more months to live, if you can call it living. I've seen what that treatment does to a person. I don't want to go through that. Losing my hair, my reflexes, my skin. Forget it. I'd rather die a whole man than a half of one."

"Look, John, I know you don't want anyone to know about your condition, but so help me, if you don't start listening to me and following my advice, I'm going to call Christie and tell her. Maybe she'll be able to talk some sense into you."

The outrage that the doctor expected from his patient did not materialize. Instead, John Sinclair returned to staring out the window, unable to bring himself to continue looking at the doctor.

"I already beat you to it, you son of a bitch," Sinclair said quietly as tears filled his eyes.

"You spoke to Christie? What did she say, John?"

"She said . . . she said she's coming to get me."

19

Beirut

THE small black car swerved through the crowded, debris-strewn streets of Beirut, knocking over a peddler's cart, dodging in and out of the sea of people trying to buy, beg, borrow, or steal their evening meal. Moussef's left hand constantly pummeled the car's horn, while his right continually shifted and grinded the gears. He was late for the rendezvous and it was imperative that he deliver the good news in person. It would help his own standing in the Organization, he felt, and he wanted to take credit for the success of the mission.

A small boy taking sheep to market blocked his path and no amount of horn blowing would move them. In disgust, he left the car where it stood in the middle of the road and made the rest of his way on foot to the café on Hamra Street.

His recent growth of beard itched annoyingly and his discomfort was aided by his own perspiration. He cursed the beard under his breath, but knew the itching would pass in a few days more, perhaps a week. In the meanwhile, it would add needed years to his visage, to say nothing of the resemblance he would bear to Arafat.

When he reached the café, the barman inclined his head in the direction of a rear doorway lined with multi-colored beads. Moussef parted the beads and entered. He was not too late.

"Es Selamu Aleikum," offered the dirty, out-of-breath messenger in the traditional Islamic greeting.

"Aleikum Es Selamu," impatiently responded the robed and bearded man seated on the divan. He took a luxuriously long puff on the hookah but did not offer a seat to Moussef. "You have news?"

"Yes," Moussef said, trying to catch his breath. "I have news. I was afraid I would be late, you see. My plane arrived late at the airstrip and then there was the drive from the airstrip. But I wanted to bring word myself, you see, knowing how important—"

"You talk too much and say nothing," the man on the divan interrupted. "Tell me the news before I die of old age."

His young face drained of all color and he felt the itching of his scraggly beard grow more intense as the perspiration rolled steadily down his face.

"It is done. The three did their jobs well and then they were disposed of. It was made to appear as if they had taken their own lives."

The man on the divan lowered the stem of the hookah,

rose casually, and, with the back of his meaty hand, struck Moussef's face, knocking him to the floor.

"Idiot! A Mossad agent was killed! That was not supposed to happen. There was to be *no* killing at the café, only shooting."

"It could not have been avoided. That was an accident. But the others—the others were not harmed."

The robed man returned to the divan and picked up a glass of hot tea. "No matter. The plan still works. The messages?"

A broad smile crossed Moussef's dirty face. "I left two."

"Ah, I see you are pleased that you managed to accomplish the task a small child could have performed."

The smile quickly evaporated.

"But it is good. He will come. And he will come soon. But he must stay alive long enough to be of service to us. Do you understand this?"

Moussef bowed deeply and touched his head and his chest with his right hand. "I heard and I obey."

"Take two good men and prepare yourself for another journey."

20

Jerusalem

ALEX, Christie, and Avi were seated around a small scar-topped table on the second floor of a trinket merchant's shop located just inside of the Jaffa Gate entrance to the Old City. The merchant, who sold very few trinkets, was nevertheless quite prosperous by local standards. The Mossad paid him well for the constant use of his shop's unique vantage point. To the well-trained eye, it was nearly impossible to enter or leave the Old City through the very busy Jaffa Gate unobserved.

The table was littered with maps of Iran, maps of Tehran, and maps and blueprints of the many buildings inside of the United States Embassy compound in Tehran. Other papers detailed locations and numbers of guards, locations of the hostages, and the times and locations of the five daily Moslem prayer offerings toward Mecca, as well as the time and location of the daily protest for the benefit of American TV news cameras.

They had been at this for hours and Mycroft's legs were cramped from sitting and stiff from walking. Avi had insisted on taking Christie on a walking tour of the Old City, in and out of the numerous bazaars, all along the Via Dolorosa, stopping at each of the stations of the cross. It was less a sightseeing tour than an opportunity for Avi's men to photograph Christie and have her observed in person by a wide variety of Mossad informants. Blume wanted to take no chances. The only time Mycroft had rested all afternoon was inside the Church of the Holy Sepulcher where he prayed silently.

Avi guided them to the breathtaking Dome of the Rock, or the Mosque of Omar, built upon what was once the summit of Mount Moriah. He explained that, according to Islamic religious legend, Mohammed rode his white horse to that spot, alighted on one foot, and immediately ascended to heaven. There are those who claim Mohammed's footprint is visible in the rock, Avi had said. Christie said she could see it ("Then, according to Islamic tradition, you are blessed," Avi interpreted), Alex saw nothing more than a rock surrounded by beautifully colored marble pillars, and Avi was noncommittal.

They crossed the small park area, removed their shoes a second time, and entered the Aksa Mosque to admire its magnificent Persian rugs and exquisite chandeliers.

"Orthodox Jews never come up here," Avi explained more to Christie than to Alex, who seemed restless. "In fact, the chief rabbis of Israel forbid it. Here, observe the warning sign. It prevents anyone from entering this most sacred area, but it is ignored by all but Orthodox Jews. They come only as far as the sign, kneel, and pray. But they never enter this area.''

''Why is that?'' Christie had asked.

''This is the most holy site for the world's three major religions. It was on Mount Moriah that David purchased the threshing floor of Ornan, the Jebusite. He erected an altar on this site to appease the wrath of a destroying angel. At an earlier time, this is where Abraham was about to offer up his son, Isaac, as a sacrifice, before God spoke to him and told him to spare his son. More importantly, it was on this site that the First Temple was built by King Solomon, and then upon the rubble of that destroyed Temple, where the Second Temple was later constructed. Legend has it that the Ark of the Covenant, containing God's commandments, and the Holy of Holies, where the Ark was housed, were buried somewhere underground as a result of the destruction. It would be a sacrilege to walk over the Ark or over the Holy of Holies.''

''There is so much excavation going on in Israel, why don't the archaeologists just dig up the Ark or the Holy of Holies?''

''Ah, it would be wonderful if we could, but it will probably never happen in our lifetime. Not knowing the precise location, if we were to dig, we probably would have to destroy the mosques. It would start a holy war without end. No, it will never happen in our lifetime, I'm afraid. Nor will the Messiah come.''

''The Messiah?''

''Yes, there are two reasons why the Messiah will never come, if you believe in Jewish legend, that is. First, you see, the Messiah will not come until the Third Temple is built on this site. As I explained, no digging or building can take place without destroying the Moslem's sacred buildings. So, it is unlikely that a Third Temple will ever be built.

"And then there is another curious reason. Before the Messiah comes, Elijah, God's messenger, must enter through the Golden Gate of the Old City to herald the arrival of the Messiah. Elijah will not pass over or through a cemetery. Now, before we reclaimed Jerusalem in 1967, this part of the City was in Jordanian control. The Jordanians, of course, discounted everything of Judaism and denied, in fact, our very existence, let alone our claim to this land. They certainly put no stock in the coming of a Messiah. But just to play it safe, they placed a cemetery directly in front of that particular entrance to the Old City."

As they walked down the narrow path from the sacred ground, Avi pointed out the Western Wall.

"Ah, our timing is perfect. It is sundown and *Oneg Shabbat,* the beginning of the Jewish Sabbath prayer service, is beginning at the Wall. I have showed you Christian and Moslem beliefs. Let us conclude our brief tour with Jewish belief."

They stood in the outer crowd filled with tourists as the rabbis at the Wall conducted the brief service. Avi pulled a yarmulke from his back pocket and put it on his head. A small boy selling paper skullcaps and paper lace for women passed by and Avi purchased one of each.

"For you," he said to Alex and Christie. "It would be indelicate not to wear them. I hope you don't mind." They each covered their heads.

"Since it is no doubt difficult for you to follow what is going on, let me just tell you a little about the Wall and why it is so sacred to the Jews," he said softly. "This Wall was the western fortress wall of Solomon's Temple destroyed in 586 B.C., and of the Second Temple, destroyed in 68 A.D. If

181

you look closely, you can see the bottom two-thirds of the Wall is built of large stones. That is from Solomon's time. When the Second Temple was built by King Herod directly on top of the rubble of the first, all that remained standing was this Wall. The smaller stones toward the top date back to the Second Temple. Since this is all that remained after the Second Temple's destruction, the Jews revere it.''

''Why do I see some people putting paper in the cracks?'' Christie asked.

''They are prayers to God. Some people wrap coins in the prayers, but they are quickly stolen by small Arab urchins. Also, after the Holocaust, when so many families were split up, many of them came here and left notes for their relatives. Believe it or not, many families were reunited that way. And because of the prayers and the tears which have comingled on this site for so many years, it is also commonly called the Wailing Wall.''

''One more question, Avi. Why are the woman standing by themselves to the right of the Wall, and the men to the left?''

''Equal rights for women has not yet found its way into Orthodox Judaism. Men and women are always segregated in an Orthodox shul, that is, in the synagogue.''

They had a quiet dinner following the service and then returned to the second floor of the trinket merchant's shop, where Avi explained in as much detail as possible the current state of affairs in Tehran.

''Here is what you must understand: how this situation actually came to pass. It is important to understand the why, perhaps as much as the what or the how.

''When we spoke of this earlier, I lost my temper a bit and referred to the hostage-takers as terrorists. In the literal sense—that anyone who takes hostages and threatens to kill them if demands are not met are terrorists—that statement is true. But first they were merely militant students who planned only a sit-in, a demonstration, in the name of the continuing Revolutionary struggle, of which Khomeini is the supreme religious leader. These demonstrations often get out of hand. They gain a momentum. Such was the case here.

"At the outset, the students were not demanding the return of the Shah and his wealth. No. They were merely demonstrating against the United States as well as their own former government. After the second day, when Prime Minister Mehdi Bazargan resigned and the Iranian civil government dissolved, the students claimed a victory of sorts and gained a momentum they never expected.

"In the early days, if Khomeini had simply said 'enough,' the students would have dispersed. But Khomeini made a remark that stirred them—that gave meaning and purpose to their actions. Khomeini denounced the United States for admitting the Shah and demanded his return. The students, the terrorists, grasped that straw as their own. They, too, began calling for the Shah's return, and the people supported them. They never expected to actually take over the embassy, of that we are fairly certain. But there was little resistance and there were many militant demonstrators who stormed the embassy behind a wall of women for cowardly protection. Your people panicked and before the dust had settled, you had lost your embassy and your people were being held captive.

"Now, there are *some* things in your favor. First, they are not totally heartless—at least not yet. As their frustration mounts with each passing day, who can say for certain what will happen? But they have already released thirteen hostages—all women and blacks. I must confess we do not know

1 8 3

for sure why they did not release *all* women and *all* blacks. But put that aside for the moment. The important point is that *some* were released. This can be interpreted by some as a form of compassion.

"Secondly, to the best of our knowledge, no one has been seriously injured—yet—and no shots have been fired—again, yet. But make no mistake: They are armed, and many are former Revolutionary soldiers. They know how to use their weapons and if provoked they undoubtedly will. But it would be a grave offense to Islam to mistreat the hostages without cause.

"Now, here is something else in your favor—something that will surprise you, I'm sure.

"You have seen the television pictures of the thousands upon thousands of demonstrators outside of the gates. They are there solely for the television cameras, I promise you. These are not the spontaneous demonstrations they would have you believe. These thousands of people do not miraculously appear each day to shout, in unions, 'Death to Carter, Death to the United States.' These demonstrators are bused in each day just for the cameras. There are cheerleaders—yes, actual cheerleaders with bullhorns—to teach them their daily chants and to goad them on to a frenzy. And when the cameras have taken their quota of pictures, these people are dispersed.

"What is truly a shock to behold is watching these scenes each day on television and then going to see Tehran. You would think from reports on television that the entire city is in turmoil. It is not so.

"Go a block—just one block—in any direction away from the embassy, and life, such as it is, goes on at a normal pace. The peddlers' carts are there selling sugar beets, leather goods, and such. If you lived in Tehran and had no access to news of any kind, you might not even be aware that anything out of the ordinary—whatever the ordinary is—was occurring. It is truly remarkable, I promise you. And it can play to your advantage if used properly.

"But make no mistake, my friends, even though a sense of normalcy pervades most of the city, armed Revolutionary soldiers patrol the streets regularly and you may be stopped at any time. But it is not as bad as you may think. And if you are stopped by anyone with a gun, first say to him *'Margh Bar Amerika,'* which simply means 'Death to America.' It will get any sort of interrogation off to a 'good' start.

"Also, there are many people in the city who, even though they support the revolution, oppose the takeover as an action that cannot possibly succeed. They would dearly love to see a quick solution to the takeover. They may be of assistance to you.

"Now let us turn our attention to the embassy compound itself.

"It is quite large, as you can see here on the map—twenty-seven acres in all, surrounded by a wall. It's very size should help you, too. It cannot be adequately protected or patrolled, although they do try. Also, there is a daily flow of people in and out of the compound. That big padlock you see on television is only on the front gate, located here, on Takhte-Jamshid Avenue. This is where all the banners are flown and where all the demonstrations occur. This main gate is very, very heavily guarded, twenty-four hours a day. Here you will find armed soldiers as well as students.

"Inside the entrance, down this path to the right, the first big building is the chancery. This is where most of the hostages are being held and, most likely, where your brother is, Christie.

"Further back, these next two buildings are the ambassador's residence and the chargé d'affaires' residence. There are some hostages in these two buildings as well.

"Over here is the barracks that also serves as a warehouse. Because of that, there are no windows in the building. And here, not far from this fence, is the consulate building."

And on and on it went, well into the night. Detail over endless detail, all virtually identical to the information Alex had received from the Deacon. The chancery would be his target.

How to get in and how to get out—alive—were details that could not even be considered until arriving in Tehran and doing his own firsthand reconnaissance. Avi had been correct when he said the situation was fluid. The maps and the other information might very well be meaningless in the morning. He had digested it all and stored it away in his mind for future recall.

Avi thought that Mycroft would be safe using the British passport and press credentials that the Deacon had given him, but he knew that Christie would need similar identification to travel in Mycroft's company. He made arrangements for it, knowing as well that it would give him a few more photographs of her.

Avi would put them on a London-bound plane in the morning. Once in London, they would use their British passports to obtain necessary visas to fly into Tehran.

When the briefing session had concluded, Alex asked, "Is the Middle East situation so precarious that Israel needs this information, or are you helping out the United States?"

Avi rose from the table and placed his hands on his lower back, arching it to remove the kinks. "Ah, Alex, that is a question I cannot answer fully. Let me merely say that the Middle East situation is always precarious for us. We need all intelligence to survive. For example, we know that Iran will soon go to war with Iraq. The best thing for us would be for them to destroy each other. Especially Iraq. Even as we speak, Iraq, with the assistance of the French, is building a nuclear reactor outside of Baghdad designed to build atomic bombs to drop on Israel."

Christie gasped inwardly. "Are you serious?"

"About such a thing I would make a joke? Yes, I am serious. What is more tragic is that it is not really a secret. The Iraqis are still more than a couple of years away from completion, but if your country cannot assist us in altering their plans, well . . ." He left the statement unfinished.

"And now," Avi said as he tried without luck to stifle a deep yawn, "it is late, we are tired, and early tomorrow you are on your way. I bid you both a good night."

Two hours later, as Christie slept soundly in one bedroom, Alex made his way quietly out of his bedroom and knocked softly on Avi's door.

"Come in, Alex."

"What did you find out?" he asked in whispered tones.

"Alas, nothing. The message, the code, as you yourself already know, is child's play. It works in any language with any number of letters in an alphabet. Our labs could find no fingerprints and the cheap paper could have been purchased almost anywhere in the Middle East. We will, of course, continue our analysis, but for the moment, nothing."

Alex sat down softly on the edge of Avi's bed. "That's the technical analysis. Now, Avi, tell me about the nontechnical analysis. What does your Jewish nose tell you?"

Avi sighed and rubbed his bald spot. "It *could* be real. But I say ignore it and go on."

"And I say it *could* be real and just maybe I should pack it in and go home," Alex replied with bitterness in his voice.

"Look, Avi, I haven't told you all of it. Just before I left the States, there was a disturbing phone call and Josh's name was scrawled on my wall at home. And now these messages. How can I afford to ignore all this? How can *you*? We're talking about my son, your nephew."

"No, my friend. That was six years ago. *If* he is still alive somewhere, what must he be like by now? An eleven-year-old guerrilla? A killer? A terrorist? The PLO start them out very young when their minds are supple. *If* he is still alive, he ceased being your son, my nephew, a long time ago."

"I could change him back. I could—"

"And how about your Obligation to the Craft?" Avi interrupted. "*That* is real. The messages could still be a hoax."

"I've thought about that. I could return and talk to John Sinclair. I'm sure he'd understand."

"*His* son, however, is *not* a hoax. And his son is your Brother."

Alex dropped his head into his hands and began pulling down on the outer ends of his lips. Softly he said, "I think you're being awfully cavalier about Josh's welfare considering that six years ago you held me personally responsible for what happened to him and to Beth."

"Alex, my friend, do not misunderstand: I still hold you responsible. If you had listened to me that night—"

Mycroft didn't want to go through the same discussion again and cut him off with the first words that popped into his mind: "Call your mother, Avi."

"Wh—what did you say?"

"I forgot to tell you earlier that I promised Goldie I'd tell you to call her." His head was still in his hands.

Avi walked over and put his hands on Alex's shoulders.

"I can only guess the torment you're feeling, my friend. But I cannot see what is to be gained by going home."

"Just this, Avi: I made a serious error in judgment on that beach six years ago. You know it and I know it. A dumb-ass kid off the street might have done what I did; but I was a trained professional. Beth was a good couple of hundred yards away from me, but Josh was standing right there with me only a few yards from shelter. When Beth was hit, I should have done the professional thing. I should have left her and sought the high ground with Josh. I should have *protected* him, Avi. A professional is supposed to know that. Then, after I made sure he was safe, then I could have gone out in the open and gotten myself killed if I wanted to. But instead, I left us all exposed because I was stupid. Because I wasn't thinking. Because I wasn't on an assignment. I was supposed to be just taking a walk on a beach. But a professional should never forget his training. And I fucked up.

"What's to be gained by going home? To avoid another error in judgment. If Josh is still alive, my going home may *keep* him alive. No matter what he's become, he's still my son, Avi. And that outweighs my Obligation to the Craft."

"But you're still a professional with fairly good instincts," Avi countered. "If you go to Iran, you may learn something about his fate and you'll be in a position to act on it. Go home and you have nothing."

"I know. I know." Alex sighed. "And that's probably why I *have* to go. That and my Obligation. That's my dilemma."

Avi patted Alex on the back and sat astride a chair in the bedroom.

"Today's walking tour was reconnaissance, wasn't it?" Mycroft asked.

"Now, Alex," Avi began with a defensive smile, but Mycroft cut him short.

"Wasn't it?" he demanded.

"You see, I told you you have good instincts. Yes, Alex, it was reconnaissance."

"Well? What did you learn?"

The Mossad agent sighed. "Alas, nothing . . . yet. She appears to be genuine and fits the general description of Sinclair's daughter."

"Give it up, Avi. There's no reason to suspect her of anything."

"There's no reason not to, either. I just don't want you to think with your penis just because she's beautiful."

"John Sinclair *told* me his daughter was against the operation. So did the Deacon."

"All right, all right. So maybe this one time my Jewish nose is wrong. So? So I'm a worried Jewish mother who is trying to protect your tuchus. So sue me for being careful."

"And I'll *be* careful, too. I promise." He was about to say something else, but his thought was interrupted as the object of the conversation knocked on the door and was admitted.

"Well, here you are," Christie said with a smile. "Are you two boys having a pajama party?" She walked over and tenderly and unexpectedly put her arms around Alex's shoulders. Mycroft felt a sudden heat from his loins just from her mere caress.

"Blame it on me, Christie," Avi said. "I insisted on talking about old times with my good friend here and we lost track of the hours. But I'm glad you're here. I have a little present I was going to give you on the way to the airport in the morning. But since it's almost time to go, you may as well have it now."

Avi produced a small velvet box and displayed a gold mezuzah on a chain, which he slipped over Christie's head and around her slender neck. Mycroft was surprised but pleased that Avi had made such a thoughtful gesture. Perhaps he was starting to come around.

"Inside is a Hebrew scroll," Avi explained. "It will bring you much mazel, much luck. So promise me you will wear it at least until you're back home safe and sound. And also I want you to have it to remember me, and Israel, by. Maybe it will help you to come back someday and really see this country properly."

"Oh, Avi, thank you. It's so beautiful. I'll cherish it and wear it always, I promise." She walked over and kissed him.

"Yes, Christie. Wear it always," he said as he stood to return her affectionate embrace. But he was looking at Alex when he said it.

And then his gaze shifted to the ring Alex was wearing. "You never can tell when a piece of jewelry may come in handy."

21

T HE bible is filled with legends. And legend has it
that when Solomon was placed upon the throne of
Israel, according to God's promise, he set out to
build on Mount Moriah the most magnificent edifice ever
constructed as a temple, a house unto the Lord. It was also
to serve as a final and permanent resting place for God's
commandments, housed in the Ark of the Covenant, the
Covenant between God and His children of Israel.

Solomon enlisted the invaluable aid of the Tyrian King
Hiram, and together they assembled 153,300 workmen:
70,000 bearers of heavy burden, 80,000 hewers in the mountains, and 3,300 overseers, or Masters of the Craftsmen.

In the fourth year of his reign, the third after the death

of his father King David, on the second day of the Jewish month Ziv, corresponding to the twenty-first day of April, King Solomon commenced the erection of the Temple.

In the eleventh year of King Solomon's reign, on the eighth day of the Jewish month Bul, corresponding to the twenty-third day of October, the Temple was completed in all its parts. And when they stood back to admire their work, they realized that the completed structure resembled more the handiwork of the Great Architect of the Universe, the Lord God, than that of mere human hands. And the structure was admired by all the neighboring tribes as *the* wonder of the world.

But toward the end of the seventh year of construction, Solomon was faced with a perplexing problem: how to disperse such a large multitude of workmen without creating disorder among them and economic chaos in the region. Solomon, in his infinite wisdom, devised a plan with the aid of a loyal artisan, a humble son of a humble shepherd, who found great joy as a cunning craftsman toiling in his Lord's service.

This artisan would undertake to fashion and design golden rings for the overseers. Those mountain hewers who proved themselves by word and by deed to be worthy would be advanced to the lofty position of overseer. Solomon would then disperse them in small groups, having first presented them with their golden rings. These rings, Solomon cautioned his artisan, would have to be unique to avoid being easily counterfeited, and to readily identify the wearers as former workmen upon the Temple. This, Solomon wisely devised, would enable them to be warmly received while traveling in foreign areas, and would assist them in obtaining work along the way.

And so great was this charge to the artisan, that Solomon

193

obligated him to protect the rings, if necessary, with his very life.

And so it fell to the artisan's shoulders to design such a ring. But because of the large number of rings that had to be fashioned, and because of the grave importance placed upon the successful completion of the task, the artisan took the plain golden bands with him to the Holy of Holies, the place of his daily devotions to God, where he prayed for divine guidance.

And because he was a good man who labored long and hard for his king and his Lord, God answered the prayers of this humble shepherd's son and showed him a triangle. And the artisan set out to engrave triangles on the golden bands.

But there were those—a small group of most nefarious hewers—who feared their work was not proficient enough to earn them a golden band, so they plotted to steal their rings from the artisan. Thinking him to be asleep, the small group stole into his bedchamber one night but were surprised to find the artisan still hard at work over his labors. But the sight of the rings and their own merciless greed overcame them.

When first they demanded their rings, and the artisan refused, they lopped off two fingers from each of his hands to deprive him of his future livelihood as a skilled craftsman.

You may lop off my very hands, if you wish, he had said, but my obligation to my God gives me the strength I need.

When still the artisan refused to relinquish the rings, the bandits plucked out his eyes.

You may have my eyes but not my sight, he had said. My Lord, my God, lights my path.

And when still he refused, they murdered him and stole one ring each.

The next day the artisan's dismembered body was discovered and word was sent to King Solomon. The rings were counted and a number were found to be missing. Solomon knew he had to distribute the rings but was reluctant to do so with some of them already in the hands of the assassins. He gathered up the remaining rings and went himself to the Holy of Holies for prayer and guidance.

And God was so pleased with Solomon's devotion and his work on the Temple of the Lord that He answered his prayers; but He answered with fire from the bowels of the Ark itself.

And the fire completely encircled the rings, but they were not consumed. God told Solomon that the metal of these rings would never be consumed, while other metals would perish in flames.

And when the fire subsided and the bands had cooled to the touch, Solomon saw that God had left His mark in the center of each triangle but had deleted one side of each triangle, had left it dark, as a remembrance of that devoted artisan, that devout son of a humble shepherd, who had suffered himself to be ignominiously slain while laboring in His service.

Solomon then dispensed the rings to the deserving craftsmen and assembled them for a final blessing before he dismissed them out into the world. And to this gathering came the unsuspecting assassins, to hear what was not theirs to hear, wearing what was not theirs to wear. They were easily and immediately apprehended and, by God's wrath and Solomon's edict, punished and then executed in manners befitting their heinous crimes:

For thievery, they each suffered the loss of their hands. For eavesdropping and attempting to gain admission falsely to the meeting place of the overseers, each suffered the loss of their ears. And for murder, each man received the gold he had so foolishly sought: hot molten gold poured down the mouth of each man until it ran out of every possible anatomical orifice.

Then Solomon sent forth word throughout the lands, that the wearer of Solomon's Ring had labored long and hard in the service of the Lord, and that anyone who did not render aid, comfort, and assistance to the wearer of Solomon's Ring would suffer the wrath of God, as had the assassins who had perished.

And Solomon decreed: *"Blessed be he who shall welcome and assist this worthy ring bearer. May his name be ever honored among the Craft."*

And through the ages, most of the rings were lost forever to all eternity.

But, according to legend, a few, just a few, survived.

22

London—January 1, 1980

ON New Year's Day, at precisely 8:50 P.M., three
men at three different windows of Heathrow Airport watched the British Airways 707 jet lumber
down the runway, gather speed, and take off on a direct,
nonstop five-and-a-half-hour flight to Tehran, Iran.

One by one, the three men—one wearing a three-piece
polyester suit and tie under a tan raincoat, the second wearing a handsome brown Beged-Or leather jacket over a black
turtleneck sweater, and the third wearing a dirty long black
coat with mismatched patches on the sleeves—made their
way to the long bank of coin phones and placed three calls
to the Middle East.

*　　*　　*

"We just missed them," said the man in the raincoat.

"Did you actually *see* them? Are you *sure* they're on that plane?"

"Well, we didn't see them. But they were positively ID'd. And I think we've got routine British surveillance photos of them."

"All right. Catch the next plane. Follow them. I'll meet you there." He slammed the phone down without saying good-bye. "Dumb shits," he said to himself. "Probably hung over from last night, that's why they missed them. God-damn dumb shits!"

The man in the turtleneck sweater just spotted the man in the raincoat as his call was being put through.

"Shalom. Yes, they're on their way."

"May God be with them."

"And they were being watched."

"Yes, I feared as much."

"Any other instructions?"

"No. Nothing else."

The phone rang in the back of a café and the man on the divan put down his tea to answer it.

"Yes?"

"*Es Selamu Aleikum,*" said the man in the long coat.

"*Aleikum Es Selamu,*" responded the man on the divan. "What news?"

"They are coming."

"Ah, it is well. It is well."

23

Tehran—January 2, 1980

"BUSINESS," Mycroft responded to the Revolutionary guard's question at the Tehran airport, wondering to himself who would be foolish enough to come here for pleasure. "We're reporters. Here are our press credentials."

The soldier examined the credentials closely, comparing the ID photos with those of the passports, and those against Alex and Christie's faces.

"You'll be required to check in with the Revolutionary Press Office in town," the soldier said and dismissed them.

"Well, that part was easy enough," Christie said as they made their way through the early morning crowds in the hectic airport that was filled with frantic travelers trying to flee the country.

But as they were just about to exit the terminal, Alex took a sharp intake of breath and froze in his tracks.

"What is it, Alex?"

"Déjà vu. That man at the curb. He's waiting for us. I can feel it."

"Are you sure?"

"As sure as I care to be. Come on, down here." He grabbed her arm and they made a sharp turn to the right and dodged in and out of people, luggage, carts, and livestock. Over his shoulder, Alex saw the man spot them and take off in their direction.

"He's after us. Let's try to make it to a cab. Hurry!"

Not being burdened with luggage, and trailing along in the swath Alex and Christie had already cut through the crowd, the man was quickly gaining on them until, suddenly, a young peddler with a still recent growth of scratchy beard, who had been casually leaning against the terminal building and watching the chase, thrust his cart directly into the man, knocking him down and spilling the contents of his sugar beet cart all over the ground.

Immediately the peddler began jumping up and down, hollering at the man on the ground, and ignoring the small thieves who quickly ran over to steal his beets. The peddler grabbed hold of the man's arm and refused to let go, goaded on by the fast-swelling crowd who echoed his cries and jeers.

When Alex and Christie, who had turned in time to see the activity, were safely in a cab and speeding away from the area, the peddler released his prey and himself vanished into the mob, leaving the upset cart and its contents to the hungry thieves.

At the small nameless rooming house that Avi had suggested, Alex registered for both of them. In front of his name, he drew three small dots, little more than pen points, in a triangular shape.

They took one room that was divided into a separate bedroom and a small sitting room with a lumpy couch that Alex volunteered to sleep on. It was also the only room with a private bath.

They decided to explore the area as much as possible before nightfall, registering at the Revolutionary Press Office only as an absolute necessity.

Once on the street, they felt free to talk. Alex had cautioned Christie in London not to talk of important matters in hotel rooms. From now on, unless absolutely necessary, he told her, we'll only talk about what we're planning in Iran if we're out in the open and moving.

In London, he had shown her how to place a piece of paper or a lock of hair in a hotel room door in order to tell at a glance if anyone had entered the room during their absence. He slipped a tiny scrap of paper into the door of the room in Tehran just before they departed.

Once on the street, they discussed the airport scene. Christie had started to talk about it in the cab, but a quick look from Alex and she got the message.

"Who do you think he was?"

"CIA probably. Avi told us they knew we were coming to Iran. They must have had the airport staked out ever since we left Israel."

"How about the peddler? Do you think that was an accident?"

"No, I'm almost sure that was intentional. But don't ask me who saved us or why. I just don't know."

They walked the rest of the three blocks to the U.S. Embassy compound in silence, Alex thinking to himself how true Avi's words were. It was not until they actually reached the embassy's main gate that they saw any noticeable signs of a takeover. Before reaching Takhte-Jamshid Avenue, they could have been walking through any Middle Eastern city in late afternoon. But standing across from the embassy, they saw the revolutionary banners, the padlocked gate, and armed soldiers patrolling inside of the compound.

A television news crew was placing its equipment away in trunks in front of the gate. Alex recognized a newsman from having seen him on the late-night news back home but could not remember his name.

They crossed the street and Alex casually asked him whether anything new was developing.

"Hey, you're an American, aren't you?"

"Uh, no, British actually. But I was born and raised in the States," Alex replied, trying to explain away his lack of a clipped British accent.

"Nah, nothin's happening. Same old shit. The kiddies want the Shah, Jimmy says screw you, and nothin' happens. Waldheim was here. You know, from the UN. But they wouldn't let him in. He just left."

"How about the demonstrations? Where is everybody?" Christie asked.

"Well, you missed it for today. One demonstration a day, that's it. I don't think they could do more than one if they had to, and judging from the crowds, I'd say soon they'll have trouble doing even one."

"Really?" Christie said.

"Yeah. You know, in the beginning it was easy. Man, they must've had a hundred thousand 'screaming-meemies' here each day. But it gets tiring after a while. People got other things to do, you know?"

Alex was reflective. "Yeah, I know."

"But come back tomorrow if you want to see a demonstration. Earlier in the afternoon."

"If the demonstrations are losing wind, why do you keep covering them?" Christie wanted to know.

"Hey, lady, there's nothing else going on over here. You gotta do what you gotta do. And my boss wants footage every day. So I cover the demonstrations. Hey, Joe," he called to a colleague. "Come here and help me with this shit. Sorry folks, gotta go."

Alex and Christie circumnavigated the compound a few times, examining the mostly brick wall as closely as they dared.

"Getting any ideas, Alex?"

"Oh, one or two," he answered noncommittally. "One or two. We'll know more tomorrow. I want to see one of those demonstrations firsthand. It may be our ticket in. Meanwhile, let's eat."

The rooming house's small restaurant was just off from the practically nonexistent lobby. But it suited Alex. Seated with his back to the wall, he was able to observe anyone entering or leaving the premises. As they were drinking their vile-tasting after-dinner coffee, Alex saw a small, well-dressed, dark-skinned Iranian enter the lobby and ring nervously for the desk clerk. The man's thick black hair flecked with gray was pasted down, but he was in need of a haircut.

The desk clerk arrived and the two exchanged a few words. Then the clerk produced the registration book from under the counter, opened it, and pointed to an entry with a grubby, nicotine-stained finger. The other man examined the entry closely, and the clerk, with a slight nod of his head, indicated the restaurant. Alex tensed as the well-dressed man approached.

"Please excuse my very rude intrusion on your meal," he said in fluent English. "I am a dealer in old jewelry and old coins. Perhaps I may be able to interest you in a suitable gift for your lady?"

Alex decided to proceed cautiously. His instincts, and the fact that he felt sure the desk clerk had shown the man the three calling dots he had made earlier in the registration book, told him he was about to be tested. If he failed the test, he might as well pack it in and go home.

"Please join us," Alex said. "What are you selling this evening?"

"Oh, I have only a few things with me, but I must say I admire your ring, sir. May I examine it closely?"

Without waiting for a reply, the man grasped Alex's hand and held it close under his face. From a pocket he produced a jeweler's loop that he thrust into his right eye to examine the ring.

"Lovely specimen of old-world craftsmanship. I don't suppose you would like to part with it . . . for the right price?"

"I don't think so," said Alex. "It's been in my, uh, *Brother's* family for many, many years."

"Yes, I can see that. Let me show you a few coins, may I?" Relinquishing Alex's hand, the man reached into a vest pocket and produced five old gold coins, which he laid out in a row in front of Alex.

"Now this could be a real find, for he who has the eye to observe."

Alex looked at the coins but could see nothing to give him a clue as to what to do. He felt each one in turn, examining both sides, finding nothing. "For he who has the eye to observe," Alex thought, and impulsively picked up the jeweler's loop and placed it in his eye the way he had seen this man and countless other jewelers do. It kept slipping out of his eye, so he held it with one hand while he looked again at the coins.

On the first three, he still saw nothing. But on the fourth he noticed three tiny, almost imperceptible pinprick-sized holes, triangular-shaped and identical to the simple design he had drawn in the registration book. When he removed the loop, he could see nothing. He checked the last coin to be sure, then gently pushed the fourth toward the man. "I am *very* interested in this coin."

"A very wise choice. A very wise choice." He pocketed the other coins and opened his small case. "While I tell you about this coin, let me show your lovely lady a few little trinkets that might appeal to her. Perhaps your lady might care to try on some of them. There is a mirror on that wall."

The case was filled with an array of precious stones, rings, gold bracelets, necklaces, and earrings. Christie's eyes opened wide at the sight before her.

"Oh, they're all so lovely," she exclaimed, and selecting a pair of intricately designed gold earrings, she moved over to the mirror to see how they looked on her.

"Where do you hail from?" the man asked Alex in a soft voice, while repocketing the lone coin on the table.

"From the East," Alex replied to the ritualistic query.

"And where are you bound for?"

"The West."

"And where do you rest?"

"In the South, at high meridian."

"Not in the North?"

"In the North there is darkness."

The man smiled and shook Alex's hand. "I hail thee, Brother. How may I be of service in these troubled times?"

Alex had to trust him, but he did not want to reveal too much outside of a closed Lodge.

"I am here to reclaim a Brother."

"An American?"

"Yes."

"You ask much. You may ask the impossible. I do not know."

"I do not expect an answer tonight. I would like to present my case to a Lodge of Masters."

The smile on the man's face quickly vanished. "You *do* ask much. I cannot take you inside of a Lodge of Masters."

"I can work my way in. Put me to the test."

"I can promise nothing, you understand? I can try to arrange it but I cannot promise."

"I understand. When and where. It must be soon."

"Tomorrow night. Midnight. But be careful, there is a curfew. Go to this address. If no one is there, it means I failed." He scrawled an address on a scrap of paper as Christie was making her way back to the table. "You will be safe here tonight. Tomorrow?" He shrugged his shoulders.

"Oh, Alex, aren't these lovely?" Christie asked. "How much are they?"

The man got up and closed his case. "Please accept them as a gift. Good night." Then he hurried from the table.

24

B Y the time Otis Blake's late-night phone call to the
Company in Langley, Virginia, was put through on
the scrambler phone, he was just opening his fourth
package of cigarettes of the day. He was tired and it showed
in his bloodshot eyes, which were already irritated from the
cigarette smoke that hung like a low cloud in the small
room.

"Yes, Langley, I'm here. Good connection."

"More problems, Otis?" the quiet voice with the thick
southern drawl asked.

"Let's call them wrinkles, as opposed to problems."

"Do you have him yet?"

"Not quite. We missed him again at the airport. One of our men was blindsided by a peddler."

"What do you make of that?"

"We were set up. Someone else is on the case."

"Mossad?"

"I don't think so. They're already on thin ice. I think they'd offer aid and comfort to them in Israel but not here. Too risky."

"How about Blume? Do you know where he is?"

"Still in Israel. We've got him under a round-the-clock watch."

"So who's left? Surely not the Iranians? Not the Revolutionary Council?"

"No, I don't think so. We're developing a lead on the PLO."

"What would be their angle? Why would they want to help Mycroft? It doesn't listen well, Otis."

"We haven't worked it all out yet, but one of their men was spotted at Heathrow when the plane took off. We traced a call he made to Beirut. We're trying to piece it together now."

"Well, something may develop, but don't give up on Mycroft. He's got to be isolated before something goes wrong."

"Yes, sir."

"What leads are you developing on Mycroft?"

"He's not at any of the major hotels, but there are a zillion smaller ones, boardinghouses, flophouses, and so on. We're combing through them, but we have to work through our contacts, you know? I mean, Christ, we just can't walk in and flash our potsies at 'em. It's gonna take time."

"I know, Otis. I know. And you know we're running low on time. But why did you risk this call? I know it wasn't just to give me this kind of report. The courier or the coded telex would have sufficed.''

''You're right. Look, I've got an idea that's so radical I was afraid to implement it without checking.''

''Go on.''

''We know Mycroft's here to try to snatch the Sinclair kid. And *we* know it can't work. So what happens? Mycroft gets caught by the Iranians. No big deal. Believe me, with that guy I can live with it.''

''Kindly leave your personal considerations aside, Otis.''

''Yeah, right. Well, he gets caught. Maybe gets killed. Maybe kills some students. Maybe gets some hostages killed. Anything's possible. The point is, whatever happens *we* look bad. The Iranians hold up Mycroft's scalp and claim *we're* responsible. That *we* were behind the whole operation. They use it as an excuse to execute some hostages by making good on their threat to ice the hostages if the U.S. tries anything. No matter how it plays, *we* lose.''

''Go on, I'm with you.''

''Or, let's say by some miracle of miracles he pulls it off. You know his background. You know what he's done, what he's capable of. Let's just say he pulls it off. We're still up the creek. The Iranians can still use it as an excuse to shoot the hostages.''

''What's the point, Otis? You're not telling me anything we don't already know.''

''The point is this: I say it's time to bring the Iranians in on this. They can help us, if we lay it out the right way. We can use it as a sign of good faith. We say: 'Look guys, we don't want anyone hurt. This guy's gotta be stopped. We can't do it alone.' That sort of thing. Meanwhile, it helps take the heat off us so that we can continue laying the groundwork for our own scenarios.''

There was a long silence over the phone lines. Blake lit another cigarette as a drop of perspiration rolled down his forehead and burned one of his already irritated eyes.

"How would you do it? You can't just approach them."

"I'd do what all of the other D.C. diplomats are doing: use the Swiss as intermediaries."

"You're right, Otis. It's radical. And it could still backfire."

"Don't I know it?"

"I've gotta go to the White House on this one. It's risky. There are too many other irons in the fire that even *I* don't know about. Someone who's got his hand in all of them has got to take a look at the *big* picture, to see how the cause and effect relationship will impact."

Christ, Blake thought, Langley's starting to sound like the rest of the Washington mush-mouths he knew. "How soon do you expect an answer?"

"On this, Otis? Soon. Very soon."

"I'll be here."

Four hours later, Blake took a call on the scrambler phone. It was the same familiar southern voice.

"Green light."

Otis Blake felt his heart skip a beat.

25

Philadelphia

THE night nurse at her station was absorbed in her paper work, so she did not notice the wheelchair rolling slowly by her desk. But when the red elevator indicator light went on, accompanied by the familiar "ding," she did glance up in time to see a young woman wheel an ill and very old-looking John Sinclair onto the elevator.

The elevator doors closed with a whoosh, and the nurse went to pull Sinclair's discharge papers. The papers weren't there.

26

▼

Tehran—January 3, 1980

ALEX went out early that morning to exchange some of his British pounds for Iranian rials, and when he rejoined Christie back at the hotel, she had just emerged from the shower and was towel-drying her hair. The skimpy towel around her body only served to accentuate her shape. Alex found himself getting aroused just looking at her but tried to dismiss such thoughts.

When she came out of the bathroom, fastening the sash on her bathrobe, he showed her the *Jomhouri Eslami* party newspaper he had picked up. The front page carried an outdated photograph of United Nations Secretary General Kurt Waldheim shaking hands with the Shah of Iran, along with a Pars News Agency story.

"Somebody at the bank translated the caption for me. It reads, 'Waldheim Hand-in-Hand with the Executioner.'"

"Do you know what the rest of the story says?" Christie asked him.

"Let's just say it's not encouraging news."

Christie took both of Alex's hands in hers and together she sat them down, face-to-face, on the bed. He watched a drop of water roll part way down one of her lovely breasts.

"Alex, I've been thinking all morning and we've got to talk."

"About . . .?"

"About Lee, about what we're doing. About *everything*. Alex, I'm scared." Tears welled up in her eyes.

"Would it make you feel any better if I told you I was scared, too?" he asked.

She pulled away slightly, wiping the tears with the back of her hand. "No! If anything, that would make me feel worse. One of us has to be strong, and I guess it's not me."

Alex gave her his handkerchief and she dabbed her nose gently. "Are you, Alex? Scared, I mean?"

"Hell, yes. Of course I am. We'd both be crazy if we weren't scared. But being scared doesn't mean doing stupid things that put us at risk. So far we're all right. And I hope we'll be more than just all right as soon as I figure out exactly what, if anything, we're going to do."

"You don't know yet?"

"Shit, no, Christie. I've been playing this thing by ear. But after we take a look at the demonstration today, and after I meet with some people tonight, I'll at least have a better idea if we stand any kind of a chance or if we go back empty-handed."

"Oh, Alex. One part of me says we both should leave. Go home now. Don't risk my life, or Lee's, or Alex's. Something will happen. Something bad. But the other part of me reminds me how much I love Lee, and my father, and how can I be so close to Lee and just walk away? It's so hard for me, Alex. So hard." She seemed so vulnerable as she fell softly into his arms and allowed her body to press firmly against his for comfort and support. He breathed deeply and inhaled her fragrance and her sensuality.

She casually, almost innocently, dropped one hand into his lap. His erection was immediate.

"Your poor body must ache from having slept in the chair last night," she cooed softly in his ear. "You were calling the name Beth in your sleep."

Mycroft closed his eyes as her hand brushed up against his swollen penis. She kissed him once lightly and then passionately and he responded as her tongue probed his mouth and sought out his tongue. But when he opened his eyes to look at her, he could see only the mezuzah that Avi Blume had placed around her slender neck, and he heard voices warning him not to be diverted.

He kissed her again, but without warmth, and pulled back. His erection screamed at him for what he was about to do.

"Let's save this moment for another time. We don't want to miss the demonstration."

She sighed quietly as he got off the bed.

27

OTIS Blake felt sick to his stomach, bent over at the waist, dry-heaving outside of the Swiss Embassy. He had neither slept nor eaten all night long and the mental anguish he felt over what he was about to do had transplanted itself into his bowels. He had spent most of last night in the bathroom, the other part on his cot, bathed in sweat and deep in prayer for the first time in his life. He had prayed his men would locate Mycroft before he had to arrive at the Swiss Embassy and, in his mind, turn over to the enemy the name of a fellow American.

His job had forced him to do many things of which he'd never been proud, but somehow his lack of conscience allowed him to put most, if not all, of those things out of his mind. He had never consorted with the enemy, though, and that was the only way he looked at what he was about to do. The hardest part was that he now found himself incapable of telling himself he was merely following orders—the soldier's eternal alibi. It had, afterall, been his idea, regardless of who had ultimately sanctioned it.

Sometime during the night, though, Otis Blake decided it was time for him to come in out of the cold. This would definitely be his last assignment. He had been offered a Stateside desk job before in the Company. But now he didn't even want that. He just wanted out. Completely.

He regretted that he had never taken up fishing. In fact, he hated fishing. *Killing* fish, he called it. But that was the *sort* of thing he wanted to do. He had heard so many people who had retired from a thousand different occupations say, "What do I do? Hell, man, I fish all day. There's nothing like it. No one around. Just you and your thoughts and your beer and your fish."

That's what he wanted—everything but the thoughts and the fish. God, he hated fish; but he hated his thoughts even more.

He popped an antacid tablet into his mouth and entered the embassy. The room the Swiss had set aside for the three-man meeting was a conference room bigger than a football field, he reflected—huge mahogany conference table under three enormous crystal chandeliers, gilt-edged mirrors on every wall. It was cavernous. The other two, the Swiss and the Iranian, were already there when he was ushered in.

"Mr. Blake," said the Swiss diplomat rising from his chair at the head of the long table, "I am Emile Barbeaux. We spoke last night." They shook hands. "And this is Rachmon Hassan." Blake was not surprised when his tendered hand was ignored by the Iranian. He sat opposite Hassan and studied him as a boxer might study an opponent in the ring.

216

He was in his mid-twenties and had thick black hair worn long with too much white showing around his burning brown eyes, giving him the look of a wild-eyed fanatic. A scar ran down his left cheek and was lost inside the collar of his green army fatigue jacket. The three of them were a study in colors: the brown-skinned Iranian, the red cheeks and ruddy complexion of the Swiss, and Blake's green gills.

"Let me begin by thanking you for coming, Mr. Hassan," Barbeaux began. "It is encouraging that you so readily agreed to a meeting with Mr. Blake—a meeting, let me add, that I hope will prove fruitful for all concerned, especially for the hostages." Spoken like a diplomat, Blake thought. Oh, well.

"I only agreed to this meeting because you assured me that I would receive vital information concerning a plot against my people," Hassan said in fluent English.

"I will go anywhere and meet anyone," Hassan continued, "if it furthers the cause of the People's Revolution."

Spoken like a fanatic, Blake thought to himself. He didn't like fanatics. They usually looked at issues in black-and-white terms. Blake had lived his entire life in gray areas.

The Iranian and the Swiss looked at Blake and waited for his opening volley.

"Your English is very good, Mr. Hassan."

"I was an engineering student at Berkeley, Mr. Blake. Later I trained as a soldier at Fort Benning."

Blake returned his toothy grin but thought to himself, Sure, first we educate you, then we teach you how to fight, and then you fuck us up the ass. But what he said was, "Well, I'd like to thank you, Monsieur Barbeaux, for arranging this meeting. Before we begin, I'd like to get the ground rules straight, okay?"

Neither the Swiss nor the Iranian responded, which Blake took for assent.

"To begin with, Mr. Hassan, would you mind if I searched you?"

"Yes, Mr. Blake, I'd mind very much," said Hassan.

"As would I, Mr. Blake. I really must protest. Mr. Hassan has come here in good faith and I don't see the reason for such a request. None whatsoever." Barbeaux's cheeks were even redder than before. He'd never make it as a poker player, Blake thought.

"I'm not interested in weapons. I'm interested in tape recorders," Blake explained, unruffled by the outburst. "I have some very explosive information for Mr. Hassan that can only be harmful to my country if he was able to prove that an agent of the United States provided him with it. On this point I will not budge."

"Is my word not good enough for you, Mr. Blake?" Hassan asked.

"If I were a diplomat, like Monsieur Barbeaux here, I'd never have asked the question in the first place. But let me be clear on that: I'm no diplomat."

"I know *what* you are, Mr. Blake, and I know *who* you are. I know you work for the CIA, the very same organization that set the Shah upon the Peacock Throne in 1953, which subsequently resulted in the most brutal and inhumane forms of torture, imprisonment, and death to countless thousands of my fellow countrymen."

"Let's skip the politics for now, okay?" Blake shot in. "I want to get down to business as quickly as possible. Will you agree to the search?"

"How do you know there are no hidden microphones here in this room?"

Barbeaux's face was almost crimson. "Mr. Hassan, I *assure* you—"

But Hassan cut him short. "I was only raising the possibility to see if Mr. Blake was also prepared to search this lovely room as well as me."

"The Swiss are well known for their neutrality; I think we can agree to that."

"Very well, you may search me, if I may search you as well."

"Agreed," Blake said, and stood up and removed his standard-issue Smith & Wesson .38 from under his armpit and laid it on the table. The Iranian also stood and removed a Browning 9mm automatic from his waistband under his shirt and laid the gun on the table facing Blake's. They met behind Barbeaux's chair and searched each other, finding nothing.

"Satisfied?" asked Hassan replacing his weapon.

"Satisfied," responded Blake, doing likewise with his .38.

"And so to business," said a heavily perspiring Barbeaux.

"Just one more formality, please," Blake said. "Mr. Hassan, with all the factions in your country right now, I want to know if you are in a position to enter into agreements on behalf of those holding the hostages. I'm not talking about your government. I want to know that you can guarantee the safety of the hostages, if it comes to that."

"I can."

"Monsieur Barbeaux?"

"Yes," the Swiss said, "Our information confirms that fact."

"Good. Mr. Hassan, let me ask you a hypothetical question: What if I was to provide you with information about a planned rescue of one of the hostages. Would you be willing to work with me to thwart such a rescue mission without, first, taking revenge on any of the hostages and, secondly, saying anything publicly about the rescue attempt?"

The Iranian thought for a few moments and then said, "Let me respond with a hypothetical question of my own: Why would an agent of the United States want to give us this kind of information? What could possibly be in it for your country?"

"To begin with, hypothetically of course—"

"—of course."

"—the rescue attempt I'm talking about is in no way—and I strongly emphasize that—in *no way* sanctioned by my government. But let us say, again hypothetically, that we came by information about an American with misplaced loyalties who was planning such a mission on his own. And let us say we knew he was in your country and we were unable to locate him, but that we were sure he was planning a possible suicide mission to try to rescue one of the hostages from the embassy. Maybe he's a relative of one of the hostages, okay? That could give credence, in his mind, to risking not only his life but the lives of other hostages."

"I repeat, what does your country have to gain by providing us with this information? Hypothetically, of course."

"Our country is trying to negotiate in good faith with your country. We are trying to secure the release of the hostages through peaceful means. You know this to be true."

" 'Good faith' are your words, not mine."

"Skip the semantics. The point is we want our American countrymen back. We want them back soon, and we want them back unharmed."

"And we demand the return to this country of the butcher Shah and his stolen wealth."

"I'm not here to talk about what *you* want. You tell Uncle Sam what you want. I'm telling you what *I* want."

"Which is precisely what, Mr. Blake?"

"I want your word that, without publicity and without revenge on any of the hostages, you'll help us to locate this particular individual before it's too late: before he breaks into the embassy and kills some of your people, before some of your people kill him, and maybe some hostages as well. He's a troublemaker, Mr. Hassan, and we are *not* looking for trouble."

"I take it we are no longer speaking hypothetically?"

"We are now speaking of saving lives. Plain and simple."

"First of all, what makes you think that anyone would be able to gain access to the embassy compound?"

"You don't know this man; I do. He's capable of almost anything. And let me assure you, he's not an amateur when it comes to this sort of thing. He's done it before in tougher situations. He's ruthless. He's hard to stop, if not impossible. Make no mistake, Mr. Hassan, if we don't stop him, he'll get in. It's what happens *once* he gets in that worries me. That's when the bloodshed will come. Because if he goes down, he'll take half your men with him."

"You obviously know him very well."

"*Very* well, Mr. Hassan, very well. He was trained by my government. And he was trained well."

"What are his plans?"

"I have no idea."

"And you have no idea where he is?"

"Somewhere in Tehran, but that's about it. We know he arrived yesterday but, for reasons I'm sure you can well appreciate, we've not been able to conduct a thorough house-to-house search."

"And suppose he is found. What then?"

"Turn him over to me. I'll take him out of the country."

"We may be able to help each other, but if he is captured alive, I must insist he remain here in Iran, in prison."

Easy, Blake, easy, he thought. Cross one bridge at a time.

"I *may* be able to live with that, but it's moot unless he's stopped."

"Yes, I agree. He would have to be stopped."

"Does that mean we have an agreement?"

"If what you say is true, yes. We have an agreement. But I warn you that if we find that you or your government is behind this is any way, or if it is a trick of some kind, then no. We will take appropriate steps to publicly expose this man as an agent of the United States."

Blake waited several beats before responding. More than once on this assignment he had allowed his emotions to color his actions. In fact, once or twice in this very meeting, he had felt close to losing his temper with Hassan. When an operative begins to allow emotions or personal feelings to interfere, then it is time to get out of the business.

He knew from years of experience all the best ways to threaten someone. His fieldwork had taught him that it is always infinitely more effective to remain emotionless, almost aloof from the passion behind the threat. "Nothing personal," he had said on scores of occasions, "just business." It was one of Blake's most effective techniques—to be able to say just the right words in precisely the right way to very calmly threaten a man into soiling his pants, merely by speaking to him in a very icy, detached manner.

For some reason, though, he felt too much passion with Hassan. He knew that part of his emotions stemmed from a sense of patriotism that he previously hadn't known existed in his psyche. Maybe it was the humiliation of the entire country being held hostage and helpless, not just those Americans in the embassy. Maybe it was that he was about to give an American's name to the enemy. Whatever it was, Blake had to force himself to suppress a macho urge to reach across the table and rearrange Hassan's dental work. He allowed himself the inner satisfaction of knowing that if Hassan fucked him over, he would cancel all bets and go after the Iranian bastard.

"Hassan," Blake began in chilly monotones, "I have heard what you said and I agree to it. You have heard what I said and *you* agree—on behalf of your government—with my terms. If *you* default on this agreement, I will foreclose on your life. Understood?"

The Iranian was on the verge of a militant reply in kind when he looked into Blake's eyes and decided that the CIA man not only meant what he said, but that deep down he was hoping to be able to actually deliver on his threat. He bit back the initial response and tried to adopt Blake's businesslike demeanor, but with little success. His voice quavered momentarily, which betrayed his true concern.

"Y—Yes, Mr. Blake. I understand you—completely. Will you tell me please for whom we are looking?"

Blake pulled an envelope from his inside pocket and removed several photographs. "There are two of them. We have a couple of pictures of the man, one recent and the others a few years old, but just one of the woman, taken a few days ago at Heathrow Airport. The man's name is Alexander Mycroft, but we don't know who the woman is yet. She may be a sister of one of the hostage's, but we're waiting for confirmation from the States."

28

WEARING their phony press credentials on chains around their necks, and pretending to take pictures with a couple of 35mm Nikon cameras they acquired in the local black market, Alex and Christie fit right in with the horde of other reporters from around the world as they stood slightly off to the side of the embassy's main gate and observed the daily afternoon demonstration. Even though they had been briefed by Avi Blume in Israel on what to expect, they were not fully prepared for the almost laughable nature of the rally.

"I've seen more organization at a high school pep rally," Alex told Christie at one point.

The buses bringing a large percentage of the demonstrators were late arriving and, once there, had difficulty unloading their passengers at the right place.

The "cheerleader" tried to teach the chanters various English phrases, but the crowd—most of them fluent only in Farsi—had trouble grasping the many nuances of the English language. A reporter nearby explained that the organizers like to denounce the United States in English "because it plays so much better on American TV when the viewers back home can understand what's being said."

They tried to teach the crowd to say, "Death to the tyrant Carter and the United States," but it came out so muddled that they finally settled for the old standby "Death to Carter."

When they went for "Return the butcher Shah and his stolen wealth," they had to settle for "Return the Shah."

After the cheerleader was satisfied that the crowd had mastered these two phrases, he tried to get them to string the two together: "Death to Carter, Return the Shah!" But half of the crowd chanted "Death to Carter" while at the same time the other half hollered "Return the Shah." The cheerleader had to shout into his bullhorn to stop the crowd, and the TV reporters grew impatient. At one point, one of the organizers yelled over in the general direction of the press section to be patient. "They'll get it in a minute," he said. He was wrong.

After a while, Alex told Christie to stay put while he went to do some reconnaissance. "I want to see how well guarded the other compound areas are during a demonstration. You'll be safe here, but if we get split up, meet me back at the room."

"Alex, please be careful."

He jumped down from the platform and made his way through the crowds and around the corner of the embassy

225

compound, staying close to the embassy wall. He noticed a couple of openings that he thought had possibilities but that still would be difficult under the best of circumstances. He was not able to spot many guards, though, and he made a mental note of what equipment he'd need if he tried to scale the wall.

As he turned the far corner, trying to act inconspicuous while wondering how a legitimate reporter might act, he was passed by a small black car weaving in and out of the parked buses. Just as the car dipped behind the far side of one of the buses, Mycroft suddenly went pale. He recognized Otis Blake as the passenger in the front seat.

Mycroft turned and began retracing his steps as quickly as he dared, trying not to run and draw attention to himself, and praying Blake hadn't spotted him. But Blake *had* seen him, and the car emerged from the far side of the bus and tried to negotiate an almost impossible U-turn.

"Shit," said Blake, "I think he spotted me. Come on, Hassan, can't you maneuver this thing?"

"I'm trying!"

"Forget it, I'm going after him on foot." Blake jumped out of the car and took off after Mycroft's quickly receding figure.

"Don't run after him," Hassan urged, as he abandoned the car, too. "Let us handle it; you may be shot."

But Blake wasn't about to stop once he had Mycroft in his sights. He had slipped out of the CIA's hands once too often and Blake was determined not to repeat his Agency's past mistakes.

"Mycroft! Mycroft! It's hopeless—wait!" He yelled after him, but Mycroft was already turning the corner and heading directly into the crowd of demonstrators. He had no good escape route and so decided to trust his luck to getting lost in the crowd. He literally dove into the sea of bodies just as Blake was rounding the corner, followed closely by a winded Hassan.

"Where is he?" Hassan asked, trying to catch his breath.

"In the crowd, but he shouldn't be too hard to spot. Come on."

"Don't be insane. You'll never find him in there."

Blake resented the advice, mostly because he agreed with it. But he felt so helpless just standing there, knowing that Mycroft was almost within reach.

Quickly, Blake surveyed the scene and spotted the raised platform used by the cheerleader. The crowd was still immersed in calling for the Shah's return. Without thinking it through clearly, Blake bullied his way onto the platform and scanned the vast crowd for a ripple that would be caused by a man going through it. When Blake saw how vast and tightly packed the crowd was, he couldn't imagine anyone making it through from one end to the other in one piece.

But suddenly, from his raised vantage point, he spotted Mycroft plodding his way by pushing people aside. The crowd was so deeply involved in following the cheerleader's instructions that they paid little attention to Mycroft's efforts.

Blake, realizing that Mycroft might actually make it through and escape, grabbed the bullhorn from the cheerleader's hands and bellowed into it at the top of his lungs, "STOP THAT MAN!" He pointed in Mycroft's general direction.

But the overwhelming majority of the non-English-speaking crowd mistook Blake's demand as a new chant. While most of them continued the "Return the Shah" chant, slowly some stopped to listen to the "new" cheerleader's message. It had an easy monosyllabic cadence that many in the crowd found appealing.

Soon, Blake's voice could be heard above the din and a few people began trying to duplicate the foreign-sounding words. When Blake's voice reached Mycroft's ears, he crouched as low as he could but then was surprised to hear a small but ever-increasing number of Iranians repeat Blake's cry. He stood to see some of them pointing their fingers at Blake, just as he was pointing his finger at them.

An English-speaking Iranian grabbed Mycroft by the shoulder as he tripped and hollered to him over the noise, "Who is the man we are stopping?" "Why Carter, of course," Mycroft replied. And immediately that Iranian took up the new chant.

Meanwhile, Hassan had scaled the platform and tried to wrest the bullhorn from Blake's grasp.

"Shut up! Shut up! Can't you see what you're doing?" Hassan had to scream to be heard, but when he finally managed to get Blake's attention, Blake was able to hear for the first time the chant he had started. He had been so engrossed in trying to get someone to collar Mycroft that he hadn't been listening to the demonstrators.

Hassan tried to rectify the damage in Farsi, but by the time a semblance of order had been restored, Mycroft had successfully negotiated the crowd and was long gone.

As Blake and Hassan walked back to the car, Hassan said, "We'll find him. Don't worry."

"We'd better. For *everyone's* sake."

They could still hear the crowd chanting "STOP THAT MAN!" as they rounded the corner and reclaimed their car.

29

CHRISTIE, standing amid the crowd of reporters atop the press platform, had witnessed Mycroft's miraculous escape, although she did not recognize the two men chasing him. She assumed the English-speaking man was Otis Blake but was surprised to see him with an Iranian. From his dress and authoritative actions, she pegged the Iranian as a member of the embassy takeover group.

She waited until they departed, then she vanished in the company of a crowd of TV reporters and photographers who had "gotten their shots for the day" and were off to file their stories and photos before deadline. She was tempted to stay in her place as long as possible in case Alex returned, but one of the reporters cautioned against it, warning that she'd get caught up in the mob of demonstrators that was due to disperse soon. Also, she reasoned, she'd stick out in the now-thinning press section.

She wandered through the streets and bazaars for a while until eventually making her way back to the small hotel.

Alex, for his part, emerged on the far side of the crowd with a small number of cuts and bruises, torn clothing, and minus his camera. He had managed to recapture his shoes that, when he stumbled in the crowd, had been plucked from his feet by an old man with a toothless grin and bare feet. Examining himself, he discovered that his press card had been taken, too, but his wallet and his emergency cigarette had somehow remained on his person.

He found his way to a small café where he took a seat behind some backgammon-playing, hashish-smoking patrons and ordered the only available drink: thick black tea. He permitted himself the luxury of inhaling deeply from time to time to fill his lungs and his nostrils with the café's heavy smoke. Feeling safe there temporarily, he stayed until dark.

At nightfall, Mycroft ducked into a small alley where he found a lone man in a drug-induced stupor. Without too much effort, he managed to relieve the addict of his clothes and hastily threw them on over his own. Keeping his head down and trying to fit in with the other street people, he eventually made his way back to the hotel.

Christie was waiting for him in the small room but gasped when he entered wearing the native rags.

"It's okay. It's me," he assured her.

"Oh, Alex, I was so worried. Are you all right?" She threw her arms around his neck and Alex felt her shudder against his body. But he was too exhausted to allow himself to be aroused.

"I'll be fine as soon as I shed these filthy clothes and clean a few bruises."

He sponge-bathed in the sink while Christie sat on the stained commode keeping him company. They briefly swapped escape stories and Christie said, "Then it was Otis Blake, wasn't it?"

"No question about it."

"But Alex, I don't understand something. I'm sure he was with an Iranian—someone who looked like a person of authority in the Revolution. How could that be?"

"I don't know for certain, but if you're right, it makes things even more difficult than before. Blake has obviously gone to the Iranians for help in stopping us."

"But how is that possible? How can the CIA go to the Iranians for help?"

"I don't know, but if there was a way to do it, it'd make sense."

"Why?"

"Well, Blake's men have tried to nab me twice that I know of: first in Tel Aviv and then again in the Tehran airport. Obviously he knows why I'm here and he's under orders to stop me any way he can. He doesn't know where I am—yet. Nor does he know my timetable. But he's got to know time is running out. When it was only the CIA looking for me, I wasn't too concerned about staying here. After all, the CIA can't just waltz around this city looking for people. They're trying to keep under wraps, too. But if he somehow brought the Iranians in, we'll be found in no time. This is their city and they're in charge. No, we'd better make plans to vacate these premises immediately."

"But where will we go?"

"I don't know yet, but I've got a meeting to attend shortly. I think I can get help there."

"Well, let's leave, then."

"Unfortunately, Christie, you won't be able to join me. But I do have an idea. If Tehran is anything like Saigon was during the sixties, there's a large hotel somewhere nearby where the reporters are staying. Also, there'll be a bar there that'll be open twenty-four hours."

"I thought the Ayotollah banned liquor."

"He did, but I'm sure that doesn't apply to the press. The Iranians want the press here and the press won't stay *anywhere* for long where they can't get drunk. Believe me, if there's no bar *serving* liquor, there'll be plenty of private bottles being passed around."

"Do you really think I'll be safe there?"

"Hey, you'll be the hit of the party, believe me. You'll be an oasis in a desert for those guys."

"But, Alex, these are reporters. I don't know anything about reporting. How do I fit in?"

"Forget you're supposed to be a reporter for the night. Just be a woman. It's a universal language."

"When will I see you again?"

"As soon as possible. Come on. Let's find that hotel."

But as he opened the door, a small package, wrapped in shreds of brown paper and tied with cord that had been leaning against the closed door, tumbled into the room.

"Stand back! Don't touch it!" he barked as Christie bent down to retrieve it.

"Alex, what on earth is it?"

"I don't know yet, but stand clear and let me look."

He got down on all fours and placed his ear to the paper but heard nothing.

"You don't think it's a bomb, do you, Alex?"

"Shhh!" he commanded.

He then began to sniff at the paper like a dog, but was unable to detect any telltale odors. He gently guided the package into the room with his foot and closed the door.

He produced a small knife from his pocket and carefully cut away the cord, allowing the shreds of paper to drop off.

It was a tape recorder.

He carried it to the bed, sat down, and pushed the play button. Christie sat down alongside of him.

At first, there was only a hollow sound, and then the sound of the water, the sea. And then the sound he dreaded:

"Daddy."

It was the same soft voice he had heard on the telephone in the hotel in Philadelphia.

"Alex," Christie began, "what—"

"Quiet!" he demanded.

"Daddy. Don't leave me, Daddy."

Then there was the unmistakable sound of automatic gunfire. He didn't recall that from the telephone call back in Philadelphia. Maybe he just didn't remember it.

"Daddy. Don't leave me."

And then it was over. He pushed the rewind button.

"Alex, what is this? What does it mean?"

But instead of answering, he pushed the play button again. And again. Three times in all. He was surprised at how calm he was—inwardly and outwardly.

"It means, Christie," Alex said as he began to compose a message in his head, "that it's time for me to start acting like the professional I was trained to be."

He rewound the tape and, using the built-in condenser microphone, recorded a message over the previous one, then hid the recorder under the bed.

"I don't understand the message," she said.

"But someone else will," he replied. "Just take what you absolutely need and let's find that newsmen's hotel."

30

"HOW'D you make out on your end?" Blake asked Hassan when they got back together after making several frantic telephone calls.

"I have been assured by our Information Ministry that there will be a complete news blackout on today's unusual events at the demonstration." Hassan said it with confidence but to Blake he seemed nervous about it.

"Langley—I mean my headquarters in the States—is on the phone right now to the heads of all the television networks and wire services. Just in case any news does manage to slip out of Tehran, they'll squelch it back home. I've no idea what kind of story they're telling the news guys, but I'm sure they'll suppress any stories about today's demonstration. Anything else?"

"Yes. I've alerted the students in the embassy to post heavier guards until further notice. I did not explain why but indicated we had information about a possible rescue attempt."

"Did you at least tell them not to shoot anyone unless absolutely necessary?"

"They have their instructions," he offered, without explaining the nature of the instructions. "I assure you, if Mr. Mycroft does somehow gain access to the embassy compound, he will not get far."

"Speaking of Mr. Mycroft," Blake said, "any word on his whereabouts?"

"As a matter fact, yes. We have reason to believe we have located his living quarters. It is a small dirty rooming house that tries to pass itself off as a hotel. It is only a few blocks from the embassy. I am on my way to meet some of my men there now. You may, of course, remain here and avail yourself of our hospitality."

"Screw you, Jack. I told you, this is a joint operation, as much as we both may dislike the idea. I'm sticking to you like Juicy Fruit on a shoe."

"I'm not quite certain I understand all of what you just said but I think the essence of your message is clear. Let us go."

31

MYCROFT had been right. The bar at the Intercontinental Hotel was swarming with reporters,
most of them deeply engrossed in consuming
large quantities of alcohol. He had also been right in predict-
ing that rather than question Christie's presence, those reporters not already under the table would fight over each
other to get her attention. She was a remarkably beautiful
sight at any time but especially to those in the midst of the
seedy chaos of a revolution-torn city.

Christie managed to pick up two distinct strains from the
numerous conversations swirling all about her. First, of
course, was the matter of that day's unusual occurrence at
the daily demonstration and the conjecturing of all sorts of

scenarios to explain the news blackout. And, secondly, there was the ever-persistent rumor that soon American newsmen would be expelled from the country.

That story, she learned in bits and pieces, came in waves. One day the expulsion was "imminent," and then it would pass. She also witnessed some American television correspondents making arrangements with British, Canadian, and Australian colleagues to provide daily "feeds" back to the States, "just in case."

Christie also managed to gently and seductively interrogate one particularly obnoxious reporter whose face was widely known to American television audiences. He told her that, despite appearances to the contrary, the embassy was considered virtually impregnable. "Oh, it can be breached, make no mistake about that fact, honey," he cooed, "but at the cost of the hostages' lives. Those fuckin' bastards'll kill 'em, sure as you're sittin' here."

While patiently rejecting as kindly as she could proposition after proposition, Christie was unaware of the particular scrutiny she was receiving from a man sitting effectively alone at a far-corner table: His companions had all passed out.

But this man with dark-tinted glasses, thick black curly hair, and a full and well-trimmed matching beard nursed a single drink the entire time Christie was in the bar.

She hadn't noticed him entering the bar a few moments after she had. But if she had, she undoubtedly would have paid no attention to him, dressed as he was in a safari-type jacket like so many other reporters in the room. He had quietly rolled a drunken reporter off of the chair he had wished to occupy, the one giving him a clear and unobstructed view of Christie, and had attracted no undue attention himself in claiming the seat. He took sips, no more, of the half-filled glass before him, then held it firmly between both hands, his eyes never wavering from Christie's shapely back.

For her part, Christie periodically glanced around the room as if searching for someone. More than once her gaze fell in the direction of the man watching her but her eyes quickly passed him by. No recognition given; none taken.

But after occupying her bar stool for the better part of an hour, she teasingly asked her latest would-be suitor to hold her seat while she went to freshen up. When she walked out of the bar and headed for a prearranged rendezvous, the man in the safari jacket casually glanced at his left wrist and followed at a respectable distance.

32

OTIS Blake and Rachmon Hassan had just completed going through the few articles of clothing Alex and Christie had left in their room.

"I suggest we make ourselves comfortable and merely wait for them to return," Hassan said.

"It's a waste of time. Mycroft's no fool, Hassan. He knows we're after him and I'm sure he figured it'd just be a matter of time before we found this place now that you Iranians are also looking for them. They won't be back."

"I disagree, Blake. Why else leave the clothes behind?"

"So some dumb shit like you would waste his time waiting in an empty room." Blake regretted the sharp remark the instant it slipped out of his mouth. "I'm sorry, Hassan. I'm just on edge."

"We all are," Hassan replied, keeping his own temper in check. "But a person just does not leave clothes behind."

"Hassan, this may be hard for you to understand because of the differences in culture and economy between your country and mine. I'll apologize in advance if what I'm about to say offends you, but in my country a few articles of clothing are easily replaceable. In a country like yours, that may not always be the case, so you tend to put a higher value on such things. No, I'm sure Mycroft left the clothes behind as a decoy. There is nothing in this room that he can't do without or replace easily."

"I do not take offense at such a typically American waste of money. We, in Iran, certainly put a higher value on the things we work so hard to achieve. That is why this Revolution to overthrow the Shah has been so successful and why your country—"

"Okay, okay," Blake interrupted. He did not wish to engage in a pointless idealogical debate. "Let's not get into a harangue about who is more responsible with their things. Just take my word for it, Hassan; they're not coming back."

"Then where do you think they are?"

"Jesus! How the fuck do I know? This is *your* country. Maybe we ought to check the embassy."

"There is no need for that, I assure you. Not only has the guard been reinforced inside but I have my own men on the outside watching for them on the streets. The pictures you gave me earlier have been reproduced and distributed."

"And the airport?"

"Also well covered, as are all other means out of the country. We will find him, I assure you."

"Yes, but will he be found in time? That's the question."

At that moment, one of Hassan's men by chance happened to peer under the bed and discovered the recorder.

"What do you make of this?" Hassan asked Blake.

"It's a tape recorder. Push the fucking button and let's hear if there's anything on it." This time Blake did not apologize for his outburst. He was angry that the recorder had not been discovered before. More precisely, he was angry with himself for not having thought to look under the bed in the first place.

Hassan pushed the play key and they listened to Mycroft's voice saying:

> "Baby. Let's call it off. Am never going to make it. Killers everywhere. Embassy too heavily guarded. Danger everywhere. Only chance is the airport. Next flight is at midnight. Take all your belongings. Guns are useless. Enemy too heavily armed. Too well trained. I need help. No way I can do this alone. Meet me back here at ten. You stay put if I'm late. Why did I ever come? Am losing control. You're my only salvation. Airport. Midnight."

Hassan was jubilant. "This is too good to be true. We will post more guards at the airport and more men here and just wait for him to walk into our trap. I told you we would find him. Allah truly smiles on the blessed!"

But Blake was pensive. "I'm afraid you were right the first time, Hassan. It *is* to good to be true. He won't return; neither will the girl. And you can be damn sure the last place he'll turn up at is the airport."

"Mr. Blake," said the Iranian smugly, "I fear our brief association has come to an end. We have discovered where

2 4 2

Mycroft will show up and you are no longer of any use to us." He pulled his gun from his waistband. "Now, I have no wish to kill you, but kill you I will if you make trouble."

Blake did not move. "Put the peashooter away, dumb shit, and listen to me carefully. You've never gone up against a man like Alexander Mycroft. He's smart, he's ruthless, and he can run circles around you in his sleep. And there's no way he'd be dumb enough to leave a message like that. Play the message again. As Hassan rewound the tape, Blake took out a notebook and began to write down the message Mycroft had left.

> Baby
> Let's call it off
> Am never going to make it
> Killers everywhere
> Embassy too heavily guarded

"See, I told you the embassy was well guarded. Even Mycroft recognizes that," Hassan boasted.

"Shut up," Blake scolded. "I'm writing."

> Danger everywhere
> Only chance is the airport
> Next flight is at midnight
> Take all your belongings

"And you said the clothing was not important," Hassan said scornfully.

"One more outburst—just one—and I'll push this tape recorder down your dumb-shit mouth, Hassan!"

> Guns are useless
> Enemy too heavily armed
> Too well trained

I need help
No way I can do this alone
Meet me back here at ten
You stay put if I'm late
Why did I ever come
Am losing control
You're my only salvation
Airport
Midnight

Blake finished writing and shoved the pad in front of Hassan's eyes.

"This is not his travel itinerary, as you suspect, Hassan," Blake lectured. "It's a message for me—a warning. String together the first letter in each line. The message reads: 'BLAKE. DON'T GET IN MY WAY. A.M.' for Alexander Mycroft."

Hassan stared incredulously at the now-deciphered message. "But this is ingenious. How did you know?"

"It's not ingenious, Hassan. It's simple. We learned it our first day in spy school. It was in the cadence of his voice."

"But how did you know the message was not real?"

"I told you: Mycroft's not dumb. He'd never leave the message you thought you heard."

"And why is he warning you to stay out of his way?"

"He's telling me—telling us—that he's through screwing around. It's hardball time, and he's pitching."

"What does that mean?"

"It means keep your head down and listen to me. We still may catch him in time. As for now, let's just leave this place and go cruising on the streets. Who knows, maybe we'll get lucky again."

"But I will leave a man or two behind, just in case he returns," the Iranian stubbornly insisted.

"Leave all the goddamn men behind you want to. Just don't bother leaving behind anyone important. Mycroft *won't* return."

33

T HEY came in their most somber clothes. They always did.

Alone, and in small groups, they silently entered the western portal of a nondescript shell of a building located at the far end of a dark, almost non-existent alley. The Byzantine pillars were missing, of course. But once inside the darkened doorway, they passed over the Seal of Solomon and under the twelve signs of the zodiac. They always did; it was the only way to enter.

Alexander Mycroft stood quietly in the shadows and watched as the men made their way in silence down the alley and through the door. He had had only a little trouble locating the address and had even boldly asked directions from an armed Iranian foot patrolman who had stopped Mycroft for identification. The forged British passport did its trick and Mycroft was sent on his way, after having been firmly reminded of the curfew.

But now, standing in a darkened alcove, Mycroft unconsciously fingered the ring and contemplated what his fate would be once he entered the Iranian version of a Temple of the Craft.

He had satisfactorily identified himself as a Brother of the Craft the night before in the restaurant as he would again be asked to do in a short while. That was not the problem. He could easily engage in "fraternal communications" with a Brother, or gain access to a regular Lodge Meeting. But he had requested—as he was forced under the circumstances to do—a hearing before a Lodge of Masters, where only the leaders of a Lodge may convene and render decisions on all important matters.

A Lodge of Masters was almost never attended by a Brother not of that particular Lodge, for requesting admission was virtually unheard-of, and gaining access extremely difficult as well as risky to life and limb. The penalty for failing the test was ancient and drawn from an obscure biblical reference: the loss of the challenger's right ear and left hand. But any comfort Mycroft might have felt at home, back in the States, in knowing that the penalty was merely symbolic and never inflicted (or at least he had never heard of it being carried out) afforded him little solace in a country known for its past and present brutality.

So-called Iranian "justice," he knew, was swift and unmerciful. Why should he expect any less tonight?

But if he could successfully recite the complex catechism (in English, he prayed) and satisfactorily demonstrate that he indeed possessed the Ring of Solomon, he could be assured only of receiving a fair hearing and of being allowed to leave alive and in peace. There were no guarantees that he would receive the assistance he required.

But he knew he'd never be able to reach the Sinclair boy without local help. His observations of the walled embassy compound convinced him of that.

The merchant from the previous night's dinner was waiting for him as he entered, and the moment Mycroft crossed the threshold, the doors were locked and bolted behind him.

"I greet you with mixed emotions," said the merchant, "for the one half of me is glad you were able to find your way here unharmed, while the other half of me had hoped you would choose not to appear."

"I understand completely," Mycroft responded, "and for whatever it may be worth, I, too, have similarly mixed feelings. May I ask your name, Brother?"

"My name is Ishmael. Are you ready to proceed, Brother Mycroft?"

"Yes. The sooner the better."

Following Ishmael's footsteps, Mycroft was led to the station of the outer guard, where he unhesitatingly took the guard's right hand in his own, embraced him with his left, and whispered into the guard's ear, "I am your friend."

The guard replied, "I am your guide."

Mycroft: "I am your Brother."

The guard: "Are you a shepherd's son?"

Mycroft: "Ein."

The guard: "Sof."

The guard released Mycroft from the embrace and said, "Pass, Brother, and may Allah be with you."

Mycroft followed Ishmael into a small room just beyond the guard's station.

"Prepare yourself," Ishmael directed.

Mycroft solemnly removed every conceivable article of clothing, jewelry, and money—all save the ring. He was given a white shroud that he tied at his waist and stood for inspection before the diminutive, rotund Iranian.

Ishmael then looped a silken noose around Mycroft's neck, saying, "I am glad you are familiar with the preparation."

"Yes, it is the same in my country."

"That is good. Let us hope, for your sake, that all else is the same, too." He produced a large curved razor-sharp cutlass from his waistband as he said this. "You know what I must do if you fail?"

"I know."

"And you are still willing to take the risk?"

"I have no choice."

"Let us proceed, then. I will guide you only so far and then you will be on your own. You will answer all questions put to you tonight. You understand this?"

"I understand and I agree."

"Then raise the alarm."

Mycroft took hold of a long wooden staff leaning against the second door—the door leading into the Assembly Hall—and gaveled it upon the door nine times, in three groups of three.

An unseen voice from beyond the door demanded, "Who comes here?"

And Mycroft responded: "A skilled craftsman, fresh from seven years labor upon the Temple of the Lord, seeking aid and sustenance while traveling in foreign parts. Open, I say unto you. Open in the name of the Almighty. Grant unto me the necessaries of life, or suffer the wrath of God."

A moment later, the great door creaked open slowly, and Mycroft and Ishmael stepped out into a desert.

Mycroft was not prepared for the vastness of it all. His own Assembly Hall back home was large, to be sure. But not so large that one was unable to see from one end of the Hall to the other.

What laid open before Mycroft and Ishmael was a Hall so vast that, standing in the dark portion of what he knew had to be a triangular-shaped room, he could not see even a glimmer of the light he knew awaited him if he traversed the path properly.

But the sand upon the floor was what amazed him most. Back home, the sand lay atop the floor in an even layer. But here there was no floor. Just a desert of sand, complete with dunes. And not a footprint to be seen.

An unseen booming voice spoke to him: "There are no footsteps to guide you, as before. We prostrate ourselves before our God as we will humble ourselves before you, should you prove worthy. Find your way to our tabernacle in the wilderness before the sun comes up this day, meet the final test, and all that we have shall be yours."

Mycroft's response: "I hear and I obey."

Still holding firm to the end of the silken cord around Mycroft's neck, Ishmael stepped three paces behind him, awaiting Mycroft's first movement. "There is no turning back, my Brother," Ishmael whispered softly.

"In more ways than one," Mycroft responded in a low voice. And then, with his left foot, he took his first step.

A chorus of voices called out: "I am your friend. I am your guide. I am your Brother. I am a shepherd's son."

Mycroft began the trek through the sand, firmly planting his staff into the ground with each step of his left foot. And as he walked, he called out in a loud voice: "I have built in this wilderness a Temple unto the Lord, the length thereof was threescore cubits, and the breadth thereof twenty cubits, and the height thereof thirty cubits. The Lord is my shepherd. I am His son."

Without warning, the sound of a windstorm surrounded Mycroft and he could actually feel a wind blowing the sand all around him. It was an eerie illusion that played on his senses. Mycroft bowed his head into the wind and continued on, saying, "And the porch before the Temple of the house, twenty cubits was the length thereof, according to the breadth of the house; and ten cubits was the breadth thereof before the house. The Lord is my shepherd. I am His son."

The wind died down as suddenly as it had appeared, and Mycroft found himself standing before a veil, from the far side of which a voice called out: "Who comes here?"

And Mycroft responded as before: "A skilled craftsman, fresh from seven years labor upon the Temple of the Lord, seeking aid and sustenance while traveling in foreign parts. Open, I say unto you. Open in the name of the Almighty."

"What is the name of this Almighty?"

"His name has forty-two letters."

"Can this name be pronounced?"

"Each letter represents a number."

"Can this number be spoken?"

"It is a number unlike any you have ever heard. Now open, open I say unto you. Or suffer the wrath of God."

The veil parted but there was no one on the opposite side. And Mycroft continued his long journey onward, onward. He had passed the first test with ease, and thought how fortunate it was that he was being asked to recite the complex catechism in English. Considering he was a stranger in their land, they had every right to conduct the ancient ritual in Farsi. At least they were prepared to meet him halfway. Had they opted to speak in their native tongue, he would have been lost.

And as he walked on, aware of the gentle pressure around his neck from the silken cord, the other end of which Ishmael held firmly in his grasp, Mycroft came upon a second veil. And he called out, "Open, I say unto you. Open in the name of the Almighty."

And from behind the veil, a voice responded, "How powerful is this Almighty?"

"Mighty to make the sands stand still," Mycroft responded. "Mighty to make the rivers reverse course. Mighty to make mountains erupt. Mighty to make the earth split asunder."

Using the tip of the staff, Mycroft drew a triangle in the sand.

"Mighty to breathe life into a baby's soul."

Then, with his foot, he erased one side of the triangle.

"And mighty to snuff out life. Now open, open I say unto you. Or suffer the wrath of God."

The veil parted. And suddenly, Mycroft found that there was light. No longer was he wandering around in eerie darkness.

At the third veil, Mycroft was again asked about the name of God.

"The whole of the Torah is the Ineffable Name," he responded. "The Torah was written in black fire on white fire. The white fire is the true text of the Torah, and the text that appears in black fire is merely the mystical oral law."

And the veil vanished before him.

He now had but one more veil to pass through. One more obstacle to overcome in order to reach his goal, to plead his case, to try to reach John Sinclair's son, to try to answer the Hailing Sign. A brief thought of Christie entered his mind, but he reminded himself that he could not allow himself to be distracted.

"My Brother," Ishmael whispered as they walked, "you have done exceedingly well. But you must know that no outsider ever has been able to progress beyond the fourth veil. I know I said there is no turning back, but perhaps there is a way—"

"Ishmael," Mycroft interrupted, "for more than a week, a lot of people have been telling me to turn back. I almost turned back before I began; but the more I'm told to abandon my mission, the more determined I am to go on. No, Ishmael, I need to talk to the High Priest. I need his help. I have come too far to turn back now."

"I understand."

"But one request, Ishmael: If I fail the final test, do what you have to do quickly . . . and cleanly."

"You may be assured of it, my Brother. You may be assured."

And then atop what seemed a distant horizon, Mycroft saw the multi-colored tabernacle in the wilderness, aglow in a bath of lights. But the distance was not as far as Mycroft had first thought. As with so much of what had already transpired this night, it, too, was an illusion.

For all their wanderings and meanderings in the desert, they still were indoors; had, in fact, never left the nondescript building Mycroft had entered at midnight. How many hours ago was that, he wondered to himself.

The flaps on the tabernacle were closed but there was a wooden block a foot high placed at its entrance. Mycroft gaveled upon the block nine times, three groups of three.

An unseen voice boomed: "Who comes here? Who dares disturb the peace and tranquility of the sanctum sanctorum?"

And Mycroft responded: "A skilled craftsman, fresh from seven years labor upon the Temple of the Lord, who has passed the three veils in the wilderness, seeking aid and sustenance while traveling in foreign parts. Open, I say unto you. Open in the name of the Almighty. Grant unto me the necessaries of life, or suffer the wrath of God.''

"What is it that you desire, traveler?''

"I desire admittance to the sanctum sanctorum and an audience with the High Priest.''

"What do you offer as proof that you are worthy of admittance?''

"I offer the Ring of Solomon, which I will surrender to the High Priest alone upon one condition.''

"State your condition, traveler.''

"The condition,'' Mycroft replied, "is that if, upon examination, he satisfies himself that it *is* the Ring of Solomon as I claim, he will admit me to the sanctum sanctorum and render assistance unto me. But if it proves not to be the Ring of Solomon, he may do unto me as he sees fit.''

"Tarry,'' said the voice, "as I make your prayer known.''

After a time, the veil parted and two swordsmen placed their blades at Mycroft's chest. One of them said, "The condition is accepted. Present the Ring!''

For the first time in eleven days, Mycroft removed the ring and pushed it onto the end of his staff. And as he did, he felt the same electric charge surge through his body that he had felt when he placed the ring on his finger in Philadelphia.

He tilted the staff forward and allowed the rod to be taken from him by the swordsmen, who then bade him enter.

It was a smaller triangular-shaped room, very similar to what he was accustomed to, one side in darkness with Members seated along the two illuminated sides.

He followed the swordsmen along a purple strip of carpeting leading to the throne of the purple-robed High

Priest. Ishmael, still behind him, no longer held the end of Mycroft's noose.

Mycroft's entourage halted at the altar and the white-bearded priest stepped down from his throne and joined them.

Like the altar back home, this one appeared to be golden and three groupings of candles encircled it. Through the fires of the first, Mycroft read the word "Emet," which he knew to mean "truth." The second group of candles revealed the word, "Emunah," meaning "faith." And the third candle grouping boasted the word, "Hokhmah," or "wisdom."

From the center of each grouping of flames, Mycroft observed the handles of three jewel-encrusted daggers.

The High Priest raised his arms and said, "Let us see if you speak the truth, traveler. Let us see if your faith is strong in your God. Demonstrate your wisdom."

Without a moment's hesitation, Mycroft plunged his hand into the fire marked "Hokhmah," grabbed the dagger from the flames, and said, "I have the wisdom to know that I cannot escape. Therefore this binding is meaningless." And so saying, he cut the noose with the razor-sharp blade.

Tossing the weapon to the ground, he next thrust his hand into the fire marked, "Emunah," grabbed the blade from the flames, and said, "I have faith in my Brother that he will not harm me and that he will keep his word to me." And immediately thereafter, Mycroft plunged the knife into his belly. The thick blade collapsed and Mycroft was unharmed.

And plucking the dagger from the fires of "Emet," he said, "But I am unafraid to face the truth. Yea, the truth shall set me free." And he placed the dagger back into the fire.

"Present the Ring!" cried the old priest, and one of the swordsmen placed it on the altar in front of him. The High Priest examined it carefully, turning it over and over in his hands, then translated the three ancient languages of the inscription with apparent ease.

" 'Blessed be he that shall welcome and assist this worthy ring bearer,' " he read three times. "The Ring appears to be genuine. We shall see."

The two guards grabbed Mycroft and placed him atop the altar on his back. Three pieces of black coal were then laid across his chest and the ring he had carried with him from Philadelphia was placed on the center piece of coal. Two other, almost identical gold rings were placed on the outer two pieces of coal.

The High Priest then knelt at the altar, saying, "What Allah has crafted cannot be put asunder by mere mortals." Then he reached up and plucked the dagger that Mycroft had returned to the fires of "truth." The blade was a glowing ember. Then he quickly touched the tip of the blade to each piece of coal. Mycroft soon had three fires burning across his bare chest.

All other lights within the tabernacle had been extinguished, and now the only illumination within the structure came from the three fires upon Mycroft's body.

The old priest began a series of long incantations in languages that were foreign to Mycroft's ears. And as the chants continued, the flames gradually grew larger and more intense.

Mycroft was horror-stricken.

He had known the ring was to be tested, but not like this. He moved not a muscle as he stared transfixed at the flames, feeling the growing intensity of the heat.

How long the prayers continued, Mycroft could not determine. He had long ago that evening lost all concept of time and motion. But although he could not understand what was being said, he soon was able to surmise that the old man's incantations were in the three ancient languages of the ring: Syriac, Chaldaic, and Egyptian.

At several points during the bizarre ritual, the priest would utter a phrase that demanded a response in unison from the two swordsmen. On and on it went. Until, at last, the High Priest began a final long litany of chants, complete with unison responses from all of the Members present. And when he stopped, Mycroft could see that the fires had extinguished and the top of all three coals were white.

Still reclining, Mycroft's right hand was suddenly grasped by one of the guards, who held it firmly, palm down. Slowly, the High Priest stood before Mycroft. Using silver tongs, he carefully lifted one of the two outer rings and placed it atop the back of Mycroft's hand.

The pain was immediate. Mycroft managed to stifle a shout but jerked his hand so violently that the ring flew off.

The High Priest examined Mycroft's hand and saw the red circular swelling already heralding the blister that was to come. The other guard then grabbed hold of Mycroft's left hand while the High Priest carefully lifted the other outer ring with the long tongs. Knowing what was to come made the inevitable searing all the more intense. This time he did cry out and again the ring flew off his hand. But the heat of the band was so exquisite that even a flickering moment on the back of Mycroft's hand was enough to raise a second circular welt.

Now the old priest, moving slowly and deliberately, guided the tongs to the center ring, the one that had been given to Mycroft by John Sinclair. As soon as the ring was snared by the claws of the tongs, Mycroft was seized by a dozen pairs of hands. They put him in a human vise in a half-raised position. Careful attention was paid to securing Mycroft's head. From the waist up, he was totally incapable of movement.

The High Priest inched the tongs toward Mycroft in an excruciatingly slow and calculated manner. Sweat streamed from his pores and the salt burned the backs of his hands where his flesh had been seared by the white heat of the two other rings.

The closer the tongs got to his face, the more the priest widened his eyes. Mycroft could see Ishmael standing just to the side, curved cutlass now in his hand in anticipation of Mycroft's impending failure.

The ring was so close now that Mycroft could see the inscriptions on the inside of the ring. The tongs hovered in that position for only a moment until the priest spoke: "Present your tongue."

Mycroft's mind was flooded with the words to portions of the ritual: *They came to hear what was not theirs to hear, wearing what was not theirs to wear. And as one of their punishments, they received the gold they had craved: hot molten gold poured down their throats until it ran out of every orifice of their bodies.*

"Present your tongue!" This time the command was sharper.

Someone pinched Mycroft's nose, forcing him to open his mouth to draw breath. He knew they would eventually compel him to do what they wanted, so he forced his tongue to creep slowly out of its hiding place and closer to the silver tongs. They released his nose and he allowed his tongue to grow to its full length. He wanted to close his eyes, but a pair of hands actually forced his eyelids open to watch what was about to happen.

With a deliberateness borne out of either sadism or fear—Mycroft didn't know which—it seemed to take the High Priest forever to reach Mycroft's tongue. Slowly, he inched the golden ring closer, ever closer, to Mycroft's nose, then his mouth, then his tongue. He was so close now that Mycroft's field of vision was obscured and he lost sight of the tip of the silver tongs.

But as the viselike grip on his head grew tighter, he felt the ring land softly on his tongue. It was cool. There was no hissing of burning tongue, no smell of seared flesh. There was no pain. There was coolness in his mouth and an awed silence in the great Hall.

The old priest stared in reverence and hesitatingly lifted the ring in his bare hands, turning it over and over, rubbing it on his cheeks to demonstrate to all assembled that it was not hot.

And holding the ring aloft with both hands, high above his white head, the old priest loudly exclaimed, *"Ecce Signum!* Behold the sign! Behold the proof! Behold the truth! Behold! The Ring of Solomon!"

And in unison, the response from the Members assembled: "Behold! The Ring of Solomon!"

Slowly, the High Priest reclaimed his throne as unseen Brothers helped Mycroft to his feet.

Ishmael, overcome with what he had just observed and the remarkable faith and courage of the man he had led to this point, quickly leaned over and kissed Mycroft on both cheeks.

The High Priest softly addressed himself to Mycroft: "You have proven yourself well, my Brother. Pray, tell us, how we may render assistance unto you."

34

▼

THERE was no possible way for Christie to know she was being followed. The man in the safari jacket, close on her trail, was never in sight. For that matter, after having left the bar, Christie was never in his sight, either. But still he knew which way she walked and up or down which streets she turned.

Had he seen her, he would immediately have noticed that she appeared to be a person who walked with a purpose. But, of course, he surmised as much anyway, merely from the speed of her gait.

For his part, he merely stayed as much in the shadows as possible, his eyesight riveted almost exclusively to a small device on his left wrist that in an instant, could be converted back into a simple, harmless wristwatch. His right hand, however, kept firmly implanted in his right ear what any unsuspecting person might easily mistake for a hearing aid. Between these two unobtrusive-looking instruments, the man in the safari jacket was quite capable of following Christie without her being aware of it.

Every so often, the man would reach up to his face to suppress an itch, each time being unconsciously surprised to find a full beard there. Then remembering it was only a hastily applied disguise, he would pat all around it to make certain the spirit gum still held it tightly in place.

After walking a while, the man stopped, puzzled by a sound he picked up in his right ear. It was the sound of someone knocking on a door, and then the door opened. He quickened his pace as he heard footsteps—two sets of footsteps, he was certain—climbing a short staircase.

He continued on and turned a corner ahead of him and walked past the small house that his left wrist clearly identified as the building Christie had just entered. He walked to the end of the block, found a hidden recess in a doorway, and waited out of sight.

He heard voices and pressed the earpiece closer to his ear. He could make out the sound of Christie's voice, but not all her words.

The walls of the old building she was in probably contained some metal, the eavesdropper thought. This would explain why her voice faded in and out and came across garbled. He was slightly familiar with the language being spoken and—even with the interference—was able to hear enough to know that she was talking to more than one man. Two. No, three. Definitely, three men.

They were raising their voices. No, *she* was raising her voice. Yes. She was angry. Very angry. They were telling her something that displeased her apparently. There was one man who did most of the talking for the men. He was not raising his voice but his voice was firm.

Yes, the eavesdropper thought, he is giving her instructions and she is unhappy.

Now, she was livid. Screaming. Hollering. Something fell over and crashed. No, something was *thrown*. Thrown in anger and smashed against a wall. Something made of glass— an ashtray, a plate, something breakable—had been hurled by the woman.

Suddenly a door flew open and he heard her coming down the staircase and out onto the street. She was alone.

He pressed himself further into the dark shadows in the event she should walk past him, but his left wrist clearly told him that she was retracing her steps, presumably back to the hotel bar. He would have liked to have been across the street from that building when she emerged to see whether he could recognize any of her hosts, but that would have been impossible to do without being seen. He wanted to give her a few moments headstart before starting out again himself.

But as he was about to step out from the shadows, he heard footsteps coming down the street toward him. Quickly, he pressed his body back against the wall just before the footsteps passed in front of him.

There were three men. Whether they were the three men from the room or three Iranian foot soldiers on patrol, he couldn't tell. But even with the absence of light, or maybe because of it, his nose told him that one of the men—maybe all of them—could do with a good bath.

The footsteps passed. The man slipped quietly out of the shadows and turned left in the direction Christie had taken.

He followed her all the way back to the bar and, converting the instrument on his left wrist back into a watch, noted that she had been gone exactly one hour.

35

MYCROFT, gratefully reunited with the rest of his clothes, was feeling more comfortable than he had in the two hours it had taken him to undergo the complex catechism. He sat inside of the sanctum sanctorum with Ishmael, the old priest, whose name he learned was Hashemi Nabavi, and four other members of the Iranian Lodge of Masters.

Mycroft had finished his story and the group sat in silence drinking tea and waiting for the priest to offer some sort of comment. Hashemi, however, merely stroked his beard and appeared to meditate through half-closed eyes. Ahmad Zadeh, who it turned out was Ishmael's younger brother, sat on Mycroft's right and thoughtfully puffed away on a Turkish cigarette, filling the confines of the small room with a rather putrid odor. He had a young boyish face but very dark and very intense eyes that belied his age.

"Just a few questions please, Brother Mycroft," Hashemi said quietly, with his eyelids still almost covering the whites of his eyes, "just to make certain we did not misunderstand anything you said. To begin with, there is no doubt at all that the Hailing Sign was given by the young Brother Sinclair?"

"No, Your Excellency, there is no doubt."

"In this room, 'Hashemi' will do."

"Thank you . . . Hashemi."

"The Hailing Sign indicates that his life is in danger. However, that does not fit in with certain other information we have received. Ahmad, would you please explain to our Brother?"

Ahmad took his time answering, still chewing on the end of his cigarette: "Brother Mycroft, this may be difficult for you to understand, but it is important that we try to explain certain political facts to you. This country is made up of many, many different groups—factions, if you please—different religious and ideological sects. It is not as simple as your country's Republican and Democratic political parties. No, it is much more diverse and complex. In this room right now, there are men of sharply opposing political and religious points of view, which, in a country where church and state are one and the same, makes life dangerous as well as merely awkward. However, as Brothers of the Craft, we put our political differences aside when we enter a Lodge. We do not bring politics inside of a Lodge. These subjects, as well as any offensive or defensive objects that may mar our harmony and good order, are deposited on the doorstep. Can you appreciate that?"

"Of course. It is the same in my Lodge, too, as I believe it is in most other Lodges throughout the world."

"True. Yes, true. But, you see, your country is not engaged in an internal revolutionary struggle as we are. For you to put politics aside when you enter your Lodge is merely to forget for a few hours which politician is running for office. Politics in your country is not something over which men shed blood. For *us* to put politics aside, even for an evening, is truly a remarkable accomplishment. But it *must* be done or the Lodge and its work will fail."

"Yes," Mycroft replied thoughtfully. "I see what you mean."

"My Brother, in this room," Ahmad continued, "there are those who despise the United States—who despise the former Shah—who think the taking of American hostages makes sense—and who truly believe in the Revolution. I am one of those."

Mycroft was genuinely surprised but did not show it.

"And then there are those who are of just the opposite thinking—who believe the Shah was good for this country—who believe we would not have grown so much economically without the aid of the United States and the oil companies—and who think the taking of hostages is cruel. My brother, Ishmael, is one of those."

Ishmael did not speak nor did he even look toward his brother. Mycroft was about to interject a thought, but Ahmad continued.

"I, myself," he said, "have been to the embassy many times. I am not a guard, not a soldier; more of what you might term an 'adviser.' I will submit to you that early on there was some physical abuse of some of the hostages—abuse such as keeping them tied for lengthy periods of time, keeping them isolated from their peers, and so on. I am not aware, however, of any instances of physical harm where any of the hostages' lives have been in danger. *Never!*"

"Perhaps," Mycroft interrupted politely, "some of your actions may have been misinterpreted by the hostages. *You* may know that you will never kill a hostage—if I may use that as an extreme example—*but do the hostages know it?*" He had raised his voice somewhat and regretted it. He knew this was a painfully uncomfortable subject for all of them—most of all, no doubt, for Ahmad.

"This may be," Ahmad replied slowly. "This may be. I have been trying to see in my mind if something such as this may be the case. I know that, in the beginning of the take-over, the bondage was necessary because we were so out-numbered and unorganized. We could have been overtaken easily. We kept the hostages separate as best we could to discourage thoughts about attacking and overpowering us. But what you say may be true; yes, this may be." He paused to light another cigarette and sip from his glass of tea before continuing.

"There, too, is the possibility, I will concede," Ahmad offered, "that there are goings-on in the American Embassy that are unknown even to me. If this is the case, I would be very distressed. I assure you that the takeover of the embassy was not planned as such. No, it was to be a demonstration; but, well, events eluded our control, so to speak." He shrugged his shoulders in a gesture of helplessness.

"I believe that," Mycroft interjected. "You have been very candid with me, so let me, in turn, make a concession to you. I will concede the possibility that Brother Sinclair, being young and understandably nervous, threw the Hailing Sign without fully realizing its consequences and without his life actually being in jeopardy. He was, after all, a Brother of the Craft a mere six months at the time of the embassy takeover."

Hashemi sat up a little, encouraged by Mycroft's statement. "Do you think that is a possibility? It would explain much if such was the case."

"I cannot say, Hashemi. But I do know that my Obligation is clear, as all of you well know." Mycroft moved his hand around to indicate his Brethren in the room. "And my Obligation to his father is also strong. He is a good friend, not only a Brother. I learned little more than a week ago that he is terminally ill and wants desperately to see his only son before he dies. Truthfully, I'm not sure if he is even alive right now. Shortly before I departed the United States, John Sinclair suffered a heart attack and was rushed to a hospital."

"You need not explain your Obligation," Hashemi said in the voice and demeanor of the High Priest. "We understand fully. And our Obligation to assist you is equally strong."

"I would like to say a few words." It was Ishmael, who had remained silent ever since the group had adjourned into the sanctum sanctorum. "My brother, Ahmad, has already explained to you how I feel about the hostage taking. I think it is cruel to make innocent people suffer, especially when anyone with an ounce of intelligence knows that the United States is not going to return the Shah." He was looking at Ahmad as he spoke but still kept his voice under control. "I am not pleased with Khomeini. I was not in favor of the Revolution. I am not in favor of what has transpired these past few months. The hostages, the daily demonstrations, it makes me ill." He pretended to spit on the floor—which he would never do in the sanctum sanctorum—to emphasize his point. "But, I most of all do not wish to see anyone get hurt or killed. Not the Americans, not the students. What is needed here is a suitable compromise solution."

"And *you* have one, Ishmael?" Ahmad asked sarcastically.

"Perhaps. I have been giving this matter some thought; hear me out. We are all agreed that if the Hailing Sign was thrown, our response to that plea *must* transcend all political and religious considerations. True?" They all nodded. "But how do we know the Hailing Sign was genuine. Oh, I don't question you, Brother Mycroft. I only meant, as you yourself suggested, perhaps the sign was thrown in haste. This could also be true, yes?" Again, all nodded agreement. "Especially if what Ahmad has said he believes—that the hostages are not being mistreated or threatened—is true.

"So, who to believe?" Ishmael continued slowly.

"If the Hailing Sign was given," the High Priest immediately decreed authoritatively, "we are duty bound to assist Brother Mycroft in saving a Brother's life."

"But," Ishmael went on, now directing his question at Mycroft, "what do *you* do, my Brother, if the Hailing Sign *was* thrown in haste—and if the young Brother Sinclair's life is not in danger?"

"I—I honestly hadn't considered that," Mycroft replied.

"Well," Ishmael countered, "let me ask you pointedly: If you were assured—beyond any doubt—that Brother Sinclair was no more than, say, inconvenienced—as opposed to being in a life-threatening situation—would you leave Iran and report back to his father that his son is safe?"

"At one time, I believe I would have said yes; but now I'm not certain. Please remember, Ishmael—all of you—that five men have already lost their lives since my mission began. One of those men was also a Brother, and he was killed even before I actually decided to come to Iran. Someone, or some group, has been trying to stop me. I have come so far, I honestly don't know if I could just walk away."

Ahmad sat forward slightly and said, "I, for one, know that the CIA is trying to stop you. I was told earlier today that the students and the soldiers at the embassy were warned about you—warned that you may try to break into the embassy. Your picture was shown around but no mention was made of young Brother Sinclair."

"Yes, I expected as much after the incident at the demonstration," Mycroft said. "But I do not believe the CIA murdered Bill Gregory, the Deacon. Nor do I think they left sick messages for me. No, the CIA is undoubtedly trying to stop me for their own reasons. There is still someone else."

"Let us get back to the subject of young Brother Sinclair," Ishmael said, slightly annoyed to have had his thoughts of a compromise interrupted. "Ahmad, you said that the students are prepared in the event Brother Mycroft tries to break into the embassy. That is just the sort of incident we would like to avoid—a break-in, a shooting, a killing. No, a break-in is totally out of the question, although I do think it is imperative for Brother Mycroft to be able to visit and speak with the young Brother Sinclair."

"And how do you propose that be accomplished?" Hashemi wanted to know.

Here Ishmael allowed himself the luxury of a broad smile as he prepared to finally speak his compromise. "It is quite simple, Hashemi. We merely take Brother Mycroft into the embassy."

"How could this be done?" Hashemi asked Ishmael.

"Ahmad could take him in," Ishmael spoke quietly. "Other outsiders have been admitted. Clergy have visited there recently. And Ahmad is, as he said, an 'adviser.' He can come and go as he pleases. Surely, if my younger brother put his mind to it, he could find a way."

"Before you answer, Ahmad," Hashemi cautioned, "remember our Obligation to Brother Mycroft. He has proven himself well and we must assist him if we can. And remember, too, what we are taught in the Koran"—the old priest closed his eyes as he recited: " 'And if any shall demand protection of thee, grant him protection, that he may hear the word of the Prophet, and afterward give him a safe conduct, that he may return home again securely.' Ahmad, is what Ishmael suggests possible?"

"Yes, yes," Ahmad responded. "Of course it is *possible* but nonetheless dangerous. Yes, I am an adviser, but there are others who hold the real power—men like Rachmon Hassan. He would never agree to such a visit."

"Then I suggest we do not take Rachmon Hassan into our confidences," Hashemi said simply.

"You mean *sneak* Brother Mycroft into the embassy? If we were caught, Hassan would hold Brother Mycroft hostage, and me as well, I'm sure."

"Then I suggest we do not get caught," said Ishmael.

" 'We?' " Ahmad looked at his brother in disbelief.

"Well, yes," Ishmael offered. "I thought that since it was my idea I should bear a portion of the risk. I am willing to go along."

"That I would love to see!" Ahmad laughed. "My older, complacent brother taking a chance, risking his well-ordered life. To see that, it would almost be worth risking my own life."

"*Enough!*" Hashemi spoke sharply. "Ahmad, we are waiting for your response. Can what Ishmael suggests be done? And will you assist our Brother?"

"I will agree. And may Allah forgive me."

"It is settled then!" Ishmael's smile returned, broader than ever. "How shall it be accomplished?"

"I will require some time to prepare," Ahmad said. "I suggest the three of us meet back here tomorrow night, at midnight. And come prepared for a long night."

As Ishmael and Ahmad escorted Alex safely back to the bar to pick up Christie, and then to deposit them both in a safe house for the next twenty-four hours, Mycroft said softly, "I know this isn't easy for you, Ahmad, and I want to thank you for your assistance."

"Do not thank me yet, my Brother, for you overlook one important detail. Even if we do remove the young Brother Sinclair from the embassy tomorrow night, there will still be the matter of you and he fleeing the country safely."

36

BLAKE was growing impatient as he listened to Hassan screaming into the phone. He didn't understand what was being said, but he didn't have to be multilingual or fluent in Farsi to know that some underling was getting his ass chewed out.

It was early in the morning and neither Blake nor Hassan had slept the night before. They alternately drove and walked the streets of Tehran, Hassan questioning his men on patrol as well as any private citizens who were foolish enough to be out on the street after curfew. Hassan had been rough on his men but even rougher on the citizens.

Blake was irritable, too, but he had expected to be until the job was done. His ulcer was acting up again to boot.

Evidently Hassan had thought finding Mycroft would be a cinch, but Blake knew Mycroft too well. When it came to losing yourself in a city, there were few better than Alexander Mycroft. More years ago than Blake cared to remember—before he left Military Intelligence for the CIA—Mycroft had been his teacher. And, at one time, his friend.

What puzzled Blake, however, was the fact that he knew instinctively that someone in Tehran was helping Mycroft. Someone local. The poser was *who*. He tried to raise various possibilities of finding the connection with Hassan but to no avail. Hassan was too stubborn to even listen.

In a little while, he'd have to phone Langley again to give a less than exemplary progress report, and the thought of it made him even more irritable. He was not accustomed to failure.

Blake was rummaging around in his pockets for a cigarette, which he couldn't find, when Hassan finally slammed down the phone in disgust.

"I don't suppose all that hollering and screaming means good news for our side," said Blake sarcastically, forgetting for a moment that he and Hassan were not actually on the same side, despite the fact that necessity compelled them to work together temporarily.

"Your friend, Mycroft, is brazen, this much I now know."

"Yeah, well, I told you that before. We're not exactly dealing here with a quivering mass of Jell-O, you know. What happened?"

"First, we now have reason to believe that the girl spent a good part of last night in the Intercontinental Hotel bar. Right out in the open! Can you believe that?"

"Sure, it was probably Mycroft's idea. You always hide where people are least likely to look for you. Besides, we know they've got forged press credentials; the hotel bar swarming with reporters was a smart move. Shit, if Mycroft had had the time, he would have gotten the girl a job as the old Ayotollah's secretary, and he would have applied for the position of bodyguard. How about Mycroft, was he with her?"

"We don't think so," Hassan said.

"And what do you hear from the embassy?" Blake asked.

"Nothing. The guard was increased but there was no activity. No one got in; no one tried. It is impossible to get inside the embassy. If your Mr. Mycroft is so smart, surely he must realize that by now. He would not be so foolish to actually try to get into the embassy."

"Hassan, I'll just tell you once more: Mycroft's nobody's fool. That means that he'll *find* a way to get in—a way we haven't thought of. He already knows the element of surprise has been taken away from him. But it might be better for us if he didn't know that. Then maybe he'd try something crazy and we'd nab him. But after that business at the demonstration, he not only knows I'm after him but he knows you are, too. That makes me nervous. And if you had any br—, any sense, it'd scare the shit out of you, too."

"So what do you suggest?"

"You said it yourself: Mycroft's brazen all right. He may very well be wandering the streets right now, but I doubt we'll find him that way. First, I suggest we don't waste any more valuable manpower, including ourselves, searching the streets. Secondly, since we know his ultimate goal is to reach the Sinclair kid, I suggest we beef up the security inside the embassy, especially around Sinclair. And third, since the most logical time to try to get into the embassy is after dark, I suggest we assume Mycroft'll try to waltz right in in broad daylight."

"In broad daylight? It is not possible."

"You and I think it's impossible, but only because we haven't figured out a way to do it. I'm telling you, Hassan, I *know* this guy. He'll try to get into the embassy in broad daylight, right under our noses."

"But how?"

"What the hell's the difference how? Forget how. Let him get in. What's the big deal? But when he tries to get to Sinclair, we'll be waiting for him. In fact, if we really want to get this thing over with soon, let's make it easier for him. Pull back the guards at the gate. Not all of them; otherwise he'd suspect something. Just thin out the outer guards enough so that he'd *try* to get in that way—*and make it!*"

Hassan mulled it over and smiled at Blake. "You are really quite devious, aren't you?"

Blake returned the smile and accepted the compliment as it was intended. "I've been in this business a lot longer than you, Hassan. I'm not guaranteeing it'll work, but I think it makes sense. It's worth a shot."

"I will order the outside guards thinned out, as you say, and move them inside, nearer to Corporal Sinclair. But as to abandoning the search on the streets, no. That I say we should continue."

"Well, if it's all the same to you, you go ahead and waste your time looking on the streets. I've got to check in with my boss. Say we meet back her in a couple of hours?"

"Until then."

The voice on the other end of the scrambler was clear, so clear that Blake could easily detect the sleepiness in Langley's voice. He glanced at his watch, trying unsuccessfully to calculate the time back home. He was never good at doing that in his head, but he realized it was still the middle of the night in Virginia.

"Problems, Otis?" The southern drawl was more pronounced through a stifled yawn.

"Minor setbacks, sir," Blake replied while almost swallowing a cigarette and lighting an antacid tablet. He threw them both away and started all over.

"Are you able to take corrective measures?"

"It's very difficult with the Iranians, sir. It wasn't until just this morning that I was able to convince them what kind of man Mycroft is. They were taking him lightly, I'm afraid."

"Yes, that would account for the incident at the demonstration. But what *progress*, Otis?"

"If you can call this progress, I managed—I think—to convince Hassan that Mycroft is capable of getting into the embassy. He thinks it's an impregnable fortress."

The southern voice allowed itself a sardonic chuckle. "Oh, Otis, how naive of them. If only our value of human life weren't quite so high, we could have crushed them on November 5th. Pity."

Blake wasn't sure if the 'pity' referred to the high value placed on human life or the Iranians' naiveté, but he continued. "Hassan's agreed to pull back some of the guards to make it even easier for Mycroft to get inside. I figure the best place to nail him is inside the embassy when he goes for the Sinclair kid."

"Yes, you may be right. By the way, we've put some of our best people, and our best computers, on Mycroft's file to try to figure out how he may do it. He may be a creature of habit and try to duplicate a mission from his past. Have you ever read his file, Otis? He's really done some remarkable things in his career."

"Yes, sir. I've read it."

"He makes a worthy adversary, doesn't he, Otis? Anyway, we think a daylight break-in may be likely."

"I've already considered that possibility, sir. Hassan's briefing his men now."

"Good, Otis, good. I'll brief the White House tomorrow—well, later this morning, actually."

"How about the girl? Have you been able to ID her?" Blake asked Langley.

"The photo wasn't a very good likeness, as you know, but it does fit the general description of John Sinclair's older daughter."

"What does Sinclair say?"

"Ah, yes. Mr. Sinclair. Well, Otis, Mr. Sinclair doesn't have much to say these days."

"Christ! Did the poor old guy die?"

"We think not. But he did, apparently, leave the hospital without permission. We haven't yet been able to track him down."

"How about his daughter, Christie? Have you located her?"

"No, Otis, we haven't. Not yet."

"So you're saying that the girl with Mycroft could actually be Sinclair's daughter. Is that it?"

"Yes, Otis. So be careful and try not to get her killed. Anything else for the report, Otis?"

Blake decided there was no point in bringing up the the screw-up in the Intercontinental Hotel bar. "No, sir. Nothing else."

"Oh, one more thing, Otis. The White House feels there's a good chance of this blowing up in our face no matter what happens. The best way to prevent that is to see that Mycroft not only fails but that he doesn't leave Iran."

Blake didn't like what he thought he was hearing and neither did his ulcer. "But what if he snatches the kid?"

"See that he doesn't, Otis."

Blake swallowed hard. "And if he does?"

"He'll still have to get out of the country. See that he *doesn't*."

"You mean actually turn him over to the Iranians?"

"Oh, no, Otis. Colonel Mycroft deserves a better fate than that. Liquidate him, Otis. Before, during, or after whatever may happen at the embassy. Do I make myself clear?"

Blake could feel a cramp developing in his right hand from gripping the phone so tightly, and his stomach felt like a volcano had just erupted inside. "And how about Sinclair?"

"*If* Mycroft gets Corporal Sinclair out, see that you put him back in."

"*Back in?*"

"Yes, Otis. It could prove, uh, embarrassing otherwise. We can make sure that Corporal Sinclair doesn't go blabbing about any of this later on, or that if he does, no one will believe him. So if he gets out, you put him back. Do I make myself clear?"

"Yes, dammit. Perfectly clear."

37

Beirut

THE dusty black phone in the rear of the café jangled, and the robed man on the divan lowered his glass of tea and answered it without speaking.

"Es Selamu Aleikum," came Moussef's distant voice through the poor telephone connection.

"Aleikum Es Selamu. Where are you?"

"Tehran."

"It is over?"

"No. It begins."

"Soon?"

"A day or two at most. But it will happen and it will happen soon. I have been told."

"And the girl? You gave her her instructions? How did she respond?"

Moussef put a hand up to touch the scar on his face, which was the result of a recent mishap with a flying plate. "She was unhappy, as you expected. She did not take the instructions well. She wants nothing more than to kill Mycroft. She longs only to cut out his heart for what he did to her years ago."

The meaty hand of the robed man swatted his glass of tea against the wall. "Washington warned me that she was unstable, but I told them she would be perfect. She must know how much is at stake, both with our relations with Iran and our dealings with the United States. The friendlier we can appear to the Americans, the more we can undermine the sympathies for Israel. Doesn't she understand the importance of trading Mycroft's son for an American hostage? Doesn't she know how valuable that could be to us in negotiations? If we had the American but no one knew, and then we were able to free him, the Americans would be more receptive to us."

Moussef could smell the hot tea breath coming through the telephone lines and could feel the anger that he thought was directed at him. The cold Iranian air did not prevent beads of sweat from forming on his forehead. "She—she *does* understand. I—I have told her."

"She doesn't have to like her orders, just obey them. Will she?"

"I think so, yes," Moussef replied. "But to a point. Clearly, her first priority is not ours. She wants Mycroft dead. No, *more* than dead. She wants to kill him herself. Slowly. Painfully." The thought brought a sharp pain to Moussef's groin and made him shudder.

The robed man shrugged into the phone. "She can have Mycroft afterward. He will be of no use to us then. Tell her again if you have to! *After* the rescue, then *after* the trade, Mycroft is hers to do with as she pleases. But not before."

Moussef breathed more easily. "As long as she believes that she can serve our needs and still fulfill her own, she will comply. But what if Mycroft frees the Sinclair hostage but will not then trade for his son?"

"Then we will have misjudged a father's love for his son and be forced to kill Mycroft and Sinclair."

"The girl asked if Mycroft's son is really alive."

"Who knows? Does it matter? We have made Mycroft *think* he is alive. That is all that matters. When we trade, we will give Mycroft a boy of the right age and color, whose tongue we will cut out. But that is not your concern. See that you are prepared for your assignments."

"I hear and I obey."

38

Tehran

THE sounds Christie was making in the tiny roach-infested kitchenette awoke Alex from a deep sleep on a hard chair. He got his bearings quickly and surveyed the cramped bedroom of the one-story house that Ismael and Ahmad had provided for them.

The single mattress, lumpy but basically clean, boasted only one white sheet serving as a coverlet. Christie had opted to leave the sheet under her as an extra measure of cleanliness, and Alex thought his best bet was on the lone chair rather than the floor. A small four-drawer dresser, minus one drawer entirely and all the handles from the rest, completed the room's furnishings.

The bathroom had reminded Alex of the many gas station

restrooms he had been forced to use over the years; rust-spotted sink, a similarly encrusted toilet, and one lone moth-eaten towel. The bathroom had no tub or shower stall, but it did have a leaky rubber hose that could be attached to the sink's faucet. There was a corroded drain hole in the floor.

Neither Ismael nor Ahmad had offered to tell them whose house they were occupying, and Alex had been unable to find any clothes or other personal effects to give them a clue.

When he exited the bedroom, he found Christie, wearing only a white T-shirt and bikini panties, stooped over in the kitchen area retrieving a pot she had dropped.

"Oh, I'm sorry. I woke you, didn't I?"

"No, not really," he lied, as he found himself consciously averting his gaze from her, somewhat embarrassed to have stumbled upon her in such a state of undress. This was certainly not like him and his feelings baffled him. "What are you up to?"

"I thought I would try to rustle up some breakfast"—she glanced at his watch—"or lunch, but I'm afraid there's not much here in the way of provisions. All I've located is some stale pita bread and tea."

"Tea sounds fine. Can you manage all right?"

"Oh, sure. Sit down and I'll bring it over."

They sipped their tea and Christie asked, "What are the plans for today? When will I be able to see Lee?"

"With luck, Christie, tonight."

She jumped up from the table in excitement. "Really? This is wonderful. Why didn't you tell me last night?"

"It's not definite. But I'm pretty certain that I'll get to see Lee tonight and, if my suspicions are correct, I won't be leaving the embassy without him."

She came over to his side of the table and hugged him

warmly. "Oh, Alex, this is too good to be true. Tonight, it will *all* be over."

Mycroft's mind was awhirl with thoughts and most prominent among them was why he inwardly recoiled when she approached him so suddenly. He was having a difficult time of late with his thoughts about her.

"Just don't get your hopes up too high," he cautioned as he sensed her excitement. "Tell me about Lee, Christie. You know, I really know very little about him."

"Oh, Alex," she said, breaking into a tender smile. "It was just the two of us kids growing up and even though I'm older, he was my protector." She walked over and sat down on the green couch. "We've been so close over the years and when this craziness started, it just about drove me nuts with worry that something might happen to him."

Mycroft got up and joined her on the sofa.

"That's why I was so upset when I learned what you were going to try to do," she continued, "and why I wanted to stop you. But now that we're here and we're so close to seeing Lee, I can hardly believe it."

Alex could sense that she would continue talking if he asked her to but that she'd rather change the subject. He complied.

"How did things go at the Intercontinental last night?"

"It was pretty much like you predicted: a lot of reporters. Most were drunk, some were hitting on me."

He stole a peek at the spot where the white of her thighs disappeared under the elastic of her panties. "I can understand that. But did you learn anything?"

It was as though she was reading his mind. She crossed and uncrossed her legs, and then repositioned herself on the couch closer to him. "It seems there was a news blackout of some kind yesterday. None of the television, radio, or newspaper reporters were able to report on the craziness at the demonstration where you were being chased."

He felt uncomfortable and shifted his position slightly away from her, and also made a conscious effort to avert his gaze. This is silly, he thought: I feel like a teenager on a first date. What the hell is the matter with me? Have I suddenly gotten shy? Bashful? Stupid?

"You mean it was an Iranian news blackout?" he asked.

"That's what I understand. One of the TV reporters I spoke to said the Iranians pulled the plug on him when he tried to send a story to the States via satellite."

"I guess that confirms that the Iranians know what we're up to, especially if they go to the trouble to issue a news blackout. Do you know if any reporters got any stories through?"

"I didn't hear of any, but that doesn't mean they didn't. Oh, wait; I did hear somebody say that someone had managed to smuggle out some videotape, but the network wouldn't air it."

"And *that* sounds like White House pressure."

"They were also talking about a rumor going around that either all of the reporters, or maybe just the Americans, might be kicked out of the country soon. But someone else said that that's just the usual type of rumor that makes the rounds in all countries experiencing a revolution."

"Well, whatever happens with the reporters, there's nothing we can do about it. In fact, there's nothing to do about anything except wait until tonight."

She moved closer and put her head on his shoulder. Lowering her hand to the upper part of his thigh, she began to almost casually run her fingernails up and down his leg.

"You know, Alex," she cooed, "if there is nothing to do but wait, we should make the most of the time we have together. You're a very attractive man and there are so very many ways—exciting ways—that I'd love to get to know you better."

Mycroft's ambivalence was bothering him. He was in the presence of the most beautiful woman he'd ever known and he could recall how aroused he'd been when he first saw her through the two-way mirror at the Mossad safe house in Jaffa. But that was from a distance and through a barrier. Now she was caressing him through his rumpled pants and sex was the last thing on his mind. "Never be diverted, men" echoed in his ear. But, no; it wasn't that.

She was still whispering about all the ways of love while she unzipped his fly and buckle and began to fondle his limp penis.

He then thought of Beth, and casually touched his shirt pocket to make certain that his glass tube was still there. But no; it wasn't Beth that was troubling him. Nor was it Josh. He'd certainly had sex in the past six years; plenty of it, too. So he reasoned that it was not the thought of his wife and son that kept him flaccid.

She was stroking the underside of his cock with her finger-nails, telling the sort of lies that make men feel good and powerful and strong. "Oh, your prick is so beautiful. Oh, I can't wait to see it grow. To *make* it grow. To take it in my mouth and—"

He tuned her voice out and thought of Avi Blume. The Mossad agent was not infallible, he knew; but that famed Jewish nose of his was right most of the time. At first, Avi had been wary of Christie, only to confess later that he was unable to find anything or anyone who could give support to his suspicions. And then when Alex had suggested Christie go home, Avi got visibly agitated at the thought of them splitting up. Avi's words came back to him: "By keeping her with you at all times, there may be danger but at least you'll be able to watch out for her. She *must* stay with you for safety's sake."

Alex had first thought it to be a warning for him, but then Avi had given Christie that lovely mezuzah which she was still wearing around her smooth neck. Maybe that was Avi's way of saying he was sorry and that his words were not a warning for Alex, but just an admonition to keep Christie— the sister of a Brother—safe.

But then Avi's other words came back to him—that Alex should stop thinking with his prick. He knew that hundreds of times in the past he had certainly been guilty of doing just that. But if that was true this time, why was he still soft? Was it because this time—for the first time—he was thinking with his mind instead?

Christie stood up in front of him and stripped off her T-shirt. Mycroft had never seen such perfection but his penis apparently was not looking.

"Oh, Alex, I know so many ways to make you feel good." She blew the words toward him on a cloud of sensuality. "So many ways to make you feel happy." She dropped to her knees in front of his lap and took him into her mouth. The sensation was all-consuming.

Something else Avi had said to him: Trust your instincts. You used to be one of the best, Avi had said to him. What the hell were his instincts telling him now? The only thing Mycroft sensed was that the more time he spent with Christie, the less attracted he felt to her. But there was another emotion growing within him in place of love or sexual attraction. It was . . . *fear*.

His body tightened and jerked with self-realization. He was actually becoming frightened of her. But *why?*

"Oh, Alex, relax, my sweet. You're so tense. Just relax your body and let me help you release your own power."

Mycroft reclined on the couch, but his mind raced through the recesses of his dark memory.

39

▼

—January 5, 1980

ISHMAEL, having picked up Alex at the house, was silent for the first part of the drive to meet Ahmad at the Temple. He drove slowly through the mostly deserted streets, not wishing to attract any attention.

"They discovered your former room," Ishmael said quietly.

"How did you hear?"

Ishmael shrugged his shoulders and waved his right hand in the air. "Oh, the grapevine, you could say. They left a few men there to stand guard in case you returned. Did you leave anything of importance behind?"

"Nothing that can't be replaced."

They continued in silence for a short while and then

Ishmael said, "Ahmad is right, you know. Leaving the country, with or without young Brother Sinclair, will be next to impossible. Have you given thought to this matter?"

"Yes, Ishmael, I have given it a lot of thought and there may be a way," he replied evasively. "But I prefer to take things one step at a time. And the first step is tonight. Have you spoken to Ahmad today?"

"Yes, and to answer your unasked question, he is very, very nervous. But he will perform. The Obligation demands it."

"And you, Ishmael? Are you nervous, too?"

"Of course, my friend," he laughed slightly. "Truthfully, I am petrified."

"I'm glad to hear that. I never did like going on missions with people who knew no fear. They were always the ones to make mistakes—usually costly mistakes."

"Ah, so that means you, too, have fears about tonight?"

"Yes, Ishmael. I, too, have fears. I have fears about Ahmad, first of all. Oh, I'm sure he'll get us in, but I think he'll panic when I go to take Sinclair with me."

"But what if Sinclair hasn't been mistreated? How about what you said last night to Ahmad? Did you lie?"

"Not really. You see Ahmad honestly does not believe that any of the hostages have been mistreated. For that reason, he readily agreed to help me spring Sinclair if Sinclair *was* being mistreated. Ahmad doesn't think he can lose, and I pity him his rude awakening. But you see, Ishmael, I've spent time as a hostage myself and I *know* Sinclair's been mistreated, if only by being denied his freedom. He may not have been beaten—that remains to be seen—but psychological scars are often the worst scars of all. Physical wounds heal; mental wounds can bleed forever. And on this subject, Ishmael, I speak from experience."

They exchanged glances briefly, but Ishmael quickly returned his eyes to the road ahead. "What other fears do you have about tonight?"

"Blake, the CIA agent who has been after me since day one."

"Yes, but you've successfully avoided him so far."

" 'So far.' That's the operative phrase. I know Blake and I know pretty much how he thinks. Most spies have the same kind of mentality."

"Do you speak from experience here, too?"

Alex smiled in the darkened car. "Yes, Ishmael. From *too* much experience. If Blake is after me, he has to know I'm after Sinclair. If I've managed to elude him so far, it only means that he'll pull back his forces and wait for me at the goal line."

"The 'goal line'?"

"Meaning at the *end* of the line. In this case, at Sinclair. Sinclair *is* the end of the line. I wouldn't be surprised if we walked into the embassy tonight and found Blake waiting for us. The fact that he seems to be working with the Revolutionary forces only means that he could easily gain access to the embassy. Yep, that's what I'd do if I were Blake: pull up a cozy little seat in Sinclair's quarters, make myself as comfortable as possible, and wait. Just wait."

"But what will we do if this happens? What do we do if this Blake *is* waiting for us?"

"Well, let's just say that that's one of the things that scares me about tonight."

Just then they arrived at their destination. Ishmael parked his car about a block from the alleyway entrance to the Temple, but when they reached the door of the Temple, Ahmad was not in sight.

"Are we early?"

"No," Ishmael replied looking at an antique gold pocket watch. "If anything we are a few minutes late. It is just past midnight. But have faith; Ahmad will be here."

And with those words, they were bathed in the glow of headlights turning the corner at the top of the alley. Quickly they both ducked back into the shadows provided by the recessed entrance to the closed Temple. They heard no sounds and realized the vehicle approaching was coasting with the engine off. When the headlights were extinguished, they peeked out to observe a truck coasting in relative silence toward their end of the alley. Finally it rolled to a stop and Ahmad jumped down from the driver's seat and looked around. He was dressed in an olive green military-type fatigue jacket and cap, and carried a rifle in his hand. Alex and Ishmael stepped out of the shadows to greet him.

"I am sorry to be late, but I had a small difficulty in obtaining the truck."

"Nice wheels, Ahmad," Alex said, taking a fast walk around the truck. It was a small military vehicle with a brown canvas top covering the flat payload area behind the small cab.

"This truck and me are our passage in and out of the embassy tonight. I have brought jackets, caps, scarves for your faces, and rifles." He reached into the cab and produced the named items. "What I propose is quite simple: I will drive us into the compound with Ishmael beside me. I do not think I will be stopped or questioned or the vehicle searched, but we can't take the chance of Brother Mycroft being spotted in the truck. If any of the guards say anything to Ishmael, well, he is after all Iranian and will be able to converse easily with them. You have no objections to this, my brother?"

"No," Ishmael replied. "That will be fine for me, but how about Brother Mycroft?"

Ahmad escorted them around to the rear of the truck. "There is a secret compartment here in the floor that we used to use to transport guns. It extends down into a false fuel tank but is big enough for two people"—he looked at Mycroft—"if necessary. Brother Mycroft will ride in there. Once we arrive at the embassy, however, we will remove him from the compartment and the three of us will make our way, as soldiers, to young Brother Sinclair. When we walk, you both will, of course, follow me. Brother Mycroft, you will pull the visor of your cap down as far as you can to hide your fair complexion. If asked, I will say you are a friend from Australia, and you do not speak Farsi. We will all place these scarves around our mouths like this." He demonstrated for them. "And, obviously, try not to speak. Let's go."

Alex climbed into the rear of the truck. "Ahmad, to the embassy, please."

Mycroft was unbearably cramped in the secret compartment beneath the truck's floorboards, but the fumes from the real gasoline tank were more troublesome. He hoped he would be able to avoid coughing or gagging, and placed the scarf over his nose and mouth to aid his breathing.

He held on tightly to the rifle, afraid a bump might discharge it accidently. He was unable to check the time, but it seemed to him that they were driving a long while. Actually, they arrived at the embassy gates in only fifteen minutes.

Mycroft overheard a conversation in Farsi that he assumed was between Ahmad and whomever was guarding the gate to the embassy. It apparently went smoothly. The gate swung open and, with a grinding of gears, the truck lurched forward and into the compound.

They didn't drive much further when Mycroft felt the truck stop and the engine shut off. He heard and felt both Ahmad and Ishmael get down from the cab, but at least five long nervous minutes elapsed before they came to claim him.

"The way is clear, Brother Mycroft. Are you all right?" There was a kindly and genuine concern in Ishmael's voice.

"Yeah, just help me up." They took his rifle and then his hands and lifted him together. "I can't say I'm thrilled about the great accommodations you guys have been providing me with lately."

"Shhh!" cautioned Ahmad. "Remember what I said: as little talking as possible. Come now, follow me closely."

Mycroft and Ishmael followed Ahmad's lead and shouldered their rifles. Ahmad left his face clear, but the other two encircled the lower portion of their faces with the scarves and tilted the brims of their caps down low over their eyes. Alex and Ishmael walked abreast of each other directly behind Ahmad.

Ahmad knocked on the door of the chancery and the door was unlocked and opened from within. He exchanged brief greetings with the guard at the door, then the three walked past him, through the reception area, and up the stairs to the second floor.

Everywhere he turned, Alex saw guards but no hostages. As they walked down the long corridor on the second floor, Alex saw only three guards seated in a makeshift lounge area about halfway down the hall. He assumed there were others on patrol.

Alex and Ishmael followed Ahmad to the lounge area. Here Ahmad exchanged greetings with the three guards.

"The blessings of Allah, Ahmad."

"And on you, my friends."

"Are you here because of the big rescue attempt?" The three soldiers laughed. "It is not like you to be dressed thusly, and a rifle, too!" Again they laughed. This time Ahmad joined in the laughter, followed by Ishmael. Mycroft smiled behind his scarf.

"So, you don't believe it either, eh?"

"No, Ahmad. Who could break in here?"

"Well, we did, for one."

"True, but the Americans were not expecting it. It was easy, was it not?" More jeers and laughter. Alex continued to smile benignly to keep the light of friendship in his eyes, though understanding not a word of what was being said.

"Yes, I know. But Hassan is such a worrier. He was afraid we did not have enough guards for this night. So look what he has dredged up." Ahmad made a self-deprecating gesture with his hands. "And I must admit, there was only one guard at the gate when we drove through."

"Ahmad, you have forgotten your manners. Who are your friends?"

"Forgive me. This is a friend of mine from school," he said, pointing to Ishmael, "Malek Nabavi." Ishmael nodded his head slightly. "And this," indicating Alex by touching his chest with the back of his hand so he would get the idea he was being introduced, "is an Australian friend who is sympathetic to our cause. This is Alan Jones." Alex heard his new name and nodded his head stiffly as Ishmael had done. "He does not speak Farsi," Ahmad added as he perceived Alex was about to be addressed.

Pointing to Alex's scarf and jacket, Ahmad said, "How do you like how we have dressed him up? Not bad, eh?"

They all laughed. "Ahmad, he could fit right in."

"That's the idea."

Alex tried to follow as much of the conversation's gist as he could. And although the talk seemed to be light banter, he could see beads of perspiration on Ahmad's forehead. Alex, too, was sweating, but most of it was caused by the scarf. And then without warning, the three guards got up and left, one of them dangling a large ring of keys from one hand.

"What's happening?" Alex whispered as softly as he could.

"I suggested they take a break from their studies," Ahmad replied. "I told them we'd take over for about fifteen minutes. Come on with me. We won't have much time."

Once again, Ishmael and Alex fell into step behind Ahmad and tried to act like sentries on parade. They passed one soldier, then another, who were walking the floors. Alex observed them going through a door marked EXIT and assumed they had other floors to patrol as well.

The three of them reached the end of the hall and stood nervously outside of a door.

"This is it," Ahmad whispered. "This is Brother Sinclair's room." He tried the door but it was locked, as expected.

Alex stepped up and examined the door closely. There were no dead-bolt locks, just a simple spring lock in the knob. The molding prevented Alex from using a plastic credit card to jimmy the lock. He reached into his back pocket and withdrew a small case containing an assortment of small picks. Quickly, he knelt down and started working on the lock.

"Hurry," hissed Ahmad.

"Don't rush me. I've almost got it."

Then, from the other side of the door, came, "Hey! What's going on! What are you bastards up to? Hey! HEY!"

"Sinclair?" Alex said as loud as he dared.

"Yeah. This is Sinclair. Who's that?"

"A friend. But for Christ's sake, shut up!"

Alex reapplied himself to the lock and in a minute more he turned the knob and opened the door cautiously. Given Mycroft's knowledge of Blake's method of operations, he was surprised to find the room empty save for Corporal Lee Sinclair, U.S.M.C., tied hard and fast to a chair in the middle of a very sparse room.

Sinclair just stared at Alex as he entered the room. Alex thought how much he resembled his father. Ahmad entered behind Alex, leaving Ishmael to stand guard alone outside the room. They closed the door behind them.

Alex immediately went to work on the rope as Ahmad stood by the door, listening.

"How you doing, Lee?"

"You—you're American? But your clothes. Wh—who are you?"

"I'm the shepherd's son you sent for, Lee, and a good friend of your Dad's."

Suddenly Lee started to cry. "Hey, don't do that," Alex said kindly. "I know you've been through an ordeal, son, but I've come to take you home. It's over."

Ahmad turned his head sharply and said, "Remember our agreement!"

"Look at this kid, Ahmad. Look at the bruises on his face. Look at the rope burns on his wrists. The circulation's been cut off. Look at him, Ahmad, and tell me he's not been mistreated. Tell me the kid's living the life of Riley."

Ishmael stuck his head in the door. "Shh! Keep it down but hurry up before someone comes." He closed the door behind him again.

"Did you throw the Hailing Sign?" Ahmad asked him.

His tears had subsided and he asked Mycroft, "Who's he? He's not American."

"He's a Brother of the Craft." Alex looked at Ahmad. "And a damned good friend. Answer his question."

"Yes. I threw it."

"Was your life really in danger?" Ahmad asked.

"Hell, yes. You want to hear about the fun these guys have with their tortures and their goddamn mock executions? Everyday it's something new."

"Mock executions?" Ahmad expressed genuine shock. "What do you mean?"

"They take some of us outside, line us up against a wall, and pretend they're going to kill us. Sometimes there are no bullets in the rifles, but they pull the trigger and it just goes 'click.' Other times they fire over our heads. I don't think they've killed anyone . . . yet. But it's a real barrel of laughs, let me tell you."

"Satisfied, Ahmad?"

"Alex, I didn't know. I swear." It was the first time he had used Mycroft's Christian name. Ahmad began to remove his fatigue jacket. "Here, start putting this on." He tossed it over to Lee.

Alex helped Lee to his feet, but the young boy just held onto the jacket, clutching it tightly between both hands, not moving to put it on.

"Come on, Lee. We haven't much time."

"You—you really came because I threw the Hailing Sign?"

"Yes, Lee. Really. Now stop wasting time. Come on, I'll help you."

"What's your name?"

"Alex. Alex Mycroft. Come on give me your arm."

Lee just stood there unmoving. "I've heard of you . . . from Dad."

Mycroft was getting exasperated at the delay. "That's wonderful. Your dad's told me a lot about you, too, Lee. Now, can we please get the hell out of here?"

"Yes, please!" pleaded Ishmael, who had just opened the door again. "I can hear every word out here. Hurry, for the love of Allah! *Hurry!*"

"Wh—where are you taking me?" Still he refused to put the jacket on.

"Alex, I think something is wrong," said Ahmad.

"I'm taking you to see your father, Lee. I'm taking you home."

He didn't really start to cry again, but still there were tears streaming down his face as he finally managed to say through quivering lips, "I—I can't go."

The only sound came from Ishmael opening the door once more. "Did I hear right? Allah have mercy on me!"

Neither Alex nor Ahmad could find any words. There was a stunned silence in the small room, and the only movement came from Sinclair's tears streaming down his freckled cheeks. Finally the young boy dropped to his knees and began to sob uncontrollably.

"Ishmael, quick! Return to your post," ordered Alex, who dropped to his knees and took the boy in his arms.

"Lee, Lee. It'll be all right. I know it will. Trust me," Alex said softly as he cradled the boy's head gently.

"You don't understand," he stammered between sobs. "I—I want to get out of here more than anything. But how c—can I leave everyone else behind? What will happen to *them* when the militants discover me missing?"

"Nothing will happen, my Brother. Please believe me," Ahmad said tenderly as he came over to the boy's side. "We—they—will not retaliate. They cannot afford to risk what might happen."

"Listen to him, Lee. He knows what he's talking about. Besides, you'll be more help to your friends on the outside."

"How?" Lee questioned as his composure gradually returned.

"First of all, it will give *them* some hope knowing someone managed to escape. And secondly, you have vital information about what's going on that the United States needs to know. They'll want to debrief you. It will help them, which means it will help your friends here. It may even help them get home sooner."

"Is that really true, Alex? Would my escaping really help the others?" Lee was quickly warming to the subject.

"Do you know that a couple of months ago the Iranians released thirteen women and blacks?"

"Yes, we heard about it. At first, though, we didn't believe it."

"How did you feel when you learned it was true?"

He thought for a moment. "Yeah, I see what you mean. I remember we all felt great for them. We wished we were *all* going along, naturally, but I remember thinking if these bastards released some of us, it meant that eventually we'd all be getting out."

"Well, that's what your leaving will mean to the others. But it'll probably mean even more."

"Why's that?"

"It's one thing to be released by your captors, but there is a certain bravado about an escape that gives all other prisoners courage to go on. I know, Lee. I've been there myself."

Ishmael stuck his head in the door again. "Please hurry, it's been almost fifteen minutes."

"Get dressed," Ahmad directed Lee. The young Brother started to comply.

"How's my Dad?" Lee asked.

"Your father's fine," Alex replied, not thinking this the time or the place to mention John Sinclair's heart attack. "And so is your sister. She's waiting to see you."

"My sister? Which one?"

"Christie. She's just a few minutes from the embassy."

"Christie is *here?* Wow! I can't believe it. How in the world—"

Ishmael rushed in. "The guards are returning. We cannot leave with the boy. It's too late."

Ahmad became alarmed. "What will we do? Alex, please. What should we do?"

Alex was silent for a moment. Then he quickly took charge again. "Ishmael, start strolling the floor. If the guards ask where we are, tell them we are patrolling other parts of the floor. Wait for us in the lounge. Keep the guards busy. Talk to them. Go, go!"

The rotund Iranian immediately did as he was told.

"Lee, off with the jacket and back into the chair, Ahmad, start tying him up again. Same as before."

Neither one of them moved.

Then Ahmad finally spoke in a whisper. "Alex, what are you doing? I didn't want to come here in the first place but we are here. I am willing to remove the young Brother. But now you want to tie him up again?"

Lee still hadn't moved. "Don't argue with me, either of

you," Alex ordered. "Tonight is not the night. We'll come back tomorrow."

"I'm going to be ill," Ahmad pleaded. "Alex, we can't!"

"Ahmad, Lee. Both of you. We have no choice. Just do as I say. Now, Lee, back into that chair. *Hurry.* I can hear the guards checking the rooms."

As he said it, all three of them could hear the distinct sound of a guard walking down the long hall, jangling a set of keys and methodically opening each door and apparently checking to make certain that all was as it should be within the confines of the makeshift prison chambers.

Lee had reclaimed his seat and Alex and Ahmad began to retie the binds that had held him, lashing his hands and feet to the chair. They moved as quickly as they could, but the shakiness of Ahmad's hands kept him from moving too fast.

"It'll do for now," Alex said, inspecting their handiwork. The problem now was where to hide.

Alex listened to the sounds of the guard as he neared Lee's room. From the sounds Alex picked up, it seemed that the doors were opened and closed rather quickly. Mycroft could only hope that meant that the guard did not enter the room but just looked in from the hallway.

One of them would be able to take cover under the cot, and Alex gave that refuge to Ahmad. Mycroft thrust himself up against the wall near the door, praying that the door would not fly into him—and thus reveal his location—when the guard opened the door. The guard was just closing and relocking the door to the adjoining room.

Mycroft stood rigid with his back against the wall, facing Lee's perspiring face and heaving chest.

Mycroft didn't know how much time he had to spare, but he knew he had to chance his next action.

He rushed over to Lee and wiped his face with a handkerchief. "Listen closely," he whispered. "Close your eyes and breathe deeply until you hear the door open. When you do, keep your eyes closed like you're sleeping. But make some noises—like snoring or like you're talking in your sleep. That way, if he sees you out of breath and sweaty, he may think that you're just having a nightmare."

Just then, they heard the sound of the key entering the lock. Alex dashed back to his spot just as the door was starting to crack open.

The door opened slightly and the guard peered in. To Mycroft it seemed that he stood there longer than he had stayed at any of the other rooms, but after only a moment, the door began to close.

Then, the guard spotted that one of the ties holding Sinclair's ankles was loose. He re-entered the room and bent down to retie it. Had he glanced to his left only a few degrees, he would have found himself face-to-face with Ahmad Zadeh. As he held the cloth in his hand, he heard, "Shh. Don't wake him."

It was Ishmael, standing in the doorway to the room. "Let him sleep," Ishmael gently admonished the Iranian guard, who quietly tightened the cloth, then silently departed, closing the door behind them.

Alex, Ahmad, and Lee let out a collective sigh of relief.

"I thought you said they didn't check the rooms," Alex questioned Ahmad, as he approached Lee.

"They didn't before. I don't know why they did tonight," Ahmad replied while he struggled to get out from under the cot.

Alex knelt down at Lee's chair. "Are you all right, Lee?"

"I suppose so," the young man replied. "But, Jesus Christ, I'm scared. What's going to happen?"

"For now, nothing. I'm sorry. But I'll be back. Promise. Expect me tomorrow night. If not tomorrow, then the next night. But I *will* be back, Brother." Then Mycroft whispered softly so Ahmad would not hear: "One more thing. In the next twenty-four hours, try to make a mental note of absolutely everything about this place—how many guards; where they are; how often they change shifts; how many usually are armed; where the other hostages are. *Everything.* Just let your mind become a camera. Do you understand?"

"Yes, Alex. I'll do it. And Alex . . . thanks."

"Forget it, kid. See you tomorrow."

"Alex, please. Think of the consequences," Ahmad pleaded. "You ask too much of me—too much of my Obligation to the Craft. Tonight we were lucky. We got in and out, and no one knew. But do not think they—we—are stupid; it cannot happen again. We tried tonight and we failed. And truthfully, was he really that mistreated?"

"Ahmad! What are you saying?" Ishmael demanded.

"Oh, Allah, give me guidance. I don't *know* what I am saying. But Alex, I implore you: Think about the consequences."

"I can't, Ahmad. I can only think about that kid and the fifty or sixty others just like him. You saw his condition; he's not having a picnic, Ahmad. Ishmael, what do you say?"

"You already know how I feel about the entire situation, my Brother. If you return, I'd like to go with you. But I caution you that without Ahmad's help, getting into the embassy will not be easy. There will undoubtedly be bloodshed, some of it ours."

Ahmad slammed his open palm against the side of the truck. He started to walk away but quickly changed his mind and returned. "My Brother," he said to Alex, "and my brother," he looked over at Ishmael. "I just do not think I can go back tomorrow night. I think there will be bloodshed whether or not I am there. The students are also my friends. Please try to understand my feelings."

"I do, Ahmad. That's what makes this a ball-busting proposition all around. I understand your feelings, mine, Ishmael's, and Sinclair's. Everyone's right, no one's wrong. But people are suffering anyway."

"Listen, this much I *can* do: First, I will think on this tomorrow and pray for guidance; secondly, whatever Allah advises, I will not say anything of these plans to anyone . . . ever."

"I suppose I can ask for no more. But if you decide to help us, we'll meet here again tomorrow at midnight. Ishmael?"

"Yes. Midnight it shall be."

40

▼

THE car carrying Otis Blake and Rachmon Hassan was passed in the opposite direction on a narrow street by the car carrying Alexander Mycroft and Ishmael Zadeh, still wearing their fatigue jackets and caps.

"Did you see that?" Hassan asked.

"What, that we were almost sideswiped?"

"No, the two men in the car. Those were my men on patrol. You could tell by their dress."

"So?"

"So it means I have had enough for tonight. My men are on the alert for Mycroft. It is only a few hours before dawn. Tomorrow we begin again."

Blake tried unsuccessfully to stifle a deep yawn. "Yeah, maybe you're right. Take me home, Hassan."

"Did you see that?" Ishmael asked.

"I saw Otis Blake, if that's what you mean."

"And I saw Rachmon Hassan."

"In a way that's good."

"How?"

"It means they're searching the streets instead of waiting for me at the embassy."

"Tonight, yes. But tomorrow is another day."

Mycroft tried unsuccessfully to stifle a deep yawn. "Yeah, maybe you're right. Take me home, Ishmael."

41

ALEX had just entered the dimly lighted hovel he had lately been calling home, when he heard—but not saw—the woman he knew as Christie hiss at him.

"Where is he, Mycroft? What have you done with him?"

"Come out of the shadows and we'll talk," Mycroft replied.

"Keep your hands where I can see them," she ordered. He obeyed by raising his hands and resting them atop his head and leaned back against the door for support. He knew from experience not to allow his arms or his legs to get too tired if at all possible.

She came out of the kitchenette area and turned on the

only other lamp in the room. Mycroft saw that she still wore the white T-shirt from that morning but she had put on some jeans. She was pointing a Walther PPK/S semi-automatic pistol directly at Mycroft's belly. She held it confidently and professionally with two steady hands, one supporting the other.

"Once more, Mycroft: where is he? Where is Sinclair?"

"He's safe. He's out of the embassy and he's safe." The room was so small that she was upon him in only three or four strides. He was about to go for her when, at that precise moment, he was distracted by two men coming out of the bedroom pointing automatic rifles at him. The momentary diversion was enough to allow her to strike Mycroft in the temple with the gun. When his hand flew up to ward off a second blow, she turned and elbowed him in the stomach and doubled him over. It was a swift maneuver.

She glanced over her shoulder and said to her two cohorts, "I told them I didn't need you to handle Colonel Mycroft." She spit on him then kicked him once in the ribs. "Get up before I kill you," she commanded.

Mycroft struggled to rest on his haunches but was too wobbly to stand. He rested against the door again to give himself support from falling over.

"Now, Mycroft, the next time I ask you a question you will answer it to my satisfaction. You will not be given a second chance. Tell me why Sinclair is not with you. What have you done with him?"

Alex labored to regain his breath and his wits. He needed time to think.

When he didn't answer, she walked over to him and knelt down beside him, wiping a few drops of blood from his face with one of her fingers. She started drawing a small circle on his cheek, using the blood from his temple, as she seductively cooed to him. "Oh, Alex, please don't fight me. We have your son and we are prepared to trade your son for the American hostage Sinclair."

He glared at her through blurred vision. "My son is dead."

She chuckled softly. "Are you so sure?"

She dipped her finger into the blood again and began drawing a line down the side of his nose. "Or, I can kill you right now. I'd love to do that, you know, Alex. I've been dreaming of killing you for the longest time. And I've finally decided how I want to kill you." She was still using her sweet seductive voice as she created another line of blood on the opposite side of his nose. Mycroft kept his gaze fixed on the two men facing him near the window. He couldn't tell whether they were able to hear what she was saying.

"What I want to do," she whispered, "is have your son watch me cut out your heart, Alex, dearest. I want your son to watch me kill you just the way I saw you kill my father fifteen years ago."

He turned and faced her again. Maybe it was the blurred vision that made her face seem dreamlike, but he finally put it together. Lord knows, he had had that dream enough times over the years. He opened his eyes wider, trying to clear his vision more, trying to see her more clearly and praying that when he did, he would realize he had been wrong.

But he wasn't wrong. And she smiled when she saw the recognition in his eyes, then she laughed softly as she licked her bloodied finger in a tantalizing manner.

"Yes, Colonel, it *is* me."

There was a sudden pounding in his ears and at first he was unable to hear his own words: "You're Méi Ling." It was not a question and it was not a statement. It was merely a nightmare come true.

"That's right," she still cooed, "and you are the man who murdered my father, Xian Ling, in Vietnam."

The thought of her father caused her to lose her attention for an instant. Mycroft made a sudden move, intending to go for her gun, but a sharp rebuke from one of the men with the automatic rifles brought him up short.

She quickly backed away from Mycroft and stood beside one of the men, who said, "So, you don't need us? Without us you would be dead by now."

She slapped him across the face with the back of her hand twice. Very calmly she said, "Never again speak to me that way."

Mycroft could see the anger rising in the man's face. The slap humiliated the man, and Mycroft wondered whether he could somehow turn that to his advantage. He also thought the mention of her father was a particular sore spot for her and thought he might have a chance of saving his own life if he could use that to provoke her into making an error of some kind.

Although it seemed to Mycroft that the only one making errors was him. It had only been a little earlier in the evening that he finally realized that she was not Lee Sinclair's sister, but he never imagined that she was Méi Ling. But then it all fit: his instincts—his fear—had been right all along. Even his prick had been right when it refused to respond to her that afternoon.

But what really troubled Mycroft was how stupid he had been to just waltz into the house tonight knowing she was an imposter. What had he expected to do? Give the little lady a stern lecture and send her on her way? He hadn't thought it through at all, and now he was paying for it. Maybe with his life.

Meanwhile, the rebuked gunman and Méi Ling were eyeing each other, but she finally turned her back on him as a further gesture of her contempt for him.

"The last time I saw your father," Mycroft said, "I seem to recall he was butt fucking you, wasn't he?"

"Don't talk about my father, Mycroft. He was a wonderful loving man who—"

"Your father was a sadistic, cold-blooded, murdering child fucker who deserved to be skinned alive and burned in boiling oil."

Her breathing started to come in short gulps, although she brought herself under physical control in only a moment or two. But the cadence in her voice revealed how deep the wound really was. "I know what you're trying to do. You're trying to get me angry. But I'm not angry, Colonel Mycroft. I'm not angry. I'm very calm. Do you want to know why? I'll tell you why I'm calm. I'm calm because of you. That's right. I'm calm because I'm asking you for the last time where the Sinclair boy is. If you don't tell me, I will kill you. You give us Sinclair and you can have your son. He's quite the handsome boy, now."

They were trying to push each other's buttons and Mycroft knew that this would not work. "Josh is dead. He drowned six years ago. That's one thing he has in common with your father: They're both dead, cunt. You want Sinclair, find him yourself."

"You heard him, you heard him," she announced gleefully, almost childlike. "You tell that to Beirut. I gave him a chance, I gave him the choice. He turned it down so I can kill him *now* without waiting."

She turned and started walking toward Mycroft.

"No!" It was the man she had slapped. "He can still be persuaded to cooperate. Remember the orders. We need the hostage."

She pointed the gun at her talkative associate and calmly shot him. The sound was deafening in the confines of the small room. "I told you never to speak to me that way again," she said evenly. The wounded man lay on the floor, the other man merely stood there, too stunned to move.

She ignored them both and any threat they might be and turned again to face her intended target.

Slowly she raised the gun and started to take careful aim at Mycroft's forehead. "Good-bye, Mycroft. I'm sorry your son isn't here to see this. I'll be sure to tell—"

But suddenly her next words were cut off by a muffled retort of what sounded like a small explosion. All three men stared at her—even the wounded man who had struggled to his feet. They were bewildered as her mouth dropped open and a slow trickle of blood appeared at the corner of her lower lip.

She started straight ahead at Mycroft; she was unable to speak. The gun fell from her hand and clattered to the floor, but her hands remained out in front of her.

Mycroft held his hands open as if to say, to her and to the two men in the room, I don't know what happened either, but don't look at me.

Her mouth began to move but no sounds emitted from her throat. She twitched her index finger spasmodically as if pulling a trigger. And then Mycroft saw the blood begin to stain the front of her white T-shirt, a small dime-sized circle of red oozing forth in the center of her chest above her breasts. None of them could understand it. If she had been shot, she had not been shot by anyone in that small room. And since she had been facing Alex at the time, which meant facing a closed front door, she could not have been shot by anyone outside of the house either. But the circle of blood grew larger and larger and now began to freely run down the full length of the T-shirt.

Her hands moved to clutch her chest, her wound. And when she did, Alex could see from the clear indentation her hands made upon her chest that the hole was enormous. The major upper portion of her chest had been blown away. No gun could have made a hole that large.

When the girl dropped to the floor, the two men instinctively raised their guns, unsure of where to aim or at whom to shoot. But their indecision was quickly removed from their minds when a vaguely familiar voice from somewhere outside the house commanded, *"Alex, hit the dirt!"*

As Mycroft immediately obeyed and dropped on top of the girl's blood-soaked body, he heard a long burst of machine-gun fire come crashing through the rear window of the small room, splashing minute fragments of the two gunmen's clothes, flesh, brain matter, intestines, and blood throughout the room and onto the walls. Their bodies in death danced like rag dolls.

It all was over in seconds. And when Alex looked up and rolled onto his side, he could make out against the early-morning light only the shadow of a very tall burly man in a long overcoat breaking away the rest of the window with the barrel of a submachine gun. The tall man in the overcoat then climbed through the window and examined the three bodies, making certain they were dead and kicking away their weapons.

Alex watched him work with his back toward him. The tall man moved like a professional, putting the barrel of his weapon against the side of the head of each body on the floor before bending over to check for a pulse. He did this with all three before laying his own weapon down and turning around to examine Mycroft, affording Alex the first clear view of the face of the last person in the world he ever expected to see in Iran.

"Hi, Cap. Nice entrance."

"You okay, good buddy?"

But before Alex could answer, the front door crashed open and flew halfway off its rusty hinges from the force of a well-placed boot. Just when Alex thought he'd been saved, along comes someone to screw it up, he thought.

Alex grabbed for Captain Stanley Harris' hand, but he couldn't comprehend why Cap ignored the figure coming through the door and persisted in checking to make sure Mycroft wasn't hurt seriously.

"You make a lot of noise, Cap," said the man in the safari jacket. "Let's get Alex out of here fast before any unwelcome neighbors show up."

As they both reached down together on either side of Mycroft to lift him gently from under the arms, the second man turned to Alex and said, *"Meshugenuh!* It took you long enough to move away from the door!"

"Avi?"

But Avi Blume just smiled at Alex and said, "Shalom, my friend, and relax. You are in safe hands . . . now."

42

Beirut

"*E S Selamu Aleikum.*"

"*Selamu Es Aleikum,*" replied the groggy voice from a small bedroom above the café. "What news deserves awakening me?"

"They are dead," said Moussef in a frightened voice.

"Dead? Who is dead? Speak clearly, you camel's ass!"

"All three. The girl and the two recruits."

"Will Allah never spare me from incompetents? And what of Mycroft? What of the Sinclair boy?"

"The Sinclair boy is still in the embassy." There was an uncomfortable pause. "And Mycroft—"

"Yes, *yes?* What of Mycroft? Speak, before I reach through this phone and rip out your black lungs!"

"Mycroft has disappeared."

There followed a long silence, and then: "How did they die? How could Mycroft have killed three well-trained fighters?"

"The men were shot. How and by whom I do not know. But the girl—the girl—"

"Yes? What of the girl?"

"It was horrible. Most of her chest had been blown away. By what means I do not know."

"All right. Heed me well. We have clearly underestimated Mycroft's cunning. We have learned our lesson but we shall profit from it. Mycroft will not try for the boy again. This much is clear, as even a fool like you could see. He will attempt to flee the country. Watch the airport, the highways, everything. Find him and kill him. He must not leave Iran. We cannot allow these deaths to go unanswered."

"I hear and I obey."

"You will obey or the girl's death will be nothing compared to your own."

The man in the small bedroom above the café hung up the phone and tried to return to sleep, despite the early-morning rays of the sun peeking through the cracks in the boarded-up window. But sleep would not come. He kept recalling once having spent an entire week in bed with that girl—an unforgettable week—and his instant erection kept him awake. He knew sleep would not come until his organ was satiated. He picked up the phone and called down to the café.

"Send up the boy. Yes, the one with the pretty mouth."

43

Tehran

"HERE, drink this, Alex. It'll help."

Mycroft sipped the whiskey from Cap's hip flask and winced as the liquid ran down his throat and burned his stomach lining. It brought tears to his eyes, but he was glad for the taste, for the pain.

"So besides being a miniature grenade the mezuzah was also a transmitter?" Alex was amazed at the ingenious Israeli microtechnology.

"Yes," Avi replied, "as well as sending out a homing signal. The chain was actually the antenna. I had the girl under surveillance ever since Israel. I could always locate her and monitor her conversations."

"And the weapon part of it worked on a simple radio frequency?"

"Well, not so simple. We wouldn't want it to go off accidently, of course. But yes, that is the general idea. Push a button and the grenade explodes.

"Amazing. Just amazing!" Alex took another, longer swig from Cap's flask and this time let the warmth spread throughout his pained body. But suddenly, Alex's mood changed dramatically. "Wait a fucking minute! If you were outside of that house the whole time and could hear everything going on *inside*, why the hell didn't you push your goddamn button sooner? I almost got killed in there!"

Avi looked over at Cap and shrugged his shoulders. "How's that for gratitude, eh, Cap? You and I, we risk our necks for this old fossil and he complains about the service!" Then Avi turned back to Alex and said, "Seriously, my friend, I know it was hard for you and believe me when I say the temptation to rescue you sooner was almost impossible to resist. It was a calculated risk but one we both thought worth taking."

"Sure," Alex said, "with my life you take calculated risks!"

"No, no. Listen, my friend," Avi implored. "It was important to find out as much as the girl was willing to impart while she thought it would do no harm if you knew certain things. You know, Alex, when people think they are *in* control, they tend to *lose* control with their mouths."

"But more than that," Cap interjected, "we wanted the girl alive if possible. Avi and I were on opposite sides of the house. Our A plan was for Avi to crash the front door open. While their attention was diverted toward the front of the house, I'd take out the two guys from the rear."

"But when we peered through the rear window, we saw

you were positioned directly in front of the door," Avi continued. "And then when the girl started talking, we were hoping you would ask her the important question."

" 'The important question?' " Alex asked. "You mean you don't think what she told me was important?"

"Oh, of course, my friend," Avi consoled him. "Naturally, it was important. Do not take offense. What she told you was important in that it confirmed what Cap and I already knew or surmised. But what we also needed to know was whether anyone else is involved besides those three. We know the PLO is involved, but to what extent? If those three were part of a larger operation, we'd like to know about it."

"Yeah," offered Cap, "Avi and I were set to take out the girl and her two buddies, but I like to know what's on the other side of the door before I open it. Like is it booby-trapped with any more shitheads."

"The Iranians we can handle fairly well, Alex," said Avi. "They are dangerous, but not subversive. Their actions are rather open and obvious. And why not? They are operating in their own homeland. We thought the information about the PLO vital enough to risk things a moment or two longer."

"I was the one who really blew it, just walking in there like that. Christ, am I an ass!"

Avi tried to console him. "You're just a little out of practice, my friend."

Alex sighed and lowered his head into his hands. "I'm more than a *little* out of practice, Avi. It took me a while to finally trust my instincts, and then when I did, it was almost too late."

"Yeah," said Cap, "but almost only counts in horseshoes and hand grenades."

The old line, delivered up by this ancient cop in a nasal

Philadelphia accent, brought a smile to Alex's face. "You're right, Cap. Now let's compare notes. First, how did you two ever hook up together? What brought you to Iran?"

Avi answered first. "I think I can speak for Cap that we both came to Iran to cover your tuchus. You knew I was suspicious of the girl back in Jaffa—from the moment she showed up to the attack at the café. There was a lot for this old Jewish nose to get wind of. When I escorted her on the tour of the old city of Jerusalem, I had her observed by informants and photographed by my people, as you already know. Someone finally thought they recognized her from one of the pictures, but you and she had already left the country. It was just a suspicion but it was enough for me to follow you here and pick up her trail through the transmitter.

"I had her under surveillance from the Intercontinental Hotel the night you went to the Temple of the Craft. I followed her when she met up with her associates, but I was wearing a disguise—a beard—in case she saw me. But it was because of *these* associates that I suspected there may be others."

"And how did you and Cap team up?"

The other two laughed at the question. "I'll let Cap answer that," Avi said, embarrassed. "It was his doing, in a way."

"I picked up your trail at the Temple," Cap explained. "But then I saw you leave with two Iranians and I had no idea who they were. So I stayed in the background. After you picked up the girl at the hotel, I noticed a guy in a safari jacket started to trail all of you. I waited for the right moment and decided to introduce myself."

Avi rubbed the back of his head where it still hurt from the blackjacking Cap had administered to that spot. "He's being modest, Alex. He jumped me and damn near killed me before we both realized we were Brothers trying to help you."

Alex was still confused. "But Cap, I still don't get it. How did you ever find your way to Iran? What in the world tipped you off?"

"The Deacon's death," the cop replied. "Or rather, the way poor Bill Gregory died. He had been sexually molested and mutilated. Actually, he had been castrated."

"Jesus," said Alex. "That *was* her style."

"That's it, Alex," Cap said. "It was her style. And the Deacon had some State Department and military files on you with him when he died. I read them and saw the references to the sexual mutilations in Vietnam. It's not your average type of killing and I figured with a sick M.O. like that there had to be a connection. Then I checked the Deacon's files and found that he had been in the same POW camp with you. John Sinclair told me about his son and the rescue and, while I really didn't know what the hell was going on, I did figure out your ass was on the line somehow. The Deacon died throwing the Hailing Sign, which I took as a warning—his warning—for you. I also knew there was one place you'd most likely show up to use that ring. I staked out the Temple for a couple of days and freezing nights until I spotted your kisser."

Alex reached over and patted the cop's knee. "Nice going, Cap. I wish I had been as sharp as either of you but I'm afraid I wasn't. She even gave herself away once and I still fell into the trap."

Avi's ears picked up. "How so, my friend?"

"When she was still playing the role of Christie, she told me that there were no brothers or sisters besides Lee. But when I was in Lee's room and told him his sister was with me, he asked 'which one?' I then remembered the Deacon telling me there was another sister, too. Suddenly I knew I had been set up somehow and that taking Lee out of the embassy last night would be a mistake. But still I walked into her trap.''

''Yes, but you walked *out,* too,'' Avi reminded him. ''The same cannot be said for her. Now tell us about the embassy and of your other friends and Brothers.''

Alex quickly detailed his successful examination at the Temple of the Craft, his alliance with Ishmael and Ahmad, and his visit to the embassy and to Lee Sinclair's room. He concluded by telling them that Otis Blake was in Tehran and apparently in cahoots with the Iranian Revolutionary Army.

''Blake may have to be dealt with,'' Avi said. The finality in his voice made his meaning clear.

''Only if there is no other way,'' Alex replied. ''I'll kick any Iranian ass that gets in my way, but I'd like to avoid spilling any blood.''

''I understand,'' Avi said, ''but with the CIA working so closely with the Iranians it will make it next to impossible to get out of the country. The embassy? Pfft''—he snapped his fingers—''it can be like child's play. But our escape from the country will require more planning.''

''Fine,'' said Cap, ''but there's no point in worrying too much about an escape before we get the Sinclair Brother out of the embassy.''

''No, Cap, you are wrong,'' lectured Avi in a stern voice. ''It is important to have all of the details taken care of first, that way—''

''Wait a minute. Both of you,'' Alex interrupted. ''You guys don't have to risk your necks anymore, you know. This is *my* Obligation.''

''Wrong. It is *our* Obligation,'' Avi said. ''Sinclair is our

Brother, too. We may have to figure out how to leave the country later, but when we do, the Sinclair boy will be with us."

"Amen," echoed Cap. "Besides, too much blood has been shed already to even think about not helping you see this through to the end. Whoever it was who said 'I have not yet begun to fight,' well, that goes double for Cap Harris."

Alex recalled Avi's words of a mere few hours ago when he had told him that he was in safe hands now. He was also in the hands of good friends and Brothers and for the first time since this mission had begun, he actually felt a sense of warmth and security—even though the most dangerous events were still to come.

"Now, whether or not we are all crazy," said Avi, "it is time to begin action. How about this Ahmad and his brother, Ishmael? Will they help us again if we try for the embassy tonight?"

"Ishmal will. He's nervous but he's a gutsy little guy. As far as Ahmad goes," Alex shrugged his shoulders, "we won't know for sure until midnight tonight. Avi, how's the arsenal? Besides the two Uzi's you and Cap have, and the small arms we picked up from Méi Ling and her friends, can you pull any more 'magic mezuzahs' out of your yarmulke?"

Avi produced a knife from a leg sheath under his trousers.

"Just a knife? That's not much," Cap said.

But Avi ignored him and used the flat blade to pry up a loose floorboard alongside his feet. "Of course, if I had known what was in store for us, I would have come prepared. As it is, though, I'm afraid we'll just have to make do with these."

Cap and Alex peered into the hole in the floor and both let out a long low whistle. Inside the concealed space were four more Uzi submachine guns, six semi-automatic pistols, a few thousand rounds of ammunition, an assortment of plastic explosives, numerous detonating devices, hand grenades, smoke bombs, stun grenades, stilettos, and bullet-proof vests.

Avi's eyes grew cold and steely hard as he waited for Alex and Cap to lift their gaze from the arsenal. When they did look up at him, he said, "With or without the assistance of Ahmad and Ishmael, we will get Brother Sinclair out of the embassy tonight." Then quietly, almost reverently, he whispered, "The Mossad does not fail."

Cap's throat was dry and his voice raspy as he said, "That's fine for you, Avi. But I'm just a flatfoot detective from Philadelphia. I've never even seen most of this stuff before, let alone used it."

"Yes," Avi replied, "but you are a *good* detective and you have courage. You proved that already. That means that you know how to *think* and are not afraid to *act*. Alex and I can teach you—we *will* teach you—how to think like Mossad and how to fight like Mossad. And before this day's sun has set, there will be three Mossad prepared to storm the American Embassy."

Cap still looked shaky, but Alex said, "Cap, I've seen the embassy, I've seen the guards, and I've seen the Mossad. It can be done."

And Avi stood up, swelled his chest to its fullest, and proclaimed, "Three Mossad against all of those Iranian tin soldiers? Hah! I pity them their inferior odds!"

44

"THE girl is dead," Rachmon Hassan said into the phone. "She was killed some time early this morning. Mycroft, unfortunately, was not there. I thought you would want to know."

"I just got off the phone with my superiors," Blake said. "I don't know who the girl was but I know who she wasn't. They just confirmed that it wasn't the Sinclair girl. The real daughter snuck her father out of the hospital a few days ago and took him to some farmhouse in Connecticut."

"And yet she was posing as the sister. A British passport in that name was found on her," Hassan said.

"Mycroft must have discovered she was an imposter," Otis Blake mused aloud. "How was she killed?"

"In a most unusual and ruthless manner. Almost her entire chest cavity had been blown away, such as from the force of an explosion. There was almost nothing left of her upper torso."

The description of the girl's corpse immediately raised the CIA agent's suspicions, but all he said was "What time are we meeting this morning?"

"I'm afraid I must postpone that for a while. I have reason to believe that Mycroft was in the embassy last night, and I'm on my way over there to interrogate Corporal Sinclair."

"What makes you think Mycroft was there? And what happened to your great security, Hassan?"

"We may have a traitor in our midst. I will know soon. But someone definitely was with Sinclair last night. When he was examined this morning, it was discovered that one of his bindings had been untied and retied hastily. We are waiting to question the guard who was on duty last night. We then discovered scratch marks on the door lock that weren't there previously."

"Jesus Christ, Hassan, didn't anyone see anything? You told me you were beefing up security over there!"

"There were three unexpected visitors to the embassy last night, but one of them is so well known to us that he was not challenged. He may be our traitor. It will not happen again, though. And at least Corporal Sinclair is still in his place."

"Look, Hassan, I want you to take me with you to the embassy," Blake demanded.

"That is out of the question."

"Okay, okay. Just hear me out first. Let's say Mycroft got to the boy last night. Why didn't he take him out?"

"I do not know but I intend to find out this morning."

"You'll find out *shit*, Hassan! Let me finish. All right,

Mycroft gets in to see the kid without any sweat. Chances are he could have danced the kid out last night, too. But he didn't, *why?* Maybe there was a snag, a hitch, an unforeseen problem. *Something.* Maybe it was the girl. Maybe she queered the deal, or Mycroft found out about her at the last minute and realized he'd been had . . . thinks he was set up.''

Blake paused to think the next thought through, running it around quickly in his mind.

"That *could* be it, Hassan. Look, we know the girl was posing as the kid's sister. Maybe Mycroft and the girl got in with your traitor last night, but the kid took one look at the bitch and said, 'Who's that?' And Mycroft figured the jig was up, she'd spilled the beans to someone, so he put her on ice and wasted her later. He told the kid to stay put and he'd come back for him. Then, who knows? Maybe he tried to get back into the embassy last night but couldn't; maybe he's planning another drop-by tonight.

"But the point is this, Hassan: whatever really *did* happen last night at the embassy, the kid's not gonna tell *you.* But there's a chance he may confide in me.''

"Why you?"

"Hey, Hassan, don't be a dumb shit all your life, huh, fella? He and I are both Americans. You know, the guys in the white hats. If it's a choice between telling you or telling me, my money's on me.''

Hassan was silent.

"Hey, Hassan. You still there?''

"I'm thinking.''

"Look, blindfold me if you want to. What the fuck am I gonna see? Don't forget, I'm the one who came to you about Mycroft in the first place. On this one issue, Hassan, you and I are on the same side, as much as we may despise each other. But Sinclair doesn't know that. He won't talk to you.''

"All right. Be ready in ten minutes. And Blake?"

"Yes?"

"No weapons this time."

"Scout's honor."

The phone call to Tel Aviv went through just moments before Hassan arrived to pick up Blake.

"Listen, you dumb shit: I thought you told me Avi Blume was still in Israel."

"Sir, he hasn't left his apartment in days."

"How do you know he's still there? Have you *seen* him?"

"Well, no, sir. But we saw him enter his apartment almost a week ago and we've had a round-the-clock surveillance on the place ever since, just like you ordered. He's still got to be inside, sir. I'd stake my reputation on it."

"Johnson, the only reputation you've got is getting worse with each passing day. I'll bet you your ass he's here in Tehran."

"Th—that's impossible! Why are you so sure? Have *you* seen him?" There was an angry arrogance in the voice.

"I don't have to see him; I can *smell* him. Plus, someone just described the remains of a body to me—the girl's body. It has all the markings of a Mossad killing. Now you break into that fucking apartment if you have to, but I want to know for sure whether he's there or not. Do it now and get word back to me P.D.Q."

As they drove through the heavily guarded embassy gates, Hassan slipped a thick smelly cowl over Blake's head, which was not removed until they were standing directly outside of Lee Sinclair's room.

"What do you make of that?" Hassan asked him.

Blake bent down to examine the door lock, and announced, "You're right. This lock was jimmied—and recently."

They entered the small room together and found Lee stretched out on the cot. He had been untied for breakfast and exercise earlier in that morning, Hassan had previously explained to Blake, and had been left that way, which was customary. They did not wish to alter his particular routine and make him suspicious if he was indeed in league with Mycroft.

Hassan stood quietly by the door while Blake positioned the straight-back chair over toward Lee's cot and flashed the young marine a toothy grin.

"Hi, Lee. Okay if I sit down?"

Sinclair immediately recognized Blake as a fellow American from his voice and his clothes, but eyed Hassan cautiously. He sat up and swung his legs over the side of the hard cot and faced Blake.

"Sure, sir."

"You can drop the 'sir' with me, Lee. My name's Otis Blake. I'm a friend of Alex Mycroft's."

"Alan who, sir?"

"Alex, not Alan. Alex Mycroft, Lee."

"Sorry, sir. I don't recognize the name."

Blake sighed audibly, erasing the smile from his lips.

"Look, son, I'm with the CIA." He proffered his ID.

But Sinclair's eyes were on Hassan when he answered: "If that's true, sir, you sure travel with some interesting people."

"Don't pay any attention to him, Lee," Blake said. "Just listen to me for a minute. We know Alex Mycroft broke in here last night and we know what he's up to. Your government is trying to win your release through peaceful negotiations with the Iranians. Anything Alex Mycroft attempts will only screw things up for everyone. Can you follow that, Lee?"

"Yes, sir. I follow you but I'm afraid I don't understand. I told you before, I don't know any Alex Mycroft, and no one broke in here last night . . . *sir.*"

"Lee, *please* believe me. I'm trying to save your life—and Mycroft's. If he tries anything, you could get hurt. People could get killed. He's dangerous, Lee."

"Yes, sir. If you say so, sir."

Blake was exasperated. He knew Sinclair was lying but he was sincere when he said he wanted to save the kid's life. And he was equally honest when he said Mycroft was dangerous.

"Lee is there anything—anything at all—that I can say to convince you I'm telling the truth?"

Lee thought for a moment and said, "Yes, sir, there is something. You can tell me who the shepherd's son is."

Blake's expression went blank. "The *what?*"

Lee returned to his reclining position on the cot and said, "That's what I thought . . . *sir.*"

Once outside the boy's room, Hassan replaced Blake's hoodwink and had him taken out of the embassy. Hassan told one of the guards to send for Ahmad Zadeh, then reentered Lee's room alone.

Lee didn't bother getting up for Hassan. He just laid on his back with his arms folded behind his head on the pillowless mattress.

"I will not even bother to ask you why you did not trust Mr. Blake," Hassan said softly. "But I will ask you what Alex Mycroft's plans are."

"Fuck you, prick!"

Lee was caught completely off guard when Hassan lifted

the side of the cot off the floor, spilling Lee against the wall and onto the floor. Hassan tossed the cot with ease across the room and grabbed Sinclair's shirt front and lifted him to his feet. Pinning him against the wall with his left hand, his right pummeled Lee's belly hard, once, twice, three times. Then he dropped him and let him crumble to the floor, gasping for breath.

Two guards, hearing the commotion from the room, rushed in with guns drawn.

"Tie him to the chair," Hassan barked. "Tightly."

The two guards lifted him from the floor and bound Lee's hands and feet to the chair. Hassan then dismissed the two guards and turned back to Lee.

"Now that I have your attention, what are Alex Mycroft's plans?"

Lee started to say something, but with his head lowered on his chest and his breath coming slowly, Hassan had to strain to hear him.

"What? What are you saying?" Hassan walked over and lifted up the young man's head and lowered his own face to hear better. When he was looking into Lee's eyes, Lee spit directly into Hassan's shocked face.

The fury balled up in Hassan's fist caused the chair to topple over backward with the force of the blow to Lee's face.

Hassan massaged his bruised hand and forced himself to bring his own temper under control before righting the chair. The scar on his face pulsated madly. His eyes were wild.

"I have wasted days looking for Mycroft. I know he was here last night and I know he'll try to come back. Tell me when. Tell me when he is coming back. *Tell me what Mycroft's plans are!*"

"Leon Sinclair, United States Marine Corps, rank corporal, service number 179—"

This time Hassan smacked him across the face twice, once with the open palm of his hand, and then on the other cheek with the back of his bruised hand. One blow caught Lee in the nose and blood began squirting from his nostrils.

"Tell me, you stupid fool. Tell me before I kill you!"

"Leon Sinclair, United States Mar—"

Hassan had stepped back to give himself enough leverage to kick Lee in the stomach. He then began pummeling him unmercifully, like a boxer who has pinned a helpless opponent on the ropes. First in the face, on the side of his head, then in the stomach. Hassan was a man possessed.

"Tell me! *Tell Me!!*"

"Rachmon, *stop it!* Have you gone mad?" Hassan, in his wild frenzy, hadn't heard Ahmad enter the room. "What in the name of Allah do you think you're doing, Rachmon?"

"Hello, my friend, Ahmad. My loyal friend, Ahmad." Hassan stepped away from his handiwork, affording Ahmad a clear view of the boy's ravaged face and body. Ahmad immediately called out to the guards to bring water and bandages.

"Rachmon, you are mad to do this. This is insane. You know our plans called for not harming any of the hostages. What if we have to turn the hostages over to the Iman tomorrow? How would we explain this boy's condition?"

"Don't talk to me about tomorrow, Ahmad; talk to me of last night!"

"What do you mean?"

"Do you deny you were here last night?"

"In the embassy? Of course I do not deny it. Since when may I not enter the embassy? You forget, I was one of the organizers of this takeover."

"And who were the two people with you?"

"Friends, Rachmon. Loyal friends, sympathetic to our cause."

"And since when is Alex Mycroft sympathetic to us?"

"Rachmon, I don't understand what you are saying. You are not talking sense. Are you questioning *me? My* loyalties?"

"You may have been one of our organizers, Ahmad, but I am in charge here now."

"Yes, Rachmon," Ahmad answered slowly. "And I think it is all going to your head, this power." Just then the guards entered. "Clean him up at once and treat his wounds," Ahmad ordered.

As the guards lifted Lee's head from his chest and began to wash away the still-fresh blood, Lee spotted Ahmad and a glimmer of recognition flashed in his eyes. Ahmad, seeing it, suddenly became scared that Lee, in his delirious state, might say something to expose him. Lee started to mumble something, and both Ahmad and Hassan pushed away the guards to get closer to hear his words.

" 'Before divulging the secrets entrusted to my safekeeping . . . ' " Lee began in a hoarse raspy whisper. Rachmon, thinking Lee was about to lay down a condition before confessing, became visibly excited.

"Yes? Yes?" he prodded. "What is it you want before divulging your secrets? *What?*"

But Ahmad inwardly relaxed, recognizing immediately that the sentence Lee was struggling to emit from his bloodied mouth was an important line from the cryptic ritual, as well as an important message to Ahmad and to Alex.

" 'Before divulging the secrets entrusted to my safekeeping,' " Lee began once again, " 'I will gladly suffer myself to be ignominiously slain.' "

Having forced the words out, Lee allowed himself the painful luxury of a broad, bloody smile. And then he spat a mixture of blood and saliva into Hassan's bewildered face once more before passing out.

45

"I can see by your face that you didn't have any more success with the boy than I did," Otis Blake said when Rachmon Hassan entered his room.

"Alas, no," Hassan responded. "He was most reluctant to talk."

Blake suddenly leaped from his chair and grabbed Hassan by the throat, pinning his neck against the wall with his left hand while repeatedly slapping him across the face with the front and back of his open right hand.

"How much did you beat him, Hassan? How hard did you work him over? Huh? Is he still alive, you bastard? I told you before what I'd do if you fucked me. If you think I was kidding, just try me!"

Hassan tried desperately to respond but was unable to articulate more than a grunt with Blake's hand against his vocal chords. Blake gave Hassan one more violent punch to his soft belly, just for good measure, before letting the Iranian drop to the floor, gasping for breath.

Finally he was able to speak. "Wh—what did you do that for?"

"I wanted to work out some aggression, and I figured I'd use you as a punching bag," Blake answered.

"You—you are . . . mad. *Insane!*"

"Fuck you, Hassan! Look at your hands. Your knuckles are raw to the bone. You beat the kid. I told you he wouldn't talk to you. So you figured you'd just beat it out of him, and all you wound up with was a sore hand. Just consider what I did to you as a downpayment on what the Sinclair kid owes you."

Otis Blake didn't know whether it was a surge of patriotism coursing through his veins but he knew the light beating he had just administered to Hassan made him feel better, more at peace with himself, than he had felt in the past week. He turned his back on Hassan as the Iranian slowly struggled to his feet, thinking about jumping Blake. Blake had a sixth sense about these things.

"Don't try anything foolish, Hassan. I'm really in the mood today and I'd just love to be provoked into doing a real tap dance on your skull," he threatened without even bothering to turn around. Hassan meekly took a seat and waited for Blake to finish lighting a cigarette.

"Okay, Hassan, let's get down to cases here. What if I was to suggest—just suggest, mind you—that Mycroft is receiving help from the Israelis, specifically from the Mossad. Would that give you any better ideas of where to look for him in Tehran?"

"How do you know the Mossad is helping him?"

"Remember, I only said it was a suggestion. I could be wrong."

"You could be but you don't think you are, do you? Go on with your suggestion."

"All right, here's the way it lays out: Mycroft was in Israel shortly before he showed up in Iran. While he and the girl were there, I know he got some kind of help from the Mossad—probably intelligence stuff on the embassy set-up and so on. By the way, do you know a Mossad agent named Avi Blume?"

"We have never met but I know of him and I've seen pictures of him. I would know him if I saw him, and, of course, we do know the Mossad is in the area. Why?"

"Blume helped Mycroft in Israel. They're very old friends. When Mycroft and the girl left for England just before coming to Iran, Blume stayed behind and I had some of my men put him under surveillance. A little while ago I found out that my guys fucked up. They had been watching an empty apartment. Blume gave them the slip, and so far they haven't been able to spot him anywhere in Israel. My hunch is he's here."

"Why do you think so?"

"Because of the girl's death. Mycroft certainly *could* have done it, but from the way you described the condition of her body, it sounds like a Mossad killing."

"How can you tell?"

"We know the Mossad has developed a cute little device that would do the sort of damage you described. I'm not gonna tell you how it works, but have you ever heard the expression 'Beware of Greeks bearing gifts'? Well, the same goes for Mossad agents! Anyway, if *we* knew the girl was a phony, chances are Blume did, too. And Mycroft. Maybe

Blume gave the gizmo to Mycroft and told him how to operate it. Maybe right now Blume's stretched out sunning himself on a beach at Eilat. I don't know. Like I said, it's just a suggestion, just a hunch. But I've been telling you all along Mycroft's been getting help from someone. I always figured it for a local—and maybe it is, too. But I wouldn't rule out Blume."

"I see," Hassan said pensively. "And you really think this Avi Blume is here in Tehran?"

"Let's just say my gut thinks so. I'm not sure about my brain. For example, it's one thing for Blume to give aid and comfort to Mycroft in Israel, on his own turf. I can buy that. But why would Blume come to Iran to risk his neck for Mycroft—especially in an operation that doesn't involve the Israelis? That's the part I can't piece together, and I have a hard time imagining the Mossad giving him the go-ahead. If Blume *is* here, he's probably operating alone and not with Mossad sanction. And, if so, he won't be able to use the Mossad's normal routes out of the country. That could help us."

"Well, it opens up new possibilities. There are some places where we can search that we did not consider previously. It's almost dark, though. Let's leave immediately."

"Hassan, before we go, let me try to reason with you once more. Watch my lips carefully: Mycroft has been one jump ahead of us the whole time. Let your men do the searching for Mycroft's Mossad hideaway. Move Sinclair to another room. And let's you and I wait for Mycroft to show up in Sinclair's old room. For once, we'll be one jump ahead of *him*."

"I've told you before, Blake, do not concern yourself with the embassy. The guards have been doubled, inside and out, day *and* night."

46

▼

AFTER dinner, which he did not eat, Ishmael Zadeh played with his three children until it was time for them to go to bed. His wife was surprised, not only that he spent so much time with the youngsters but that he also insisted on putting them to bed himself. Ishmael bathed them together in the kitchen sink, helped them into their bedclothes, and rocked them to sleep on his lap as he hummed them an Iranian lullaby that he recalled from his own childhood. His wife silently observed all this in wonderment. When the children nodded off, he kissed each one tenderly as he piled all three into the same small bed.

"Ishmael, my husband, are you feeling well?"

"Sit down, woman, I have something for you." He

reached into his pocket and produced a brown sealed envelope and handed to her.

"I must go out again tonight. If I do not return, you are to open this envelope. Inside there is money for you and for the children."

"Ishmael! Where are—"

"*Silence*, old woman! Do not question Ishmael Zadeh!"

"But, my husband, *please!* When will you return?"

"I will return when I return. Or when I do not," he responded in a slightly confusing manner.

"But where are you going, Ishmael?" There were tears in her eyes.

"First, I am going to the mosque for evening prayer," he answered as he slipped on the military-green fatigue jacket, cap, and scarf. "Then I have things to attend to."

"But you are not dressed for prayer, Ishmael."

"For the sort of praying I must do tonight, I am dressed appropriately."

He started out the door but suddenly, impulsively, and totally out of character for him, he hurried back and kissed his wife softly, tenderly on the lips. The tears in her eyes prevented her from seeing the tears in his.

"Lose some weight, woman!" he growled as he turned to leave. "Who would want to marry a fat woman with three screaming children if I was not around?"

"Come back to me, Ishmael," she cried after him. "Ishmael, I love you!"

But Ishmael was already out the door.

47

▼

—January 6, 1980

A T precisely midnight, Alex walked alone and with extreme caution to the alley entrance way leading to the Temple of the Craft. Avi and Cap were at opposite ends of the block, standing in the shadows of the deserted street. The three of them were connected to each other through earpiece receivers and miniature voice transmitters, provided by the Mossad agent, on the inside of their respective left sleeves. But they each maintained silence while waiting for Alex to reach his destination.

"I'm here," Alex's voice squawked into Avi and Cap's earplugs. "I think I'm alone."

"A car just cruised by slowly," Avi reported. "A driver,

no passengers. Keep a look out, Cap, I think he's headed your way."

"Got him in sight," Cap said. "He's cruising all right, like he's looking for something . . . or someone. Wait! He just pulled up at the end of the street. He's put out the lights but he's sitting in the car. Hold it, he's getting out now. Hard to make him out. Looks like an older guy, short, heavyset, but he's wearing a fatigue jacket. He's heading this way!"

"Stay out of sight," Avi whispered.

"Just went past me. Heading your way, Alex."

"Right. I can see him now."

The figure approached the alley cautiously, stopping but for a moment at the end of the alley to see whether he was being watched. Satisfied that he was alone, he quickly ducked down the alley toward the almost hidden Temple entrance. He'd gone only a few short steps in that direction when Alex's arm reached out of the darkness and grabbed him from behind. Mycroft's left arm was around the man's neck and a stiletto stood poised in his right hand, ready to plunge into the stranger's back if he should be an enemy.

"Allah be merciful!" Ishmael cried out softly and Mycroft recognized the voice and spun him around. "Alex, it's you!"

"Hello, Ishmael. Glad you could make it."

Alex spoke softly into his left sleeve: "It's Ishmael."

"Wh—what are you doing?" asked the confused Iranian.

"It's all right, Ishmael. I brought two friends—and Brothers—along to help. Any word from Ahmad?"

"Alas, no. I tried all day to locate him but no one seems to know where he's gone. I fear we'll be on our own tonight."

"We'll manage. I'm glad you remembered to bring along

that fatigue jacket because tonight you'll have to play Ahmad's part."

"Alex!" Cap's voice came through on the earpiece. "Another car—no, wait, a truck—coming this way. Can't make it out too clearly; the lights are aimed my way."

"Don't let him see you, Cap," Avi ordered.

"It's turning down this street," Cap reported. "Coming right for Alex. Hang on, guys, it's a military half-truck."

Alex said, "It could be Ahmad."

But Avi cautioned, "Yes, and maybe not. Check it out carefully, Alex."

Alex and Ishmael dropped back into the shadows and watched as the truck pulled up and stopped at the head of the alley, then extinguished its lights. The driver stayed behind the wheel and lit a cigarette. From the glow of the match Alex recognized Ahmad.

Alex raised his left sleeve to his lips: "Cap, Avi, come on in. It's Ahmad."

Alex stepped out of the shadows and walked over to the driver's side of the truck. "Ahmad, it's Alex. Brother, am I ever glad to see you!"

But when Ahmad turned his head toward Alex, Mycroft thought he saw tears in the young man's eyes.

About a hundred thoughts flashed instantly through Mycroft's mind, but he had been in this business long enough to know that they all added up to trouble. He knew he had been set up.

"Alex," Ahmad said quietly, "there was no other way. I'm sorry."

Mycroft wasn't about to waste time asking what the young Iranian was sorry about, and he immediately ducked down just as a Revolutionary soldier who had been crouched down on the seat of the cab alongside Ahmad raised a gun at Mycroft's receding figure and fired.

But at the same instant, Ahmad grabbed for the gun, which sent the shot wide.

"No! No!" Ahmad cried. "You promised no shooting!"

The diversion gave Alex the few moments he needed to rush back to his temporary refuge of the alley's darkness and throw Ishmael down flat on his rotund stomach.

"Stay down," he ordered, and reached for the Uzi submachine gun he had deposited in the small niche. "It's a trap," Alex barked into his sleeve.

When the shot was fired, the canvas tarp covering the rear of the truck flew back and six Revolutionary soldiers jumped out and headed for the alley. They fired blindly down it, never anticipating Mycroft to return their fire. He immediately killed the first soldier, and the others ran for cover at the top of the alley.

Cap and Avi, seeing the flash of the guns and hearing Alex's warning, readied their own Uzis, released the safeties, and scurried as fast they could toward the center of the street from opposite ends of the block, staying across the street from the alley entrance.

Ahmad, meanwhile, had the soldier's pistol in both hands now, but the soldier alongside of him was not encumbered by a steering wheel. With that freedom of movement as leverage, he easily twisted the gun around and fired two shots into Ahmad's chest. Ahmad collapsed forward onto the truck's horn.

Judging from the flashes from the soldiers' rifles as they continued to fire down the alley, Alex reported to Cap and Avi, "I figure about a half-dozen, minus one I already nailed." He fired a few brief bursts up the alley, trying to draw the soldiers' fire and pinpoint a target or two: When he did, and they fired in his direction with more accuracy, Alex rolled across to the opposite side of the alley and returned their fire.

"Cap and I are in position," Avi radioed. "We'll set up a cross fire."

At that moment, the soldier who had just shot Ahmad jumped down from the passenger side of the truck and was starting to run around the front of the truck to join his men. But before he had turned the corner in front of the truck, a short burst from Avi's well-trained Uzi fell him in his tracks.

The soldiers at the top of the alley panicked at the sound of the unexpected gunfire behind them. This was not part of their plan. This American, Mycroft, was supposed to be unarmed, but he had already demonstrated with deadly accuracy that he was well armed. And he was supposed to be alone, save for Ahmad's older and non-violent brother. But suddenly there were unexpected shots from behind them. Two of the soldiers turned to engage Avi. But as they started to fire in Avi's direction and the Israeli easily maneuvered for cover, Cap, standing further up the street with a clear view of the two soldiers who had just fired their rifles, picked them off easily with a long series of bursts from his Uzi.

"Don't waste ammunition," Avi said in Cap's ear. "But thanks, my friend, just the same. Alex, how many on your side of the truck?"

"Two or three. No more than that."

There were three soldiers left. Three scared and badly confused Iranian Revolutionary soldiers, unsure of where to go or what to do. Their leader, unbeknownst to them, was dead. And now there were three deadly men with submachine guns who had them hopelessly pinned down. They were totally unprepared for this.

They decided their only recourse was to make a run for the truck and flee for their lives. But as they stood to cross the top of the alley to reach the truck's cab, Alex managed to drop two of them.

One, however, made it across the top of the narrow alley and pried open the driver's side of the cab. But as he struggled in vain to remove Ahmad's body from behind the wheel, Avi fired from directly across the street, through the open passenger window, killing the last remaining soldier.

After a few minutes of silence, now that Ahmad's body was no longer lying on the truck's horn, Avi said, "Alex, you and Ishmael stay put while Cap and I check things out."

Together, Avi and Cap cautiously circled the truck, each of them keeping the other covered, as they made sure that there were no more soldiers waiting for them. They satisfied themselves that all the soldiers they had shot were dead.

Cap radioed down the alley: "Alex, there's one still breathing. I'm not sure but I think it's Ahmad. He's calling your name."

Mycroft and Ishmael came running up the alley together.

Ahmad's shirt front was covered with his own blood, but Cap had been right. He was still alive—barely—and was struggling to speak through the blood in his mouth.

"It's Alex, Ahmad. Save your strength."

"Alex, Alex. Forgive me, Alex. It was not meant to happen this way." Ahmad's voice was a low whisper, interspersed with coughing.

"Ahmad, don't talk. We'll find a doctor."

"No, Alex . . . no time. Hassan found out we were there last night . . . thinks I'm traitor . . . he beat Sinclair . . . may be badly hurt . . . I couldn't bear to leave my beloved Iran . . . Shemran is so peaceful. . . ."

"Alex," Avi whispered with a sense of urgency, "he's

going fast. Ask him if anyone else at the embassy knows about tonight's operation. Ask him if there will be another ambush. *Hurry!*"

Alex repeated the questions.

"No . . . no one else knows . . . tell Ishmael I always loved him . . . have you seen the statue of the mountain climber in Shemran . . . Alex? . . . don't feel anything . . . I don't—"

Ishmael leaned forward and closed his dead brother's eyes, then kissed him.

"Ishmael, I'm sorry," Alex said.

"So am I," Ishmael said quietly. "So am I."

Cap looked at Alex and said, "Well, what happens now?"

But it was Ishmael who answered bravely. "Now? Now we do what we came to do."

48

"I think we found it," said Blake. "Look at this stuff."
Hassan walked over to where Otis Blake was
thoughtfully examining a few seemingly meaningless
scraps of crumbled and partially burned paper lying in a
table ashtray.

"I can't read this shit," Blake said, "but it looks like
Hebrew. What do you make of it?"

Hassan bent down and declared, "You're right. It's certainly not Farsi or any other Arabic language I know of. I
don't know enough Hebrew to read it, but I can recognize
it."

Blake, continuing his examination of the small Mossad
safe house where Alex, Avi, and Cap had been only hours

before, turned over the contents of a wastebasket and found a soiled towel.

"This looks like dried blood," he said. "Not much of it, but it looks like somebody bled a little."

But Hassan was busy examining something he found on the floor. "What do you think this is?"

Blake took it from him and said, "I don't *think*, I *know*: It's a shell casing from a Uzi submachine gun."

They continued searching the sparse room and discovered the weaponry hiding place beneath the loose floorboard. But it was "Empty," Hassan declared, save for a few loose shells.

"All right," Blake mused, "let's think for a minute. From that scrap of paper, we can assume a Jew was here. Let's further assume it was Blume. From the towel, we know someone was bleeding but not hurt seriously. It could have been Blume or it could have been Mycroft. Either one of them could have gotten hurt—or even just some blood splattered on them—when the girl was killed. Okay, let's assume Mycroft and Blume have been here. The next question is who was the third person?"

"Third person?" Hassan asked. "How do you know there was a third person?"

"Three glasses on the table."

"*Ahmad!*"

"Who's Ahmad?"

"The traitor I mentioned earlier. When he came to the embassy last night, there were two other people with him. Earlier we assumed Mycroft and the girl, dressed like a man, were the other two visitors. But now we know it was Mycroft and Blume."

"All right," Blake thought out loud, "that might fit. Except, what's the connection between this Ahmad character and Mycroft and Blume? The Israelis and the Iranians don't exactly get along, and neither do the Iranians and the Americans. So, the way you figure it, you've got an Iranian, this Ahmad, playing footsie with an American *and* an Israeli. Does that make sense to you?"

"I must confess, no. What makes even less sense is Ahmad's actions, *period.* He was one of the founders of our movement, one of the original organizers."

"We're still missing a piece, Hassan. But, no matter, let's get moving."

"And where would you propose we go at"—he glanced at his watch—"one o'clock in the morning?"

"For one thing, to find someone who can tell me what's on this scrap of paper. Do you know anyone who can read Hebrew?"

"Yes, of course. But at *this* hour?"

"I'll make a deal with you, Hassan: You stay, give me the keys to the car, tell me where the fuck we are and how to get back to civilization. Back to the embassy."

"The embassy? What about your theory that Mycroft will try his rescue in broad daylight?"

"If you're right about last night, my theory's already blown. But it's more than that. It's—it's this place."

"This place disturbs you?"

"No, not disturbs, more like . . . *reminds* me. I've been in dumps just like this one all over the world. And this place has the feel of a place you leave just before you go on a mission."

"This sounds like nonsense to me."

"I don't expect you to understand it, Hassan. But my ulcer sure understands it. And there's something else: Those three glasses sitting together like that on the table, almost touching the way they are."

"What about them?"

"I think they drank a toast just before leaving. It's the sort of thing Mycroft would do." Blake paused for a minute, thought, and then very quietly said, "Hassan, they're at the embassy. *Now*. I know it; I can *feel* it!"

"All right, we'll leave. But first we'll find an old Jew I know in Shemran who will tell us what these papers say. Then we'll go to the embassy."

"Forget the old Jew in Shemran for now. I'm telling you Mycroft's at the embassy. He's there *now*, Hassan. Let's go."

Hassan confidently replied, "I have faith in my soldiers at the embassy. They are prepared for any eventuality. No, Blake, we will do things *my* way: first, the old Jew to tell us what this paper says. Then, to make you happy, we'll visit the embassy." He turned to leave.

Blake cursed under his breath and caught up with Hassan outside of the house.

"You know something, Hassan," Blake said as they got into the car, "you're a dumb shit. The biggest goddamned dumbest shit I've ever met, and boy, let me tell you some day about some of the dumb shits I've met in my time. But you, Hassan, *you* take the cake!"

49

▼

AFTER they had disposed of the soldiers' bodies, changed into their uniform jackets, and taken some of the less bloody clothes for Lee Sinclair to change into, they piled into the truck Ahmad had been driving and reached the embassy gates. It was one-thirty in the morning.

Ishmael was driving with Alex beside him. Avi and Cap crouched in the rear of the truck. By mutual agreement, they had discarded the notion of using the floorboards as a hiding place. In the event of any trouble, Avi and Cap wanted to be readily available. Alex kept them informed by talking into the transmitter in his sleeve.

Ishmael drove around the entire compound twice, slow-ing each time he passed in front of the main gate. They counted only three guards stationed there.

"Are the guards on the inside of the gate or the outside?" Avi wanted to know.

"Inside."

"How does everything else appear? Normal? Quiet? Lights on or off?"

"Quiet," Alex answered. "Not too many lights on in the chancery."

"Okay," Avi said, "drop us off at the end of the street."

Alex directed Ishmael to a spot at the end of Takhte-Jamshid Avenue, and Avi and Cap climbed out of the rear of the truck.

"Check your watch, Alex. Give us exactly thirty minutes."

"Thirty minutes. Check."

Cap and Avi each carried a long canvas duffel bag with back straps. They ducked unseen around the corner of the quiet street. Cap opened his bag and produced a grappling hook attached to a rope. He hefted the hook over the twelve-foot brick wall, made certain it caught, then gave Avi a boost up the rope. At the top of the wall, Avi stayed low and peered around as best he could through the trees and foliage decoratively planted along the inside of the wall. It obscured his vision but would also provide much-needed cover for the work he and Cap had to do.

Avi announced that it was all clear and reached down as Cap hoisted the two duffel bags up to him. With more effort, owing to his bulk, Cap huffed his way over the wall to join Avi on the inside of the twenty-seven-acre compound. Mossad intelligence long knew—and had passed along to the United States—the fact that it was easy to breech the compound. It was too large for adequate protection and the

Iranians limited their outside show of public security to the mainly ornamental front gates. Inside the several buildings, however, security was not as lax.

They crouched stealthily along the inside of the wall, staying behind the trees and shrubbery, stopping about every twenty paces to plant small but powerful explosive devices in the ground adjacent to the wall that was parallel to Takhte-Jamshid Avenue. They carefully worked their way toward the main gate.

After they had covered most of that section of the walled compound, Cap, who had been checking his watch constantly, quietly said, "Time."

Avi looked at his own watch to confirm that they had taken twenty-seven minutes of the allotted thirty. They had just three minutes to reach the main gate from the inside as Ishmael and Alex were due to approach that entrance from the outside.

Avi and Cap still had about twenty yards to go when they spotted the truck turning in and stopping at the gate. They waited until Ishmael turned his lights off—the signal that the guards were at the gate.

The signal came and Avi grabbed a remote control device and affixed it to his belt. Then he and Cap left their duffel bags against the wall and continued creeping along in deadly silence.

Neither Avi nor Cap had any idea what Ishmael was saying to the three guards, but whatever it was, he had the undivided attention of the three bored gatekeepers. None of them made a move to unlock the padlocked gate, not that it was really expected that Ishmael would be able to talk his way in.

In the dimness of the darkened cab, Alex squinted to see the luminous hands of his watch. Avi did the same. Exactly twenty-nine minutes had elapsed.

Casually, slowly, Alex stepped down from the cab and walked directly up to stand alongside of Ishmael, facing the three guards, as Avi and Cap simultaneously approached them from the rear.

One of the guards continued arguing with Ishmael as Alex, still as nonchalant as his rapid heart beat would allow, pulled out a silencer-equipped semi-automatic pistol and aimed it at the center guard.

As the guards made a move to ready their own weapons, Avi and Cap grabbed the two outer guards from behind. While Avi used a vicious karate chop to the base of the neck of the soldier he had grabbed, Cap favored his trusty blackjack to put his man into oblivion. As the middle soldier, ignoring Alex, turned around to point his rifle at Avi and Cap, Alex merely reached through the iron bars of the gate, grabbed the soldier's jacket by the back of its collar, and pulled the back of his head repeatedly into the iron gate, knocking him unconscious.

Total time elapsed: thirty minutes for planting the explosives, and six seconds for eliminating three soldiers.

"They don't have the key to the padlock," Ishmael quickly explained. "That is what they were telling me. They were going to go get the soldier with the key, but I thought it best not to let any of them go, so I kept them talking."

Alex patted Ishmael's cheek. "Good thinking, Ishmael. We'll make you a soldier of fortune yet."

Cap came puffing back with the two duffel bags from which he and Avi produced rope and gags for the three soldiers. Avi then took out a small wad of plastic explosive, which he gingerly applied to the huge padlock and inserted a short fuse.

"Stand back!"

Ishmael put his hands to his ears, but the only noise was

a brief "pffft," like someone blowing out a match, and the padlock fell open.

"Amazing!" Ishmael said.

Avi and Cap swung wide both gates to let the truck pass, reclosed the gates, and affixed the padlock to make it appear to the casual observer that it was still intact. They then climbed aboard the truck as Ishmael drove it to the same spot under the trees near the chancery where Ahmad had parked the night before.

After he had selected a weapon of his choice, Ishmael was left to guard the truck. Alex, Avi, and Cap crept around in the shadows of the chancery to the front door that Ahmad had easily walked through only about twenty-four hours earlier. Alex left his two companions behind in the bushes and sidled up against the wall to peer through the door.

"Heavily guarded inside," he whispered when he returned. "I'd judge at least a dozen, maybe more. Certainly more than last night. Most of them are armed, and most are wearing heavy coats and fatigue jackets like these. They're probably outer guards who just came in to get warm."

"We'll give them heat, all right," said Cap. "Plenty of it."

But Avi ignored the humor and said, "That would explain why there were only three guards at the gate. No matter, the plan will still work. Ready?"

The other two nodded and proceeded on their bellies close to the front door. As all three readied stun grenades and smoke bombs, Avi pushed the first button on the device he wore on his belt and detonated the first of the many explosives he and Cap had planted along the wall.

The devastating roar of the blast sent the soldiers inside the chancery scurrying for cover, unsure of the cause or even the direction of the explosion.

A heartbeat later, the three stood back as one of Cap's stun grenades was detonated at the foot of the front door, sending its shattered remains flying off in a hundred different directions. Without waiting for the smoke or debris to clear, the three of them affixed their gas masks and Avi and Cap followed Alex as he lobbed two smoke bombs into the frenzied scene in the lobby of the chancery. Avi detonated two more explosions at the wall and the three men unharnessed their Uzis and rushed into the midst of a chaotic swirl of orange smoke and frantic yelling. The rescue had begun.

Otis Blake had waited in the car when Rachmon Hassan banged on the door of the undistinguished house in the village of Shemran, awakening its elderly occupants.

"Was he able to translate it?" Blake asked when Hassan returned to the car and began negotiating the less than favorable mountain road heading back toward Tehran.

"We were right that it's Hebrew," Hassan replied. "But it's unimportant—nothing more than a weather forecast."

"*Jesus H. Christ!*" Blake shouted. "A weather forecast! For what day of the week? What area of the country?"

"The old Jew didn't say. Why is that so important?"

"*Why?*" Blake was incredulous at the density of the Iranian's limited brain. "Use your head, man. It could be weather information to fly a small plane in or out, say for an escape. If we knew what day it was for, or what general area of the country, it might help us to figure out their plans. Turn back, now! I want to talk to that guy. Besides—say, is that a fire down there?"

Blake was looking down on Tehran through the trees along the high mountain road. Hassan pulled the car over to get a better look.

"What the hell is it, Hassan?"

"It's the embassy! I'm sure of it!"

From their vantage point high above the city of Tehran, they were too far away to hear the explosions but they did see clearly the blasts from the second and third of the explosives Avi Blume had detonated.

"Christ! That's not a fire; those are fucking explosions! I told you they'd be at the embassy, you dumb shit. Come on, Hassan, let's move it! How far are we from the embassy?"

"At least thirty minutes, maybe more."

"Move the hell over; I'm driving. I'll make it in half that time!"

.

At the sound of the first three explosions, the scene at the Intercontinental Hotel a few blocks away changed from subdued drunkeness and occasional sleep to mass exodus and chaos as reporters, cameramen, and photographers gathered up their equipment as fast as they could and ran through the streets of Tehran toward the embassy.

The confusion inside the lobby entrance of the chancery, coupled with the thick clouds of smoke, made it both rough and easy going for Alex, Avi, and Cap, dressed in their recently acquired soldiers' uniforms. Those who did see them paid them no mind. They hovered momentarily against the inside wall as an occasional coughing soldier bumped into them on his way out of the building in desperate search for fresh air.

Avi detonated the fourth explosion by the outer wall a moment before Avi and Cap grabbed hold of Alex's jacket. He blindly led them from memory across the lobby floor to the stairs leading up to the second floor.

As they pushed open the door to the stairs, where the smoke bombs had not yet penetrated, they were met by two soldiers just starting down from the top of the stairs to investigate the commotion. The soldiers, recognizing the

.

three as dangerous interlopers, immediately raised and aimed their rifles in their direction. At the same moment, Cap tossed another stun grenade at the soldiers, and the three Brothers ducked back out into the lobby until the grenade did its intended job.

The three rushed back through the door and climbed the stairs two at a time, stepping over the prostrate forms of the two unconscious Revolutionary soldiers. At the top of the stairs, Alex peered cautiously through the small glass pane built into the door. He managed to duck his head just before the glass was shattered by rifle fire from the opposite side.

As they prepared to throw open the door and toss additional stun grenades and smoke bombs down the second-floor corridor, rifle fire from the stairs below forced them halfway up the stairs leading to the third floor.

With his Uzi at the ready, Avi jumped over the the handrail onto the stairs leading from the first floor to the second and provided cover for Cap, who hurled a stun grenade in the direction of the rifle fire.

Quickly returning their attention to the second-floor door, the three prepared to storm it a split second after Avi detonated the fifth, sixth, and seventh explosions by the outer compound wall.

The repercussions from the three simultaneous blasts shook the building and knocked out windows along the front of the chancery. Even from their insulated position, they could hear soldiers outside of the building firing into the direction of the blasts. Each blast, exploding closer and closer to the main gate, drove the bewildered soldiers further and further from the gate.

Avi kicked the second floor door wide as Alex and Cap, kneeling on either side of the door, tossed a series of stun grenades in various directions along the second-floor corridor. They then retreated almost to the top of the third floor as the ensuing explosions rocked the second floor. A moment before crashing through the second-floor door, Cap filled the stairwell with thick plumes of orange smoke. When the three of them did burst through the door, they fired continuous bursts from their weapons up and down the corridor the moment they hit the floor. They could have saved the ammunition, though, since there was no movement from the small handful of soldiers who had been knocked out of commission by the effective stun grenades.

According to plan, Cap stood guard on the second floor near the stairway, amid the rubble of falling plaster and shattered glass, as Alex and Avi made their way unimpeded down the hall to Sinclair's room.

The journey down the long corridor seemed an eternity to Mycroft. It was not that the passage required an inordinate amount of time to negotiate; rather, Mycroft felt his heart being tugged at each door he passed. From behind some, he heard shouts demanding to know what was happening; and from a few others, he heard the plaintive cries of frightened hostages. More than anything, he ached to open each door and set free all of his fellow Americans, or, at minimum, to offer words of comfort and encouragement. And yet he knew that to attempt anything more than the planned objective would be disastrous for all. *Never be diverted, men,* reverberated through his mind. *Get in, get out. One, two, quick, men.*

Trying unsuccessfully to shut off his mind to these thoughts and his ears to the sounds of the hostages, he made his way quickly to the end of the long hall.

Just as Alex was about to put his foot to Sinclair's door, he noticed it was slightly ajar. Kicking it in anyway, he jumped back in time to avoid the single rifle fire that whizzed mere inches from his head.

"I will kill him unless you surrender immediately!" came the shrill and frightened voice from within the room.

"What do we do now?" Alex whispered to Avi while their backs were flat up against the corridor wall.

"Surrender, naturally. I'll cover you."

"All right," Mycroft shouted. "I'm coming in! Don't harm the boy!"

Mycroft held his Uzi out away from his body and cautiously stepped forward into the room.

"That's far enough!" shrieked the lone and petrified soldier who was using Sinclair's body as a shield. His rifle was pointed at Mycroft. "Throw down your gun!"

Mycroft could see that Sinclair was hurt, remnants of the morning's beating still evident on his bloodied face.

"The boy's hurt," Mycroft said. "Put him down in the chair."

"Not until you do as I say: Toss down your weapon!"

Mycroft did as he was told.

"How many more of you are out there?" asked the soldier nervously.

"The same as you," Alex said for Avi's benefit. "I'm all alone. Now lower the boy slowly. He's hurt. That's right, ease him down slowly. Don't worry about me. I'm all the way over here. I'm not going to do anything stupid while you've got the rifle on me. That's right, ease him down. Slowly. Nice and easy. *GOOD!*"

At that word, Alex ducked as Avi appeared in the doorway, surveyed the room in a fraction of a second, and killed the guard with a short burst from his Uzi.

Alex ran to Sinclair as Avi checked the soldier.

"Dead," said Avi.

"Alive," said Alex.

"I'll be okay, Alex. Just help me up," said Sinclair.

Alex carefully slipped his left arm around the boy's waist and lifted him to his feet.

"Can you walk, Lee?"

"Yeah, my legs are okay. I think I've got some cracked ribs. They taped 'em, though. I'll manage. Got a weapon for me?"

Avi reloaded his Uzi and handed it to Lee.

"Can you use one of these?" Avi asked.

"Sure, no sweat, sir."

"Good lad," said Avi as he pulled another Uzi out of his duffel bag and checked the corridor. He then lifted his sleeve to his lips: "Cap?"

"Yo!"

"We're on our way back. How's it look?"

"You're clean and green all the way."

Avi led the way through the door and out into the corridor as Alex kept his left arm around Sinclair's slender waist. Alex holding his submachine gun with his right hand, Lee holding his with his left.

There was an uneasy quiet as they rounded the corner and headed for Cap's position. They found him just finishing tying up the last of the four unconscious soldiers.

"All quiet," Cap reported when they reached him. "Too quiet if you ask me."

"Then let's stir things up a bit," Avi said and detonated two more explosions along the outer compound wall. "Okay, Cap, let's get us home."

As Avi and Cap ran past the doorway leading to the stairs, they dropped two smoke bombs down the stairwell and then waited a few moments before seeing whether the coast was clear.

Alex kept one eye on the door while the other followed

Avi and Cap's progress through the door and down the stairs.

"It's almost over, Lee," Alex consoled. "You gotta hang tough."

"Don't worry about me, Alex. I'm a marine!"

"I hope you won't hold it against me if I tell you I used to be regular army."

"Alex, I'll never be able to repay you for this. You know that, don't you."

Alex was about to tell Lee that he owed him nothing, that an Obligation to a Brother of the Craft was a sacred honor, and that Lee also had the same Obligation if he was ever in a position to save a Brother's life. But before he could say any of this, Avi and Cap returned.

The reporters clamoring around the main gate of the embassy were being held at bay by armed Revolutionary soldiers firing shots over their heads.

Some of the American reporters, caught up in the tension and anxiety of not knowing what was going on inside the embassy—save for the all-too-frequent sounds of gunfire and grenade explosions—abandoned their primary roles as reporters and became Americans first and foremost.

"What's going on in there?" some of them shouted.

"You harm those hostages and you'll pay with your own blood!" screamed another.

"Open the gates and let us in, you fucking Iranian bastards!" yelled others.

The panic-stricken guards, who had come to know two quiet months of passiveness from the press, were leaderless and at a loss over what to do. Firing over the heads of the newsmen, however, seemed to keep them from storming the gates. So round after round went sailing off into the black night.

The reporters, unbeknownst to them, were aiding in the rescue by keeping the guards occupied at the gates. The guards had not really believed anyone would be foolish enough to try to pull off a rescue attempt. But, nevertheless, what they had been told to expect was a lone man, not several, not submachine guns, not smoke bombs, not stun grenades, not explosions along the wall, and certainly not hundreds of newsmen crying out for vengeance. The guards were frightened, they were scared, they were nervous, they were panicked. And many of them cowardly fled for their own safety.

The concussion shock from another explosion against the wall—this one closer to the main gate than the previous ones—sent both newsmen and soldiers scurrying for temporary cover.

Television cameramen stood poised with cameras in hand, filming the frenetic action when they themselves were not taking an active part in it. Pandemonium reigned outside the embassy, while inside it was unnervingly quiet.

"How much longer?" demanded a perspiring Otis Blake.

"Ten minutes, if you don't kill us first," answered an equally nervous Rachmon Hassan.

"I told you that fucking bastard was dangerous, you dumb shit!"

"Yes, but not as dangerous as your driving—*Watch out!*"

Blake swerved the car just in time to avoid crashing into an oncoming truck and depressed the accelerator to the floor once again.

"How's Lee holding up?" Cap asked.

"Don't worry about me," the young Brother answered for himself. "I can handle anything."

"Avi, what's the word?" Alex asked.

"It seems too quiet," the Israeli replied as he checked his watch. "Exactly fifteen minutes since the first explosion. They may have had enough time to regroup and organize. They could have pulled back and be waiting for us outside."

As he spoke, Cap produced a flak jacket and a military fatigue jacket and began helping Lee into the garments.

Avi reached into his duffel bag and secured a gas mask for Lee. "Try it," he ordered.

Lee complied and tested it out for a few breaths. "No sweat," he reported. "Just like standard general issue in the marines."

All four Brothers of the Craft checked their ammunition and supply of grenades. Avi disappeared for a few minutes and checked the stairs and lobby once more and then reported that all still appeared calm and clear.

"Then let's go for it," Alex said as he gingerly lifted Lee to his feet.

"I can't be sure," Avi reported, "but I think there are reporters outside of the gates, along with a hell of a lot of guards. There's some kind of small mob out there, and I think I see television camera lights. Whatever it is, they appear to be keeping the guards occupied."

"Let's hope they keep it up for a few more minutes," Cap offered, "and that they don't get hurt when we bust through that gate."

Avi checked his watch again. "Twenty minutes. We're behind schedule. Let's go!"

Avi led the way down the stairs, followed by Alex supporting Lee. Cap brought up the rear. As Avi had said, the stairs were deserted save for the telltale odor and lingering wisps of the smoke bombs that had gone off before, and two still unconscious soldiers. Avi bade the others stay as he peered out into the lobby. Seeing no one, he motioned for the rest of the party to follow him. But when they were halfway across the lobby area, two soldiers hiding behind a reception counter stood up and opened fire on the group.

The first bullet went wide, but the second struck Lee's flak jacket, leaving him shaken but unhurt.

Avi, Cap, and Alex simultaneously aimed their Uzis at the two soldiers, splattering their blood along the far wall as they fell down behind the counter.

The noise from the gunfire alerted some of the soldiers outside who began running toward the chancery just as the group of four emerged. Avi detonated two more explosions as Cap fired at the approaching soldiers' feet. Alex hurled two stun grenades in that general direction just as some of the reporters, realizing at last that the padlock was a sham, burst through the gate.

Avi quickly turned left and headed for the lightly wooded area where they had left Ishmael and the truck. The group followed and Alex and Lee fired blindly into the emptiness behind them.

They reached a frantic Ishmael just as the car carrying Otis Blake and Rachmon Hassan turned down Takhte-Jamshid Avenue on two wheels and sped for the open gate.

Many of the reporters who had crashed through the gate were repelled by the gunfire and the two successive explosions at the wall. They began heading backward, reconverging on the narrow opening at the gate as Blake furiously blew his horn, screeched on his brakes, and tried desperately to get through the crowd without running over anyone.

With the truck's motor still running, Ishmael jumped behind the wheel with Avi alongside of him. Alex, Cap, and Lee jumped in the back, stumbling over the body of a dead soldier, a stiletto still protruding from his neck.

"Good old Ishmael," said Alex.

"You said it!" answered Cap.

"You remember what to do?" Avi asked Ishmael.

"Yes, I drive straight and run over anything in our way."

"Okay, Ishmael. Show us what this baby's got under the hood," Cap cried from the rear, and the truck sped off with a jump just as some of the soldiers came within sight of the rear of the truck.

The three in the back opened fire when Alex ordered, "Shoot over their heads, or in the dirt in front of them. Just enough to make them scatter." They needed no second invitation.

The truck sped along over the grass leading behind the chancery and emerged on the far side just as Blake and Hassan were entering the gates.

"Car coming," Avi hollered. "Get ready."

Alex and Cap stood up and threw back the canvas top of the truck, positioning themselves behind one of the metal frames that held the canvas in place. Lee stayed low and protected their rear flank. As Ishmael skidded back onto the narrow road, he headed straight for the oncoming car.

"You're doing fine, Ishmael," Alex yelled as the wind roared into his open mouth. Avi detonated one more explosion just as Blake swerved at the last possible moment to avoid a head-on collision. Ishmael never once removed his foot from the accelerator.

More guards along the fringe of the roadway opened fire, which was answered by four Uzi submachine guns from both sides, front and rear of the speeding truck.

Ishmael was now within twenty yards of the embassy gate, plowing through the congested reporters who quickly scrambled for cover while shooting as many pictures as they could. The truck was soon awash in a sea of flashbulbs and strobe camera lights as it headed straight for the gate, throttle opened wide.

Blake turned the fast car around and began following the truck as Avi let loose with the remaining three explosions right in a row.

"Alex, that car's following us. And it's gaining!" warned Lee.

But Alex and Cap needed no further invitation. They sprayed the car with gunfire and obliterated the tires, headlights, and engine of the oncoming car. Hassan dove for cover, but the CIA agent was desperate to try anything.

"Mycroft! Mycroft! Don't do it!" Blake was screaming at the top of his lungs. "Alex, for God's sake, come back here! *ALEX!*"

Mycroft just smiled and half-saluted. Then he banged on the roof of the truck's cab. "Let's go home, Ishmael!"

And the truck sped off into the dark night, trailed for a very short while by the flash of camera strobes.

The first part was over.

A Brother was a hostage no more.

An Obligation had been paid.

The Hailing Sign had been answered.

50

OTIS Blake had been kept under armed guard in a holding area, while Rachmon Hassan surveyed the damage to the chancery and completed a thorough bed check of the remaining hostages.

"At least three of my men are already dead and many are critically injured," he reported when he returned. "And Corporal Sinclair is missing."

"Missing? Sinclair's not missing, you dumb shit. He's escaped. He's been rescued by Mycroft and Blume and I don't know who else in that truck. I told you he would walk all over you, Hassan. But you were too fucking stupid to listen, you goddamn dumb shit, you."

Hassan was too stunned to pay much heed to Blake's

tirade. The Iranian numbly stared out the window toward the still reigning chaos in front of the embassy gates. It was dark, but if he lifted his gaze, he imagined he could see the mountains where the original germ of the takeover idea first took root. Who could have known, who could have predicted it would come to a night such as this? Hassan felt an urge to cry but suppressed it as Blake's continuous monologue interrupted his reverie.

"All right, the game's not over yet. The first thing you do is beef up security at the airports, train stations, everything. But don't forget about private airstrips. If Blume was interested in weather reports, it's my guess they've got a plane coming in for them somewhere. Now you get right on—"

"STOP TELLING ME WHAT TO DO!" His voice pierced the small confines of the room. "I'm sick of you, Blake. You, your CIA, your government . . . all of it. It makes me ill. Why don't you leave us alone!"

"Hey, don't get your bowels in an uproar, pal. You want us to leave you alone, release the other hostages."

"When your country has returned the Shah, we will—"

"Ah, can it, Hassan. You're like a fucking broken record. You're pissed because I warned you not to underestimate Mycroft and you fucked up! You said you had plenty of guards—well, you're damn lucky they didn't kill more than three. And judging from what I saw just in the few minutes before they made good their escape, I'd say they could have done just that, too. No, Hassan, Mycroft didn't want bloodshed; he was being kind to you and your boy scouts. All he wanted was the Sinclair kid. He came, he saw, and he took, like candy from an Iranian baby."

Hassan sat down and lowered his head between his knees. "Leave me alone, Blake. Please, just leave me alone."

"All right, Hassan. I'm going to get some sleep. You should, too. Call me later, after you've cooled off."

"Yes, yes. Anything you say. Now just leave me in peace. Please."

After Blake had left, one of the guards said, "Do you want me to follow him, Rachmon?"

"Don't be stupid. He'll spot you and kill you. I've had enough death for one night."

"Oh, then you have heard about Ahmad."

It didn't register with him at first. "Ahmad? What of Ahmad Zadeh?"

"Rachmon, Ahmad is dead. He and seven others were killed some time tonight. They—they were all shot."

"Ahmad? Seven others? Three more just now? No, no, *no! This cannot be happening!*" He gripped his head between his hands. Slowly he stood and spoke to one of the guards.

"Take me to Ahmad."

The other guard asked, "Is there anything we can do, Rachmon?"

"Yes. I want the guard increased immediately. Here, at the airport, train, and bus stations . . . and especially at all private landing strips. AT ONCE!"

51

"THIS is very distressing news, Otis. Yes, indeed. Most distressing."

"Well, it's no fucking picnic over here, you know." God, how he hated talking to Langley lately. The acid buildup in his stomach increased each time he was forced to report to the Company on the scrambler phone.

"The White House will most assuredly be displeased, Otis. They're already under constant attack from Congress on our activities, as well as pressure from the American people to settle this crisis as soon as possible."

"Look, I have all I can do right now without worrying about the White House's feelings. All I want you to do, *sir*, is see if you can put some real pressure on the Israelis. I *know* I saw Blume in the front seat of that truck's cab. Can't they bring him in? Don't they have any damn control over their people?"

"Try to stay calm, Otis. We're trying to work with the Israelis, but they claim they don't know where Avi Blume is."

"I know where he is, dammit! He's here, fucking us over with his pal Mycroft. And I'm telling you there was another American in the truck with Mycroft and the Sinclair boy. I'll be damned if I can figure that out, unless it was another of the hostages."

"Is that possible, Otis?"

"Shit and double shit! *Anything* is possible. Hassan said only Sinclair was missing"—he remembered how he had lambasted Rachmon Hassan's use of that word—"I mean, had escaped. But who the fuck knows what these bastards know for sure? Or how much of what they say to believe. And it looked like an Iranian driving the truck."

"Yes, so you said," dripped Langley's southern drawl.

He lit another cigarette, inhaled deeply, and started talking as the smoke wafted from his mouth with each verbal utterance. It burned his throat but he ignored it. "Why the fuck would an Iranian be helping Mycroft? An American, an Israeli, and an Iranian. This doesn't figure, does it?"

"I agree. On the surface, that dog won't hunt."

Blake ignored the southern metaphor. "Even so, you may want to run that type of scenario through the computers and see if it turns anything up. I'd sure like to know who the others are, especially that other American."

"Very well, Otis. I'll have the names run. Anything else?"

"Yes, sir, just one more thing: If there *is* a second hostage out besides Sinclair, can I assume the previous orders are countermanded?"

"No, Otis, you may not. If anything, the previous orders are more firmly etched than before, if you get my drift. The hostage—"

"—*Former* hostage, or hostages, you mean," Blake interrupted.

"The *hostage*, or hostages, are to be returned to the Iranians, Otis."

"And Mycroft?"

"You have your orders concerning him, Otis."

52

"*E S Selamu Aleikum,*" said Moussef on the telephone from Tehran.

"*Aleikum Es Selamu,*" responded the man in the Beirut café. "What news? Have you killed Mycroft yet?"

"No. He—he broke into the embassy last night and rescued the American. There was much shooting and several Iranians are dead."

"He did *what?* How in the name of Allah is that possible?"

"I—I am not certain. We were not expecting it and, as you instructed, were concentrating our meager resources on airports and highways and—"

"Yes, yes, yes. *Enough!* This should at any rate make

your task easier. Mycroft still must flee the country, only now he must attempt escape with the hostage. This will be difficult for him but easier for you to spot him. Do not fail!'' He hung up.

''I hear and I obey,'' said the young man with the scratchy beard into a dead telephone.

53

▼

—January 13, 1980

I SHMAEL hurried into his house just before dawn and leaned against the door as he slammed it shut behind him. The others watched him anxiously but allowed him to catch his breath and give his report at his own speed.

"It is no use," he finally blurted out. "The Brotherhood has considered the request carefully and fully appreciates its urgency. But they have followed the strict letter of the Obligation in rendering their decision and turning us down. As long as you are here, they have decreed, you are safe and your lives not in danger. To remove you from this house might jeopardize your lives, and they cannot be a party to that. Therefore, they will not assist. I am sorry." He lowered his gaze to avoid returning the stare of the three pairs of eyes on him.

Cap muttered, "Shit," and Avi said something softly in Hebrew.

"We knew it was a long shot," said Mycroft. "They've already done plenty."

"We've been hiding out here for a week," Avi said. "All of my sources have dried up. We don't know if that plane ever made it to the private landing strip and there's no way to get in touch with them again."

"The city's tighter than a drum," said Cap. "But the longer we stay here, the riskier it gets for Ishmael and his family. We've got to move on. Anybody got any ideas?"

The silence was broken by Mycroft. He walked over to close the door to the bedroom where Lee was taking his turn sleeping.

"I've got one idea but I don't want the boy to hear it," Mycroft said quietly. "The only way out as I see it is with the Iranians' help. We've got to swap our way out by offering to trade in exchange for them allowing Lee out of the country."

"That's great," said Cap, "but what the hell do we have that they want?"

"Me," said Mycroft.

"No!" Cap bellowed. "Don't screw around!"

"My Brother," Ishmael said at almost the same time, "you can't be serious."

"I'm *very* serious; it's the only thing that makes sense. I've got to get the boy home—all the way home, not just out of the embassy. We can't move anywhere in the city and the longer we stay put, the more likely it is that we'll get picked up in a door-to-door sweep. Besides, you said it yourself, Cap: Think of the risk to Ishmael and his family."

"And what happens to you?" Cap demanded.

"I can fend for myself after Lee is on his way home. For now, though, it's the only way."

"Avi," Cap pleaded, "say something; talk some sense into him."

The Mossad agent was momentarily lost in reverie, thinking of how paternalistic Alex had become since the rescue. He couldn't help noticing in the past week how many of Mycroft's references to Lee were filled with a paternal warmth and protective air. But he quickly turned his attention to the matter at hand.

"Actually," Avi responded, "I was about to suggest the very same thing. Alex's idea is the only thing that does make sense."

"You're both nuts, I swear it," Cap said. "You can't trust these fuckin' Iranians to make a deal with them." He caught Ishmael's wince. "Sorry, Ishmael. You know what I mean."

"I agree that Hassan can't be trusted," Alex said, "and that no matter what he agrees to do, it'll just be lip service. He won't swap the way we'd like him to—me for Lee's safe passage and yours; but he will *agree* to a swap if he thinks there's a chance of nabbing me *and* Sinclair. That'll be the bait."

"And," Avi chimed in, "it will force the issue; it will make something happen. It will create a fluid situation to which we will have to be ready to respond just as fluidly."

Cap slammed his meaty fist on the table. "I still don't like it. What if something goes wrong?"

"The way I see it," Alex said slowly, allowing his idea to form in his mind, "we can set it up so that the worst thing that happens is what I'm prepared to do anyway: stay behind and take the boy's place.''

''And how do you think Lee is going to feel about that?'' Cap asked.

''I *know* how he'll feel, which is why I won't tell him until the very last minute.''

54

THEY glared at each other across the highly polished conference table under the opulent chandelier in the Swiss Embassy. Responding to a message delivered to him by a pudgy Iranian, Otis Blake hastily arranged for the meeting on the neutral ground of the Swiss compound.

Hassan sat next to Blake and the two of them locked eyes with Alex Mycroft and Avi Blume. Emile Barbeaux sweated at the head of the table, but he was ignored.

Mycroft had just concluded his pitch and Hassan laughed at him. "This is madness," Hassan roared. "Why would we agree to this folly?"

"You don't have to agree," Mycroft countered. "We're

smart enough to admit that the city is too buttoned down for us to get out without a lot more bloodshed. But you should acknowledge that you're never going to find where we're hiding. If you keep searching and wasting valuable manpower, pretty soon your security at the embassy will be so weak that someone else will break in." Suddenly the smile vanished from Hassan's face. "And if you call off the search for us," Mycroft continued, "there's a damn good chance that we'll *all* get out of the country anyway. Be smart and face facts: You're running out of time and options."

"So the deal is you for Sinclair?" Blake interrupted. "I arrange for an air force evac plane to fly in, Sinclair flies out, and you stay behind at the mercy of the Iranians. Is that it?"

"Close enough. Take the deal, Otis; it's the only one you're gonna get."

"How about Avi?" Blake asked.

"He stays with you here while you make the arrangements. Then he goes to the airport with you and Hassan but he leaves with Sinclair. Until then, he keeps an eye on you both to make sure there are no surprises tonight."

Hassan jumped up and started to protest, but Blake grabbed him by the arm and pulled him back into his seat. "Shut the fuck up, will ya, Hassan." Blake demanded.

"Jesus, Otis," Mycroft said, "how the hell have you been able to put up with this guy?"

"It hasn't been easy, Alex."

Mycroft turned his attention to Hassan, who was still sputtering. "Listen to what I'm saying: Right now you're holding your dick. The kid means diddly squat to you, except maybe to your pride because he escaped from the embassy. But he's just a kid; he's worth nothing to you. I'm offering to take his place. Think of the propaganda value you'll have with *me*."

Hassan suddenly brought himself up short. Mycroft's words began to sink in and make sense to him. Hassan looked at Blake, who nodded. "Deal," said the CIA agent. "I'll arrange for the transport."

Mycroft got up to leave and was halfway across the room when Blake called out: "Just curious, Alex, but how much is Sinclair's father paying you for this?"

Mycroft kept walking. "Not enough, Otis. Not enough."

55

WHEN the landing lights of the C-9—the military version of the DC-9, more commonly referred to as a Nightingale—were first spotted coming through the thick early-morning fog hovering over Tehran Airport, Otis Blake picked up a walkie-talkie from the front car seat and began giving landing instructions and taxiing orders to the pilot. Hassan, who had arranged for the airport to be closed to all other traffic for the duration of the exercise, turned to the Israeli agent in the backseat of the car and asked, "Where are they? The plane is here, the airport is closed. Everything you have asked for."

"It will be over soon," Avi said. "Blake, get the plane into position."

Blake flipped on the car's headlights and radioed the appropriate message to the pilot. When the plane was in position on the dewy wet tarmac, Blake gave orders to lower the rear landing steps. The plane was about one hundred yards in front of them and Blake started the car's engine, preparing to drive closer.

"No," Avi instructed. "We stay here. Let's get out of the car. And leave your guns on the seat."

Immediately, Hassan started to raise his voice. *"I will not—"* But he was cut off by Blake's more even tone.

"Cut the shit, Hassan, you're giving me a headache," the CIA agent said as he dropped his Smith & Wesson onto the front seat. "I don't care if I'm standing here balls naked: That plane's not going anywhere until I give the pilot the right signal. Blume knows it, Mycroft knows it, and the pilot knows it. They can't overpower the pilot because they can't get into the reinforced cockpit. So what're they gonna do, blow the fuckin' thing up? Forget it. Give up your piece and let's get this thing over with. It's just a simple little swap."

Hassan didn't like it but did as he was told and the three got out of the car and walked to the front to stand in the limited warmth of the headlights. Avi, who knew everything Blake had said was true, still held onto his Uzi and stood a few paces behind Hassan and Blake.

A few minutes passed in silence until a military truck driven by Ishmael came bounding across the field. It circled the plane once and then drove over to circle the area where Hassan and Blake stood with Avi. Ishmael then maneuvered the truck to a standstill, the rear abutting the side of the terminal building at a spot about halfway between the plane and the area where Hassan nervously shifted his weight from side to side. The early-morning cold was making a beeline straight to his bladder.

But Hassan's concentration, as well as Blake's, was focused on the truck, whose door opened slowly to discharge one passenger. Alex looked over at Avi, who gave him a wave to indicate that all was as it should be on his end.

The huge form that was Cap Harris emerged next from the rear of the truck.

"Who the fuck is *that* guy?" Blake demanded as he spun around to face Avi.

"He was not part of the trade," Hassan joined in.

"Never mind who he is," Avi responded evenly. "If you didn't know he was here, you won't miss him when he's gone."

About fifty yards away, Alex and Cap watched the action and could just make out the rise of animated voices.

"What do you think is going on?" Cap inquired.

"They're discussing your future health. This is the first time Blake or Hassan have really seen you and they're not happy that suddenly there's another person involved in the swap. Let's just wait it out before we bring the boy out from the rear. But remember, once he's out in the open, he's your responsibility, Cap. Keep him with you and be sure, no matter what happens, he boards that plane and takes off."

"You can count on me, Alex," the big cop responded.

Across the field, Avi finally won the argument and signaled once more to Alex.

"Okay, Cap," Mycroft said. "Dig Lee out of that fake floor in the rear."

In no time, Lee Sinclair joined Alex and Cap on the tarmac and the three of them made their way slowly toward the plane. The fact that Mycroft was heading to the plane with Sinclair did not sit well with Hassan.

"This is a trick. This is a trick! Stop them, Blake. *Stop them!*"

Blake ignored Hassan's ranting, but he, too, was concerned. "What are you guys trying to pull?" he asked Avi. "Whatever it is, it won't work. The plane won't budge till I say so."

"No tricks, Blake," Avi told him. "They're just saying good-bye."

The three of them were nearing the plane and Alex put his arm around Lee's shoulders in a fatherly gesture.

"Look, Lee, there are some things you have to know. First, we're not all making the trip at the same time."

"What are you talking about, Alex?" the young marine demanded. "What's going on?"

"*You're* going on, Lee. You're going on that plane and so are Cap and Avi. I'm staying behind."

"You can't do that! You've *got* to come."

"There is no room for debate. The deal's been cut."

"Then I'm staying with you."

"Listen carefully, Lee. I said there were some things I had to tell you. The other concerns your Dad."

They were almost at the rear stairs of the plane, but Lee stopped short.

"Dad? What's the matter with him, Alex? Is Dad okay?"

"He's very sick, Lee. Ishmael learned it last night from the Iranian Brotherhood. They had received word from our Lodge in case they heard from us. He was in the hospital when I left the States, but he's much worse now."

"Why didn't you tell me, Alex?"

"There wasn't any point before. But now you see that you've got no choice. You're getting on that plane and you're taking off for home. I'm over here because of your father and the Obligation. If it's within my power, I've got to get you home so your father can see you before it's too late."

Tears began welling up in the boy's eyes and he grabbed hold of Mycroft's arm. "Alex, please don't leave. Please." But Mycroft shook him loose in a rough gesture.

"Cap," he barked, "get him on board." Mycroft threw the young Brother into Cap's waiting bear hug and started walking over to where he would change places with Avi. Cap struggled to drag Lee onto and up the plane's rear stairs.

"Alex, come back," Lee cried out, but Mycroft ignored the shouts. "Please don't leave!"

On the opposite side of the field, Avi started to move out to meet Alex halfway. "Stay here," he directed Blake and Hassan.

Avi's path toward the plane and toward meeting Alex took him directly along the headlights of the car pointing that way. Alex was just coming into the tip of the headlights' reach and all eyes were on the two of them when the first shot rang out from the roof of the terminal building.

Everything on the ground came to an immediate standstill as the reality of what had occurred settled into everyone's consciousness and they scanned each other quickly to see who had cried out and who had been hit.

Through the crosshairs of the assassin's high-powered rifle, the first of his intended victims still stood in shock. Moussef prepared to squeeze off another shot. The biting wind brought tears to his eyes and a slimy mucous to his nose, both of which he wiped away with his dirty fingers.

Moussef had been watching events unfold through the gun's telescopic sight and had awaited a moment such as this when, if Allah's blessing be upon him, he could rid the world of all three of his intended targets: the American spoiler Mycroft, the Israeli Mossad agent Blume, and the young hostage Sinclair. But it wasn't until the moment he fired the first round that all three had been in the open.

Then he had to decide which of the three to go after first. He allowed his logic to dictate the answer and offered a silent prayer of thanks that logic coincided with his own personal preference. Only one person on the field had a weapon that he could see, so his first bullet found home in Avi's back. Moussef's second shot was as true as the first. The Mossad agent sank to his knees before collapsing on the tarmac.

Alex had seen the muzzle flash out of the corner of his eye, but he had been looking directly at Avi when his brother-in-law was hit. Avi took the bullet but it was Mycroft who cried out in pain.

"No! Jesus, no! Avi!" Mycroft paused only a second before he started a foolhardy sprint in the open to try to help Avi, now sprawled face down on the tarmac. Mycroft knew he should seek cover and get out of the headlight glare, but the sight of Avi overcame his better instincts and his training, and he continued as fast as he could to travel the almost fifty yards to reach the Mossad agent.

Hassan initially became so unnerved by the events that he momentarily lost control of his bladder as he dove for cover on one side of the car. He didn't know who was on the roof, but the sight of his sworn enemies, Americans and Israelis, under fire began to rekindle a Revolutionary passion he hadn't felt for months.

Blake had already sought refuge on the other side of the car. His mind was on trying to retrieve Avi Blume's Uzi, but he was helplessly pinned down.

At the plane, the sound of the shots so surprised Cap that he lost his grip on Lee for a moment, which was all the young marine needed to bound down the plane's rear stairs and start racing across the tarmac without any regard for his safety, just for his savior's.

"Alex! Alex!" Lee cried out. "Come back. Take cover here. Alex!"

Mycroft heard the young voice and stopped for only an instant and hollered at the boy. "Go back, Lee. Go back. Get him, Cap. Get the kid!"

Cap was in hot pursuit and tackled Sinclair from behind as a couple of Moussef's shots that were directed their way went wide. Cap struggled to drag the boy back while Alex continued his run to Avi.

Blake had reached into the car and pulled out his Smith & Wesson to try to return fire. But at that distance, there was little he could do except provide a small diversion to help Mycroft.

Cap and Sinclair were still in the open but back in the shadows far enough so that they were not as visible as they had been before. Only Mycroft was still in the glare of the headlights. As soon as Blake realized this and saw what Mycroft was trying to do, he reached up and opened the car door to try to douse the lights. He was met, however, by Hassan staring at him from the other side of the car seat, pointing his retrieved gun at the CIA man.

"Let's leave the lights on just a bit longer, Blake," the Iranian said with a smile. "I want a good view for the end of Alex Mycroft's life."

"Don't do this, you bastard," Blake spit back. "He's a sitting duck out there."

"I think the phrase is 'dead duck,'" Hassan laughed.

"Give him a chance, you fucker!"

Hassan allowed the smile to drop from his lips and raised his gun a little higher. "Back out of the car, Blake. I've tolerated your name-calling and your foul language long enough."

Whatever response Blake was prepared to deliver was checked as the assassin fired off round after round that landed at Mycroft's running feet. Moussef toyed with his prey for only a moment or two, for when he raised his sights, he caught Mycroft on the side of his chest with the first bullet.

The burning sensation made Mycroft rasp for breath, but he struggled to continue the run until he was only ten yards from Avi's body. Moussef's next shot shattered Mycroft's kneecap and sent him sprawling along the tarmac. As he hit the ground, the glass tube popped free of his shirt pocket and went skittering across the tarmac with him.

To Mycroft, it all was happening in slow motion, and he had a clear and unobstructed view of the action. He landed on his belly and a combination of his speed and the oily, wet ground sent his body sliding straight for Avi's still form. And as the progress of his body was propelled forward, it spun a full 360 degrees. He saw the glass tube slide along with him and he reached for it before his body began to spin around. As he came around full circle and softly landed against the Mossad agent, he was able to reach out and gently place his hand atop the glass tube.

He brought it close to his body and whispered, "Beth," and then lost all consciousness.

Moussef then started to fire with abandon. While he could not quite make out where Lee Sinclair and Cap Harris were in the shadows, he had a close enough approximation to fire in that general direction and keep them from reaching the plane. He knew that Rachmon Hassan and Otis Blake were at the car, and he periodically fired into and around the car. Occasionally Blake would harmlessly fire his handgun in Moussef's general direction, but as far as the assassin could determine, there was only one other gun of significance to be concerned about, and it was the Jew's Uzi, which was out of reach.

What Moussef did not know was that directly under his vantage point, Ishmael sat behind the wheel of the military truck, watching in shocked disbelief. Through the truck's windshield, the portly Iranian had taken in the entire scene of devastation. He saw two of his friends gunned down before his eyes. He couldn't tell whether they were dead or alive but knew that if they were alive, the longer it took to get them help, the lower their chances of survival.

He reached down and opened the box of Avi's hand grenades and scooped up several of them. If he could lob one onto the roof of the two-story building, he prayed that he might get lucky and kill the assassin.

Kill the assassin, he thought to himself. Listen to what I am saying! I am a jeweler who before last night never committed a violent act in my life. Now, look at me. I am grabbing hand grenades and talking to myself about killing assassins!

But he managed to shut off that stream of thought long enough to work on the real problem he was going to face: trajectory. He was too close to the building to toss a grenade onto the roof. The trajectory from that angle was almost straight up and down, and if he missed, the grenade would fall to the ground near him. What he needed to do was move further away from the building so he could lob the grenades in a gradual arc. His problem was how to get into position without being observed and getting killed himself.

He would have to use the truck but was afraid to start the engine and alert the sniper. He released the brakes and climbed quietly out of the cab and moved behind the truck.

He squeezed his portly frame between the rear of the truck and the building and began to push the truck so that it would roll away from the wall.

It gathered a little speed and Ishmael jumped in back as it rolled down a small drainage area; but it did not escape Moussef's eye. The assassin fired several rounds into the truck's cab, but he was not prepared when the canvas top in the rear was thrown back and Ishmael lobbed one, two, and then a third grenade onto the roof with precision.

Moussef jumped to the top of the balustrade, rifle in hand and a final Islamic prayer on his lips. But it was lost, as was he, in the resultant series of explosions. The debris rained hard on the truck and Ishmael had to pull the canvas back onto the frame and take cover for several minutes.

The pilot revved the massive jets and Cap helped Lee to his feet. The two of them stood silently for a moment, not quite certain whether the shooting was over. It might have been, except for Hassan's dash to retrieve Avi's Uzi. Now that Mycroft was out of the way, the Iranian had no intention of honoring his word and letting the Sinclair boy out of the country. Hassan was determined to either recapture the soldier or kill him.

He grabbed the Uzi and started shooting. Cap's swift reflexes brought them both down before any of the shells found home.

"Hassan, stop it. Stop it!" Blake hollered as he ran to where the Iranian prepared to fire again. "We had a deal. Let them go."

"Never. Never!" He turned to fire again.

"Let them go, Hassan. I'm warning you."

"No, I want to kill them. I want to kill the Americans. Kill the Americans!"

Blake slowly pulled his Smith & Wesson and stuck it into Hassan's left ear. When he cocked the hammer, Hassan suddenly shut up.

"Hey, asshole, *I'm* an American. And you, you dumb shit, are dead." Then he pulled the trigger.

Blake turned to Cap and hollered toward him, "I don't know who the fuck you are and I don't care. But get that kid on the plane in the next ten seconds or plan to wave goodbye to it. 'Cause that plane is outta here, now!"

Cap and Lee stood uncertainly and looked at where Alex and Avi lay. Blake knew what they were thinking.

"Don't worry about them. I'll take care of things here and do what I can for them. Now, get the fuck outta here!"

Blake spoke into the walkie-talkie. The plane's engines revved again and the rear stairs slowly began to close.

"Now!" Blake screamed over the roar of the jets. "Move!"

Cap grabbed Lee and the two of them raced for the stairs. When Blake was sure they were safely on board, he radioed the pilot and gave him the word to take off.

As the lumbering plane gathered speed down the runway, Blake turned at the sound of the truck's engine grinding and coughing its way to life. He turned his attention back to the runway as he watched the plane take off into the dawn's haze. Behind him, Ishmael drove as fast as he could to retrieve the fallen bodies of Alexander Mycroft and Avraham Blume.

EPILOGUE

Philadelphia—May 7, 1980

THEY came in their tuxedos. They always did.

Alone, and in small groups, they silently entered the western portal of one of the oldest and most ornate buildings in the world. They passed between the Byzantine pillars, over the Seal of Solomon, and under the twelve signs of the zodiac. They always did; it was the only way to enter.

For the first time in twelve months, Lee Sinclair was among them; but it was not a joyous occasion. They came to perform a memorial service for a deceased Brother.

He had spent close to a month in a U.S. Air Force Hospital in Wiesbaden, West Germany. The marines then shipped him Stateside and issued him a medical discharge. Since then, Lee spent as much time as possible at his father's hospital bedside.

The disease that continued to ravage John Sinclair's body finally took the Master's life early the previous morning. Lee knew that his father's death was a blessing and that now the pain had stopped for good. No one should have to suffer like that, he felt. Still, he had cried when his father closed his eyes for the last time, while Lee held his hand.

Tomorrow, Lee's Brothers of the Craft would perform a fraternal graveside funeral service over John Sinclair's body, as was the custom. And tonight the Craft would hold a brief memorial service in the triangular Assembly Hall, also customary. It was to that memorial service that Lee was now headed as he climbed the grand staircase and signed his name in the outer guard's ledger.

"Hello, Lee," said a familiar voice. "I'm awfully sorry about your father."

"Cap! God, it's good to see you again!" They embraced affectionately.

"When did you get back, Lee?"

"About three months ago. I—I thought about calling you, Cap. Honestly, I did. But that business at the airport hit me kind of hard."

"I know it did, son. I know it did. Listen, we've got a little bit of time before the service begins. Let's go into your father's old chambers and chat for a while."

"Sure, Cap. I think I'd like that." Lee led the way, being forced to stop every few feet to shake hands and receive condolences and welcome-home wishes from those Brothers he hadn't yet seen. But finally they reached the office at the Apex of the Assembly Hall.

Cap opened the door and stood back to let Lee pass through first. A man with thick wavy brown hair, a matching beard, and piercing blue eyes was standing in the room. He was examining a framed photograph while pensively stroking his mustache with his left hand; his right hand rested on a wooden cane with an ivory handle. He smiled as Lee entered.

"Oh, excuse me," Lee began, "I—" and then he stopped dead in his tracks.

"Alex? *Alex!* It's really you! Holy shit, you're alive!"

He ran to throw his arms around Mycroft, who returned his embrace warmly.

"They told me you were dead, Alex. You and Avi."

"I know," Mycroft answered as he allowed Lee to step back. "Otis Blake arranged it to cover up Hassan's death. They put out the word that I killed Hassan and Blake killed me. That way there wouldn't be any reprisals against any of the other hostages."

"And Avi?" Lee asked tentatively.

Alex and Cap exchanged glances briefly, and then Cap said, "Tell him, Alex. The boy's got a right to know."

Mycroft took a breath. "Avi didn't make out as well. He's paralyzed from the waist down and the doctors say he may never walk again. He's in a rehabilitation hospital in Haifa."

"That's terrible," Lee said.

"Tell him all of it," Cap prodded.

Alex paused for a moment, and then said, "So far, he refuses all therapy, despite the doctor's telling him that there is a chance for some recovery. His depression is still pretty deep. I was with him until yesterday when I heard about your Dad."

Silence followed for a minute or two, and then all three of them started talking nervously at the same time. They let Lee have the floor.

"Why the disguise, Alex? Does it have something to do with the Iranians?"

Alex pulled down on the corners of his mustache and laughed. "Oh, you mean the beard and the hair color?"

"That's no disguise, Lee," Cap interjected. "That's actually the *real* Alex Mycroft."

"I don't understand," Lee said.

"This is what I *used* to look like, Lee," Alex explained. "And then, about six years ago, my hair turned gray and I shaved the beard."

"How come you grew it back and dyed your hair?"

"Well, Lee, it's a long story; but basically I've been giving some serious thought to trying to locate a lost relative that I haven't seen in about six years. The last time he saw me, this is the way I looked. And *if* I find him, I want him to recognize me."

Just then a knock on the door signaled that the service was about to begin.

When they left the Temple of the Craft about an hour later, Cap peeled off, explaining that he had to go on duty soon.

"After that escapade in Iran, all I pull are night shifts. But at least they gave me my old job back."

As they watched Cap's receding figure, Lee suggested going out for a drink.

"Not on an empty stomach," Alex protested. "I'm not sure, but I don't think I've eaten since I left Israel. Plus, I've got to start sometime cleaning up a pretty big mess in my house. And I want to get up early tomorrow and pay my belated respects to Bill Gregory's widow and young boy."

Lee was about to respond when they both noticed an

attractive woman standing on the opposite street corner waiting for the light to change. Staring across the street, Alex could feel his heart begin to race as he realized who she was. He had just been looking at her picture in the Master's Chambers.

"Oh, I almost forgot my sister was meeting me here," Lee said. "Christie! Christie," he hollered as the light turned green and the young woman began crossing over toward him. "Christie, this is Alex Mycroft! This is the man I told you about. He's the one who rescued me from Iran. Can you believe it? He didn't really die after all!"

But Christie bypassed her young and exuberant brother and walked directly up to where Alex was standing. He could scarcely believe the soft radiant beauty of her face, and his legs were rubber as she shook his hand tenderly.

"Hello, Alex Mycroft," she said gently. "Thank you . . . for everything."

Alex couldn't help staring at her. Her beauty took his breath away for an instant.

"Listen," Lee interrupted Mycroft's thoughts, "I've got a *great* idea. Alex just told me he was starving. Why don't the three of us—"

"Why don't we go to my apartment?" Christie offered, returning the gaze of the man who had saved her brother's life and granted her father's last wish; a man about whom her father had told her so much, but about whom, suddenly, she felt she wanted to know more. So much more. "It's just a few blocks from here and I'm really a very good cook."

"I'm sure you are . . . Christie." He once thought he would never again be able to utter that name. "But I think I'd better take a rain check. I've got a lot to do."

She didn't show her disappointment but instead reached

inside her handbag for a pen. For paper, she had to settle on a book of matches, which she used to write down her phone number and handed it to him.

"Will you call me sometime, Alex?" she asked. "I really would like to hear from you."

He slipped the pack of matches into his shirt pocket without looking at it. "Sure," he said. "I'll call."

She kissed him briefly on the cheek and Alex shook hands with Lee. He watched them recross the street as he stood under a street lamp and allowed his heart to return to a normal rhythm.

"Daaaaddy!"

He turned his head quickly and saw a father and his young son running toward him. They were wearing sneakers and carrying a baseball bat and gloves and were late coming home from a park.

"Mommy's gonna kill us when we get home," the father yelled behind him as he easily outdistanced his son. "It's so late."

"Daaaaddy! Wait for me! I'm running as fast as I can!"

Mycroft watched them speed past, his heart again racing.

He closed his eyes and instantly was transported back to the beach at Netanya, and to his son's plaintive wail: *"Daddy! Don't leave me!"*

He quickly opened his eyes and reached into his shirt pocket. It was hard to make out the writing on the glass tube, but he knew it, of course, by heart: "Break Glass In Case of Emergency."

He closed his eyes for an instant and was back at Netanya. "Goddammit, Beth!" He yelled into the quiet evening air. "This *is* an emergency!" Then he slammed the glass cylinder against the street lamp and retrieved the fallen cigarette from among the broken shards of glass.

He rolled the cigarette around on his fingertips, then nervously placed it between his lips as he produced the book of matches Christie had given to him. He opened the cover and read her name and phone number, then struck one of the matches and applied it to the cigarette.

Watching the match burn, another voice echoed in his mind: *Never be diverted, men.* Then, just as the match was about to die out, he applied it to the other matches in the pack and watched as Christie's phone number was slowly engulfed by the flames.

The cigarette was unmercifully stale and it made him choke. He dropped his cane and grabbed hold of the lamp post with one hand for balance, then caught his breath.

He closed his eyes to wipe away the tears brought on by his coughing and heard his son's voice again: *"Daddy! Don't leave me!"*

Between spasmodic coughs, he took two more drags on the cigarette in rapid succession, then tossed it away, expertly flipping it with his fingertips.

The bells in the City Hall clock tower were starting to chime the hour.

"I'm coming for you, Josh," he vowed over the din of the bells.

Then he removed his hand from the post.

More gripping fiction from Headline:

The ultimate courtroom drama

THE

JUDGEMENT

HOWARD E. GOLDFLUSS

Christmas Eve. Beautiful millionairess Andrea Blanchard
lies dead in her apartment – brutally strangled. The police
move fast to arrest the obvious suspect: her toy-boy lover
has a key to the apartment and is found right outside the
luxury skyscraper.

A twist of fate brings Jorgensen to trial before the
distinguished judge Allen Sturdivant – ironically the very
man who should himself be in the dock. . .

So begins a superb courtroom drama of unrelenting tension
and suspense. By its nail-biting conclusion, the scales of
justice are brought shockingly back into balance.

FICTION/THRILLER   0 7472 3095 1   £2.95

Headline books are available at your bookshop or newsagent, or can be ordered from the following address:

Headline Book Publishing PLC
Cash Sales Department
PO Box 11
Falmouth
Cornwall
TR10 9EN
England

UK customers please send cheque or postal order (no currency), allowing 60p for postage and packing for the first book, plus 25p for the second book and 15p for each additional book ordered up to a maximum charge of £1.90 in UK.

BFPO customers please allow 60p for postage and packing for the first book, plus 25p for the second book and 15p per copy for the next seven books, thereafter 9p per book.

Overseas and Eire customers please allow £1.25 for postage and packing for the first book, plus 75p for the second book and 28p for each subsequent book.